"I SHOULD WARN YOU, MADEMOISELLE, I HAVE LITTLE INTEREST LEFT IN THE TRUTH. IF YOU HAVE SOMETHING TO SAY, YOU HAD BETTER SAY IT NOW, BEFORE IT IS TOO LATE."

There was no mistaking Stephen's excitement. His eyes glittered wildly now, his nostrils flared. His grip upon her had tightened, and his body throbbed urgently against hers.

"I have nothing to say," Mary said hoarsely.

"Good." He lifted her in his arms. Their gazes locked and her will died. She had never known her body could be so hungry.

"The time for words is over."

BRENDA JOYCE is

Brenda Joyce

PROMISE OF THE ROSE

AVON BOOKS
An Imprint of HarperCollinsPublishers

This is a work of fiction. Names, characters, places, and incidents are products of the author's imagination or are used fictitiously and are not to be construed as real. Any resemblance to actual events, locales, organizations, or persons, living or dead, is entirely coincidental.

AVON BOOKS
An Imprint of HarperCollins*Publishers*
10 East 53rd Street
New York, New York 10022-5299

Copyright © 1993 by Brenda Joyce Senior
Cover art by Paul Stinson
Inside cover author photograph by Roy Volkmann
Library of Congress Catalog Card Number: 93-90339
ISBN: 0-380-77140-3
www.avonromance.com

First Avon Books printing: November 1993

Avon Trademark Reg. U.S. Pat. Off. and in Other Countries, Marca Registrada, Hecho en U.S.A.
HarperCollins® is a trademark of HarperCollins Publishers Inc.

Printed in the U.S.A.

20 19 18 17 16 15 14 13

For my mother, my best friend,
a very great and special lady.
I love you.

The Players

The House of Northumberland:
Rolfe de Warenne, the Earl of Northumberland
Lady Ceidre, the Countess of Northumberland
Stephen de Warenne
Geoffrey de Warenne   }   their sons
Brand de Warenne,
   Isobel de Warenne, their daughter
Neale Baldwin, Constable of Alnwick

At Court:
King William II (Rufus the Red)
Prince Henry (Henry Beauclerc)
Roger Beaufort, the Earl of Kent
Adele Beaufort, Roger's stepsister

Other Players in England:
Roger of Montgomery, Earl of Shrewsbury and Arundel
Henry of Ferrars, Castellan of Tutbury
Duncan, son of Malcolm Canmore and Ingeborg

In Normandy:
Roger Courthouse, the Duke of Normandy

In Scotland—The House of Dunkeld:
King Malcolm III (Canmore)
Queen Margaret, his wife
Edward
Edmund
Ethelred
Edgar   }   their sons
Alexander
David
Mary
Matilda (Maude)   }   their daughters

And in the Hebrides:
Donald Bane, Malcolm Canmore's brother

Another Player:
Doug Mackinnon, Laird of Kinross

Part One

The Rose Challenged

Prologue

*A*gain, he could not sleep. He lay upon his pallet, his cheek pressed into the straw, listening to the snores of the knights around him—and the drunken laughter and conversation coming from the solar above.

He had only been in the King's household for three weeks, but it was not long enough for him to forget home and to cease yearning for the open moors of Northumberland or the cheery warmth of the great hall of Aelfgar.

The little boy shivered, for it was the dead of winter and he was cold. He tried to snuggle more deeply into the straw and the thin wool blanket he had been given. He did not want to think about Aelfgar, for then he would think about his brothers, his parents. How sorely he missed them. If only he could forget his mother as he had last seen her. Lady Ceidre had been waving to him as he rode away amidst the King's men, her smile brave yet forced, and he could see the tears that streaked her face as she wept without making a sound.

Stephen gulped. Then, as now, the haunting image threatened to unman him.

"Men do not cry," his father had told him gravely when he had taken him aside earlier on the day that he left for Winchester. " 'Tis a great honor to foster with the King, Stephen, a great honor, and I know you will do your duty as a man always does, and that you shall make me proud."

"I promise, my lord," Stephen said, his heart swelling with determination.

His father smiled and gripped his shoulder, but the smile did not reach his vivid blue eyes, which were inexplicably sad.

But Stephen had not counted on the loneliness. He had not understood what separation from home and family truly meant. He had never dreamed he would yearn so terribly, so secretly, for home. Still, he had yet to give into unmanful tears, and *he would not*. One day he would return to claim his patrimony, a man full grown, a knight with spurs, and his father and his mother would be proud of him.

"Wake up, brat."

Stephen stiffened. Duncan leaned over him, another boy fostering with the King, a few years older than he himself, and in far graver circumstances. For Duncan was not just fostering with King William, but he was a hostage as well. He was the son of Scotland's King from his first marriage. In theory Scotland's King Malcolm would cease his vigilant warfare against England now that King William had his son Duncan well in hand.

Stephen felt sorry for Duncan, but the boy was so nasty that he could not like him. And Duncan, for some reason, seemed to hate him.

Warily Stephen sat up, brushing straw from his cheek.

"The prince wants ye," Duncan said. "Ha' ye been crying?" he sneered.

Stephen stiffened. "I'm too old to cry," he said stiffly, standing. He was six. "What does the prince want?"

"I dinna ken," Duncan said, but he was smirking, his tone belying his words.

Unease pricked at Stephen, although there was no reason for it. He did not mind being summoned to the prince. Rufus had befriended him shortly after his arrival, and was his only friend amongst all the boys in the King's household. Being the youngest and the newest boy, Stephen was either ignored by the other boys, or bullied and teased. Stephen had quickly learned when to fight back and when to retreat. Now, of course, he was perplexed. He had never been summoned by Rufus before, and especially not in the dead of the night. Stephen increased his stride to match Duncan's as they slipped from the hall and outside.

Stephen wondered where they were going but asked no questions. Before leaving home, he had been warned by his father to watch closely, listen well, and reveal little of what he thought or felt. He had been advised to trust no one but himself. So far, these past few weeks had underscored the value of his father's advice.

Upon the threshold of the stable, Stephen froze. Rufus was not alone; he was surrounded by a group of his friends, other young men close to the prince's own age of sixteen years. They were all deeply in their cups. One of the boys was singing a raunchy song. A serving wench was amongst them, and two of the lads each had an arm around her. Her tunic was torn and gaping open, revealing taut nipples and lush breasts. For an instant Stephen stared, then he flushed beet red and looked away as one of the boys fondled her.

The prince was staring at the six-year-old boy. For some unfathomable reason, Stephen's initial unease soared. Rufus was flushed from drink and his eyes glittered wildly. He crooked a finger, calling softly. "Come here, sweet Stephen."

Stephen did not move. Not only were the prince's eyes glittering and overly bright, he had his arm around a younger boy in a very intimate manner. Stephen did not recognize the younger boy, who wore the shabby clothes of a villein. Clearly he was not the son of a great lord sent to foster with the King. Stephen felt a flash of piercing sympathy for the lad as their gazes met.

His father had warned him that there were men at court who liked young boys, and that he must be careful to remain aloof. Stephen had vaguely understood. He had seen lust in most of its forms even if he had not comprehended it. Now there was sudden, startling, frightening comprehension.

But surely he must be mistaken! This was *Rufus*. The King's son.

The prince approached, having forgotten the young boy. "Good eve, Stephen," he said, smiling. When he smiled he was quite good-looking, despite his unruly flaming red hair. He threw his arm around Stephen's small shoulders and pressed him close. "Share my wine. 'Tis uncommonly good, from Burgundy."

The prince was his friend, Stephen told himself as his heart began to race and pound. He had been kind to him since he had arrived at Winchester—the only boy to be kind. But Stephen did not like the hungry way the prince was gazing at him, nor did he like the look of expectation and amusement on the faces of all the prince's friends. He did not like the look of relief on the young villein's face. Not only did Stephen feel as if he was the butt of a vast joke, he felt as if it was a cruel one—a dangerous one. He felt trapped. He pulled away from the prince's embrace.

"No, thank you, my lord."

Rufus rubbed his back. "So formal this eve, lad? Come, sit with me, tell me why you appear afraid of me all of a sudden."

Stephen did not want to understand what was happening. But he did. He comprehended that the prince's intentions were not simple friendship. He comprehended the prince's unnatural lust.

As he stood, torn, not wanting to believe the worst, not wanting to give up his single friend, yet knowing he was in danger, knowing he must move, and flee, an unfamiliar young voice rang out. "Leave him alone, Will. Let him be!"

Stephen started as a youth he had never seen before shouldered forcefully through the boys. In size he did not appear any older than Stephen himself, but there was shrewdness and authority in his tone. Although his features were far more even, his hair far less bright, his resemblance to Rufus was unmistakable. This then was the King's youngest son, Henry.

"Who asked you to interfere?" Rufus said coldly.

Henry's smile was just as cold. "Are you stupid? Would you abuse the boy who would one day be Northumberland? Who would one day be your greatest ally?"

Stephen began to shake as final, full comprehension sank in. His heart was pounding now in fright and anger. The prince's interest in him tonight had nothing to do with friendship—had never had anything to do with friendship. The betrayal—and disappointment—was vast.

"You will be sorry for this," Rufus cried.

Rufus suddenly lunged at his brother, perhaps to throttle him, his face red with rage. Henry ducked, and as one, Stephen and Henry began to run. They raced out of the stable and into the bailey.

"This way!" Henry shouted, and Stephen followed the youngest prince back towards the donjon. A moment later they were safely in the great hall amongst the sleeping men.

They fell onto Stephen's pallet together, panting and out of breath. To Stephen's horror, he felt tears well. The same tears he had been fighting ever since he had ridden into the King's household. He had the horrible thought that he wanted to go home.

But he would die before letting Henry see, so he turned his face away and regained control. When Stephen could speak, he said, "Thank you."

"Forget it," Henry said easily, the straw rustling as he sat up. "Didn't anyone tell you to be careful of my brother, who is far fonder of boys than girls?"

"No." Stephen stared at his hands. "He was kind. I thought he was my friend." It hurt. He had no friends after all. Not here at court. He was far from home, and alone. Then he glanced sideways at Henry, who had come to his aid without being summoned. "Why did you help me?"

Henry grinned. "Because I do not like my brother. Because one day you will be Northumberland—and we will be allies."

For the first time in his life, Stephen had an inkling of the power that would one day be his. "And if I were not Northumberland's heir?"

Henry looked at him, no longer smiling. Finally he said, "I would be a fool to prick at my brother if it did not serve me well."

Stephen could not help being disappointed. William Rufus had not been his friend, and neither was Henry. Henry had come to his aid, not in an offer of friendship, but for reasons politic.

Henry crossed his arms over his knees. "You are such a baby. You will never survive to become Northumberland if you do not grow up."

Stephen was annoyed then. "You are no older than me."

"I am seven. And I have been raised at court, both here and in Normandy. I know of what I speak." Then he smiled his winning smile. "An ally is far better than a friend."

Stephen's temper cooled and he thought carefully about it. Henry was right. Tonight had proved that. "Then we are allies," he decided, his tone so firm that Henry slanted him a glance. "And I will stay away from your brother." His lips thinned. He began to feel rage. How dare the prince treat him as he had the villein, when one day he would be Northumberland.

And one day the prince would be his King. Stephen sobered. One day Rufus would be his leige lord.

"Usually Rufus is better behaved," Henry commented, "but in your case, because you are only a hostage, he assumed no one would care if he did as he willed."

It took Stephen a full moment to comprehend what Henry had said. "I am no hostage."

"Oh, come! You mean, you do not know? No one told you? Your father did not tell you?"

There was only disbelief. "I am no hostage. I foster with the King."

"You are a hostage, Stephen. Just as Duncan is a check upon his father's power, so, too, you are a check upon your father's power."

"But—my father and the King—they are friends!"

Henry was grave. "Once they were friends, but I know well of what I speak. I have heard my father rage about Lord Rolfe de Warenne. He is afraid, for he has given him too much, and what he has not given, Lord Rolfe has taken. You are here to guarantee that Lord Rolfe continues to support the King against his enemies."

Suddenly Stephen felt even more alone than he had earlier. "He d-did not t-tell me," he whispered, closing his eyes.

Henry said nothing.

Stephen could not move, could not breathe. His father had not told him the truth! He was no fostering youth but a hostage, and 'twas no great honor aftcr all!

Stephen opened his eyes and clenched his fists. Rage engulfed him. How he hated the King for forcing him from his home, for forcing his father to give him up! His father—whom he loved—who had lied to him as well! Anguish ripped him apart. Now he understood his mother's tears. Now he understood it all.

"I am sorry," Henry said as if he meant it.

Stephen looked at him warily, then forced his anger down, at the same time fixing a smile upon his lips.

" 'Tis better you know," Henry said with a shrug. "What will you do?"

"Nothing changes," Stephen stated, his tone not that of a six-year-old boy, but of a man. "I do my duty."

But in that moment everything had changed, forever.

Chapter 1

Near Carlisle, 1093

A lovers' tryst. Mary could not help smiling to herself as she hurried away from the keep, careful not to be seen. It would be her very first such rendezvous, and excitement filled her.

She was in disguise. She had shed her fine outer tunic with its long, jewel-encrusted sleeves for a peasant's coarse woolen shift. Her gold girdle had been exchanged for a braided leather belt, her pointy silk shoes for wooden clogs. She had even been clever enough to borrow a pair of rough wool socks from the dairymaid, and an old linen veil covered her blond hair. Although her lover was her betrothed, a clandestine meeting was out of the question for any lady, much less herself, and she was determined not to get caught.

Mary's smile broadened. She was immersed in visions of her handsome laird sweeping her into his arms for her very first kiss. Her marriage had been arranged for political reasons, of course, so she knew very well how lucky she was to have fallen in love with Doug Mackinnon, a young man who had been her friend since childhood.

The sound of voices slowed Mary. For an instant she thought that Doug must have company, but then she realized that the voices were not speaking in Gaelic or English. With a gasp of fright she scrambled behind a big oak tree, crouching down in the grass. She peeped around it. For an instant she could not move, frozen with disbelief.

Norman soldiers filled the small glade in front of her.

Abruptly Mary haunched down even more, her heart slamming against her ribs. All thoughts of her tryst with Doug fled. Had she taken just one more step out of the woods and into the sunny glade she would have walked right into their camp!

Mary was afraid to move. She had been teased by her father many times that she was far too clever for a girl, and now her mind was already spinning out its own conclusions. Why were Norman soldiers there, on Scottish soil? Did they know of the wedding of the Liddel heir that would take place on the morrow? Liddel was an important outpost for her father, Malcolm, holding Carlisle and this part of the border for Scotland against the marauding, treacherous Normans. A fragile peace had reigned in the past two years since Malcolm had sworn fealty again to their Norman king, Rufus the Red, at Abernathy. Had the Normans been so clever, then, knowing that Liddel would be so preoccupied with the wedding festivities that they could camp under its very nose and spy—or do worse? Outrage swept through Mary. They were up to no good; she must relay this information immediately to Malcolm.

Her knees began to ache from squatting behind the tree. She raised herself slightly to take another peek at the Normans. They were making camp despite the fact that it was still several hours before dark. Scanning the group of men in front of her, she instantly saw why. Her eyes widened. One of the Normans was hurt. Two of the knights were helping a huge man dismount from his destrier, blood pouring down one of his powerful legs. Mary hated the sight of blood, but she did not look away. She could not. For she was looking at a man she had seen just once before, but had been unable to forget.

Suddenly it was hard to breathe—her lungs felt crushed and her mouth had gone dry. If only she had been able to forget him. Two years ago at Abernathy he had stood behind his rotten King, William Rufus, towering over the King's head of flaming red hair, his face a hard mask, while Rufus was openly smug. And beneath Rufus, on his knees in the dirt, had been her father, Malcolm, the King of Scotland, forced at the point of a sword to swear allegiance to the King of England.

Mary had been the only maiden present—women were not welcome at such events—and she had come in disguise. It had been a gathering of armies, after another attempt by Malcolm to invade and conquer Northumberland. She had been surrounded by much of the Scot army, all loyal to her father. Yet their numbers had been pitiful in comparison to the forces facing them—the most brutal in the land— that of the Earl of Northumberland. The man she could not remove her gaze from was bastard heir to the earl, Stephen de Warenne.

He had not noticed her then. She had been standing behind her brother, dressed as Edgar's page, careful not to draw any attention to herself, she certainly did not want her own family to recognize her, for more than a scolding would come. Edgar had been an unwilling participant in her escapade, for he, too, knew how angry their father would be for this.

Mary had been mesmerized by the bastard heir, staring at him from around her brother's shoulder. Once his gaze had connected with hers, a mere coincidence. The moment had lasted less than a heartbeat.

As she stared at Northumberland's bastard now, Mary's fists clenched. Her gaze was riveted on the man. He was one of her father's worst enemies. She prayed his wound would cause him to die.

He did not appear to be at death's door. Although he had to be weak from loss of blood and in great pain, he wore an expression similar to the one he had worn at Abernathy— hard and inscrutable. She knew he was ruthless; never had he showed the Scots any mercy. Was he incapable of feeling? Was he even immune to physical pain?

One large black tent had been erected in the open field, and the Northumberland banner already flew beside it. It was a striking flag, its field divided into three diagonal bands of black, white, and gold, in its center a short-stemmed, bloodred rose. Mary watched as a page dragged fur pallets inside the tent while the two knights supporting de Warenne helped him limp within. The tent flap closed behind them.

Mary collapsed. She was perspiring heavily, her mouth absolutely dry. This was worse, so much worse, than she had first thought. Stephen de Warenne was not just ruthless but a great military commander, exactly like his father, and his prowess was undisputed. He was also ambitious. The family's astonishing rise to preeminence from a history of landlessness was well known, and the whole realm feared the ambition of all the de Warennes. What was he doing here? What disaster did he intend to unleash upon Scotland now?

Mary knew she must return to the keep and seek an audience with her father. Yet she was terrified of moving, for to be caught by these men would be a catastrophe. Nothing could be worse. Despite her fear, somehow she must dare to creep backwards, farther into the woods, until she could safely turn and run.

The camp was busy. The horses were being unsaddled and fed. A small, smokeless fire had been stoked. Broadswords, battle-axes, lances, and shields were placed carefully by the heavy leather saddles. Every indication told Mary that this was a serious war party. If she did not escape now while the knights were still preoccupied with setting up their camp, she would have to wait until they slept, and then there would be watchful guards posted. Mary positioned herself in a crouch, refusing to give in to her fear. A twig snapped as she shifted her weight, but no one heard it.

She let out a long breath, backing up a step, never taking her gaze from the camp. At that exact moment a breeze materialized, moving the branches of the big oak tree right above her head. Mary froze, praying.

Several of the knights nearest to the woods—and to her—turned, staring directly at the tree she had been hiding behind. They saw her at once. Mary did not need any more encouragement. She lifted her skirts and fled.

"Halt! Halt now, wench!"

She heard them crashing through the woods. She ran as hard as she could. Having been raised with six brothers, she was a good runner, fast for a girl, but she was unused to the clumsy clogs. Abruptly she tripped hard and went sprawling down in the grass.

"Oh ho!" shouted one of the men with lecherous laughter. Just as she gained her feet, he was upon her, his hand closing on the folds of her tunic at the nape of her neck. He jerked her back to him.

Mary screamed as he reeled her in, and when she was close enough, she tried to kick him in the groin. He easily evaded her, and both he and his companion laughed at her very real efforts of resistance.

He immobilized her, enfolding her in his arms. Mary writhed, but quickly she went still. There was no way to escape his hold. She fought to catch her breath.

"What's this?" Her captor's eyes widened as he got his first glimpse of her. His friend was startled into silence as well.

The veil had slipped, and they could clearly see her features. Mary was well aware that she was beautiful, for she had been told so many times. Indeed, traveling minstrels frequently sang about Princess Mary and her incomparable beauty. She had a pale, perfect complexion, a small, slightly upturned nose, high cheekbones, and an intriguingly heart-shaped face. Her eyes were almond-shaped and green, her mouth full and red.

Yet Mary knew that beauty of the flesh was unimportant. That concept had been drummed into her head by her mother since she was a child, so she had never cared one way or the other about her looks, until Doug had told her how beautiful he thought her to be just yesterday. And until now. Until she was caught by these two Norman knights whose intentions were obvious. Desperately she tried to think, her wide, catlike eyes filled with a mixture of defiance and fear.

"Ha!" the young knight laughed, pleasure transforming his countenance. "Look at this! Look at what I have found!"

"Ahh, Will, *we* found her—*we* found her," his cohort responded. The other men in the camp had heard Mary's screams and began to gather around the trio.

"Usually I don't mind sharing, Guy, but not this time," Will replied, tightening his hold on Mary's arms.

But Mary wasn't struggling. Wasting her energy was pointless, especially if she needed to conserve her strength in order to resist these men. The two knights began to argue over her fate, while another dozen knights ringed them, jeering and leering. Despair welled and her cheeks flamed. Unfortunately she understood Norman French perfectly and missed not one of the lecherous remarks. She thought rapidly. She would be raped like any common peasant unless she revealed her identity. But if she revealed her identity, she would be held hostage, at great cost to Malcolm and Scotland. Both outcomes were unacceptable. She must find a middle ground.

A flash of dull silver color caught Mary's attention. She saw a knight emerging from the tent, striding towards them. Both Will and Guy fell into silence as the older man approached, elbowing through the circle of men. "What's the ruckus?" His cool gray eyes fell on Mary. "You are disturbing Stephen. What have we here? Tonight's entertainment?"

Mary had had enough. "I nae be amusement fer the likes a yae!" She had decided to continue her disguise for as long as possible, and she spoke in a heavily accented burr. "Norman pig!"

"Come now, girl, don't you like Normans?" The older man was slightly amused.

"I hate ye all, damn ye to hell!" Mary spat. She was quaking inside, but she would never let them know it. Then her heart lurched. For behind the man, the tent flap moved again, this time to expose Stephen de Warenne.

He limped out, leaning heavily on a staff. His face was drawn in pain and gray in pallor, but his eyes were bright and keenly intelligent. They lanced the small group. "What passes?"

Mary inhaled. Although a stone's throw separated them, he was bigger than she remembered, bigger and more powerful and more frightening. And he was close to being naked; he had shed his mail and most of his clothing. He wore only a short undertunic which just covered his groin, calf-high boots, and a cloth bandage, high up on one of his powerful thighs.

Intently he met her regard.

Mary swallowed. She had seen men's legs bare before, of course, but Scotsmen, decently clad in knee-high kilts and tall leggings. Now she quickly looked away, her face already flaming at the male nudity facing her.

"Will appears to have caught us tonight's repast, Stephen," the older man said.

Mary tensed, glancing up. Stephen's gaze turned to one of inspection. He did not respond to Neale as his gaze slid down her slim body. Mary's heart thudded. She did not like the way he was looking at her, and if he thought to cow her, he would not—even though she *was* cowed. She glared furiously back.

"Bring her to me, Neale," Stephen ordered, and then he ducked and disappeared back into his tent.

Neale suddenly chortled, a sound at odds with his stern, battle-scarred face and cold, iron-gray eyes. "It appears that his lordship is not as badly off as it appears, and I do think he has settled your argument, lads."

Mary was paralyzed by the meaning of Stephen de Warenne's words. The old knight's comment brought her to life. "No!" she cried. Then, remembering her disguise, she reverted to her burr. "Nae! Nae!"

Despite her protests, Neale grabbed her arm and propelled her towards the tent. Mary was a small, slender girl, but nevertheless she fought him every step of the way, digging in her heels, twisting, frantically trying to kick him. He ignored her, dragging her with him as easily as if she were a small child.

Laughter sounded. The men found her pathetic struggle and imminent fate amusing. Hot tears blurred her vision as she heard the coarse jests being bandied about. She could not help but understand what was being so crudely said. Graphic references were made about the sexual prowess and physical endowment of the man she was being brought to. "His lordship will probably kill her," someone finally joked.

Terror seized her. And then it was too late. Neale was pushing her ahead of him into the tent.

Inside it was dark. Mary stumbled when Neale released her but caught herself before falling. She was trembling and out of breath as her eyes adjusted to the shadows. She finally saw him. Her enemy was half-sitting on the pallet of fur-lined blankets, propped up by his saddle. His presence seemed gigantic in the small tent, and a feeling of claustrophobia and imminent doom swept over her.

Stephen sat up straighter. "You may leave us, Neale."

Neale turned. Mary cried out. "Nae! Do na gae!" But Neale was already gone. She whirled to face Stephen, panicked, slim hands raised. "Do nae touch me!"

"Come here."

She froze. His words were soft, but unquestionably a command. The kind of command one automatically obeyed, but her feet did not move, and now her mind was frozen, too.

"Woman, come here, *now*."

Mary searched his countenance. There was no innuendo in his tone to confirm that her fate was about to be a violent rape—an act that, according to all she had just heard, would most likely murder her. Nevertheless, she was shaking.

Her gaze found his again; he had been studying her, too, with growing impatience. "What do yae want with me?" she managed.

"What do you think I want?" he gritted. "You are a woman. I am in pain. Come here and tend my leg properly, now."

Mary started and then relief flooded her. "Is that all yae want?" She was incredulous.

His jaw flexed. "I am used to instant obedience, woman. Come here and do what you have been trained to do."

Mary knew she must obey, for his rising temper was obvious, but if she did not reach an agreement with him now, while she had some tiny portion of power, she never would. "I will gladly tend ye, if ye promise tae release me unharmed after."

He was openly incredulous. "I command—and you make demands?"

She knew she had pushed him as far as she should, that she should not push him any further, but despite herself, she said, "Aye, I do."

He smiled. It was a cold and dangerous smile that did not reach his dark, glittering eyes, and it was infinitely frightening. "Very few men have dared to disobey me, and even fewer have survived to see the light of another day."

Mary inhaled, unable to turn her regard away from his, unable to even blink. Whatever power he possessed consumed her. Her knees had turned soft, threatening to give way. And something dangerous and terrible in its potency seemed to reverberate between them. "Do yae threaten me?" she whispered hoarsely.

"Only your sex spares you."

She had not a doubt that if she were a boy, she would now be dead. He was her single most hated enemy, the enemy of her people, of her family, of her father, the King. Her situation was dire, but she must not give in to her growing panic. Mary stiffened her spine. If ever was the time for heroics, it was now. "Sae do ye agree tae my terms?"

He stared. "I think you are either the most stupid lass I have yet to meet, or the bravest."

She stared back, hardly complimented and too frightened to be furious.

"You heal me and you shall be released."

Mary gasped. She had attained what she sought, but she was certain she could not trust him, not as far as her youngest brother could spit. She had no choice, however. Grimly Mary came forward, determined now to see to his injury, to tend to him as quickly as was possible, praying she would be freed as he had promised so she could immediately reveal all that she had so far learned to her father. She tried to ignore his brilliant gaze, which never left her person. Swallowing, she knelt by his side. "What happened tae ye?"

"A maddened boor. My horse broke its leg just before the kill, leaving me in the creature's path. I slew it, of course, but not before this."

She did not reply. Her gaze was on his hard, dark-skinned, naked thigh. The bandage was already stained crimson. The wound was high, perilously close to his privates. For a moment her glance was drawn there, where she had no business looking—at the dark shadow between his legs.

Heat suffused her. Her hands shook, and she clenched the folds of her skirt.

She saw only a blur of movement, and his huge hand was clamped around her small wrist. A scant second later, she was lying flat on his rock-hard chest, chin to chin with him. When he spoke, his breath touched her lips. "Why do you wait?"

Her gaze left his mouth and flew to his eyes. For the first time she saw the stark pain there. Something twisted in her heart, compassion she refused to entertain. She must not think of this man as human, or as being hurt and suffering. She must only remember him as an inhuman monster, one capable of single-handedly and cold-bloodedly killing her people to suit his aggressive nature.

She nodded, unable to speak, the feel of him warm and solid and disturbing beneath her breasts. He released her. Mary scrambled onto her knees at his side. She touched the bandage. Cautiously she began to unwrap it.

She winced. The wound was open, bleeding and ugly, but not too deep. Water and lye soap had been brought to clean the injury. " 'Twill hurt."

He met her gaze, saying nothing. In the dim light his eyes seemed as jet black as his hair, and this close, they were unquestionably beautiful. She pursed her mouth, refusing to dwell upon such thoughts.

As she worked over him, trying not to hurt him, she was aware of his black regard boring into her, making her terribly warm and uncomfortable. She felt small and vulnerable next to him, dwarfed by the power he exuded even while hurt and momentarily at her mercy. It was a ludicrous notion. A man like this even briefly at her or anyone else's mercy. He would never submit to another's domination, not even while wrenched with pain, and especially not a woman's.

The wound was finally clean. Mary paused, wetting her dry lips, looking at him. "It needs tae be stitched."

"There's a needle and thread and fresh linen behind you."

Mary looked over and nodded. She picked up the needle, hesitating. "Perhaps yae want some wine."

His brow lifted. "So you do have a heart beneath those pretty little breasts?"

She tensed. "I have nae heart fer yae!"

"Do it."

What did she care if he suffered even more at her hands? Unfathomably angry, trembling with agitation, she picked up the needle. She had stitched up wounds before, but she would never grow accustomed to the procedure. Her stomach roiled. She bent over him, working diligently and precisely, aware of his gaze on the top of her head, unable to forget his words. When she had finished she knotted the thread and cut it with her small, white teeth. She straightened, relieved that the surgery was over.

Mary expected to see him drained of all color, his face a mask of pain. Instead, his eyes were entirely lucid but brilliant, dangerously brilliant, holding hers. Quickly Mary picked up a fresh piece of linen, dropping her gaze.

She was greeted with a sight she did not want to see, had no right to see. She had moved his tunic aside to perform the surgery, exposing his heavy genitals, and now, now she quickly settled it back into place. Her face flamed, stinging. She pressed the linen to his leg, trying not to think. But those men were right. If he raped her, he would kill her. Her hands, small and delicate and white, contrasting sharply with his dark, powerful legs, trembled as she quickly tied the bandage.

The exact instant she was done, his hand cupped her face, forcing her chin up and her regard to his. "You dress like a hag, but act like a lady."

Mary was frozen.

His gaze left her eyes, sliding over her features one by one, finally lingering on her lips. "No peasant woman I have ever seen has a face such as yours."

She opened her mouth but found herself incapable of summoning a self-defense. Her stunned mind could drum up only one terrible image, and that was of her captor pressing her down beneath him on his pallet.

His hand left her face, but caught her own palm, turning it over. "Milk white, silk-soft."

Terrified and mute, aware that she had not a single callus, she was drawn to his glittering gaze. She recognized the intensity there now even though she had never been faced with such an uninhibited display of male lust before.

The corners of his mouth lifted—an attractive, perfectly formed mouth, Mary could not help thinking—in an expression that could not be described as even the semblance of a smile; rather, it hinted at aggression and triumph and primitive satisfaction. Mary drew back, a second too late. He had already slipped her veil from her hair. As he leaned close, nuzzling her cheek, he said, "You hair is clean and it smells of flowers." He straightened, staring. "I have little doubt that if I looked beneath your clothes, I would find skin as clean and as sweet-smelling."

Mary lurched to her feet. She did not get far. He gripped one wrist, jerking her immediately back down on her knees beside him. "Am I correct?"

"Nae! Na' at all! I swear tae yae—" Mary's words were cut off when his hand snaked up her leg, beneath all of her clothing, a caress of hard, callused palm on soft, naked skin. Mary cried out, shocked at the violent sensation sweeping through her. She was staring down dumbly at the entire length of her bare leg, from where her wool socks ended at her calf to the very top of her thigh, which he had just exposed.

"As I thought," he said, and now there was a change in his tone, one Mary immediately recognized despite her inexperience, one that tightened every fiber of her being and made her pulse soar.

"I . . . I can explain," she whispered.

"Soft, so soft, and clean," he said, locking regards with her again. He did not cover up her nakedness. He did not remove his hand from her thigh, his fingertips perilously close to grazing the ripe plumpness at the apex there. Instead, nostrils flared now, he leaned close, his face—his lips—brushing her neck.

Mary gasped. Her eyes fell closed, her body jolted as thoroughly by his kiss as if by a bolt of lightning. There was no air to be had in the cramped space of the tent. His mouth moved with growing fervor on the vulnerable underside of her neck. His thumb slipped through her pubic hair and up against the cleft of her flesh. Mary could not contain herself. She moaned. Her mind, once filled with hostility, was now dizzily blank, receptive to nothing but the stunning sensation he dealt her as deftly as he might a sword's fatal blow.

He crooned in her ear, his mouth against one lobe, his thumb against another, "So who are you, my lady? And more importantly, what are you, if not a spy?"

Chapter 2

Stephen de Warenne watched her wrench away from him with a cry of fright. Had he thrown icy water over her head, he could not have shocked her more. She did not get far. His grip was iron on her wrists. Casually he pulled her back to him, until her nose almost touched his.

He was indifferent to women, with precisely two exceptions, but he was not immune to females he found attractive, and this one was probably as close to perfection as anyone would ever come—in face and form, at least. Despite the fact that she was no common wench—that undoubtedly she was an experienced courtesan sent to whore for him and spy upon him by his enemies, of whom he had a few—he was hardly indifferent to the entire length of her naked leg, now clamped between his, or the softness of her breasts, crushed against his chest, or the astounding beauty of her face, just inches from his own.

Blood had long since surged to his phallus. He was heavy and impatient. Their position was so intimate that she could feel every inch of him, but wasn't seduction her intention? Why else would such a woman be sent to him in such an

elaborate disguise? He attributed her wide, frightened gaze
to his having ascertained the truth.

For a moment, despite his better intentions, he longed to
take her, then and there, hard and fast, and be done with
it. Answers could come later. But he was his father's son
and heir. Furthering the interests of Northumberland had
been his overriding ambition since he had won his spurs
at thirteen. His reputation as a keen and ruthless leader
had been earned, not given. Answers could not wait. If
his enemies knew he was there, the King's plans were in
jeopardy.

"Wh-What?" Mary finally managed to gasp.

"I think you heard me very well, demoiselle," he said
coldly. Because his blood was so overheated, he set her
down on the pallet beside him while keeping a cautious grip
on her wrist. Inherent politeness made him refer to her as if
she were a lady when she was obviously the furthest thing
from it, although to look at her, a man would never guess
so. For some reason, he was disappointed that her angelic
facade was only that, a facade. "Who has sent you here to
spy upon me? Montgomery? Roger Beaufort? The King? Or
is Prince Henry once again up to his infernal tricks?"

She stared at him as if mesmerized. He was a hardened
man, yet a pang of empathy swept him. She was young, very
young. The courtesans he knew—and so frequently used—
were older and widowed. This girl looked to be no more
than fifteen or sixteen, but again, looks deceived.

"I am nae spy," she gasped out.

"Do not treat me as a fool," he said coldly.

"Yae promised tae release me!"

"I am not yet healed." He watched her absorb his statement. Instantly she understood his meaning, rage suffusing
her features. He should not be surprised at how quick she
was. Only a very clever woman would be sent to work her
wiles upon him.

"Yae deceived me!" she cried. "Yae made me believe
yae'd let me gae after I tended tae yer wound!"

"You believed what you chose to believe." His patience
was at an end. "Enough. I demand answers and I demand
them now. Who are you and who sent you?"

She shook her head, tears coming to her eyes, tears that could not, he told himself, affect him. He knew from many years of experience that, with very few exceptions, women were not to be trusted. This one was not one of those exceptions; indeed, she should be mistrusted more than most. She was young but no innocent and no child. Undoubtedly her fear and tears were theatrics.

"I am nae spy."

Another thought had occurred to him. "Or did Malcolm Canmore send you?"

She started. "Nae! He dinna! I dinna even know him! I am nae spy, I swear tae yae!"

She was lying. He was certain of it. Just as he was certain now that Malcolm Canmore was behind this treachery. Newfound anger made him doubly grim. "I warn you, demoiselle, I have the means of forcing information from you, and once provoked, I am merciless."

"Please! I can explain tae yae,'tis not what yae think!"

"Then I suggest you do so now."

"I—I am a bastard. Me father is Sinclair o' Dounreay Castle, me mother a dairymaid," she blurted, fast.

He did not raise a brow. Such a claim was only possible if she thought to dupe him, given her absurdly ill-fitting disguise. And it was possible that she was actually some laird's by-blow. Yet he was certain that she was lying, and she would only be lying if she were a spy. "Eager now to volunteer information, demoiselle? Where is Dounreay?"

"As far north as ye can gae." She worried her hands in her lap, not meeting his eyes.

It was an excellent lie. He would not be able to confirm her parentage in a timely manner, although confirm it, he would. He almost felt a grudging respect for her; she was no fool. And to come to him on such an errand took a great deal of courage. "As far north as you can go," he repeated. "As far north as the Orkney Islands?"

She smiled in relief. "Almost."

He sat very still, regarding her. It was the first time that she had smiled since he had laid his eyes upon her, and if he had thought her beautiful before, she was glorious now. The interrogation had distracted him from his carnal inclinations, but now his blood roiled and his shaft reared rock-hard against his short shift again. Grimly he probed on. "I see. And what brings you so far south to Carlisle?"

She was flushing crimson, tearing her gaze from his loins. He could almost see her mind working. It was clear to him that she thought frantically for a plausible answer, which puzzled him. If she were as clever as he was becoming convinced that she was, she should have memorized her story far in advance of their meeting. Nor did he understand her blushes.

"I am from Liddel. My mother was from Liddel."

Stephen leaned back against his saddle, clapping his hands twice. "A memorable performance, demoiselle."

"Yae dinna believe me?!"

"I do not believe a single word you have said."

She froze, her eyes huge and riveted to his.

"You have ten seconds, demoiselle, to tell me all of the truth. If you fail to do so, you shall suffer the consequences as forewarned."

She gasped, pulling away from him. He knew her intentions the moment that she did. She lurched to her feet, intent on escape. Although there was nowhere for her to run to but into the arms of his men, Stephen responded as any red-blooded male would. Despite the pain that shot through him, he staggered to his feet, too. He caught her at once. She screamed.

Without another thought, Stephen turned her in his arms and gripped the back of her head and covered her mouth with his.

He had touched her intimately, but he had not really kissed her. Not in the manner he had wished to, from the moment he first gazed upon her extraordinary face. His kiss was openmouthed and thorough. His hands slid down her back, each palm cupping one of her buttocks. "Let's try again, *petite*," he said hoarsely, lifting her up against his raging erection. He moved his mouth down on hers.

"Nae," she began, but was cut off. His mouth opened hers quickly. Stephen plumbed her warmth with his tongue, each thrust becoming more and more forceful, more rapacious. Tentatively she met one, and the tips of their tongues touched.

He could not help himself, his body surged even more wildly, more impossibly, in response to her—he wanted complete, instant surrender. He expected it. He needed it—now. But to his amazement, she suddenly pulled her face away from his. "No—we must not."

"Do not tease me now," he gritted, catching her chin in one hand. He forced her mouth up to his again.

She cried out in another halfhearted protest. She raised her small fists against his chest, then clutched his tunic. Stephen would have laughed with primitive elation except for the fact that he was too intent now to laugh about anything. Their mouths were fused, their tongues mated.

Suddenly she tore her face away. She writhed frantically in his iron embrace, as if to escape, yet her every gyration, brushing his manhood, was as artful and agonizing as a whore's purposeful caress. As an actress, she was superb. For it was almost as if she were not a seductress, as if, knowing the end was near, she was truly panicked. Despite his brief confusion, he could not stop himself now. He managed to reassure himself that she deliberately provoked his confusion to incite him even more wholly.

Stephen had had enough of these games. He had no desire to spill his seed upon them both, which he feared he might actually do. He pushed her down on the pallet. She continued to play the unwilling woman, her fists bouncing pitifully off of him, making small, fearful sounds. He took her mouth again. When their loins touched as he settled himself upon her, she went still.

Lightning appeared to have struck them both. "I cannot wait," he whispered, words he had never whispered before.

The eyes he gazed down into as he spoke were wide with emotions he could not identify. Her face was flushed pink and sheened with perspiration. She did not move. And her palms curled about his massive shoulders, gripping him tightly.

Stephen spread her legs wide with his knees, beginning to shake fiercely. He was aware of the drops of sweat that rolled down his face and onto hers. He flicked her long tunic up to her waist, and for a single moment, was poised above her.

Their gazes met, held. She opened her mouth but said nothing. Stephen looked at her breasts, heaving beneath her gown, her nipples tight and erect. He touched one. She closed her eyes and sobbed, the sound laden with anguish.

He looked down at her and could no more help himself from touching her now than he had before. He slid his hand between her legs and found the folds of her flesh swollen and heavy with the pulse of her blood. She was as hot for him as he was for her, spy or not. This was no act. He thrust a finger into her.

He froze. There was no mistaking the barrier he had come up against. He was shocked. She could not be a virgin— she was a whore sent to spy. But she was a virgin; it was a fact.

And in the midst of confusion there was a sudden and sweeping sense of elation—she had never known a man; he would be the first.

This far aroused, he had never denied himself. But he had never taken a virgin before—unlike many men he knew, rape had never excited him. And if she was a virgin, then she was no whore sent to spy upon him.

Stephen's mind reached these astounding conclusions in mere seconds. It was probably the hardest deed he had ever done, but he launched himself off of her. Dazed and panting, he lay unmoving on his stomach beside her, wishing that the fur pallet he was pressing himself into was much, much harder.

Sanity returned swiftly despite the persistent ache in his loins. There were no virgin whores, no virgin spies. Was it possible that she had been telling him the truth? Was her father some northern laird, her mother a dairymaid? It was plausible, yet he doubted it. Her hands had never seen rough labor, but she was dressed as one who labored. If she was a bastard, she had been raised as a lady. This costume was a disguise. Why?

Suddenly she moved. She slid from the pallet, as quick as a wild vixen. Stephen was even quicker, reaching out and grabbing her before she took a second step, without moving from the furs. His leg hurt too much now for such antics. The force of his grip caused her to fall in a heap at his side.

Restraining a groan, he sat up and extended his hand to her. "Mademoiselle?"

She was panting. Although he saw that she was furious, he allowed her to take his hand and he lifted her to her feet. It was a mistake. Immediately she drew back her fist and hit him with all of her strength in his jaw.

He didn't move, stunned speechless.

"Norman bastard! You are a pig and a brute! And a liar!" she shrieked. She raised her fist to hit him again.

This time Stephen reacted. He caught her wrist, pulling her forward. She wound up in his lap.

"No!" she screamed, twisting to leap free of him.

He held her in place. "You have deceived me, struck me, and maligned me," he said harshly, shaking her once. She went still. "I thought you brave, but now I am beginning to think you very foolish—or mad."

She lifted her chin, a defiant gesture, despite the fact that her eyes were glazed with unshed tears. "I am not mad."

His jaw tightened. "You have lost your burr, demoiselle."

She paled. "When can I leave?"

"You were not so eager to leave me—and my bed—a few moments ago."

She flushed. "No, I am eager to leave your bed—to leave you. This minute is not soon enough."

"Who's the liar now?"

"I speak the truth!"

"I think not. Indeed, thus far you have not spoken a single word that is true. I ask you again, who are you and why are you here?"

She swallowed, meeting him stare for stare. He felt her mind working. "Please unhand me," she said huskily. "And I will tell you all."

Giving her a skeptical look, he did as she asked. She scooted to her feet and put the length of the tent between them, standing with her back to the exit, hugging herself defensively. Her posture made him see her as a child, not a woman, and he was suddenly ashamed of his behavior. By all the saints, he had treated her as he would a whore, and she was a young virgin, certainly not more than sixteen. Perhaps the real question wasn't who was she, but *what* was she? Virgin or whore, villein or lady, child or woman? Spy or innocent? "You may begin with your name."

She wet her lips. "Mairi. Mairi Sinclair. My father is Rob Sinclair. My mother is dead, and she was a maid at Liddel." She flinched from his gaze. "And you were right—these clothes are a disguise."

Tersely he said, "Were you sent to me to spy?"

"No!" She was pale. "I was in disguise because I was meeting someone. A—A man."

And Stephen understood. "Ahh, I see now. A man."

Again her small chin lifted. " 'Tis not what you think. The man was, I mean, he is my betrothed."

His stare was ice. "You have yet to explain your disguise."

" 'Tis unseemly for a lady to tryst with a man, even when that man is to be her husband, and you know it well."

"And who is this paragon of manhood who lures you to an undoubted fall from grace?"

She bit her lip. "What does it matter?"

It shouldn't matter, except for the fact that he intended to verify every word she said. "It matters." He was not pleased to realize that he was peeved—perhaps even jealous—that this woman obviously coveted another man. "Do you love him?"

She was furious. "That, Sir Norman, is none of your affair!"

It wasn't. He stood stiffly, finding his staff in order to lean upon it. Then he limped to her until he was towering over her. He had to admire her; she stood her ground. "To the contrary, demoiselle, you are now wholly my affair. And until I am satisfied, you shall be detained."

She lost the little color she had. "*Until you are satisfied, I shall be detained!* What do you mean?"

"I mean," he said grimly, "that I intend to unearth the truth, the entire truth, about you, and until I do, you are my guest." He hobbled past her, raising the tent flap.

"Your guest!" she cried after him. "You mean that I am your *prisoner*! But why? What have I done? I have done nothing, Norman!"

He paused and turned. "To the contrary, demoiselle. You have whetted my very jaded appetite, and my even more jaded interest. If you are indeed of little import, I think we shall suit well, you and I, for a time, at least."

Mary stared after his back as he limped from the tent, leaving her alone. What did that last remark mean? Oh, dear God! She dared not delude herself. He suspected her deceit, intended to find the truth, and whether he did or not, she was in great jeopardy!

She sank down on the hard dirt floor, limp and drained. Rolfe de Warenne, the Earl of Northumberland, was one of the most powerful lords in the realm, first having been an intimate adviser to King William the Bastard, and now an intimate adviser to the Bastard's son, the rotten King William Rufus. The earl was also her father's worst enemy, and by extension, so was this man, his bastard son and heir. Malcolm and Northumberland had clashed on too many occasions to count. The earl had been nothing but a penniless, landless knight when he had followed Duke William to England, though 'twas said he was the younger son of a great Poitevin family. Shortly after the invasion, he had been awarded a small fief in Northumberland; one that, today, reached Newcastle-on-Tyne in the south and the River Tweed in the north. Though the heart of Malcolm's kingdom lay between the Moray Firth and the Firth of Forth, well north of the Tweed, the Kings of Scotland had long claimed the right to rule all of the territory south of Lothian as far as Rere Crossing. The de Warennes were interlopers. Malcolm had spent his entire adult life attempting to regain Scotland's lost territory. The existing border between Scotland and Northumberland had been brutally and bloodily fought over for many years. Mary had delivered herself right into the hands of her father's worst enemy.

The Norman's parting words echoed, a frightening refrain. If she understood him, he intended to assuage his lust on her if he thought her to be of no importance to anyone. Thus, if he did not learn the truth of her identity, she would be taken and used until he tired of her and discarded her. She would, in fact, be ruined. Doug would no longer want her. Of course, he was no fool and he would still marry her. After all, she was a princess with a great dowry.

She almost wept. The only thing worse would be if the Norman learned the truth. If he discovered that she was the daughter of Malcolm Canmore, she would be a hostage until her father paid whatever exorbitant ransom her captor demanded. She did not fool herself for an instant. The Norman would do his best to cripple her father. He would demand far more than gold and coin; he would demand land. Precious, priceless Scottish land. Land that Scottish blood had been spilled over again and again.

And after the ransom was paid—and her father would pay it—the border would once again be plunged into a fierce, bloody war. Two years' fragile peace would disintegrate like the wisps of yesterday's dreams.

She clenched her small fists, sucking in not just her breath but her courage. Her situation could not possibly be worse. Now she was fiercely glad she had not revealed her identity to him.

The Norman was a brute, she thought grimly—he had proved that beyond hearsay—but he was no fool. He had proved that, too. He had been quick to see through her careful, elaborate disguise, and he doubted the tale she had invented, a tale that was not unreasonable and might have fooled a lesser man. She would need every ounce of courage she had and then some; she would need all of her shrewd wits as well. She must not let him even guess who she was. For having met him, Mary realized the extent of his power and his will. If there was a way for him to discover the truth of her identity, the Norman would undoubtedly find it, and once he did, her father and Scotland—and she herself—would suffer the horrible consequences.

Just as her father used spies all the time, this man would certainly use them, too. By this evening there would be a crisis at Liddel over her disappearance. A Norman spy would eventually report this. Was her captor shrewd enough to guess the truth once he learned that Malcolm's daughter was missing? How could he not comprehend her identity in such circumstances!

Mary closed her eyes. How could she keep her identity hidden yet still hold him at bay for any length of time? It seemed an impossible task. Escape was the only solution, but for the moment, that, too, was an impossibility.

She wiped her eyes. Tears solved nothing. She must ready herself for their next war of wits and wills. So far she had not done very well. And she did not want to repeat what had just passed between them—the encounter that had drained her so, yet left her feeling disturbed and agitated and so strangely ripe.

What had just passed between them. Mary made a choked sound, her mind flooding with fresh memories. To her horror, she could still feel his touch, his mouth on hers, his hard loins on hers, and her body began throbbing. She covered her face with her hands. Mary could no longer avoid her shame. It overwhelmed her.

Exhaustion overtook her. She would not brood upon the bastard heir anymore. She shifted to look longingly at the fur pallet. She could only guess whether the Norman would return to sleep there or not, and she was too fatigued now to think clearly. But it didn't matter. She could not lie in his bed, even alone; the very idea was atrocious.

Mary sank down on the dirt floor, huddling into a small ball. Finally numbness settled upon her aching mind, but sleep eluded her. She drifted restlessly, listening to the sounds of the night and the camp, the nickering of horses, a hooting owl, the men talking quietly outside, until the last of their voices died down. As the human sounds faded, she tensed, waiting for inevitable footsteps—footsteps she was certain would come. She lay rigid for a long time, but they did not come—he did not come.

Mary awoke to find the Norman's face close to her own. For one instant she did not move, dazed with sleep, gazing into glittering eyes that were not black but a rich maple brown. Then reality hit her with violent force and she jerked away from him.

He had been leaning over her, to touch his face almost to hers, but now he straightened. "I hope your story proves to be the truth, demoiselle."

His meaning was not lost upon her. "Get away from me!"

"What frightens you so this morn, mademoiselle? Is it me you fear—or yourself?"

Mary found her tongue. "I do not fear myself. I fear big black Normans for whom rape is as casual a sport as hawking."

He laughed. "I can assure you, mademoiselle, I have never participated in that particular act of violence, and I never will." He added, very low, "I have never needed to, and when you join me in my bed, it will be with enthusiasm—the same kind of enthusiasm that was in evidence last night."

His blunt reference to her appalling behavior yesterday infuriated Mary. "You will never see such enthusiasm from me again!"

He lifted a dark brow. "Do you challenge me?" His smile was genuine. "I enjoy challenges, demoiselle."

She shook her head vehemently, her heart tripping. "You have no power over me."

"To the contrary, I have an ancient power over you, mademoiselle, the power of a man over a woman."

"I am not like other women."

"No?" His teeth flashed. "You appeared to be a woman as any other last night, when you lay mewling beneath me, a woman both in my power and at my mercy. But if it makes you feel better, I will concede that you are far more interesting than all the women I have so far met. Far more interesting, far more intriguing, and—" he smiled again, his eyes suddenly warm "—far more beautiful."

Mary fought the seduction that simmered in the intensity of his gaze. She bristled. "I do not mewl, Norman! And you may say whatever you like, you may think as you undoubtedly will, but it does not change what I feel, and what I feel for you is better left unsaid."

He eyed her for a long moment, assessingly. "Beneath the anger there is much to explore, I think. Nevertheless, we are wasting not just words but time. We leave in a quarter hour.

I suggest you take a few private moments to do what you must. This dispute can be concluded at Alnwick."

De Warenne turned and limped away, moving remarkably well for a man who had recently suffered a gore wound. Mary stared after him, relieved that he was gone. Every encounter she survived—intact—seemed to her no small victory.

But she was also dismayed. Alnwick was the new seat of Northumberland. The earl, the bastard's father, had spent some fifteen years completing it, and rumor held it to be an impenetrable fortress. If that was true, it meant that once she was imprisoned there, she had no hope of being rescued.

It flashed through Mary's mind that by this morning, Malcolm and her brothers would be scouring the countryside looking for her. Perhaps she could be rescued before being imprisoned at Alnwick. She *must* be rescued first! It was her only hope.

What if she were to leave a sign for Malcolm? How could she do this?

Quickly she shoved aside the fur she had been covered with, trembling with excitement. Someone had brought her a bowl of water, and Mary quickly washed. She hurried from the tent and stopped.

Horses were being saddled, the camp packed up. Everyone appeared absorbed with their tasks. Mary saw her captor talking with another knight, his back to her.

Mary took a calming breath, praying that Stephen de Warenne would not notice her. But he suddenly turned to face her. Mary ignored him, hoping her sudden excitement did not show, walking to the woods. She was well aware that a knight trailed after her, obviously instructed to guard her. Her spirits dimmed somewhat, but not her determination. Mary disappeared behind a tree and some bushes to tend to some pressing needs. In the process she tore off a piece of her fine silk chemise, worn beneath both peasant tunics, one well laundered and bone white. Her hands were shaking so badly that it took several attempts to tie the bright piece of fabric to a branch of the tree. When she had succeeded, she tore off several additional strips, stuffing them up her sleeves. She hurried around the bushes to where the knight stood, his back to her. Her hopes soared. Surely one of the Scots searching for her would find the flag she had left!

The knight escorted her back to the camp and her captor. The Norman was in conversation with the man who had captured her yesterday.

"Liddel?" Will was saying. "It should not be a problem, Stephen; after all, by tonight everyone will be well crocked from the wedding feast. I can find out what you want, my lord." He flashed him a cocky smile.

Stephen smacked his shoulder. "Godspeed." He smiled at Mary. "Is there a message you wish to give someone? Your beloved, perhaps?"

Mary was frozen, but only for an instant. "Do you have eyes on the back of your head like some misshapen monster?"

He was amused. "Did you really think to eavesdrop? If you wish to know my intentions, you need only ask, mademoiselle."

"Why is he going to Liddel?"

"Do you have something to hide?"

"Of course not."

"Then you have nothing to fear."

He was toying with her, testing her, and she was justifiably anxious. "Why are you doing this?"

His amusement faded. "Because I cannot help myself."

They stared at each other. His gaze was briefly penetrable, and Mary saw dark desire and even darker determination. He exerted a magnetism upon her that she was powerless against. She shuddered with a sudden foreboding she dared not comprehend. It was far safer to ignore whatever had passed between them, to pretend it did not exist, had never existed.

He broke the spell he had so effectively cast. "Come, we are leaving; you shall ride with me."

Mary did not move.

He dropped the hand he had extended. "Is something wrong, Mairi?"

"I wish to ride with anyone else but you."

He planted himself in front of her and stared down at her. "But I am not giving you a choice, mademoiselle."

He smiled slightly. "Besides, riding with me will be very entertaining."

She understood the innuendo and could feel her face flame, but at least his frankness was something she could deal with. "You are so typically cocksure."

He laughed. "Did I hear that remark from a lady's lips?"

"I do not care what you think of me," she gritted. "Where is your damn horse?"

He pointed, laughing again, his teeth flashing white.

Mary marched to the big brown destrier, his laughter echoing in her mind. She resolved to outwit him no matter what the cost, and when she did, she would fling her triumph in his face. Then she would be the one laughing.

Stephen lifted her into the saddle effortlessly, then swung up behind her with the grace of a much smaller man. Mary tried to ignore the feel of his body. She gripped the pommel tightly. It was going to be a very long day; of that she had no doubt.

They traveled northeast at a rapid trot, away from Carlisle, through rocky, rolling hills. September had swept much rain across the countryside, and the land was green and verdant. It was clear to Mary that he was intent on reaching Alnwick that day. Obviously whatever mission the Normans had been about had been accomplished. She brooded upon the possibilities. She was determined to learn what the Normans had been doing in the vicinity of Carlisle and Liddel.

And every hour that passed, Mary let a piece of her chemise slip from her sleeve and flutter to the ground.

Their pace did not let up until they stopped to water the horses at noon. By then they were surrounded by the harsh Northumbrian moors and an endless gray sky. Occasionally gulls wheeled above them. Mary thankfully slid to the ground, drained from having to endure the intimacy of sharing a saddle with her captor for so many endless hours. She thought that it was as close to hell as she might ever come.

No one was paying any attention to her. Around her the knights spoke in low tones, their mounts drinking deeply. Mary edged closer to a single gaunt tree. She sat down with a show of fatigue, and let slip another piece of chemise. When the knights had remounted and reassembled a few minutes later, she got to her feet and ambled back to the group. Stephen de Warenne rode his great destrier slowly towards her.

"Enjoying the scenery, demoiselle?"

She glared. "What is there to enjoy in this scene? Nothing surrounds me but ugliness."

"Spoken like a true Scot." His gaze pierced her. "Are you a true Scot, Mairi?"

She stilled. Was he the devil—and a reader of minds? Or had he guessed her identity? Her mother, Queen Margaret, was English. Margaret's brother was Edgar Aethling, a great nephew of the Saxon King Edward the Confessor, and he had been heir to the throne of England before the Conquest. When Duke William the Bastard invaded England, Margaret's widowed mother had fled to Scotland with her children, seeking refuge, afraid for her son's life. Malcolm was smitten with Margaret at first sight, and when his first wife, Ingeborg, died, he married her almost immediately.

"I am a Scot through and through," Mary said, meaning it.

"You do not speak like a Scot—except when you choose to. Your English is flawless, better even than mine."

Of course her English was flawless, not just because her mother was English. Over the years Malcolm had anglicized his court in deference to his wife. "Perhaps Normans are too stupid and dim-witted to learn to speak English well."

His jaw tightened. "Perhaps this Norman has been dim-witted, indeed." He slid from his horse, giving her an enigmatic look. Mary did not like his words or his tone. She froze when, instead of lifting her into the saddle, he walked right past her.

He walked directly to the misshapen tree where she had been sitting. Mary's heart skipped. He stooped and retrieved her piece of chemise. His strides were hard as he returned to her, clenching the silky fabric in his fist. "What a clever little minx you are."

Mary stepped back.

His hand shot out, jerking her forward. "If you are so eager to shed your clothing, demoiselle, you need only say so."

Mary could not summon up a suitable response, especially not in the face of his fury.

"For how long have you been leaving these signs, demoiselle? *For how long?*"

Chapter 3

"**Y**ou're hurting me!" Mary cried.

Stephen instantly released her. Mary backed away from him, rubbing her arms. "Did you really think you could take me prisoner without a fight?"

Stephen was regretting hurting her, but her words made him itch to shake her again. This child-woman was determined to fight *him*? "For how long?"

"Since this morning."

Stephen was incredulous, stunned by her wit, her audacity, and her bravery. "I have greatly misjudged you," he said harshly. Then he shouted, "Neale!"

The older man was at his side instantly. "My lord?"

Stephen did not remove his furious gaze from his captive. "This shrewd little minx has made fools of us all. She has been leaving a trail. Alert the men; we may have pursuit."

Neale wheeled his destrier.

Stephen reached out and pulled Mary closer as she began to sidle away. Her body stiffened at the contact; he had to drag her with him. "Just whom were you alerting, demoiselle? Your lover? Your father?"

"Yes!" she cried. "Yes, yes, yes! And soon, so very soon, you shall be skewered by my father's sword, Norman, for he is the greatest warrior in all of Scotland!"

Stephen halted. "Is he, indeed? Then surely I must know of him."

She set her mouth mulishly.

"Your father is not this Sinclair of Dounreay as you so prettily insist, is he, demoiselle? Such an insignificant man would never attack me, and we both know it. So who are you expecting, Mairi? Is that even your name?"

She said nothing.

Very angry, he propelled her roughly towards his mount. Mary stumbled, then had to skip to keep ahead of him and out of his reach. Stephen did not care. He abruptly caught her, and heaved her into the saddle as if she were a sack of grain. He leapt onto the destrier behind her, signaling his men. The cavalcade rode off at a fast canter.

Mary closed her eyes, giving in to a moment's despair. She should not be distraught, she knew that; she should be elated. She had outfoxed the Norman with her trail of scraps. But she did not feel like gloating; she felt something close to terror. The bastard heir was enraged. Every instinct Mary had told her that there would be hell to pay for her small victory.

They rode harder now. Mary found herself frequently looking over her shoulder, hoping for a glimpse of her kinsmen upon the horizon. She saw nothing, and as every mile passed, her hopes sank a little bit more.

Where, oh where, was her father?

Now they climbed a long, gradual rise, and when at the summit, Stephen abruptly drew his mount to a halt, clamping her to his powerful, mailed body. His words quelled any protest she might have made.

"You have lost, mademoiselle," he stated. "For we are here. Look. Alnwick."

Dread rushed over her and she was heedless of how harshly she gripped his thick forearm, cutting her fingertips on his chain mail. They had arrived—and she was lost. Ahead lay Alnwick—ahead lay her prison.

The sun was setting. Partly obscured by gloom, Alnwick's stone walls appeared dark and unbreachable. The fortress lay on a huge natural motte with impenetrable man-made ditches surrounding it. The thick brown outer walls of the bailey were interspersed with watchtowers, tall and imposing; beyond them, the taller, crenellated tower of the keep could be seen, drenched in fading apricot-hued sunlight. Mary felt an acute dismay.

If she failed to escape—and escape was unlikely—and if she was not set free or ransomed, she would have little hope of ever seeing home and kin again, because no attack could be sustained for long against such a place as this, not even an attack by Malcolm.

They rode across a drawbridge and through a raised portcullis into the outer bailey, saluted by a dozen armed guards. There were a dozen buildings within—stables for the horses, shops for the keep's craftsmen, quarters for excess knights, and pantries and supply sheds. People were everywhere—women with hens underarm for the cook pot, children herding pigs, carpenters working with their apprentices, farriers and grooms and horses, servants and bondsmen. An oxcart laden with barrels of wine had entered ahead of them; other carts were being unloaded near the wooden stairs at the entrance to the keep. The noise was deafening. Amidst the human cacophony was the barking of hounds, the squawking of hens, the whinnies of horses, the ringing of the smith's anvil, and the banging of the carpenter's hammer. There was scolding and laughter, terse shouted commands. Mary had never been inside such a large fortification before—it was larger than most Scottish villages and larger even than her home, the royal fortress at Edinburgh.

They reached the steps at the front of the keep, and the Norman easily swung her to the ground. Mary stumbled a little, her legs stiff from the day's long ride. Stephen slipped to his feet beside her and began to guide her firmly to the stairs. Mary jerked her arm free. "Do not fear. There is obviously nowhere for me to run even if I wished to."

"I am glad you have the sense to think so."

"You would not be so pleased if you knew what I *really* think."

"To the contrary, I would be very pleased if I knew your innermost thoughts."

Mary looked away, goose bumps creeping up her arms. She feared his tenacity would be greater than hers.

They entered on the second floor into the Great Hall. Two large trestle tables dominated the room, at right angles to each other—one elevated and empty, where the earl would sit with his family, no doubt. A number of household knights and men-at-arms sat at the lower tables, partaking of a supper repast, served by kitchen wenches quick to evade the more amorous men and overseen by the keep's chamberlain. Other retainers gambled, drank, and diced. Beautiful, vivid tapestries hung from all the walls, and a fire curled in a massive stone fireplace. Fresh rushes, sweetly scented with herbs, covered the floors. Mary realized with surprise that there was not a single hound in the place. Two large, carved, cushioned chairs sat in front of the hearth, identical to the two at the head of the elevated table. For a moment Mary froze, thinking the Earl of Northumberland was in residence as she spotted the back of a golden head in one of those chairs.

But it was a young man only a year or two older than herself who sat there alone. He rose to his feet with unusual grace when they entered and strolled towards them. He was golden-haired, blue-eyed, and very handsome, his fair skin tinged faintly golden from an excess of summer sun. "Greetings, brother," the handsome man said. But his dark blue gaze was centered wholly on Mary. The slow smile he finally gave her was devastating.

"Might I assume your presence here is significant?" Stephen asked dryly. His tone changed. "And, Brand, she is mine."

Brand finally looked at his brother. He swept a mock bow. "Of course. I defer to the heir. And yes, I am an envoy from His Highness, as you have undoubtedly guessed."

Mary stiffened. Protesting Stephen's casual statement of possession became irrelevant. It flashed through her mind that she was in a position to learn the enemy's most secret plans, that she could very well be invaluable to her father during her forced stay here—if she became the spy her captor had already accused her of being.

"All is well, Brand; relax." Stephen placed his large hand on Mary's rigid shoulder. "We will speak later. When must you return?"

"Immediately." Brand eyed Mary, again smiling, the curl of his lips almost mocking, with little or no trace of humor in his eyes. "What's this? No introduction? Are you afraid she will prefer me? And do we not have enough maids here to please you, or have you already sampled them all?"

Stephen ignored the obvious teasing. "Mademoiselle Mairi, this is my bigmouthed little brother, Brand, a captain of the King's household troops. You may disregard his attempts at humor as they are quite dismal. Besides, *he* is the lover, not I."

Mary sincerely doubted Stephen's last words. Both brothers were undoubtedly unrepentant predators when it came to the fair sex. Their looks were quite different, one so golden, the other so dark, but they were both striking, and no female would be immune to either one of them. Mary did not return Brand's smile as she regarded him warily.

Brand's bold gaze turned questioning, moving from Mary to Stephen.

"She is my guest," Stephen said shortly, clearly dismissing any further inquiries.

"How fortunate you are," Brand murmured. Giving them both another last look, he walked a short distance away, in order to contemplate the fire.

"I am *not* your guest," Mary said angrily, unable to restrain herself and shaking off his hand. "Guests are not mistreated. Guests are free to come and go. Do you not speak the truth even with your brother?"

The gaze Stephen leveled upon her was cold. "You accuse *me* of mispeaking the truth?"

Mary flushed hotly, but recklessly refused to back down. "Yes, I do."

He raised his hand. Mary did not think he intended to strike her, but nevertheless she flinched. His forefinger slid over the curve of one cheek and lingered by the corner of her mouth. "Come now, demoiselle,'tis you who plays a masquerade, is it not?"

"No," Mary croaked, pulling away, "I have explained my manner of dress. I have explained all. You must release me, at once."

"You are appearing desperate, demoiselle. State your true identity now, and *then* we shall discuss your freedom."

"After you have raped me!"

Stephen glowered at her. "As I have previously stated, there will be no rape."

Her gaze locked with his. Why was it that she was within a hairsbreadth of believing him? Why was it that she was almost disappointed? Surely her dismay was in response to the sum of her predicament and not his avowal.

Stephen revealed his teeth in a slow, wintry smile. "When I take you to bed, demoiselle, you will enjoy it."

Mary could not move, could not respond.

"Yesterday you were fortunate. Today . . . today I grow tired of this game."

She found her voice, which was far too husky to please her. " 'Tis no game."

His smile was colder than before, but his eyes were far brighter. "If you wish to spare your maidenhead, you will reveal yourself to me immediately."

She gasped.

"I have never been able to resist wielding the final blow, demoiselle," he added very softly, "when engaged in battle. The time for surrender has come."

"No," Mary whispered. Heat unfurled like a stream of smoke in her frozen body.

"Yes," he murmured seductively.

"But . . ." Her mind was dazed, making coherent thought difficult. "I thought you were going to send spies to Liddel to learn whether I am telling you the truth or not! Surely that takes time!"

"Obviously if you are of any import, you will tell me before I ruin your worth to another man."

Her heart pounded. Their gazes remained fixed, the one upon the other. Mary was finding it difficult to breathe, to think. She only knew that she could not, must not, tell him who she was.

"My patience is at an end. If you are who you say you are, after this night you will be my mistress," Stephen said flatly.

Silence fell like the blow of a sword between them. Mary was white. She gripped her hands together tightly, desperately trying to sort out the dilemma he had put her in. If she continued to insist that she was Mairi Sinclair, he would take her to his bed—very shortly. Images of him naked and aroused filled her, and she wasn't sure if she felt anticipation or dismay. But she could not reveal her true identity to him, she could not. She spoke through dry, stiff lips. "I am Mairi Sinclair."

His response was immediate. "My chamber is the first one upstairs. Go and await my pleasure there."

Her jaw clenched. Her breasts heaved. She did not move, nor did she remove her gaze from his.

"Go and await my pleasure there," he commanded again, low.

Their gazes clashed, held, locked. It occurred to Mary that, faced with her doom, she was crazy to war with this man. She could not win. She should give in, surrender as he had insisted she do, reveal herself to him. Hazy, passionate images flooded her mind, of an amorous couple, twisting and entwined. Of her and Stephen de Warenne . . . She could *not* betray and beggar her father, her King, whom she loved and worshiped more than anyone.

Mary squared her shoulders, raised her chin, and slowly she turned her back on him.

For an instant Stephen did not move, watching her as she walked to the twisting spiral staircase. Then he snapped his fingers, pointing. One of his men-at-arms materialized from across the hall, to escort Mary to his chamber. Both brothers watched her go, the hall eerily silent.

Then someone guffawed. Laughter followed and conversation resumed. One of the knights slapped a maid sharply on her rump as she refilled his wine, causing her to squeal and jump and spill some from the flagon. Dice rolled, bets were wagered.

Brand turned to Stephen with a raised brow. "What is this? An unwilling maid?" He was droll. "Is that why she fascinates you so? My oldest brother does not lust, he merely takes when moved to do so."

Stephen walked to the dais, climbed it, and sat down at the table. The chamberlain materialized at his elbow with a vessel of red wine from Burgundy. Stephen nodded to him and he poured his lord a drink. "She is an uncanny woman, Brand, and it is her deception which intrigues me."

Brand slid into the chair beside him. "Indeed?" He was skeptical. " 'Tis not her exquisite face?"

Stephen was exasperated. "So I am human after all. What difference does it make? She will reveal herself this eve, and I will not have to make good my threat."

"If she is as you suspect, a lady of some worth," Brand said, "she will bend before the deed is done. No lady will give away her virginity for naught."

"Yes," Stephen said as a maid came and laid trenchers of meats, pasties, and cheeses on the table. "Bring food and wine to the guest who waits in my chamber," he said to the blushing girl.

"And will you spare her your attentions even then?" Brand asked with cool doubt.

"I will have to, will I not?" His expression was hard, his gaze unfathomable. She *would* bend, revealing herself to him as some lady of importance—and he would send her on her merry way, although perhaps he would be a bit richer afterwards from the ransom.

"Do not do anything foolish," Brand warned, no mockery in his tone now. "Remember what you have just said."

"Thank you, little brother, for your confidence."

Brand shrugged. "The King is anxious to know what you have learned."

Stephen lowered his voice. "Carlisle can be taken. But we end the peace."

"He is not interested in the peace, Stephen, he is interested in securing the North so he may turn his attention elsewhere."

Stephen grunted, already knowing this.

"You shall give me a full report?"

"On the morrow," Stephen said with a sigh.

Brand nodded, picked up his cup of mead, and leaned back in his chair. His mouth curled. "I bring you tidings."

Stephen helped himself to a large slice of bread. "From Father?"

"No, from Adele Beaufort."

Stephen said nothing.

Brand fingered his eating knife. "She sends you her warmest regards."

Stephen said, "And I send her mine."

Brand shifted to face him directly, all blandness gone. "But not in the manner that you shall send your regards to little Mairi this night, if you find that she is in truth little Mairi."

"Enough."

"You do not know Lady Beaufort. You have barely spoken to her. I, however, have had much opportunity to observe her since she has come to Court. She is no ordinary woman, Stephen. The lady you wed in three months time will be most unhappy if she hears you have installed a beautiful mistress in your chamber."

"Do not fear," Stephen replied harshly. "I have no intention of jeopardizing my relations with Adele Beaufort."

Stephen stepped out onto the ramparts. There were only a few watchmen on the towers, and he was as alone as he could possibly be. He stalked to the northernmost wall and stared out over its crenellated edge. It was a nightly ritual when he was at Alnwick, to stand thus and gaze upon his domain.

As far as the eye could see, the land belonged to his father, Rolfe de Warenne, and one day it would be his. Ancient Northumbria. Stephen felt a fierce rush of pride and possessiveness. His father had come to England with his overlord, William, the Duke of Normandy, and fought by his side at Hastings twenty-seven years ago. He had been the landless younger son of a Norman comte, seeking the spoils of invasion in a new land. He had been the Conqueror's most trusted military commander from previous campaigns in Maine and Anjou, and his reputation had grown after Hastings. Soon he had been awarded Aelfgar for his loyalty and military prowess. With the Conqueror's permission and encouragement, Rolfe had gradually pushed his borders north and west until they encompassed all the territory that was now theirs. And with it, all the power.

Stephen was very aware that one day all the power of Northumberland would be his. He had been born a bastard—his parents had not been able to marry until his father's first wife had died—but he had been made his father's heir. It was a vast responsibility, a heavy burden, one he had assumed the very day he had been sent to foster at the King's court at the tender age of six. But he had never questioned his duty to his father and Northumberland, not then, not now, and not in all the years in between. A man did what he must, always. He had learned that lesson the same day he had ridden away from home with the King's men, not returning for nearly a decade. Marrying the Essex heiress, Adele Beaufort, was merely another duty he would bear.

They had been betrothed for two and a half years, and they were finally to be wed this Christmastide now that she was sixteen. Rolfe had wanted the union to take place two years ago, but Adele's guardian would not hear of it. She would bring Stephen a large estate in Essex and, more importantly, much silver coin. Coin was something his family always needed. Unlike most of the King's other great magnates, Northumberland carried the huge military burden of maintaining England's northernmost defenses, one that was costly in the extreme.

On the one hand, Stephen's marriage to Adele Beaufort would make Northumberland dangerously independent, something the King could not be pleased about. But the King was desperate for revenue himself, determined as he was to wage his own wars against his older brother Robert in order to reunite Normandy with England. The King did not need the additional expense of subsidizing Northumberland in its wars with Scotland. So he allowed this match between the two powerful houses of Essex and Northumberland.

Stephen realized that his thoughts had generated a pulsating tension within him. It was his duty to keep the North secure, and for two long years he had walked a tightrope to maintain a fragile peace, responding to every incitement by the border reivers blow for blow, yet knowing he must not strike back so fully that he would shatter the reigning truce. It had been no easy task.

He was tired.

He looked forward to his marriage, for Adele's dowry would ease the burden generated by constant warfare that was forever upon his back.

Brand's warning words mocked him. Goddamn it, he was a deliberate man, neither impulsive or rash, but there had been nothing deliberate or careful about his decision to take the woman calling herself Mairi his prisoner. She had intrigued him with her beauty and her deceit, and he had abducted her. He had hoped to discover her to be of little value, so that he could take her to his bed. He still hoped, even while he doubted it.

No man in his position would jeopardize marriage to an heiress for another woman, no matter how desirable she might be. And he had no intention of doing so. A brief liaison, if he was fortunate enough to have it come to that, did not jeopardize his alliance with the Beauforts. But she could not remain in his chamber. In sending her there, he had again acted rashly, for it was a dangerous breach of etiquette. Adele Beaufort would be justifiably furious should she learn he kept a woman in his room. As soon as their next confrontation was waged, he would remove her from his bedchamber.

His jaw clenched. And he would solve the mystery she presented. When faced with imminent ruin, he had not a doubt that she would confess her deception. She would confess her deception, revealing herself to be a highborn lady, and he would send her upon her way, no worse for wear, as he had sworn to do. Stephen could not imagine letting her go without bedding her, but if she revealed herself to be highborn, he would. And in three months, he would wed the Essex heiress.

There was no pleasure in the thought. Not anymore.

Stephen was irritated to find that once again Mairi had disobeyed him; she was not awaiting him in his chamber as he had told her to do. He stripped down to his braies, the heavy muscles in his back rippling, his arms thick with sinew, every tendon defined, his biceps bulging with each slight movement, his stomach flat and rock-hard. His was a knight's well-used body, one honed by years of practice with sword and lance, and years of combat.

Stephen was more than annoyed. He was disturbed by his moment of self-doubt, and perplexed by the confusion he had suddenly felt in regard to his marriage to Adele Beaufort. How could his prisoner, beauty or not, raise such alien emotions in him?

He was angry. It was safer to be angry with her. Already his blood boiled, and she had yet to enter the chamber. For the first time, Stephen wondered if he could exert the self-control necessary to deny himself her body, which he must do once she unmasked herself. He reminded himself that he had no choice.

His sister entered without knocking. Her rude interruption into such disturbing thoughts was welcome, although he was not pleased that she should glimpse him in his state of undress. "Knock, Isobel," he warned, turning away from her and shrugging on his undertunic. She was a very precocious ten, and even more astute. He was afraid that one day she would discover him in some pursuit not fit for any lady's eyes, much less such a young one.

She stuck her tongue out at him. "Why?"

Stephen bit back his smile. He had yet to see Isobel since his return. She had been up to some mischief in the bailey, no doubt, for she was inclined towards perpetual trouble-making. "Because 'tis polite." He tried to scowl. "What greeting is this?"

She beamed and ran into his arms. He held her briefly and set her down, unable to restrain a rush of pride. She was everyone's darling, certainly his. His little sister was a clever thing, already too gorgeous and not yet betrothed. Stephen knew Rolfe was biding his time, but soon he would find her a husband and make another powerful alliance for the de Warennes. Stephen thought, but was not sure, that their father intended to wed her to the King's younger brother, Henry Beauclerc. The prince had little land but much silver, for his father, the Conqueror, had given Normandy to his

oldest son, Robert, and England to William Rufus, leaving
his youngest son only great wealth. Stephen knew him well
from the long years he had fostered in the Conqueror's
household, still he was not sure he approved of the match.

He gazed at her with affection. "Where have you been
this evening?"

"Oh, around," she said mysteriously, but her smile was
quick and angelic. "Why should I knock? You're alone. I
listened at the door to make certain."

His eyes went wide. She stepped back, giggling. "I'm not
a baby anymore, Steph," she said haughtily. She was the
only one who dared bastardize his name. "I know what you
do at night with the maids."

He could not believe it. He didn't know whether to laugh
at her or scold her. "Just what *is* it you think I do with the
maids, wench?"

She gave him a knowing look. "Father says if there is one
more bastard born on Alnwick, he's taking a whip to you as
if you were a boy of twelve!" She was gleeful.

"Oh, he does," he managed, choking on laughter and
despair. "You still haven't answered my question, Isobel."

"Do I seem stupid? You make babies, Steph, and the
maids like it, I know, for I've heard them talking about
you."

This time he went still. "You've heard them talking . . ."
He sputtered. "And what, pray tell, Big Ears, do they say?"

"Well—" she rolled her dark blue eyes "—they say 'tis
big and strong and very randy . . . but sometimes quick, too
quick . . . and sometimes—"

Stephen was scandalized. "Enough!" He pounced on her,
but she dodged him with a laugh. "I hope you have no idea
what you're talking about," he growled. "And I intend to
tell Mother that you are eavesdropping—on the servants,
no less!"

Isobel looked hurt, well and truly hurt. "Mother will send
me to Father Bertold," she quavered. Her large, luminous
eyes held his, as soft and innocent as a fawn's. "I promise
not to listen anymore, really I do. Don't tell Mother."

He sighed, exasperated. She was a handful, had always
been a handful, and one day would undoubtedly rule her

husband with no contest. "I won't tell this time," he said. "But, Isobel, don't test me."

She bit her lip, serious now. They both knew she could only manipulate him so far. "Why is Mairi a prisoner?"

"Ah. So you've met the mysterious Mairi. I prefer to think of her as my guest."

"She says she is your prisoner—and that you must release her at once."

"Did she send you to me with such a message, Isobel?"

"I only know whât she told me." Isobel was wide-eyed and expectant.

Stephen was very exasperated with his guest again. Did she think to maneuver him through his sister? Could she be so shrewd? "Where is she?"

"In the women's solar. Why have you frightened her so?"

"Your curiosity into the affairs of others will one day be your downfall, Isobel. If you are wise, you will mark my words and fight your inclination."

Isobel was disappointed but undaunted. "Does that mean you aren't going to tell me what you've done to her?"

"I have done nothing to her," he said, then added, "yet."

Isobel blinked, fascinated.

"Go and send Mairi to me." He leveled a hard gaze on his sister. "And then you may join Brand downstairs." He did not want her snooping outside his chamber door.

Isobel nodded, still wide-eyed, and ran off. Unsmiling, Stephen shrugged off his undertunic. It was time to make good his intentions—it was time to make Mairi Sinclair reveal the truth about herself.

Chapter 4

The heavy wooden door of the Liddel keep swung open to admit a group of men. They were soaked with rain and covered with mud, for outside it was storming fiercely, the sky black, the wind howling. Thunder boomed and lightning lit up the sky. Queen Margaret sat by the fire in the smoke-stained hall, motionless and despairing, unfinished embroidery at her feet. At the first sound of their entrance, she leapt up. "What news?"

Malcolm entered ahead of the other men, flinging off his sodden mantle, a servant unable to catch it before it fell into the muddy rushes on the floor. Immediately he strode to his wife. "We have not found her, Margaret."

Margaret made a sound of fear, clutching for his hands.

Four men, all wet and weary, trekked into the hall behind him. Malcolm and Margaret's three eldest sons, excluding Ethelred, a priest, were removing their dripping outerwear and reaching for cups of warm wine which servants hastily brought forth. The fourth man paused to stand and stare blindly into the hearth's roaring flames, a puddle forming at his feet. He made no move to shed his soaking cloak.

"You have found something," Margaret cried, clutching

Malcolm's hand. "You are hiding something from me!"

"We have only speculation, nothing more," Malcolm said grimly. But his face was flushed darkly, telling Margaret that he was furious and barely able to contain his anger.

"What is it? What have you found? Mary cannot have just disappeared!"

Edmund whirled. Tall and lean, he was the image of his craggy-faced father. "Show her," he demanded. "So we may know for sure."

Edward, the oldest brother, grabbed his arm and jerked him back. "Leave Mother alone," he warned. "There is no sense alarming her further."

"You will get nowhere with this attitude," Edmund scowled. He was a year younger than Edward and of them all, he most resembled Malcolm. "Do you want to find Mary or not?"

"Of course I do!"

"Stop it!" Margaret cried, her usual calm completely shattered. "How dare you fight now! Malcolm! *Tell me!*"

Malcolm gripped her hands. "There were Norman soldiers here yesterday, Margaret, not a mile from Liddel."

Margaret gasped. "You don't think . . . ?"

"Show her, Father," Edmund demanded. "Ask her if it belongs to Mary."

Edward shoved past Edgar and hit Edmund with his fist in the shoulder, but Edmund was bigger, and the blow only unbalanced him slightly. Immediately Edgar came to Edward's aid, ready to jump upon Edmund, until a roar from Malcolm ceased the fisticuffs.

Malcolm withdrew a piece of wet, white cloth from his belt. Edward made a sound of protest. Edgar, hardly a year older than Mary, was ashen. Malcolm ignored his sons, carefully unfolding the scrap, watching his wife. "Could this be a piece of Mary's shift?"

Margaret's eyes widened and she gasped. "Where did you find that?"

"Where the Normans had their camp," Malcolm said grimly.

Margaret swayed.

Malcolm and Edward caught her at the same time, steadying her. "Do not fear, Mother," Edward said soothingly, but his jaw was tight. "We shall find her and return her to you in no time at all."

"Just the time it takes to find the whoreson bastard," Edgar said darkly, glancing quickly at the silent man who still stood staring into the flames. Because of the proximity of his and Mary's ages, he was closest to her of all the siblings. As children, he and Mary had been as inseparable as possible for a brother and sister. Even now, when Edgar was not fighting, he could usually be found with Mary. "If they have hurt her . . ."

"I will kill them all, every last treacherous Norman!" Malcolm roared. "Every last one!"

"Let's go now, Father," Edgar urged. His green eyes blazed. "If we ride through the night, we can be at Alnwick by dawn."

"*Alnwick?*" Margaret asked. " 'Twas Northumberland?"

"His troops were seen in the area this morning," Malcolm replied harshly. " 'Twas the bastard whelp, not the damned father, who is still at his wretched King's court. And who else would dare to abduct our daughter—who else?" Recently, with the earl away so often, Stephen de Warenne had become the thorn in Malcolm's side.

Margaret was as white as death. "My poor Mary, dear Lord Jesus, protect her," she moaned, praying not for the first time, and not for the last. "Please see her returned to us unharmed!"

" 'Tis my fault," the man standing in front of the hearth said abruptly, turning to face them. His russet hair flamed in the firelight. "Had I not been detained, I would have been with her. and never would I have let her fall into de Warenne's hands."

The agony the young man felt was etched in the lines of fatigue on his face. Margaret hurried to him, intent on comforting him despite her own pain. " 'Tis not your fault, Doug. Mary knows better than to wander outside these walls, or any walls, alone." Tears filled her eyes. "How we have warned her time and again to behave as befits a princess, not an orphan of the burgh. If it is anyone's fault, it is mine, for failing to rein in her spirit."

"It is not your fault, Margaret," Malcolm said, his tone softening. "Mary is to blame, and when I get my hands on her, she will not sit down for a week." He was angry again. "How could she be such a fool!" He turned to face Doug Mackinnon. "And you are equally to blame, for enticing her to a rendezvous as you did. I will deal with you after I have dealt with her."

Doug said nothing, but his mouth was tensely drawn.

"Malcolm, we must know for sure where she is," Margaret cried.

"Do not fear, Mother," Edward consoled, taking her hand. "We are certain 'twas Northumberland's bastard heir. We found two more pieces of linen before it became too dark to continue to follow the trail, and obviously they were heading northeast. Who else but our Mary would be so bold as to leave these little flags for us? At the very least, her spirit remains unbroken."

Margaret sank into her chair. Her heart was pounding too rapidly and she felt faint. "I must send for Maude," she murmured, referring to her pious younger daughter, already a novice at the Abbey of Dunfermline. "I need Maude, Malcolm!" But the sore truth was that she needed Mary; how she needed to know that her darling, headstrong Mary was unhurt.

Malcolm took her hands. "I will send a man tonight; she will be here with you on the morrow."

Margaret gazed at him gratefully. He was a hard man, even a difficult man, but she knew 'twas no easy thing to be King of the Scots. She had never blamed him for his faults. And he had yet to let her down, not once in their long marriage. She knew that Maudie would be with her on the morrow, and that if anyone could rescue Mary, it was her husband.

"We are wasting time," Edgar cried. "We know it was de Warenne, so let us besiege him immediately!"

"Do not be such a fool," Edmund said. "We cannot see in the dark, and there is no rushing a siege—if a siege is indeed called for." His tone was skeptical.

"You would leave Mary there to rot, wouldn't you?" Edgar cried.

"I did not say that," Edmund said coldly.

"No one is leaving Mary to rot," Edward stated, directing an ice-cold glance at Edmund.

"Stop it! I cannot stand this bickering, not now!"

Everyone turned to look at Margaret.

"There will be no war!" she cried, standing. Rarely did she give commands, and never did she interfere in matters politic, but now she shook with the force of her determination. "Malcolm—you will pay whatever ransom it is that Rolfe de Warenne demands. You must!"

"You are not to worry," Malcolm said. "Dear heart, why do you not go upstairs to rest?"

Although Margaret knew she would never rest this night, not with Mary missing, she nodded and obeyed. There was silence until she had left the hall.

"What are you planning to do?" Edward asked uneasily.

Malcolm smiled, and it was chilling. "I will do what must be done, my son. Harken well. There is a benefit to be had from this, and I intend to reap it."

The first few drops of rain began to fall, pattering steadily upon the battlements of Alnwick.

Inside, Mary paused in the open doorway of the Norman's chamber. She had not considered refusing his summons, even though she was nearly paralyzed with fright at the thought of what might happen. He was wearing only his linen braies, and his lack of dress was all the confirmation she needed. Her face, paler than the costliest ivory, stung with sudden heat. Mary turned her gaze away from the sight of his hardened loins bursting against the fabric of his braies.

He regarded her without expression. The sound of the rain, now beating determinedly down upon the roof, filled the silence of the room.

Mary's back was to the open doorway. She cast her gaze around wildly, her heart tripping. She had considered revealing herself to him. Though she had not had much time, less than an hour, to contemplate her dilemma, she had brooded over her alternatives as carefully as possible in the face of her growing panic.

And until the minute Mary had come to his chamber, confronted with her enemy and his obvious desire, she had harbored desperate hope. She would not accept her ruin, at least not meekly. She had been determined not to bend to his will in the ensuing contest, a contest in which her virtue and her pride were at stake. She would fight him. If she remained firm in her resolve and if she refused to allow herself to be seduced as she almost had earlier, and he had been speaking the truth of his aversion to violence, then he would not condescend to rape her.

But any hope she'd had died a sudden death. Facing him in the flesh, pinned beneath his glittering gaze, she did not believe him capable of desisting from brutality. She knew what her fate would be. For in the end it was better to be a martyr, accepting her own ruin, than to reveal herself to be the princess Mary and hand her captor such a priceless gift.

Outside, the wind roared, and for the first time that evening, thunder cracked almost directly overhead. Mary jumped.

Stephen said, "Do storms always make you this nervous, mademoiselle?"

Mary looked at him. Her jaw tightened. Lightning sliced across the sky, and for a moment the ink blackness outside the narrow slit became white. Mary turned her gaze away from the narrow window. "Be done with it."

His brow rose.

He was studying her. Mary fought to keep her eyes on the casement window, watching the rain as it fell now in heavy, silvery torrents. It wasn't an easy task. His presence was compelling, overwhelming. Her gaze sidled to the canopied bed. He stood in front of it in the middle of the room. The bed curtains had been pulled open, the furs and blankets folded aside.

The chamber was too warm, Mary thought. It was becoming difficult to breathe in a normal fashion. Despite the inclement weather, she wished the fire would die down to mere embers. She wished he would stop staring at her and she wished he would do something, anything, to end this torment, this suspense.

He finally moved. His strides were tightly controlled,

giving no hint of the impatience his body must be feeling, as he crossed the room. Thick rugs covered the stone floors, and his bare feet made no sound. He drew her into the chamber, closing the door behind them.

Mary lifted her gaze to his, wide-eyed, trembling. There was such finality in his action. She felt as if he had just slammed the door on her fate. Perhaps he had. Determined to remain mute for as long as he, she met his stare, hoping to appear fierce and uncowed.

He smiled.

There was such carnal intent in the curling of his lips that Mary staggered backwards. Stephen easily caught her. And instead of steadying her, he reeled her up against him. "There is no need to be afraid of me."

"I am not afraid of you—Norman!" Mary gasped. But she was already in his embrace, and his chest was slick and damp against her rigid palms, an indication that he felt the heat, too, and his groin felt like the blunted tip of a sword thrusting against her abdomen. She tried vainly to push away from him.

"Do you think to insult me?" He was amused.

"Bastard," she hissed, momentarily ceasing her struggle. She was panting. He was too strong. As she had thought, she was doomed.

"True enough," he murmured. "I fear I cannot change the circumstance of my untimely birth. Do you really think to wound me with such words?"

"No, but you will wound me, will you not? A man such as you!"

One of his large hands swept down her back. She shivered. "Ahh, you are afraid. I know 'tis too much to ask you to trust me. I will not hurt you, mademoiselle, not after the first time; all women, even one as small as you, are made to accommodate a man, even one like me."

Mary's small breasts rose and fell harshly. His statement summoned up a recollection of his heated touch the day before—and an anticipation she was determined to deny. She would fight him, for martyr or not, that was her clear-cut duty. Her will must be stronger than her body. It *must*. Mary ground her teeth together. "I—will—fight—you."

"I don't think so." His suggestive—and amused—smile flashed again. "Of course, we can end your dilemma easily enough. You need but speak two words—the name of your father."

"No!" Mary wriggled against him. He forced her to become still instantly, gripping the firm mound of one of her buttocks. Mary was frozen. "Shall we test your resolve?" he murmured in her ear.

Mary could barely speak, due to the strategic placement of his fingers. "Be—done—with—it."

For a moment he was unmoving. "An invitation I cannot refuse. Does such acquiescence signal your intention to remain tight-lipped, does it mean that you will forfeit your virginity instead of your identity?"

Mary stared. She had discerned a subtle change in his tone, which was no longer quite so casual; tension rippled beneath the surface of his words. His eyes had grown brighter, his nostrils flared, and his grip upon her had tightened. And still his manhood throbbed urgently against her. He was trying to hide it, but there was no mistaking the heightened pitch of his excitement now. Mary nodded once. She was incapable of speech.

Slowly he smiled. "At this point I should warn you, mademoiselle, my interest in the truth wans. If you will speak, speak now, before it is too late."

Mary thought, dazed, that it was probably already too late. She realized her hand had found his hip. It was hard and free of fat, his skin warm even through the thin linen of his braies. His words sank in. She had to use great effort to remove her hand from his body. "I have nothing to say," she said hoarsely.

"Indeed?" There was a catch to his voice. Abruptly he lifted Mary in his arms. Mary knew she must make some effort at resistance.

Their gazes locked. Her will died then and there. She had never known her body could be so hungry. She realized she was holding on to him instead of pushing him away. The blaze in his eyes made her grip tighten.

They were a step away from the bed. Unsmiling, he slid her onto the center of the mattress. Mary found herself on her back, her gaze, like the rest of her, dominated by him.

" 'Tis your last chance," he said harshly, and she saw that his fists were clenched. "Tell me no lies."

She was having trouble remembering the issues at stake. She whispered, "I-I am Mairi Sinclair."

His lips curled. He leaned over her. His gaze slid over her flushed face, then lower, to her heaving breasts, and lower still, to the outline of her slender legs. "The time for words is over, demoiselle."

She gripped the covers of the bed. She was oblivious to all existence. She had forgotten the stifling warmth in the room, did not hear the crackling fire, the sound of which mingled with the sound of the rain, blurring together into nothingness. Lightning brightened the night sky behind Stephen's head, but she was unaware of that, too. All of her senses were focused on the man standing before her, and on the painful pulsing of her own body.

He slid onto the bed beside her and pulled her into a sitting position, his touch strong but gentle. He did not hurry; how well he masked any urgency he might be feeling. Mary made a sound low in her throat, one that sounded suspiciously like a moan. Their gazes locked. Without looking at what he was doing, he slowly slipped off the veil she had borrowed from Isobel, freeing her waist-length gold hair. His hands shook as his fingers navigated their way through the length of her hair, beginning at her scalp and ending in the curls at her hips. Deliberately he fanned the tresses out. Mary wondered if he was going to kiss her. Stephen smiled at her.

She could not move.

And then he ripped her clothing apart and tore her tunics and shift off of her body.

Mary screamed.

"I will take you naked," he said as she tried to leap off of the bed. Mary screamed again, in fury. Stephen caught her, this time throwing her down upon the mattress. He flung the shreds of her clothing aside. Before Mary could scramble away from him, he was on top of her, pressing her down.

Only a thin layer of linen separated his engorged phallus from the tender flesh between her thighs. He throbbed

strongly against her, a hairsbreadth from being within her.
"Who in God's blood are you? You will reveal the truth,
demoiselle, and you will do so now!"

Mary looked up at him, consumed with an answering rage.
"So it will be rape after all!"

He laughed. When her hands came up, her fingers curled
into claws, he caught her wrists, wrestling them down above
her head, pinning her to the bed. He stroked his shaft against
her. He stroked her until her anger died, but her pulse did
not dim. To the contrary, it accelerated madly. Mary moaned
helplessly.

His mouth came closer to hers, his breath feathering her
face. His eyes were glittering dangerously now. "Your story
has substance," he said, low. "But that only proves what an
adept liar you are. Know you this. I have been surrounded by
intrigue and deceit my entire life. I have had much practice
at ferreting out the good from the rotten. I do not believe
you to be some barnyard bastard of the laird Sinclair. Every
instinct I possess tells me you are far more than you claim.
Give your name to me now."

Mary met his gaze, goaded beyond all resistance.
"Never."

His eyes widened incredulously. It was the first time that
she had admitted she was lying—that she was not Mairi
Sinclair—that there was a truth to be revealed. Indeed, the
gauntlet had been thrown.

He smiled without mirth. Simultaneously he reached down
between them, the back of his hand brushing the swollen,
aching folds of her flesh. Mary cried out. A moment later
she realized what his movement meant. He had ripped off
his own braies, freeing himself. He was slick, and so was
she. "We have yet to conclude our business, demoiselle."
His expression was hard, sweat streaked his high cheekbones.
"Make your choice. You may give me your identity—or your
virginity."

Mary could not move, could not speak. It had become
terribly hard to understand his words when he pulsed naked
against her so purposefully, so urgently. She managed to
breathe. Her hips twitched involuntarily, invitingly.

His hand cupped the globe of her breast. "Who?" he

whispered roughly, his gaze locked with hers. "Who are you, demoiselle?"

She struggled for sanity. "No," she said, her whisper as rough as his. "No—never!"

His smile was mirthless, a minute baring of too white teeth. It was dangerous. Still smiling, he slowly lowered his head.

Mary was rigid and frozen. His tongue touched the distended tip of her nipple. She bit her lip to keep from crying out. He had freed one of her hands, and she fisted it to stop herself from grabbing him—from clinging. A moment later he had taken her breast into his mouth. Mary finally heard herself moan.

He lifted his head, his face close to hers. "Tell me who you are, tell me now. You do not want to forfeit your maidenhead, demoiselle, you do not. You are dangerously close to doing so."

Mary could not respond. She knew an intense pleasure— and an intense need. Her fisted hand had raised itself, to settle slowly upon his bare, hard shoulder. Her fingers opened, curling against his skin. He flinched.

"Who are you?" he whispered. His voice was so rough and broken now, it was barely audible. His eyes had become wild. "Tell me who you are."

Mary could not remember who she was. She stared at him blankly, at his eyes, at his mouth. She was making small, mewling cries. How she wanted his mouth.

He half-smiled and half-grimaced. He touched her breasts. Then his fingers slid lower and lower still. Mary cried out. He parted the moist folds shielding her virginity, manipulating her with his thumb. Mary's head fell back and she was lost to all coherent thought. She began to whimper mindlessly.

"Give to me before it is too late!" he demanded. "Who are you?"

She would do anything he asked. Anything, if only he would continue to touch her. "Mary," she whispered.

"God," he cried, low and raw and agonized.

Mary felt something else then, something electric flaring hot and bright between them as he rubbed the heavy head of his shaft against her swollen lips, and she cried out. At some point he had freed her other hand, and she gripped him fiercely.

"Mairi," he moaned.

"Yes, please, Stephen!"

Their gazes locked, his wide and stark with agony and frustration. He was raised over her, his face close to hers, his eyes hotter than the sun, and he was rubbing the huge tip of his phallus against her again and again, as if he, too, were helpless in the face of his passion. Mary writhed in animal pleasure, whispering his name, sobbing his name.

"God help me," he said. "I no longer care!"

His mouth came down on hers. Mary's cry of elation was cut off by his kiss. Eagerly she opened to him, wrapped in his strong embrace, sucking his tongue deep into her throat, urging him to come into her in every way. He made a deep, low, urgent sound, prodding more forcefully against her womanhood. Mary flung her legs around his hips, locking them tight. She rocked her loins against him. *"Please,"* she gasped.

"Mairi," he whispered, his arms tensing around her.

He thrust into her. The pain lasted less than a heartbeat, for with it came an explosion of rapture so intense, she was stunned senseless. Her earthy moans filled the stone chamber, convulsions racked her body. In that moment, Mary died the most exquisite death and was totally reborn.

Slowly she surfaced. She was limp, as if drugged, her limbs heavy, her body replete. She became aware of the storm outside. The wind howled, the rain pounded, and every few moments lightning outside brightened the night and the chamber she was in.

Mary felt him. He was still on top of her, still inside her, still partially erect. Her dazed mind began to come to life.

She became lucid. Lucid enough to feel bruised and worn, aching now from the invasion of his large body into her small one, and worse, much worse, lucid enough to feel horrified.

What had she done?

Stephen raised himself up slightly on his elbows, and their gazes collided. He saw the horror in hers. His jaw tightened.

Before Mary could push him off, she felt him stirring to life inside her, lengthening, swelling. She tensed.

"Later," he said roughly. "Later you can entertain regrets."

Mary opened her mouth to protest. Then his lips covered hers, his hips moving, and she was lost.

Chapter 5

*T*he sun was just rising when Stephen broke the night's fast at prime. He was alone. His household was dutifully at mass in the family chapel with Father Bertold, a duty Stephen himself shirked this day. The woman calling herself Mairi was still asleep in his bed.

Abruptly he pushed the slice of white bread he had been toying with away. What in God's name had he done?

She had not revealed herself. He had never dreamed she would choose ruin over confession. There was still not a single doubt in his mind that she was a highborn lady. He could have pressed her further, brought her to the edge without actually taking her, forced the truth from her innocent lips. But he had not. He had taken her instead, ceasing to care about the issue at stake.

His jaw flexed. Why had he, a man of great experience and even greater self-discipline, acted like a beardless boy presented with his first courtesan?

Briefly he closed his eyes, for the first time that morning aware of a pounding behind his temples. He had failed himself last night. He was afraid. Secretly afraid that he would fail himself again.

For the woman calling herself Mairi was still in his chamber and still in his bed. Already he thought of the night to come. Already he anticipated their union. He could hardly think of anything else.

But he must send her away. Now, before she truly endangered his marriage to Adele Beaufort. He *must*. His duty, as always, was to Northumberland, and a mistress who threatened his advantageous marriage threatened Northumberland itself.

He was uneasy. He stared at the warm loaf of bread on the table before him. Mairi's image came to him as she had been in his bed last night, with a passion that matched his own, a passion he had never witnessed before, not in any other woman—not even in himself. She had brought something out in him he had never allowed himself to acknowledge before. What was wrong with him?

He could not regret what he had done, and he knew he would not send her away—not yet.

But what price would he pay for such folly?

Stephen quaffed his glass of ale. He told himself that in another night or two he would tire of her and send her on her way. Before any damage was done. He had no choice.

Purposeful footsteps brought him abruptly back to the present. Stephen was glad to be diverted from his brooding. His brow rose slightly in surprise when he glimpsed his brother, Geoffrey. Geoffrey rarely had the time or inclination to come home to Northumberland. "What brings you so far north, brother?"

Geoffrey regarded him with the faintest of smiles. "What greeting is this, after so much time has passed?" he asked drolly, striding across the hall, his long robes flowing about him. There was no mistaking his relationship to Brand. He was tall, muscular, and golden, a devastatingly handsome man whom women always turned to look at twice. Even now, entering the hall where he had spent his first childhood years, a place where his face was familiar and occasionally seen, he caused the serving maids to blush with interest. "Do I not deserve some display of affection?"

Stephen did not blink. "I am not in the mood to display affection."

"So I have already noticed." Geoffrey lithely climbed the dais and slid into the seat beside his brother. A dagger materialized in his hand, one too large and too pointed for the sole purpose of eating. He casually speared a slice of cold meat.

"As always, you are astute," Stephen remarked. "When did you arrive? Last night?"

"At matins. What has you so somber? After the morning's first mass, I had hoped to catch a few hours sleep, but alas, there was such noise emanating from your bedchamber, 'twas hopeless." Geoffrey wiped the dagger clean and sheathed it in his heavy, plain belt. When he smiled, faint dimples showed, at odds with his mocking tone and gleaming eyes. "Your leman was most vocal. I would think you to be in high spirits this morning."

Stephen stared coldly, refusing to comment on that. "Is this a family visit, or something else?"

Geoffrey's smile was gone. "You know I have no time for family visits. I have news. The King is in his sickbed." He held up his hand, a hand both tanned and callused, the hand of a man who was physically active and often out-of-doors. " 'Tis not grave, the physics say, but he has appointed Anselm Archbishop of Canterbury."

Stephen was silent. Then, "The King must think himself at death's door."

"He does."

"How does this affect you? And us?"

Geoffrey's fine nose flared. "He is a good man. 'Tis long overdue that our dear King appoint someone to follow in Lanfranc's footsteps."

"And?"

Geoffrey's jaw clenched. "I gain an ally in my battles against the Crown's attempts to bleed Canterbury, I hope."

"You hope?"

Geoffrey's tone held some small amount of self-derision. "Anselm is much like Lanfranc, a true and saintly man. We may seek the same ends, but I'm not sure he approves of me." His smile was twisted. "Perhaps I gain a new enemy."

Stephen looked at his too handsome brother. In some ways they were so alike, and in those ways Stephen understood his brother well. Geoffrey would do what he had to do, but wasn't that the lot of a man? "Better a friend than a foe. See to it that he loves you as Lanfranc did."

Geoffrey looked at his older brother. Sadness showed for the barest instant in his eyes. "Lanfranc was more a father to me than our own father, as well you know. Despite my worldliness, he was forgiving—and understanding. In truth, I am now torn. I both seek and do not seek the day of Anselm's election. In the beginning we will be friends, out of need to protect the see from the King, but in the end?" Geoffrey shrugged.

"Anselm is a holy fool if he does not see the powerful ally that he has in you," Stephen said abruptly.

"Some men will not—*can*not—compromise their morals."

Stephen looked at his brother's face, trying to glimpse Geoffrey's soul in his eyes; but Geoffrey would not meet his gaze. "You are not immoral."

"He has asked me why I am not ordained."

Stephen stared. It was hardly surprising that Anselm would want to know why his archdeacon had yet to make his final vows—Stephen had wondered about it himself. He believed, but could not be certain, that it was Geoffrey himself who delayed the event. And Stephen suspected he knew why. "And what did you reply?"

Geoffrey raised his gaze. It was hooded. "That I am no Lanfranc."

Stephen was disappointed with the response, but he should have known that his brother would keep his own dark secrets. To break the tension, he smiled. "Thank God."

Geoffrey laughed, his mask back in place. Stephen joined him. The moment of tension—and frightening intimacy—had passed.

" 'Twas inevitable, was it not, that Rufus appoint a successor?" Stephen said, pouring them both ale. "How long could he keep the see vacant? No matter how he bleeds Canterbury's coffers, the lack of an archbishop was too mighty a matter for even the King. Surely you have been prepared for this day."

Geoffrey folded his arms and looked at his brother, his eyes glittering. "In the past three and a half years since Lanfranc's death, I have prepared for this day, by administering the see to the best of my ability, with the help of my able, and loyal, staff, and by guarding its coffers in a losing battle." His face was hard. "Anselm will find his ship easy to navigate, but the course he must steer is frought with peril. Too, I think that Anselm will be far more fanatical in his dealings with the King than anyone anticipates."

Stephen looked at his brother, the Archdeacon of Canterbury. He had been awarded the appointment by his mentor, the Archbishop Lanfranc, when Lanfranc was on his deathbed four years ago. But even before his appointment, he had been Lanfranc's most trusted personal assistant. With the death of his friend and mentor, he had continued his duties, the first being to administer the see until a successor took office. Not only had he done so, he also had to fight the King in a constant hidden battle over control of ecclesiastical revenues.

"I have other news as well," Geoffrey said. "I have been summoned to Court. My spies have told me I am to be asked for a precise accounting of my holdings, especially of the knights and men-at-arms in my service." Then he flushed. "Rather—an accounting of the see's holdings."

This was news. It could pertain to the new archbishop, or it could not. Stephen raised an eyebrow at the news and replied, "And I was sent to Carlisle to ascertain if it is ripe for the taking."

"Is it ripe?" Geoffrey asked, drumming his long fingers upon the scarred table.

"Yes."

"Well, for the moment you can rest assured that Rufus thinks not of invasion but of repentance for his sins," Geoffrey murmured.

"Perhaps his fear that he lies dying will change whatever his plans were," Stephen said darkly. "We have maintained such a fragile peace for such a short time. I hate to see it ended, especially by us."

"Even if the King decides against invasion," Geoffrey said, "and you can be sure that Father is doing his best to turn him from this purpose, undoubtedly that scoundrel Malcolm will break the peace. He is a barbarian; he will not change his ways."

Geoffrey was right. Stephen knew it was only a matter of time before that precious peace was broken, one way or another. Malcolm Canmore had sworn fealty to William Rufus at Abernathy two years ago, but that would not stop him from treachery. It never did. It was inevitable that sooner or later Malcolm would invade Northumberland. His last invasion, while not successful, had still inflicted much damage upon Stephen's northernmost manors. Those manors had lost their harvest, and last winter Stephen had been forced to use sparse coin to import extra stores so his northern vassals would not starve. Some of his mercenaries had yet to be paid in full for that campaign. His marriage to Adele Beaufort would solve that particular problem, as well as many others. Suddenly Stephen found himself thinking not about war and peace but about his captive. Why on earth had she continued to defy him until it was too late?

"So who is the vocal wench?" Geoffrey asked, as if he could read Stephen's mind. His tone was openly teasing now.

Despite himself, Stephen flushed. Had his thoughts been so visible? "She is my mistress and we shall leave it at that."

"Your mistress!" Geoffrey mocked incredulity. "Shame on you, my lord, for taking a mistress upon the eve of your wedding. Shall I determine your penance?"

"Thank you, no."

Geoffrey's tone became serious. "I am surprised you have brought a leman here, brother. Tread softly. News travels far too quickly, especially news with the potential to destroy. You would not want to wreck your alliance with the Essex heiress. Lady Beaufort does not strike me as an understanding—or forgiving—woman."

"First Brand, now you," Stephen said with real anger. Geoffrey's words were an unpleasant reminder of the quandary he had fallen in. "I am not a stupid boy to be chastised thus. Lady Beaufort will stand with me at the altar this Christmastide."

At that moment, before Geoffrey could reply, a noise made both brothers turn towards the stairs. Stephen started as his captive stumbled around the corner and froze, staring at him. Apparently she had lost her balance as she hung on to the wall on the bottom steps, eavesdropping. She regarded only him, and if looks could kill, he would now be dead.

Slowly he smiled. He found himself on his feet. He was aware of the rushing of his blood, not just through his veins, but to his loins. He found that he could recall the past night in instant, vivid detail. He recalled her defiance; he recalled her surrender. He was far from sated. "Were you spying upon my brother and me, mademoiselle?" He stepped down from the dais.

She straightened, her back against the wall. "No."

Stephen still smiled, a smile he had worn upon many occasions when facing a particularly dangerous enemy. He paused in front of her. Their gazes clashed.

"Ahh, the wench of last night," Geoffrey remarked with genuine interest, regarding them both. "You have never chosen better, Stephen. She is a beauty."

Stephen tossed his brother a dark look over his shoulder. "I am in complete agreement with you." There was no mistaking the territorial tone.

Mary clenched her fists, shaking. That he should discuss her as if she were not present infuriated her, almost as much as the fact that they had been so casually discussing her when they thought her to be absent. But what completely enraged her was what she had just discovered—that the arrogant Norman bastard was betrothed to another.

"He is not going to introduce us," Geoffrey said pleasantly, causing her to look at him. The gleam in his intense eyes was not even remotely polite. "Undoubtedly he is afraid you will compare us and find him lacking." Geoffrey smiled at her.

Mary glared at him. He did not fool her for an instant. He wore a prelate's long, dark robes, but there was nothing holy about him. No man of God should have such a face, or such a gaze. He was unmistakably male, he was unmistakably powerful, and most important, he was a de Warenne, which made him the enemy as well. "I do not have to compare you both to find him lacking," she snapped. Her gaze had already returned to Stephen.

Geoffrey started—and laughed.

Stephen was also amused. "You did not find me lacking last night, demoiselle."

Mary turned crimson. "You prove yourself a brute at every turn, Norman," she hissed, her fury knowing no bounds. "Only a beast would speak to me in public in such a way."

She turned her back on him coldly. She had come downstairs because she was awake and unable to sleep, much less remain in bed as if awaiting the Norman's pleasure. In fact, she had barely slept at all, only pretending to do so when he had finally given her the chance to rest. While he had slept deeply and soundlessly beside her.

Her shame knew no bounds. Her virtue had been intact when she had gone to him, and she had intended to resist him. Had he raped her, she would have more than just remnants of her pride left, but it had not come to that. Her resistance had been pitiful; he had seduced her effortlessly. While he slept and after he had left her bed, Mary was haunted by every detail of their encounter, no matter how she tried to shove such recollections aside. She did not want to face what he had brought her to in bed. It was impossible to dismiss.

Mary was excruciatingly aware of having failed her country and King, of having failed both of her parents, of having failed Doug, and of having failed herself.

She strove to derive what comfort she could from the fact that she had not lost the entire war—he still did not know that she was King Malcolm's daughter. And he would never know, she vowed, even if it meant sharing his bed time and again. She tried not to think about that probability, dared not think about it. Instead, she must concentrate upon survival.

Mary felt Stephen's eyes upon her, and her skin tingled. She found herself facing him again. His gaze was bright and intent; she flushed in spite of her rage.

Adele Beaufort. The fury surging through her was nothing like the anger she had entertained earlier. *Adele Beaufort.* Who was Adele Beaufort? They had spoken of her with some respect; apparently she was both beautiful and an heiress. Oh, how she wished she could tell him that she was King Malcolm's daughter—that she was a princess and far more important than any English heiress!

Stephen spoke, drawing her complete attention. "You may call me whatever you wish just as you may choose to make the worst of this situation, mademoiselle, or you may make the best of it. It will not change my intentions; you succeed only in arousing my interest. I suggest you take advantage of the fact instead."

"You have indeed gained what you sought," Mary said unsteadily. "You are stronger than I, and obviously far more experienced. But that does not change my intentions. I will not be your mistress, regardless of what happened last night. I am your prisoner, and nothing more, forced to suffer your attentions. Mark that, Norman."

"I prefer to mark actions, not words."

His smugness was more than she could bear. "Then you should have marked all of my actions! I was not as willing as you wanted, Norman."

He looked at her.

In case he failed to understand, she smiled. "You won only one battle last night. One that I consider much less significant than the battle over my identity. Indeed, I do believe I won the war."

The blood rushed to Stephen's face. Above him on the dais, apparently only pretending not to hear them, Geoffrey choked.

Mary trembled. But she could not stop now. Victory was so sweet. "Never," she flung. "Never will you get the answers you seek—not from my lips."

A very long moment passed while Stephen struggled for self-control, his jaw tense, his fists clenched, his face dark. Mary refused to cringe, although her heart pounded with real fear. Any other man would have long since beat her for her daring and her insolence. She regretted her brave words.

"Demoiselle," Geoffrey said, already moving from the dais to stand beside Stephen. Mary saw that he had a tight hold on his brother's arm. "Desist. My brother does not even beat his dogs, but I fear you push him too far."

Before Mary could reply, Stephen barked, "No! Let her speak as she wills." His smile was ruthless. "How you amaze me, demoiselle. But do not fear. I do not care that I have not mastered your mind, I care only that I have mastered your body. Beating is too good for you. I have far better, and far more entertaining, punishment in mind."

Mary blanched.

"Mademoiselle?" he challenged.

For an instant she was frozen. She was remembering what it was like when he mastered her body, and she could imagine the exquisite torture he would inflict. Suddenly robbed of air, she was unable to summon up a reply.

"What do you hide?" Stephen demanded.

Mary said nothing. She was still consumed by his words.

But Stephen had regained complete control. He looked at his brother. "Wipe that smirk from your face, Geoff. This lady has refused to reveal her identity, choosing instead to give me her maidenhead. Undoubtedly some border lord is about to seek vengeance. I have other duties to attend to, as you know."

Geoffrey was startled. "You are not thoughtless. You are not rash."

Stephen did not respond to him. Abruptly he held out his hand to Mary. "A truce, mademoiselle. I declare a truce."

His tone was firm with authority. Worse was his gaze, which had become soft and seductive, perhaps with memory. Although he was unsmiling, he was undeniably attractive, much more so than either one of his brothers. Mary stared at his hand. It flitted through her mind that she could accept his offer of peace, and cease all defiance. That she could accept him.

As if sensing her thoughts, Stephen stepped closer, a second later catching her palm in his. "Give to me, mademoiselle," he coaxed. "Instead of fighting me when you are going to lose, why not bend? There is much to be said for anticipation. Even now, I anticipate being in your arms again—and I believe you share the same feeling. I am going to pleasure you regardless of your willful pride, and we both know it."

"I believe you are trying to seduce me even now!"

Stephen straightened, his height and breadth overpowering. "And if I am? What upsets you so? That you find me as desirable as I find you? If you bend to me, you will more than enjoy your stay at Alnwick."

"I desire you, it's true," Mary said slowly through stiff lips, hating admitting it, even to herself, "but I do hate you more. Whoreson bastard!"

His grip tightened; he almost smiled. "I much prefer the sound of my given name coming from your lips."

There was no mistaking to what he was referring. "Do you prefer the sound of your name coming from my lips— or from Adele Beaufort's?" Mary hissed.

Stephen froze. Then, "She has never spoken my name with the *relish* that you have."

"Oh?" She was shaking, as much in hurt as in rage. "So she is too good for you to abuse? You only abuse maids you abduct, sirrah? Even when they are not as they seem? Or is it because I am a Scot? Is that why you took my maidenhead without a care for the consequences? I am a *Scot*, but your heiress is an *Englishwoman*!"

Red tinged his cheekbones. "I did not abuse you, so cease with your abominable hypocrisy. And what is done is done. I do not regret my actions. I am sorry, though, for the price you must bear. When the time comes, demoiselle, I will provide for you. You need not worry on that score."

She drew back as if he had slapped her. Already he referred to the time when he would grow tired of her and send her away. Tears stung. "And I should be relieved that you will not toss me aside penniless? Oh, how noble you are!"

Mary turned to flee. His grip clamped down on her wrist and she was jerked around to face him. Very low, he said, "You might remember that a man cannot mate alone, and you were as willing a wench as any I have ever taken to my bed. More so, in fact."

Mary cried out inarticulately and tried to yank her arm free. She failed.

"You could have revealed yourself to me," he said, his eyes black and blazing. "You were a partner to the deed, demoiselle, and you may choose to forget it, but I do not."

"I am returning upstairs. I am no longer hungry," Mary said with great dignity. The truth burned. She had been a willing partner to his passion, no matter that her ambition had been only to continue her deceit. She refused to give in to the rising tears which had no rightful place in this bitter confrontation. "But I am very tired. If you would excuse me?"

Stephen stared at her. Finally he said, "Go then, to the women's solar. I will send your break-fast to you. And remember, demoiselle, I wish a truce, but I alone cannot achieve the peace."

Chapter 6

Mary contemplated disobeying him yet again. But in the end she rushed into the solar as if it were her refuge. Closing the door, she leaned upon it, out of breath. Her mind spun. All she could think of was their recent encounter, the one last night, and the one that would occur this evening.

She did hate him. He had ruined her uncaringly; he had said he did not believe her to be Mairi Sinclair, yet he had continued his lovemaking, taking it to its final conclusion. He was ruthless, vain, and self-serving. Mary knew without a doubt that he would never ravish his English bride, he would not even ravish the daughter of an insignificant English knight. The difference was that she was a barbarian Scot.

A barbarian Scot, yes, but a princess, Mary reminded herself. Had he known the truth—that she was Malcolm's daughter—he would not have taken her to his bed. Mary was certain of that. She reminded herself that her loss of virtue was insignificant, that she had consciously chosen to martyr herself instead of revealing herself.

But what, she wondered with despair, awaited her now? When he tired of her and freed her, then what? It had been somehow easy to think of returning home to Doug before last night. How could she ever face Doug again? What if the Norman used her so mercilessly that he got her with child? Mary froze with the thought.

She was diverted from her brooding. A light rapping upon the door reminded Mary that he said he would send her break-fast. She bid the serving maid to enter, and was surprised when his little sister, Isobel, skipped into the chamber as well.

They had met yesterday. In her distress, Mary had barely paid attention to the child, answering her inquisitive questions automatically. Now, when the maid left, she found herself alone with the girl. For the first time she really looked at her. She was a beautiful child, one who promised to become a stunning woman.

"Do you mind my company?" Isobel asked with a pretty smile.

In truth, pleasant companionship would be refreshing. Mary sank into a chair, aware for the first time that day that she was exhausted and overwhelmed from all that had passed, not to mention a sleepless night. She was tired of thinking. "I do not mind. I could use some company." In fact, she could use a friend. "Would you like to break the fast with me?" A hopeful note had crept into her tone.

Smiling, Isobel came closer, shaking her head negatively. "I have eaten." She inspected Mary openly. "But I will gladly keep you company."

Mary smiled.

"You are very beautiful, my lady."

Mary took a bite of oven-warm bread. "Not half as much as you," she said earnestly.

Isobel tossed her head, looking pleased. "They say I am a great beauty. Do you think it's true?"

Mary's eyes widened. "Real beauty comes from within," she heard herself say, quoting her mother exactly. Then she grinned. "But you are indeed a great beauty. However, my mother has always said that vanity is a sin."

"Who is your mother? Is she very pious?"

Mary started. Isobel gazed right into her eyes, unblinking. Mary wondered if she could possibly be trying to discover her identity, or if she was just succumbing to her natural curiosity. "How old are you, Isobel?"

"Not much younger than you, I daresay," Isobel said quickly. "I am ten."

Mary knew Isobel did not mean to insult her, but her size, which always made people assume her to be younger than her age, had always dismayed her. "I am *almost* seventeen. Far older than you."

"Old enough to be wed."

"I am a maid." Mary thought about her captor for the first time since Isobel had entered her chamber.

"You are so small, not much bigger than me, that from a distance, one would think you a child."

"And you are very tall for such a young girl."

"Undoubtedly my husband will be much shorter than I." Isobel laughed at the idea. "But I do not care what he looks like, as long as he is powerful and strong."

Mary stared at Isobel as her earlier statement sank in, her heart jumping. *She and Isobel resembled each other*.

"Stephen is powerful and strong," Isobel said rather coyly.

Mary did not respond. She did not even hear Isobel. Her mind whirled. It was true. She and Isobel had similar appearances. Not only were they about the same height and size, they were both fair and long-haired. Mary thought that, in shadow and from a distance, a man would not be able to tell the two of them apart, not if Mary bound her small breasts and wore Isobel's clothes.

"Lady—is something wrong?"

Mary was quivering with excitement and fear. She gazed blankly at Isobel. "I beg your pardon?" *It was her duty to escape*.

Isobel repeated the question, but Mary did not listen. Instead, she knew that it was more than her duty to escape, it was a necessity. For in time, whether it be a day or two or even a week, Stephen de Warenne would learn from his man Will or other spies about the disappearance of Malcolm's daughter. He would instantly comprehend that she was the Scots princess.

"Madam?"

Mary jerked to attention. "I am sorry, I did not sleep well last night, and my concentration wavers." But her mind raced on. Somehow she would have to borrow Isobel's clothes and get into the bailey, and as there was no way she could do so by walking past her captor or his brothers, perhaps when Isobel went out, she could join her. And once in the bailey, without escort, thought to be the young girl, there would be opportunities for escape. There must be.

Isobel was asking, with a sly smile, "Don't you like my brother now?"

Mary realized that Isobel was waiting for a reply. With an effort she recalled the question. Then she comprehended the child's meaning—that after last night, a night she had spent in Stephen's chamber, she must have some fondness for her captor. Her eyes were wide and she stood up. "No, Isobel, I am sorry to say that I do not!"

Isobel started. "But how is that possible? All the maids I know pray for him to take them into his bed. And afterwards, they are always very pleased—indeed, they pray he might notice them again."

Mary folded her arms very tightly against her chest. "I suppose he—Stephen—takes ladies to his bed often."

"Very often," Isobel said, not quite smiling. "But not ladies, just kitchen maids and strumpets. You look peculiar."

Mary said nothing. She walked over to the window slit and stared out of it. She decided that she would attempt to escape immediately. She hugged herself harder.

"Do you not find Stephen handsome?"

Mary refused to answer. She was having trouble dislodging an unwelcome image from her mind, of Stephen and some hussy in a torrid embrace. She gripped the rough stone ledge. Her back was to Isobel. "Isobel, as we are the same size, is it possible you might find me a garment that is more pleasing to look upon than these poorly mended rags I now wear?"

Isobel blinked.

Mary's heart pounded. She had hardly been subtle. But the urge to flee was one she now could not resist.

And Isobel beamed. "Of course; why did I not think of it? You are a lady, and no lady could tolerate those filthy clothes for long. I am happy to give you something of mine."

Clad in an ice blue tunic and a silver girdle, silver hose, and dark blue slippers, her purple mantle lined in squirrel, Mary slowly descended the staircase with Isobel. As the morning had passed, they had become good friends, and Mary regretted using her. Isobel was clever, witty, and headstrong, and she reminded Mary in no small way of herself. There were more similarities between them as well, for, like Mary, Isobel had been raised with a batch of brothers by powerful yet fond parents. Mary thought that if circumstances were different, their friendship would blossom when the child matured into an adult.

But of course, that was not to be.

Mary tensed. The Norman was below, and she could clearly hear his voice as they went downstairs. He was immersed in affairs of the estate in the hall below with his chamberlain, his steward, and both of his brothers. Mary listened to his strong, slightly husky tone. Apparently he was with a tenant as well, one who now was asking for some small boon.

Would she be allowed to leave the keep with Isobel?

With some encouragement from Mary, Isobel had offered to show her her pony, which happened to be from the Hebrides, not only a group of western islands belonging to Scotland, but the place of her uncle Donald Bane's exile. Mary had accepted. Undoubtedly this would be her one and only chance to escape before nightfall. Mary did not want to think further than that, about what awaited her if she did not succeed in escaping now. There seemed to be a thick lump in her chest.

Isobel grasped her hand firmly. "Do not be afraid of him. He is not as bad as you think."

Mary wet her dry lips. "I am not afraid of your brother, Isobel."

Isobel appeared skeptical.

"But I am quite certain that your brother will not allow me to go with you out of this keep."

Isobel snorted. "He will if I ask him!"

Determined to be calm and not give away her scheme, Mary followed Isobel into the hall. Gaily Isobel ran to her brothers. While Geoffrey greeted her with some joke that made her giggle, Stephen ceased his directives abruptly, favoring Mary with an interested and speculative stare. She was aware of the admiration in his gaze as he eyed her clad in his sister's fine clothes. "A vast improvement, mademoiselle," he murmured.

Mary tensed her jaw, refusing to hold his regard. Her heart was beating so wildly, she was afraid he could hear it, and guess that all was not as it seemed.

Isobel interrupted. "I want to show Mairi King Rufus, Steph. Can we? Please?"

Thinking of escape, waiting for his reply, Mary was sweating.

Stephen barely looked at his sister. "Interested in ponies?"

"I adore horses," Mary managed.

Stephen eyed her for another lingering moment, then patted Isobel. "You may go."

Isobel shrieked and hugged him, then flew across the hall. Mary turned to follow, unable to believe her luck, feeling his gaze on her, burning holes in her back.

"Beware," he said softly, ominously. "You will not be able to leave Alnwick, mademoiselle, in case you happen to think otherwise."

Somehow he guessed her intentions, somehow she did not miss a stride. But nothing was going to stop her now, nothing.

Outside, Mary was pulled along by Isobel, who chattered away. Mary did not pay her attention. Had he really surmised that she intended to escape? Or were his last words merely a warning? Surely if he guessed her plans, he would not allow her from his sight!

They traipsed along to the stables, Isobel skipping ahead while Mary, her throat dry and her pulses skittering, began to look for an opportunity to seize. She began to lag behind Isobel, which was not difficult as the child raced on.

The bailey was as crowded as it had been yesterday when Mary had first entered its confines. A bevy of laundresses were washing clothes in a huge cistern, other servants were moving purposefully to and fro, on business for their master, the blacksmith was still at work, his anvil ringing, and a shepherd had brought a small flock within, no doubt for the cook pot. His herd was milling everywhere, creating more confusion and more noise. Two small, shaggy dogs were taking frantic pleasure in chasing their charges while the shepherd ran to and fro, chasing first a ewe, then a lamb. Two knights were riding through the portcullis.

Far ahead of her now, Isobel paused, calling, "Can't keep up? Want to race?" Laughing, she took off at a run.

Mary came to a halt, watching the child disappear in the throng of bondsmen and freemen. She looked around carefully, but no one was observing her. Abruptly she darted into the long shadows of the knights' hall, where she paused.

She was out of breath, trembling with fear and excitement. Quickly she raised her cloak, pulling it up over her head. Two men in leather hauberks, wearing swords, strolled past her. Mary looked away from them. One of them waved at her; Mary waved back.

Her heart pounded. She had been assumed to be Isobel— her plan was working.

Mary glanced around. Her gaze settled on the carpenter and his apprentices, unloading a wagon of lumber near the small building that they were constructing. It was apparent to Mary, as the oxen remained hitched, that the wagon's work was not done for the day. Mary sucked up her courage and left the safety of the shadows. Keeping her face downward, she approached. Her steps slowed. Mary stepped closer to a mountain of stacked wine caskets. The men finished unloading the lumber and returned to their work, while the carter climbed back onto his seat. The wagon was now empty, except for a tarp which had previously protected the wood from any rain.

This was her chance—maybe it was her only chance. The carter would be leaving in a moment. Mary was frozen, her heart tripping wildly. She looked around. There were so many people running and milling about—but no one was looking at her. Those who were not going about their business were watching, with much laughter, the antics of the shepherd chasing his flock. She looked at the wagon. It had started to move forward. The carter cracked his whip, yelling at the oxen.

Mary did not pause. Her heart in her throat, she hoisted her skirts and scrambled into the back of the wagon.

She skinned her knees in the mad climb. She dove under the sacking, curling up, her heart banging madly, waiting for cries of discovery. She had made noise as she dove aboard; surely the carter had heard her. She was afraid to move, afraid to breathe. She closed her eyes and prayed briefly to the Virgin Mother.

Miraculously, no one whipped the sacking from her, no one hauled her by her ear from the wagon. No shouts of alarm went up. The wagon continued to roll forward.

Stephen pounded down the narrow spiral staircase. He was grim and unsmiling as he strode into the hall. Will had returned from Liddel, and if he had returned so quickly, it meant that he had undoubtedly found out his captive's identity. He was no longer sure he wanted to learn the truth. Foreboding filled him.

Will was already at the table, quaffing wine and being served refreshments by one of the maids. Geoffrey stood near him, arms crossed, looking on. Brand, seated by Will, was asking wryly, "So what have you discovered?· Is my brother's little captive little Mairi after all? Or does she belong to some great Scottish lord?"

Will grimaced. When Stephen paused in front of him, he instantly knew that his vassal had discovered Mary's true identity and that the discovery foretold trouble. At Stephen's entrance, Will leapt to his feet, his eyes dark with warning. "Stephen," he said, hesitating. "Liddel is in an uproar."

"Speak up."

Will swallowed. "And Malcolm Canmore is in a rage."

Brand's mocking smile vanished. Geoffrey stared. And Stephen was silent. Already grasping what was to come, but unable to believe it, his mind reeled. He echoed, *"Malcolm Canmore?"*

"She is no laird's by-blow, I fear," Will said grimly.

And Stephen knew the worst. *"Who is she?"*

"King Malcolm's daughter."

A stunned silence filled the hall.

As if he thought they did not understand, Will said gingerly, "You have taken the princess Mary as your prisoner, my lord."

Stephen still reeled. For another moment he could not speak. *"Malcolm's daughter?* Are you sure?"

Will nodded.

Stephen was stunned, too stunned to think clearly. *Malcom's daughter, Malcolm's daughter*—the refrain chanted in his head. He saw his brothers, equally shocked, exchange glances. "Jesu," he said hoarsely, "what have I done?"

"His full-blooded daughter," Will added, another blow. "She is betrothed to Doug Mackinnon, heir to the laird of Kinross. I did not linger to gain more information, but you may be certain that you have the princess. And—" Will grimaced "—'tis already known that it was you who abducted her—many locals saw the red rose."

Stephen winced. But his mind had come to life with a vengeance. If Malcolm Canmore knew that he had his daughter, Stephen could expect to hear from him immediately. And knowing Malcolm, he had best prepare his defenses. He turned to his brothers. "She is betrothed to Kinross. How come we have not heard of this alliance before?"

Geoffrey's gaze was sharp. "They must have gone to great ends to keep it secret."

The brothers all looked at one another, each of them fully understanding all of the myriad political implications unfolding with the facts. Malcolm's brother was in exile in the Hebrides. He was a legitimate contender to the Scottish throne, for any adult male kin could be nominated tanist during the King's lifetime to succeed him. Donald Bane enjoyed extraordinary support among the people of the Hebrides— the Isle of Ust, of Skye, of Lewes, and along the coast in northeast Scotland. These were areas where many of the clan

Mackinnon ruled. By wedding his daughter to a Mackinnon, even one not residing in the Hebrides, Malcolm was hoping to lure the rest of this powerful clan to his cause, which was well known. He wanted one of his own sons named tanist before he died.

"You have truly outdone yourself this time, brother," Brand remarked.

Anger began to seep into Stephen's veins. "What a fool she must think me. What a fool I have been." It flashed through his mind that she had indeed been the victor in their battle of wills and wits. He had not been able to seduce the truth out of her, which had been his ambition when he took her to bed. He had not intended to take her virginity, yet he had, unable to stop himself from completing what he had begun.

Stephen's anger died. He had lost that one battle, both with himself and with her, but he had hardly lost the war. *For a man must pay the price for a lady's virtue.* There might yet be a way to turn this to his advantage.

"What could she have hoped to gain?" Brand asked, puzzled. "Did she really think to deceive you for any amount of time? If she had told you the truth, you would not have lain with her and you would have ransomed her back to Malcolm."

Stephen knew that Brand thought he spoke the truth, but Stephen was not so sure. If he had discovered her identity, would he have kept his word, left her untouched and freed her? He was not a man who gave his word lightly—always before it had been inviolable. Perhaps this time the temptation the princess offered would have been far greater than he could resist—in more ways than one.

Stephen turned his thoughts to the immediate future. "Malcolm will seek vengeance."

"He will seek your head," Geoffrey said bluntly. "And rightly so. Apparently *you* are the one to bring another war down about our heads, not Malcolm and not King Rufus."

"Not necessarily," Stephen said. A strange smile, both hard and determined, changed his expression. His eyes were narrowed, focused not on those around him, but on the distant future. The peace was so dear. It did not have to be destroyed. If he could head off Malcolm, and convince him to acquiesce, and of course, convince Rufus . . .

Stephen turned abruptly, striding for the stairs. In the next second he recalled that Mairi—no, *Princess Mary*— had left the tower with his sister. A premonition of disaster filled him. He had not one doubt, not now, knowing of her royal blood, that she was intent on escaping. The stakes had changed. They were far more precious than he had dreamed. She was now the crucial pawn in a war that had outlasted generations. Mary was a great prize could he but win her, a prize that promised hope, and peace.

And he would win the prize. He would take the princess Mary to wife.

She must not escape. He wheeled, running to the door. At that precise moment, Isobel flew through it, weeping copiously. And Stephen knew it was too late.

He grabbed his sister. "Where is she?"

At his harsh, fury-filled tone, Isobel covered her face with her hands and sobbed harder.

"Do not indulge in theatrics now, Isobel!" Stephen said. *"Where is she?"*

Isobel dropped her hands, wide-eyed and tearless. " 'Twas not my fault," she cried, looking from Stephen to the others. "She was following me, and when I turned around, she was gone! I've looked everywhere," she howled, and then she covered her face again, with more tearful shudders and moans.

"Raise the alarm," Stephen ordered. Geoffrey was already rushing up the stairs to the ramparts to sound the horn. Stephen hurried through the hall, Brand and Will on his heels, Isobel chasing after him. "You stay here!" he snapped.

"Am I in trouble?"

Stephen did not answer; he was already out the door. "I think you are in a great deal of trouble," Brand said harshly. "Go to your room Isobel, and await Stephen there." He followed his brother outside; Isobel fled up the stairs.

His men had already gathered. Stephen gave crisp orders and they began to search the bailey. All work was temporarily suspended, all of the keep's inhabitants assembled and questioned. No one had seen the prisoner in the bailey, much less escaping the castle's gates. It had already occurred to Stephen why his captive princess was so invisible. As she was clad in Isobel's clothes, no one had paid any attention to her, thinking her to be his sister. Stephen hurried to the barbican. One thought filled his mind. *She had outwitted him—again.*

Within a matter of minutes Stephen had learned that an empty wagon had left the keep not more than half an hour ago, and that prior to that, Isobel had been remarked loitering nearby.

Stephen was already calling for his horse. He ordered the search to continue within the bailey, although he had little doubt that the clever princess was long gone. He galloped beneath the raised portcullis and down the drawbridge, his steed sending clods of dirt flying from its powerful hooves, a dozen knights behind him—in case they should ride into the midst of Malcolm's men. Above their heads the banner of the rose proudly waved.

She had outwitted him, not once but numerous times. Grudgingly he had to admit that her efforts were admirable. Her sense of honor was more fitting a man. But did she truly think she could escape Alnwick, escape him? Men cringed to confront his wrath, yet she dared to do worse, she dared to provoke it.

His admiration congealed. She was every bit a royal offspring, for only such bloodlines could explain her peerless pride and boundless bravery. Yet with the surge of admiration, there was apprehension. He could not help but compare her to her father. Malcolm was one of the most wily—and treacherous—men he knew. Stephen did not like the thought that Princess Mary was far more like her father than any man or woman should be. A tingle of foreboding ran down his spine.

Such a premonition was best ignored. For it did not suit his purposes.

Within a few minutes Stephen had overtaken the wagon and its lumbering oxen. The carter pulled up at the sound of his galloping approach, visibly frightened. "My lord, what have I done?"

Stephen ignored him, riding his massive stallion over to the wagon and reaching down for the sack. He yanked it from the cart.

She lay huddled in a ball. Quickly she sat up. The defiance he had come to expect blazed in her eyes, but he also saw misty tears of defeat. Despite himself, the hard edge of his anger lost its knifelike sharpness. For one instant, she appeared a helpless and frightened child. For one instant, he felt a strange softness for her.

In the next instant it was gone. She was no child. He had only to recall her sensuous body and her uncanny nature to know that. This sweet facade was only that—there was nothing innocent or helpless about her. Another tingle of foreboding raced down his spine. Would he have to be on guard with her forever after this day?

"Did you hope to beget a war, demoiselle?" he asked coldly.

Mary stiffened.

Stephen jumped from his horse and lifted her from the wagon. She cried out, jerking against his brief embrace. Stephen set her down and apart instantly. Still, the feeling of her flesh lingered. There were many facets to his satisfaction, to the victory he must score. His blood was hot with more than anger.

The driver was screeching now that he knew nothing of this circumstance. Stephen ordered him to return to the keep. With alacrity, the carter obeyed.

The wagon moved away. The knights were mounted behind Stephen in a semicircle; Geoffrey held Stephen's destrier. One and all were quiet, so quiet that Stephen and Mary might have been alone. The endless moor stretched away from them in a ragged pattern of gray and green. The sky above was darkening rapidly. A hawk circled overhead, and a breeze lifted Stephen's cloak and the trailing curls of Mary's blond hair. A vast silence settled upon them.

Stephen stared down his prisoner. With some satisfaction, he saw that she was afraid. Yet despite her creeping tears, she stood straight and so proudly; her nobility was unmistakable. "You should be afraid of me."

"It was my duty to escape."

"Of course it was, *Princess*."

She started, becoming deathly white.

"The carter did not know I was there," Mary finally said hoarsely. Her eyes were huge, riveted upon his face.

"You would be wiser to defend yourself, not him," Stephen said. He smiled, but it was chilling. "Princess?"

She inhaled. "It was my duty to escape—just as it was my duty to deceive you."

"Was it your duty to give me your maidenhead?" Stephen did not care that all of his men heard him; it was his intention that the whole realm know that Mary had slept in his bed.

Her breasts heaved. She was red. "Far better to lose my virtue than to become your hostage."

His brow lifted. "You sacrificed your virtue to save your father a ransom?" He was incredulous.

"I know you!" Mary cried, her fists clenched but shaking. "You would cripple him, would you not? You would demand far more than silver—you would demand land!"

He stared. "Indeed I shall demand far more than silver coin."

"When?" Mary demanded, but a tear trickled down her cheek. "When will you ask this ransom? When will I go home?"

"Malcolm and I must meet."

Mary nodded, the single fat tear rolling to her chin.

Stephen almost flicked his finger against her smooth skin to wipe away the lonely tear. The urge disturbed him, made him uneasy. It was very clear that she was distraught by her predicament and that she wished to leave him. Last night had not made her yearn for him. Undoubtedly she would reject any effort he made to soothe her. He hesitated, torn. He told himself he must be wary of this child-woman. Finally he said, unsteadily, "You need not cry, mademoiselle. In the end, there will be much to be gained for both of us from this circumstance."

Mary raised her fist and rubbed her wet cheek, the gesture absurdly childlike, increasing Stephen's discomfort. "No," she whispered, "you will gain, not me and mine. For I have failed. I have failed my country, my King."

He was astounded yet again. "Spoken like a man! A woman is not expected to best a man, mademoiselle. In fact, you have played a man's game, a game in which you could not possibly understand all of the consequences, a game you could not possibly win. 'Twas most unwise."

"I understand the game well enough." Mary raised her chin, her mouth pursed. "I did as I had to do. I am Scotland's daughter."

Something in him became fierce. "You are amazing, mademoiselle," he murmured. And he thought of the son she would give him, shrewd and strong and proud. Then, "Come, let us return, and let us begin again." He held out his hand.

She glared at him through her tears. She did not give him her hand. "We begin nothing! My father will kill you! And I shall dance on your grave!"

Stephen realized that he still held out his hand. He flushed dully and let his gauntleted arm fall to his side. "Malcom might try, but if I were you, I would do my best to dissuade him, for your father is no longer young, and I am in my prime."

She lost all her color. "You would cross swords with my father?"

He regretted his words. Not for the first time, he wondered at her love for such a scoundrel. "Only if forced to do so."

"Jesu," Mary moaned. "I can see the two of you when you meet to discuss the ransom!" Mary took a step towards him. "Do not kill my father. Please!"

It was only correct that she be loyal to Malcolm, but Stephen was inexplicably angry with her now for that loyalty, especially as she had just rejected him in no uncertain terms. Of course, it did not matter one whit whether she hated him or not; hateful wives abounded in this life. "Perhaps you might use pretty words and pretty manners to convince me? Perhaps you might act as a woman should?"

She blanched. "Knowing who I am—you wish me to warm your bed again?!"

"I did not say that, demoiselle. Perhaps 'tis you who wishes for another encounter like the one last night."

At first Mary did not respond, but her face was pinched, her eyes huge. "How I wish now that I were more like my sister, Maude," she whispered.

All the strange sympathy, even mixed-up as it was with anger, fled. "I did not know that Malcolm had another daughter," Stephen said sharply. Another daughter could change everything. Mary could become a political sacrifice as long as Maude was there to take her place in Malcolm's plans. Stephen wondered if he dare force Mary to the altar should Malcolm refuse to sanction the alliance.

"She is a novice in the Abbey at Dunfermline. She is very pious, very good." Mary's voice trailed off. But she added, "Unlike me."

"Do not berate yourself; it is not becoming," Stephen said sharply.

But Mary gasped. "Oh, dear Mother of God! How could I have been so thoughtless! They will betroth her to Doug, will they not? And it is me, *me*, that they will send to a convent!"

"Do you cry for your lover now?" He was furious. There was no mistaking his jealousy. His hands gripped her shoulders, his face came close to hers. "After the night we have passed?"

She shook her head. "No! No! I am not such a hypocrite!" She pressed the back of her hand to her mouth, in order to hold back sobs. "To be locked away in a convent, surely I will die!"

Stephen's hold eased. "You are not going to be locked away in any convent, mademoiselle."

Suddenly her gaze beseeched his.

"You are going to be my wife," Stephen said. And he smiled. "My princess bride."

Chapter 7

"*W*hat?!" Mary cried, disbelieving.

"I am going to take you to wife, Mary."

Mary backed away from him, her eyes wide with horror. "No! Never!"

He stared at her, his face hard with displeasure, his gauntleted fists on his hips. "You have no say in the matter, demoiselle."

"No, I do not, but Malcolm does!" Mary cried.

"That's correct. 'Tis a matter for Malcolm and me to decide."

She was filled with panic, hysteria. "Malcolm will never, *never*, give me to you. He *hates* the Normans, he *hates* Northumberland!"

Stephen was as still as stone. Then he said, after a long pause, "Perhaps when you are calmer, you will be more rational. We can discuss this union at Alnwick." He turned, dismissing her, but not before she saw how furious he was.

"No!" And fool that she was, Mary ran after him, tripping in her haste, grabbing the hem of his tunic. Stephen stopped abruptly, and Mary careened into him. She did not

99

care. Righting herself, she demanded wildly, "And when he refuses you? Then what? Then what will you do?"

He was clearly making a great effort to control his rage; he was shaking, not touching her. "He will not refuse me, not once he understands you might be carrying my child."

"I am to marry Doug!"

"I doubt he will wish to have you, demoiselle, in your ravished state." His anger spilled forth, twisting his features. "No one will have you in your ravished state, unless you wish to be the wife of some impoverished laird, the mistress of a crumbling shack filled with sheep and pigs!"

Mary felt as if he had struck her physically—so awful was the truth. "Then so be it," she whispered.

He gripped the bodice of her tunic, dragging her close. "You would prefer a life of drudgery to what I offer you? One day you would be the Countess of Northumberland!"

"Never," she cried into his face. "I will never be your wife, I promise you, for Malcolm will reject your suit. He will! He *hates* you!"

"Then I shall wed you anyway, *chère*."

Mary froze. Then her heart began to work again, pumping in huge and painful bursts. *"I hate you!"*

"I do not care," he said, clipped, his face dark. He turned his back on her abruptly. His strides long and hard, he moved towards his horse. He gestured once at Geoffrey, who leaped from his mount and went to Mary, taking a hold of her arm. Mary came to life. She writhed like a crazed vixen caught in a snare, but Geoffrey was unaffected. Stephen leapt upon his stallion. Mary ceased struggling, panting and desperate and out of breath. But she would have the last word.

"You are exactly as they say!" Mary shouted. "You have a care for no one other than yourself, a care for nothing other than your own power! Your ambition is a fearsome thing!"

He whipped his stallion around to face her, so brutally that the beast reared. His jaw was clenched hard, and the skin stretched across it had turned white. He spurred his destrier forward, coming dangerously close to treading over her slippered feet. But Mary did not move, in one of the bravest displays of her life—for she was quaking. Even Geoffrey, who held her tightly, stiffened and pulled her farther back and more closely up against him. The big brown stallion danced, its huge, iron-shod hooves just inches from her toes.

"And my fearsome ambition is to wed with you," Stephen said harshly, his eyes glittering. "A union that will take place, Princess, regardless of your distaste."

Mary had nothing left in her; she collapsed back against Geoffrey, her face stark white, her eyes never leaving Stephen's enraged face.

He yanked on his stallion's reins, whirling the beast around. He lifted his hand in a terse signal to his men, and a moment later Mary found herself astride Geoffrey's mount in the midst of the thundering cavalcade, imprisoned once again.

Several hours had passed since her failed escape. Mary had been sent to the women's solar the moment Stephen had returned her to Alnwick. Despite that confinement, she was well aware that shortly after her recapture on the moors, despite the encroaching night, a group of knights had left the keep, displaying the proud Northumberland banner. Mary had not a single doubt that these men had been sent on a mission that involved her fate.

Had they been sent to Scotland, to Malcolm? Sometime this night, would he be apprised of her whereabouts, and asked to give her in marriage to his age-old enemy?

Was her fate to become Stephen de Warenne's wife?

Mary shivered again. The night had grown inky black, the wind whining, perhaps in prelude to another storm. It would never happen. Malcolm hated Stephen de Warenne, and ravished or not, he would never agree to the union.

Tears gathered hotly behind her lids. She pressed her cheek against the cool stone wall. Dear Jesus, what if she were already with child?

Mary's distress increased. She closed her eyes, refusing to cry. She must pray she was not with child, she must not get with child, and she must not entertain an image of herself holding some swarthy newborn babe.

Mary's heart beat harder. They were in a game much like chess. She must anticipate and forestall his next move. She knew what his next move would be. He would be merciless in his attempt to get his son upon her. If he did, Malcolm might be persuaded to give in to the alliance. Mary did not think her father would allow her to be stigmatized with a bastard child.

Mary hugged herself. Undoubtedly the bastard would visit her tonight, soon, and continue to do so until she became pregnant. Too well she recalled the feel of his unyielding body against hers, within hers. Would she be able to resist his lovemaking now, knowing the ultimate stakes?

Her nerves were stretched so taut, they felt as if they might snap. She felt as if *she* might snap. The sounds coming from the hall below did not soothe her, far from it. Apparently a group of traveling players had arrived at the keep just before dark and had gained admittance. They had been entertaining the lord and his retainers all evening with their fine voices, their lutes, and their merrymaking. Once or twice Mary had heard the deep rumble of Stephen's laughter, and it made her furious.

He was not disaffected, oh no. To the contrary, he was well pleased with the turn of events.

Mary stood for a long time beside the parchment-shuttered window, embracing the cool stone wall. The hall below became quiet, and the knot of tension in Mary's belly grew. Isobel returned to the room. She would not speak with Mary, still angry at being used. Mary was too upset to make an overture to the child. Isobel stripped off her clothes and slid into the bed, taking up all of it when they were to share.

The rain pounded more forcefully. Silence reigned in the keep. Isobel appeared to be sound asleep. Mary made no move to light the dying tapers. She listened to the fast, hard staccato drops of rain, a rhythm not unlike that of her heart. She tried to listen through the drumming beat, for the sound of his footsteps. There was only the rain.

Mary tried to envision her life as the mistress of some small, isolated northern keep, where pigs and sheep ran in the hall, and she imagined attending the holy day feasts, when all the great clans gathered, with her faceless husband at her side, and her heart sank. Pride was a sin, but she was not sure she could lose hers—the thought of such a marriage appalled her. It was far easier to imagine herself as the next

Countess of Northumberland. In the next instant, she was appalled with herself.

Mary did not know for how long she stood at the window, consumed with dismay, with fear, with anger. It was all his fault; how she hated him.

Mary heard footsteps. Her body stiffened. She recognized the deceptively soft tread instantly. Her breath seemed to catch. Slowly Mary turned away from the arrow slit and gazed through the darkness at the indistinguishable door.

Too well she recalled the impossible rapture she had attained in his arms. Too well she recalled his every manipulative caress, his every deliberate touch. Too well she recalled the feel of him within her, hot, hard, and huge. She had become weak-kneed.

But he did not come.

Many long, interminable minutes passed. He did not come. He was not coming.

Mary swore that she was not disappointed. She did not move, unable to, not until she had recovered her scattered senses and control of her limbs. Finally she stumbled across the chamber, drained, to creep into the bed she would share with Isobel. She lay on the edge of the bed, the totality of her predicament overwhelming her. Monsters materialized in the night, monsters of loneliness, hopelessness, and fear. Monsters of desire. She rolled up on her side in a ball, pressing her legs tightly together, her fist to her mouth. How could she feel at once a child Isobel's age, one lost and desperate to find her way home, and at the same time like a worldly wanton capable of dying of desire for a man?

Finally, softly, she sobbed.

Eventually Mary fell asleep in sheer exhaustion, her final thoughts of a shabby single-room keep, filled with pigs and sheep, and although he had no right being there, of her captor, Stephen de Warenne.

"You do not appear to have passed a good night, brother," Brand remarked as he entered the Great Hall.

Stephen had not passed a good night; sleep had eluded him. He sat not at the long trestle table, but in a chair in front of the hearth. "Why are you not in the chapel with the others?" His tone was sour.

"I follow your example." Brand grinned, coming to stand in front of him. He leaned one hip against the wall. "Besides, this morning I must return to London, as you know."

"Say nothing about the princess," Stephen instructed. "Later, if Rufus questions you, you can defend yourself by saying that you left before we learned of her identity."

Brand nodded, grim. "It will be best for me to remain aloof. You send Geoffrey to Father, then, with the news of the princess's capture?"

"Aye. He will travel with you." Stephen dropped his head in his hands. Today he was physically tired, a very different feeling from the weariness he so often felt in his soul. But that weariness seemed to have grown overnight, as well.

He sighed. "Be careful," he told his brother. Because Brand was one of the King's household knights, it was important for him to remain loyal to his king—without jeopardizing Northumberland's interests. He walked a treacherous tight-rope—as all loyal men did. Thus he would have Brand pretend ignorance of what had passed these last few days. Geoffrey would inform their father of Mary's capture, and Rolfe would proceed as he thought best.

"Do not worry," Brand said, his wry facade gone. "Father will undoubtedly agree that marriage to the princess is far better for you than marriage to the Essex heiress. And if anyone can persuade the King, he can."

"I have little worry on that score, although Rufus can be most difficult," Stephen responded, his lips thinning as he thought about the King.

"What is wrong, Stephen?" Brand asked quietly, his blue eyes somber.

Stephen met his youngest brother's gaze. "She will drive me to insanity," he said just as softly.

"I thought so." Brand smiled then, patting his arm. "Have no fear. In no time at all you will have her in your bed—as often as you choose."

"That is only the half of it," Stephen muttered. "Did you notice how she hates me?"

"She does not hate you in bed, I daresay."

"For some reason, that thought hardly eases me."

"She will come to accept you with her mind as well. She will have no choice."

"But her sense of honor is a man's! Never have I heard a woman speak as she has—she thinks she has failed her King!"

"I heard," Brand admitted. " 'Tis most unusual, I admit."

A shadow passed across Stephen's face. "I am tired of fighting secret battles, brother. I am sick to death of intrigue. Last night it struck me—I choose to wed not a helpmeet, but a hate-filled enemy."

"When she makes her vows, Stephen, that will change."

"Will it?" he asked. "Or will she forever be a viper in our midst?"

"Would you change your mind?" Brand asked quietly.

Stephen threw back his head with a harsh, bitter sound. "Oh, no! I value the peace she might one day bring far more than the wealth of Adele Beaufort's dowry. But God's blood, Brand, I am tired."

Brand's gaze was sympathetic. "You are father's heir," he said at last. " 'Tis your duty to do what you must do, and marrying the Scot princess is the greatest alliance you can make for Northumberland." He left unspoken the chastisement—that being tired or sore of heart had little to do with duty.

"I know well that you are right," Stephen said at last. But his smile was feeble and flitting. He had not voiced his darkest fears. That if Mary clung to her sense of duty, she would forever be his unwilling wife. Too well he recalled what it was like to be at the mercy of powerful men and unkind circumstance—too well he recalled being powerless and a prisoner.

Mary awoke after the sunrise. Isobel was gone, undoubtedly rousing early in order to attend the morning mass in the family chapel with the rest of the household. Mary felt a twinge of guilt. She needed God's help, and it would not do her any good to miss any more masses.

She could not abide another moment in the chamber. She could not abide being alone with the kind of thoughts she had entertained last night. Mary had slept in her clothes, and now she performed her ablutions as quickly as possible, using a pitcher of water left for that purpose, and brushed out her hair. As she prepared to descend the stairs, she heard many voices below, as the family and retainers entered the hall to break the night's fast.

Mary lifted her chin, her eyes flashing. Some sleep had done her a world of good. It would be good, too, to face her captor, even to be challenged. It would be far better than remaining alone in the chamber, dwelling upon a dark and dreary future, or the bloody war that would decide her fate.

Mary slipped from the room and down the stairs. Her captor was not yet at the table, although many vassals were. He stood in front of the hearth, a fireplace so oversized that its mantel was level with his chin. Upon hearing her, he abruptly turned, his dark gaze pinning her to the wall. She paused, unable not to stare back. Tension throbbed in her.

He stalked towards her. He wore tightly fitting black hose and calf-high boots with spurs, a dark brown cote, and a black surcote over that. Both tunics had small embroidered bands in black and gold at the hem, sleeves, and throat. While his clothing was made of finely woven, expensive wool, it was exceedingly plain. His belt was thick, heavy, black leather, the gold buckle studded with a few precious stones his only adornment. She had realized for some time that he cared little about his appearance. Yet his garments did not detract from it; to the contrary. One was aware not of the clothes, but only of the man.

He paused in front of her. "Good day, mademoiselle. I am relieved that you have decided to join us for the break-fast."

"I do not like confinement," Mary said tersely.

"No one likes confinement." He took her arm. Mary stepped away from contact with him and walked with him towards the table. "You were not confined. Why did you refuse to come downstairs last night to sup?"

Mary tensed. He was displeased, but subduing it beneath a veneer of civility. "I haven't been hungry, Norman, and can you blame me?"

He stared. For a long moment he did not speak. "I see a night of rest has hardly thwarted your spirit."

"Did you think a single night might make me change my mind?"

"I had hoped you would see the inevitability of our union."

"There is nothing inevitable about it!" Mary snapped.

He had paused. "Are you certain?"

Mary felt her cheeks sting. His gaze had slid over her, quite frankly undressing her. He had taken her arm, and his large, warm hand closed over her wrist firmly. The air between them throbbed.

"No man, or woman, can defy fate," Stephen said softly.

Mary twisted once, sharply, to free herself, but failed. "You are not my fate. How arrogant you are to think yourself my fate!"

He just stared at her, his gaze dark and enigmatic, probing hers too deeply. Mary had to look away, flushing furiously. "If you think," she said low when she could finally speak, "that my capitulation to you in bed is an indication of fate, then you have gone mad!"

"I think, perhaps, that you have forgotten what it is like to be beneath me," he said slowly, watching her face.

Mary was scandalized. Especially as she had hardly forgotten his prowess in bed—or her own behavior with him. This time she succeeded in jerking free of his grasp. "That you speak to me in such a manner—"

"I speak the truth. I have not forgotten the feel of you, Mary, nor the taste," he said, his tone low and intimate.

Mary could not move. She was stricken with a recollection of his mouth nibbling at her thighs—perilously close to the juncture there.

He smiled. "Soon I will remind you of your fate with far more than words," he promised her.

Mary had forgotten to breathe. She gulped in air. She wondered what had kept him from taking her to his bed last night. It made no sense.

"Come," he said, his tone seductive. "Enough bickering." Mary forced herself out of her daze. This time she allowed him to lead her to the table and was seated on the dais as his guest of honor.

"Surely prisoners eat below the salts," she finally said in a feeble attempt to antagonize him.

"You are not just royalty, but soon to be my bride, and to be treated accordingly," Stephen said calmly. He pulled a loaf of warm white bread forward, and a trencher of cold meat left over from the night before.

Mary barely saw the food or what he was doing. Geoffrey had taken the seat on her other side, hemming her in. Although she did not physically touch the Norman, she felt the heat of his hose-clad thigh against hers. "I have told you, my father will never give me to you," she said hoarsely. "He loves me too much to sacrifice me to you."

He gave her a long, thoughtful look. "Does he, indeed?"

Mary tensed. From his tone, she gathered that Stephen doubted her words, and she was angry. "He does! So mark what I have said, Norman, least you later forget who is right now and who is wrong."

His eyes gleamed. Mary realized that she had leaned into him in her rage. Immediately she pulled away. Mary recognized the brilliance in his eyes. It had nothing to do with anger; it was carnal. *Why had he failed to come to her last night?*

"Do you still think to best me?" He had a dagger in hand, one long and lethal and not meant for eating, and with a motion too fast for her to follow, he had sliced the bread. A moment later he skewered it and held a piece out to her.

"If only that were possible," Mary said, her gaze flitting from his knife to his face. How could such a big man move with such grace? Was she the mad one, to even think of fighting him?

"You will not best me, demoiselle, you shall only weary us both. Needlessly. Come, take what I offer."

Mary looked from his well-shaped lips, pursed ever so slightly, to the slice of bread held aloft in the air on the tip of his knife. She refused to accept the bread. Just as she refused to accept him. But sweet Mother of God, he frightened her, for he was so powerful that she could not really imagine him not succeeding in anything he chose to do. And now, now he was choosing to wed her.

But Malcom was powerful, too. Mary shuddered, thinking of the meeting that must soon take place between the two of them, a hostile meeting that in all probability would degenerate into violence. And then what would happen to her?

"I will marry you anyway, chère," *he had said.*

Mary was seized with a sudden hopelessness. "Could you not content yourself with a ransom?" she heard herself plead.

Stephen did not immediately respond. He was holding the knife to her again, now offering her a morsel of cold pheasant. Mary's gaze flashed to his. He was treating her as he might his betrothed, his bride, or his wife. Worse than his disconcerting chivalry was the intensity she sensed behind it. That same intensity was mirrored in his dark eyes. How would she ever outwit him when he could so easily scramble her wits?

Stephen sighed, tossing the pheasant aside. "No. I will not. I cannot."

Mary stared. His words hung between them. She felt their significance, but was afraid to understand it. Surely he did not care for her in some small way? And for just an instant, Mary dared succumb to illicit dreams.

She shook herself free of the moment of insanity. "You will start a war."

Stephen moved the knife to her lips. Mary's words died. Its point was long and sharp. Before she quite knew how he had accomplished it, the pheasant was in her mouth and she was chewing it, and he had not even cut her. He skewered a piece of cold lamb. "I have no intention of starting a war," he murmured. "Long have I worked for this peace."

Mary sputtered with disbelief.

Stephen's eyes darkened. "What is so amusing, demoiselle?"

"As if you do not know!" She almost crowed. "You—a de Warenne—interested in peace. You must truly think me a mad fool."

He stared at her. "What do you think interests me? Other than your sweet body?"

Mary flushed. He was dangerously annoyed. "Why do you ask me to say what the whole world knows?"

"Speak." His smile flashed, unpleasantly. His knife also flashed, tossing the lamb to the hounds. They fell upon the small piece, snarling. "What does the whole world know of Stephen de Warenne? What do you know?"

Mary trembled. "I know of your ambition," she finally flung, unable to resist temptation.

His eyes grew black. "Ah, yes, my fearsome ambition."

" 'Tis fearsome! For it rules all that you do. I know that peace is your last concern, and that if you could, you would put your son upon my father's throne!"

Stephen sent his dagger into the table at the same time that he lunged to his feet. The blade quivered, the hall fell silent. Mary blanched but held her ground. For years Malcolm had accused Northumberland of coveting even more of Scotland than what they already had. She had only spoken the truth.

"*Our* son," Stephen said, his eyes glittering. " 'Twould not be my son—'twould be our son."

Mary could only wet her dry lips.

"You are not as clever as you think you are, demoiselle," he said, towering over her. "I do not want your wretched land, filled as it is with dozens of warring clans. I want only peace."

Mary pursed her mouth tightly shut, wisely refraining from ridicule.

"But I do not care what you think, not now, and not later, when you are my wife."

Mary managed not to cringe beneath his furious glare. He strode from the dais, calling for his steward. Mary watched as the man came running. A moment later Stephen had whirled from the hall.

Mary trembled then, slumping now that he was gone. Whatever had possessed her to accuse him so? She did not doubt his ambition, but to fling it in his face was an invitation to disaster.

"You will go far with a pretty smile, Princess, and winning ways, but to enrage him so is surely folly."

Mary's gaze flew to Geoffrey's.

"Why do you seek to push him to his limit?" the archdeacon asked. He was not smiling—his look was very somber—but he was not unkind.

Mary stared at him. "In truth, I do not know."

"Perhaps you should consider the fact that Stephen never fails in what he is determined to achieve. That you are going to become his wife, because he has never been more determined. You are no fool, Princess, so knowing this, why do you not cease sowing the seeds of discord?"

Mary looked at Stephen's dagger, where it stood upright, its lethal blade buried in the table nearly to the hilt. Most women would realize the folly of defiance and the inevitability of the marriage and act accordingly. But she was not most women. "How can I?" she whispered, finally meeting Geoffrey's intense blue gaze. "When I know my father—my King—demands such loyalty?"

Geoffrey's mouth narrowed.

An alarm sounded, interrupting them both.

Mary started. Geoffrey, Brand, and the many retainers in the hall instantly broke into action. Mary had recognized the blast of the horn as one of danger and warning. Now it was followed by the frantic ringing of the chapel's bell. "To the walls," Brand shouted to the men.

The men raced from the hall. Mary did not move. Isobel was being herded by her two ladies and her nurse into the solar, where they would undoubtedly wait out the crisis as ladies should. Isobel balked. "I want to go with my brothers!" she shouted. "I'm old enough—I want to know what's happening!"

"You will come with me this instant, young lady," her nurse, Edith, cried, boxing her ears sharply.

Mary made an instant decision. She raced across the hall, ignoring the cries of the ladies behind her. She chased after the men.

Her skirts raised to her knees, she flew across the bailey with the speed of a deer. She reached the bailey walls as Stephen and his brothers began to rush up the steps to the watchtower. Mary flew after them.

There was too much chaos for her appearance to have yet been remarked. But Stephen suddenly whirled upon the steep stairs, as if alerted to her presence. Instantly he saw her and his gaze widened with shock.

Mary did not stop her headlong flight.

"Jesu! Gerard, take the princes........e keep, now, and see that she remains there!" Stephe.........wed. And then he disappeared from view.

Strong hands caught Mary from behind, lifting her off of her feet. Mary screamed, struggling wildly. She was carried back across the courtyard and into the hall and then to the solar, where the ladies had all assembled. Abruptly she was deposited back down on the floor.

Mary stumbled, furious. One look at this knight's annoyed, set expression told her her cause was lost. Panting, she turned to face the assembled women. One and all, even Isobel, were staring at her in shock.

" 'Tis Malcolm," Mary cried. " 'Tis Malcolm Canmore, King of Scotland, come for me at last!"

Chapter 8

*I*f Malcolm Canmore had not been flying the white flag, Stephen would have never left the impenetrable safety of Alnwick with the knights he had on hand, so little did he trust the man. As he rode through the barbican at the head of his men, the banner of the rose flying above them, excitement gripped him. He had been waiting for this moment ever since he had learned the truth about Mary and decided to make her his wife.

He must proceed with care. So much was at stake. He must convince Malcolm to give him his daughter for a bride. Finally peace was a distant glimmer upon the horizon—one until now red with blood—and nothing must stop him from attaining it.

Malcolm's appearance was no surprise. Stephen had been expecting the Scot King, and his men had been prepared for the worst. Behind Stephen, two dozen of his best knights were fully armored and fully armed, and behind them, the walls of Alnwick were heavily manned with crossbowmen who could easily launch an onslaught against the Scot army if it dared any trickery. Geoffrey and Brand rode beside him.

Malcolm Canmore waited for him on the other side of the moat, at the head of a huge army that numbered several hundred. Only a third of their number was mounted; the rest was on foot, but all were battle-ready with sword, axes, and arrows. As Stephen rode across the bridge, his men behind him, Malcolm and three men separated themselves from their army and rode slowly forward to meet him.

Stephen had been at Abernathy two years ago when Malcolm had sworn homage to William Rufus. Malcolm had also sworn fealty many years before to Rufus's father, the Conqueror, breaking it time and again as he willed. He had only pledged himself at Abernathy to William Rufus after having been soundly defeated and failing in yet another attempt to extend his border south. He was a shrewd and treacherous man, and not to be trusted.

Stephen had already thought long and hard about how he would handle this interview with Malcolm. Although he was determined to wed the princess, not only did he need Malcolm's agreement, he also needed both his father's and his King's approval—which would not be forthcoming until Geoffrey reached London, spoke with Rolfe, and Rolfe in turn spoke with the King. Therefore Stephen was in a precarious position. He was usurping tremendous authority in negotiating his marriage, but he had little choice if he was to attain his goal and take Mary to wife.

He was prepared to offer Malcolm whatever he must, and he was not worried about his father; he fully expected the earl to be pleased with the sudden turn of events. King William Rufus was a different matter.

Would Rolfe be able to persuade the King? Thinking about Rufus caused Stephen's expression to tighten, his eyes to darken. He was a loyal vassal, as duty demanded, but that did not mean he liked his King, whom he had never forgiven for his betrayal so many years ago. Somehow, the little, lonely boy still lived on, somewhere deep in the shadows of his soul. Rufus had not changed in the ensuing seventeen years since Stephen had first arrived at court as a hostage for his father's continuing support. He was treacherous, he was shrewd, he was arbitrary. Too often he acted upon whim, seeking only his own pleasure and his own satisfaction. Stephen could not be sure that William Rufus would agree to this marriage. He might perversely enjoy thwarting the de Warennes, he might perversely enjoy thwarting Stephen—which was far more likely. Or he might hesitate, understandably so, to join Northumberland with his deadliest northern enemy.

The two groups of riders stopped, facing each other. Stephen was flanked by Brand and Geoffrey, the latter an oddity on this battlefield, in his cross and dark robes. Malcolm sat a magnificent chestnut stallion, surrounded by three men Stephen recognized as Malcolm's sons.

Malcolm edged his mount forward; so did Stephen. The Scot King's lined face was as immobile as carved granite. Only his blue eyes burned with rage. "What do you demand, swine of swine?"

"No formalities?" Stephen asked.

"Do not mock now! You had no regard for formalities when you kidnapped my daughter, bastard!"

Stephen did not flinch. That his enemies still called him bastard was to be expected—nothing could change the fact of his birth. It was not pleasant, but he had learned to ignore such insults as a young boy. "When I happened upon your daughter, she was ill dressed and chose to tell me that *she* was the bastard, the bastard of some puny northern laird."

For a brief instant, that threw Malcolm. He recovered as quickly. "God's blood! She was always too damn original! What do you demand of me, de Warenne?"

"A bride."

The men facing him all stiffened, stunned. Except for Malcolm, whose eyes flashed. Then one of them reached for his sword, drawing it. Before he had even finished the action, Brand had unsheathed his blade as well, with Geoffrey suddenly wielding a mace, and so quickly did everyone move that it was almost a single simultaneous flash of dulled metal. Then, as Edgar cried, "Skewer him!" both armies drew their swords. The plain clanged with the vibrant sound of a hundred blades being swept from a hundred scabbards at the same time.

Only Malcolm and Stephen remained unarmed, yet both men had their hands upon their hilts, their knuckles white.

Sweat dotted Stephen's brow. A similar glimmer stained Malcolm's face. Tension vibrated visibly between the two armies; the moors crackled with it. No one moved, no one even breathed, and Stephen knew that if someone did, the two armies would leap at one another instantaneously.

"Peace," Stephen said firmly, his words carrying. "You come in peace, I wish to speak in peace." No man, of course, sheathed his weapon, but some of the tension seemed to drain out of the many armed men.

" 'Twas not very peaceful of you to take my daughter," Malcolm mocked. " 'Tis easy, is it not, to speak of peace now?"

"As I have said, she was dressed like a villein, she even disguised her speech and manner, then dared to tell me her name was Sinclair."

"Perhaps I will kill you anyway—whoreson," Malcolm hissed. His eyes glittered.

Instantly Stephen spoke, for it was obvious to him that Malcolm was more interested in battling him than in speaking of his daughter. "Perhaps there is much to be gained for the both of us from this circumstance."

"The only thing that I wish to gain, you have," Malcolm said with a cold smile. "Your life and your patrimony."

Stephen's hand tightened on the reins. His stallion, conveyed an imperceptible message, began to dance, readying himself. Yet Stephen truly wished to avoid battle. His goal remained unchanged, to gain Malcolm's approval for Mary's hand, and he would do what he had to do, say what he had to say, in order to achieve it. "Let us cease this warfare. Let us think on the future. For once and forever, let us unite our families. Let me take her to wife. And one day, her son shall rule Northumberland."

Malcolm shrieked a terrifying war cry, raised his sword, and brutally swung it at Stephen as he rode forward. Their steeds clashed, two tons of animal, the one against the other. The heavy broadsword, swung with both hands, hit the heavy shield Stephen quickly raised. The blow sounded loudly. Malcolm swung again; and again Stephen deflected the sword with his shield, making no attempt to raise any weapon of his own. The sound of metal clashing echoed across the moors. Men on both sides of the battle stood tensed and ready. Mercilessly swinging his sword again and again, Malcolm drove Stephen backwards. If Stephen were not one of the foremost warriors in the land, if he were only a fraction less strong, he would have not been able to take the powerful, ruthless blows. One such thrust, should it be successful, would cleave him in two; Malcolm wanted to kill him. Had it been Stephen's daughter, he would try and kill the usurper of her innocence as well. But he knew that Malcolm sought to kill him for the simple fact that he hated him.

Malcolm's blows grew slower, as if the huge sword he wielded grew heavier. Stephen's arms, shoulders, and back ached from absorbing the full impact of each stroke; even his hands hurt from their relentless grip on his shield. Sweat began to interfere with his vision; it also drenched Malcolm, whose face was nearly purple from exertion. Finally the King of Scotland tried to raise his sword and failed; abruptly he let it hang. "Fight, damn you!"

"I will not. Think, Malcolm Canmore, *think!* Do not let your passions interfere with your wisdom. We can unite our families to both of our benefits!"

Malcolm panted heavily.

Stephen, his arms in agony, feeling as if they were wrenched fully from their sockets, slipped his shield back on his shoulder, not even flinching from the instant screaming pain. He did not wipe the sweat from his brow and his temples, either, nor did he labor to catch his breath.

"Even now," Stephen said, "honor demands that I wed your daughter."

Malcolm was not surprised by his admission, nor had Stephen expected him to be. Obviously he had already assumed his daughter to be ruined. "She is betrothed," Malcolm finally said heavily, still breathless.

A savage satisfaction stirred within Stephen. That Malcolm would now discuss the issue was a victory—another one. "Betrothals are made, they can be unmade," Stephen said.

"Father," Malcolm's oldest son, Edward cried, spurring his mount forward, his face flushed with anger, "before this goes any further, let us see Mary, so we might know that she is unharmed—and alive!"

Silently Stephen applauded the young man for his concern for his sister. "Do you wish to see your daughter?" he asked Malcolm.

Malcolm nodded curtly. "Send for her."

Stephen did not have to say a word; he merely glanced over his shoulder. Geoffrey had already turned and was cantering towards the drawbridge, which began to lower to admit him.

The silence thickened, lengthened, became endless. Horses stomped restlessly, nickered. Saddle leather creaked. A breeze whispered about their heads. Stephen held Malcolm's stare, aware of how much the other man hated him—and how much he was enjoying this confrontation.

Stephen shot a glance at Brand and then over his shoulder. There was no sign of Geoffrey and Mary. Where were they? His impatience turned to apprehension. Had the clever minx decided to use the furor to escape?

"Perhaps she is dead!"

Stephen's gaze riveted to the youth who had spoken, a slim boy hardly older than Mary, pale with tension and distress. "Your sister is not dead."

The youth fixed him with a look of wrath. "You bastard, I would kill you myself!"

His oldest brother placed a restraining hand upon the boy's arm.

"Here they come!" Brand cried, relief in his tone.

Stephen shifted in the saddle. Geoffrey rode towards them at a gallop, Mary behind him, her long gold hair waving like a banner. He pulled up his mount abruptly, causing the animal to rear. Geoffrey kept a firm hold on Mary, who was white with fright and wide-eyed. Stephen knew her fright had nothing to do with the mad gallop from the keep.

"I'm sorry," Geoffrey said shortly. "I had some difficulty finding her—she was not in the solar, but on the walls."

Stephen's gaze pinned her, but she was looking only at her father. "Father!" she cried. Then she stared at Stephen, appearing dazed. "You did not kill him," she whispered.

Malcolm spoke, not that Stephen intended a reply. "Daughter, you do not appear hurt. Are you virgin?"

It did not seem possible, but Mary, already white, blanched even more.

"Daughter?" Malcolm's gaze was hard.

Stephen was furious. "Did you bring her here to see that she is unharmed—or to humiliate her?"

Malcolm moved his mount closer to Mary. "Well?"

"No," she said, so softly it was hardly audible. Tears had formed in the corners of her eyes.

Malcolm turned to face Stephen, smiling in a hard, dangerous way. "Mackinnon brings me vast support. What do you bring?"

For a moment Stephen was so taken aback, he could not speak. His voice harsh, he said, "She may be with my child." He found himself looking not at Malcolm, but at Mary.

She sat unmoving behind Geoffrey, her face a mask of shock and horror.

Malcolm was cool. "There is always the cloister."

"Father?" Mary whispered in abject disbelief.

"Enough!" Stephen snapped, livid. He gestured at Geoffrey hard. "Take her back. Take her back, now."

"No!" Mary cried, but it was too late. Geoffrey was galloping away.

Stephen was shaken. Recollections of his own captivity flashed through his mind. Firmly he shoved them away. Now was not the time to dwell upon the bitter past. Not in the midst of a war of wits with Malcolm over the prize of his daughter. "Do not let your hatred steer you, Canmore. There is much to be gained, and you know it. An alliance between our families can mean peace."

"You offer me peace. Hah! There will never be peace, not until I regain what is rightfully mine!"

Stephen knew he spoke about Northumberland, not about his daughter. "You have spent some thirty years trying to conquer this land, land given by another Conqueror to my family, land we hold now without dispute. You will never seize Northumberland from us, and you must face the fact. You are old. Your sons are young, but do you really think they can achieve what you have failed to do?"

Malcolm almost smiled. "What a silver tongue you have."

"The best you can hope for, before you die, is to know that one day one of your line will inherit a land that once, many generations ago, was ruled by ancient Scot Kings." Stephen added, "And think about what is also dearest to you, and on the might of Northumberland."

Malcolm did not hesitate, which told Stephen that the shrewd King had already guessed where he was leading. "What do you offer?" Malcolm demanded. "Other than peace and your patrimony for my grandson?"

For some men, that might have been enough, but not for Malcolm, as Stephen had already known. The time had come to reveal his hand and set in motion the dangerous course it would take him on. "I promise you the might of Northumberland." Stephen smiled then. "For your eldest son. I will swear upon whatever you may choose that, when you are dead, I shall see him crowned Scotland's King."

Stephen's thoughts were spinning as he rode through the barbican and into the bailey. He had pledged upon a holy relic, a small pouch containing true slivers of the holy cross, which Malcolm carried in his sword hilt, to use his power to make Malcolm's eldest son, presumably Edward, Scotland's King. The pledge had been made in the presence of Malcolm's three sons and his brothers, all of whom were witnesses, and all of whom had afterwards been sworn to secrecy.

Stephen could not be sure that his father would have made the same pledge. As much as Stephen disliked the thought of Rolfe's death, it was inevitable that one day he himself would become Northumberland's earl. He had every right, then, to choose policies he would act upon in that future time. And though Malcolm was not young, for he was sixty, he had the heart and soul of a man in his prime. Barring an unfortunate accident, Stephen thought that the Scot King might live for many more years. Any actions he might have to take to fulfill his oath would not be anytime soon.

Stephen dismounted, his thoughts turning to Mary. He was far more concerned about her than he was about the promise he had made to make Edward Scotland's future King.

He trembled with suppressed rage. How could Malcolm not have shown the slightest concern for his daughter? Mary's white, shocked face haunted him.

Stephen entered the keep, several of his men just ahead of him. His loyal knights were smiling and elated because of his success. Although his pledge was a secret, his forthcoming marriage was not. Hearing them, the ladies came hurrying out of the solar, Isobel first. Stephen said, "Where is Mary?"

"She is in the solar—she will not come out," Isobel cried. "Steph, what happened? Why has she been struck dumb?"

Stephen barely heard her, hurrying past his sister. He paused on the threshold of the solar, his gaze flying to Mary. She faced the window, unmoving, her small body held tense and still. His heart clenched. He understood well her feelings of betrayal and disbelief.

"Mary?" he said softly.

She flinched. Slowly she turned her head, her eyes glazed with tears she refused to shed, trembling. "Wh-What happened?"

Stephen hesitated. What would his stubborn little bride do when he told her of her fate? Stephen did not delude himself; he did not think she would melt into his arms. "We are going to be wed," Stephen said gently. "You and I, in four weeks time."

"Sweet Mother of God," Mary gasped, collapsing.

Stephen caught her, cradling her in his arms. He had seen her shock, and her anguish. Understanding her as he did now, he was not angry. He was fiercely moved.

In his embrace, her breasts crushed beneath his chest, her thighs against his rigid loins, she went from being pliant with grief to rigid with denial. Her fingers curled, digging into his mail. She gazed up at him. "I do not believe this!"

"Your father and I have agreed," Stephen said carefully.

"I do not believe you!" Mary pushed away from him, and he let her go. She faced him in horror, her bosom heaving. " 'Tis a trick!"

"You were there." He ached for her.

" 'Tis a trick!" Mary cried again. "Malcolm hates you and your family more than he hates anyone other than your wretched King! He has railed against Northumberland ever since I can remember! He would never give me to you, *never!*"

Stephen could not be angry. It had been obvious to him for some time that Mary dearly worshiped her father. She saw him as a god, not as a scoundrel. She actually did not believe that Malcolm had consented to their union. And not only had he consented, he had done so for his own purposes, to fulfill his own ambitions; not once had he even asked after his daughter's welfare. Stephen was a man who dealt in realities, but this time he wanted to spare her the truth.

Mary was shaking her head, as if in bewilderment. "Is it not a trick?" she begged.

Stephen wanted to sweep her into his arms and hold her as he might Isobel. He found himself touching her cheek. "I am not tricking you, Mary."

She did not jerk away. She was wide-eyed, misty-eyed.

He would hide the truth of her father's real nature from her. He smiled kindly. "Malcolm wanted to kill me because of what I had done, but upon learning of your loss of virtue, he had no choice but to succumb."

"He . . . did?" There was hope in her tone.

"You need not know all the details, for they are far too grand, but the alliance serves us both well in the end. This marriage will not be so reprehensible, Mary; in truth, once you come to accept it, it will be far from abhorrent for us both."

She was unmoving. Stephen smiled another kind smile and leaned closer. He took her chin in his hand and bent to brush her mouth with his. It was a sweet kiss, nothing more, hardly intimate, but desire shafted him. As he hovered over her, his eyes turned black and all thoughts of kindness became obsolete.

He still touched her chin. The kiss had rekindled Mary, too. She swatted his hand away, then jumped back from him. "I do not need your pity, Norman!"

"I hardly pity you, mademoiselle."

"And I do not need your kindness!" Tears filled her eyes. She directed a disparaging glance at his bulging loins. "I know exactly the kindness you intend!"

"Mary." He tried to touch her again.

She shook him off, crying. "I thought to save my father a ransom by giving you my virtue, but it seems that instead, I handed you your greatest ambition. This changes nothing! This union serves you well—not me!" With that, she turned, tripped, and fled.

Stephen fought himself so as not to go after her. He, too, knew where his kindness would lead. How adept she was at dousing his compassion and arousing his anger. Nevertheless, a softness had been rekindled in his heart. It was a softness he had not yielded to in seventeen achingly long years.

Part Two

The Princess
Bride

Chapter 9

*A*dele Beaufort saw him the instant he entered the hall. Quickly she looked away. The archdeacon of Canterbury seemed to part the crowd as he moved through it.

Adele had been at Court for several months now, since she had turned sixteen, and she much preferred it to the routine existence she had led at her stepbrother's home in the heart of Kent or on one of her own estates in Essex. Currently the Court was in London at the Tower. Here there was never a dull moment; newcomers were always arriving, some with private messages for the King, others with petitions, and others just to curry favor with their sovereign. Here, amidst the gaiety and glamour, the intrigue and scandal, amongst the dashing courtiers and their bejeweled ladies, amongst the warlords and the courtesans, Adele felt at home. After she married Stephen de Warenne, she intended to spend most of her time at Court.

As usual, she was surrounded by admirers. A dozen men, some young, some old, some powerful, some not, vied for her attention. She rarely tired of their amusing anecdotes, the pretty flattery and the outrageous flirtation. When she chose to, she rewarded her favorites with a smile and a seductive look. But Adele did not have to act coy to arouse men; no man could look at her and be immune to her dark, sensual beauty. She was well aware of it. She had been aware of it since she was twelve years old.

Sometimes she thought that her betrothed was immune to her appeal, though. They had conversed on exactly three occasions, but Stephen de Warenne had never flirted with her or flattered her, and if she had not seen him appraising her full breasts and long legs, exactly once, the very first time they had met, she would have wondered if he was indifferent to her. That one time had reassured her. Nevertheless, if she were not so sure of her allure, she would think he did not lust after her. And that was impossible.

Raising her fan—a gift from the King himself—so that only her large, dark eyes were visible, she stole another glance at the archdeacon of Canterbury.

She stared at him. Her pulse throbbed strongly now, in her throat, between her breasts, and between her legs in the folds of her femininity. Her face was warm and she used her fan more strenuously. He was the most striking man she had ever seen, and she had certainly seen her share. God, he was beautiful. His oval face was carved with precise perfection, his nose fine and straight, his eyes piercingly blue. His jaw was tight and hard, his cheekbones bold and high. And he was lightly tanned, so that his complexion was golden, not pasty white. Adele had noticed that when he entered the hall, all its occupants remarked him immediately—even the men.

His frame was tall and broad-shouldered and obviously lean. Adele wondered at his body, hidden as it was beneath his long robes.

He also reeked of strength. He was no pampered, soft, spoiled, and self-indulgent prelate. Indeed, his very history, a history that was well known, spoke more loudly than anything else could of his determination, brilliance, and ambition. Adele knew he had been sent to foster in the harsh Welsh marshes with Roger of Montgomery, long before he had become the Earl of Shrewsbury. Montgomery was one of King William I's most able and most powerful generals, as was Rolfe de Warenne. In those years the two men had been not rivals but friends.

In choosing to send his second son to Wales, Rolfe was obviously choosing a territory as yet unconquered, torn by strife and rebellion. Geoffrey was not daunted. It was well known that he had won his spurs at thirteen—the same year that he had cast them aside and entered the cloister.

Adele, thinking about it, shivered. What young boy made such a choice?

His rise had been stunning, for he was the protégé of the Archbishop of Canterbury, who was an appointee of the Conqueror and another friend of his father's. But he could not have risen as he had if he had not been brilliant at his studies. Within three years he had earned a position among Lanfranc's staff as one of his clerks. By the time of Lanfranc's death, he was the archbishop's most able and personal assistant. His appointment as archdeacon came just weeks before his mentor died.

Adele swallowed, then licked her dry lips. She shifted her weight uncomfortably. Most archdeacons were ordained priests, but not Geoffrey de Warenne. He was not such an oddity. The last Bishop of Carlisle had been unable to read or write in any language, much less Latin, and when he had died, he had refused the Sacraments. Many in the Church had been scandalized, as had many laymen. Some of these same clerics were disapproving of Geoffrey de Warenne, even though he was well learned and devout.

Adele was certain that he had taken the customary vows of chastity when he had joined the cloister. But was he celibate? It did not seem likely. For he also reeked of virility.

Adele was flushed. She knew she was only one of the many women present who watched him, coveted him, and found him fascinating. She did not care about the others— she had no rivals, not at Court, not anywhere. But the archdeacon had never given the slightest indication that he found her desirable. Adele wondered, not for the first time, if, like the King himself, Geoffrey's virility was spent on boys.

Then she sighed. She would never find out. She was betrothed to his brother, Stephen de Warenne, one of the greatest heirs in the land, and she would never jeopardize her forthcoming marriage.

Adele was so absorbed in her thoughts that she did not realize that she was staring. Not until the archdeacon abruptly turned his head to fix her with his gaze. For one brief moment their glances held. A shadow crossed his face, perhaps annoyance, and he quickly turned away.

Adele was stunned and breathless. The meeting of their eyes had been so brief and was over so instantly that she almost thought she had imagined it. Now his back was turned solidly to her.

Adele's heart slammed hard against her breastbone, and she gasped. She quickly raised her fan, attempting to compose herself.

"Are you all right, lady?" Henry Ferrars, Lord of Tutberry, asked, his eyes narrowed.

Adele wanted to kick herself for acting like a pubescent girl. She managed a rejoinder, but her mind was not on Ferrars or any of the men in her circle of admirers.

Geoffrey de Warenne had never spoken a single word to her, not even in a polite greeting. And since she had come to London several months ago, their paths had crossed a half dozen times, because of her betrothal to his brother. It occurred to her now that perhaps he purposely avoided her—perhaps he lusted after her like all the others.

Her stepbrother, Roger, as fair as she was dark, pushed into the throng surrounding her and pulled her aside. "Your thoughts are obvious."

Adele shook him free. She fanned herself, to cool her blood. "Hello, my lord. How pleasant you are—as usual."

Roger's stare pinned her.

Adele fanned herself harder.

"What is he doing here?" Roger asked, again looking at Geoffrey. "I have heard he has been summoned. Too, that his brother came with him."

Adele's eyes widened and she froze.

"Not your beloved, so you can rest easy. He returned with Brand."

Adele resumed fanning herself in relief. She preferred not having Stephen here at Court. Her gaze settled on the archdeacon again, but at the look on his face her fan stilled once more.

"Something is afoot," Roger said. His face was tight. "God's blood! The King reveals nothing to me now! I must get back into his good graces!"

"Then you will just have to devote yourself to doing so, won't you, Roger?"

"And what will you devote yourself to, sister dear, while my back is turned?"

Adele ignored him. She smiled at her stepbrother. "Soon you will not have to worry about Rolfe de Warenne's power or his sons." Her tone was husky. "Soon I will be his son's wife and privy to every happenstance."

His dark gaze held hers. Suddenly his hand snaked out and gripped her elbow, yanking her fully against him. It was so crowded, busy, and noisy in the hall that no one noticed, and if someone had, Roger Beaufort, Earl of Kent, would not have cared. "But will I be able to trust you, darling?"

Adele was furious. Her black eyes blazed and she jerked herself free of her brother's grasp. "Time will tell, won't it?"

An ugly expression crossed his face. "We don't have time, Adele. Every instinct I possess tells me something is afoot. Why is the cleric here? Why has he been summoned for a private audience with the King? Why was the other brother sent to the North? Does another war loom—one I am left out of?"

Adele was frozen once more.

Roger was grim. "You appear fascinated with him." Their gazes locked. She knew he was not speaking of her betrothed. "Are you not?"

Adele's pulse was rioting. "Every woman in this room is fascinated with the archdeacon."

Roger said, "But every woman is not like you."

Adele raised her fan, hiding her expression. Only her gleaming eyes were visible. "I will find out what passes, brother dear."

"Have a care," Roger warned softly. "Do nothing indiscreet."

And Adele threw back her head, exposing her long, lovely throat, and laughed. "I am never indiscreet, my dear, as *you* should know better than anyone."

Geoffrey informed the King's ushers of his presence—although by now Rufus was undoubtedly aware of it, for the King had more spies lurking about than anyone—and went to find himself a seat at the table in the hall to wait for the royal summons. There was no seat to be had. Geoffrey was tired from the long, hard ride, and he worked his way to a solitary corner, in no mood for light, much less probing, conversation. His appearance at Court had already raised much speculation; most of the world knew he came only when summoned, and then to do battle with the Crown. As he was weary, his thoughts turned to the night to come. Rolfe had several small manors in Essex, and one was just across the Thames. Geoffrey intended to spend the night there instead of returning directly to Canterbury.

His second but more important reason for being in London was to speak with his father and inform him of all that had passed at Alnwick, an urgent necessity now that Stephen had arranged for a marriage to Princess Mary. Geoffrey intended to speak with Rolfe before retiring to Essex that evening. He had already sent the earl a private message.

He thought of a warm, soft bed. A moment later a woman backed into him.

She stumbled and he caught her automatically. Even as he lifted her, for one moment her soft body pressing against his lean one, he knew who it was. He didn't have to see her to know. But he felt her, smelled her, and being as virile as his brothers, he responded in kind. She turned around in his arms. Seeing him, she gave a small cry of surprise, which he did not, for a moment, believe.

For one more beat he held her. Up close, she was more alluring than from afar. Her skin was tawny and dark, from Mediterranean forebears, perhaps, her brows thick black wings above her almond-shaped eyes. Her mouth was full and large, and above the right corner was a dark mole. She was very tall, her eyes almost level with his, and she had a lush, full-breasted body, which she showed to her advantage in a thin silk surcote that fit her like fine hose. Geoffrey released Adele Beaufort, the woman his brother was still officially betrothed to.

"Thank you," she said throatily. Her scent was not just strong but musky. It brought forth images of hot nights, sweaty limbs, and sex. "You saved me from a twisted ankle."

He did not return her smile. "Did I?"

His doubting tone brought a flush to her olive skin. "The floors are very hard, my lord. Surely I would have hurt myself if you had not caught me."

He crossed his arms and eyed her, leaning his back against the wall. From this distance he saw that her large nipples were raised against her red silk gown. Would he never be able to control his body? But what man could when confronted by Adele Beaufort? She was the reincarnation of Eve, all that was female, unholy temptation, pure provocation to sweet, sweet sin. He said nothing, immersed in very base thoughts.

She smiled, touched his arm very briefly. " 'Tis a surprise to see you here, my lord."

He cocked a brow.

She seemed to sway closer, her smile infinitely seductive. "Are you on Church business, my lord?" She touched him again.

"Do the affairs of God interest you, Lady Beaufort?"

Her lashes fluttered. "All affairs interest me, my lord."

He took a deep breath. How easily he could imagine her affairs. It was a very good thing that Stephen was not wedding this one. And he was determined to stay away from her, too, before he gave in to his damnable need. "If you would excuse me." He turned abruptly. Although he fought his virility in a never-ending battle, in the end he always lost. The sooner he returned to Canterbury, the better. He would immerse himself for a single night in the ripe body of a very lusty widow. Tam was open, honest, and kind. She was no dark seductress, she had no guile, she made no demands.

But Adele Beaufort gripped his wrist, her long nails almost but not quite clawing his skin. "Wait!"

His jaw clenched, he turned.

"Have you word, then, from Stephen?"

"How would I have word from Stephen, madame?"

"Were you not in the North?"

His smile was cold. "You appear well informed, my lady."

She flushed. " 'Tis no secret that Brand was in the North, and as the two of you arrived together . . . I merely thought . . ."

He cocked his brow again.

"In truth . . ." Her voice trembled, her breasts heaved. Geoffrey damned himself for not looking away. "Perhaps a private moment . . . You might . . . We might . . . I must repent my sins."

Geoffrey's smile was twisted. He knew without having to be told exactly what sins she spoke of. His loins were very thick beneath his robes. Adele was the kind of woman to kindle sinful thoughts. "You do not appear penitent, Lady Beaufort. You appear in dire need of saving." And so was he.

"Do you—do you wish to save me?"

"Lady Beaufort, I do not think we understand one another."

"Then we must communicate more thoroughly," she whispered, and her hand stroked his arm from the elbow to the wrist.

He was frozen, rock-hard with lust, so close to an imminent explosion. There was no mistaking her meaning. And, dear Lord God, all women were forbidden him, but this one, a purposeful temptress, truly seeking his downfall, was far worse than any other—and far more tempting. For he could only imagine what it would be like to spend himself on her exquisite body.

His smile was twisted when he finally managed to summon it. "You know where the chapel is, and Father Gerard would be most willing, I am sure, to hear your confession if you truly wish to repent your sins."

Her gaze locked with his. The tip of her tongue wet her lips. It was not a nervous gesture, and Geoffrey knew it. "I do. I do. Would *you* hear my confession?"

His smile vanished. He could also imagine what her confession would be. He felt close to succumbing to her seduction. "I do not hear confessions, Lady Beaufort," he said harshly. He was furious, with her, and as always, with himself.

She saw his anger. Her eyes gleamed wildly. Before Geoffrey could go, she moved closer, blocking his way. The hard tips of her breasts actually brushed his chest. "I was only trying to thank you for saving me from a fall, my lord."

He laughed harshly, facing her. He did not move away, could not. Heat steamed between them. She still gripped his forearm. "We both know that I have not saved you, madame, although I would that I could. And we both know that you hardly wish to thank me. I will not be seduced, madame."

Her black eyes flashed. "You mistake me."

"I do not mistake you, Lady Beaufort. That would be impossible."

As seductive as she had been, she was now enraged. "Apparently I have mistaken you!"

He did not answer, for her words were a complete lie— she had recognized him from the first, recognized his huge, misplaced lust, recognized that in a way, they were exactly the same.

And then her next words made him forget himself completely. "I mistook you for a man, despite your robes! But you are no man, are you? You are no man, you are one of those others, one of those boy-lovers!"

Geoffrey forgot that they were in a public place. He caught her wrists and had her up against him a scant instant later. Her dark eyes widened when she felt his engorged manhood, then they turned to smoke.

The obvious invitation issued there brought him to his senses. He released her, stepping back from her. His smile was twisted and harsh. "Never doubt my manhood again."

"In truth," she whispered, "I never did!"

But Geoffrey had already shoved past her. Behind him, he heard her cry his name. His strides lengthened, as did his determination. But he was shaken.

* * *

Not an hour later, the Earl of Northumberland was ushered into the King's chamber after having had a very private meeting with his son, Geoffrey. He was an older version of both Geoffrey and Brand, all hues of bronze and gold except for vivid too-blue eyes. Like all of his sons, he exuded an unmistakable virility, and women ran after him hoping to entice him into their beds. He ignored them—he was still extremely fond of his wife.

His aura of power was unmistakable. It was the power of a King-maker; indeed, he was called such behind his back, both by friend and foe alike. He found the nickname somewhat amusing, but secretly it pleased him. Once he had been nothing but a mercenary knight, and he would never forget those times.

The King's apartment was one of the largest chambers in the Tower, half as large as the hall outside, dominated by a massive carved and canopied bed, covered with furs and velvets. Chests and coffers abounded, filled with the King's most prized and valuable possessions.

Rolfe approached and knelt before Rufus. The King was a big man. Once he had been all heavy muscle and almost handsome despite his flaming locks; now the excesses that drove him had faded his looks and added more than a layer of fat to his big build. For a moment he continued to sprawl indolently in a chair massive enough to suit his frame and weight. He took another sip of rich red wine from France, his face flushed from its effects, as if in no hurry to greet his vassal. Finally he said, "Rise, dear Rolfe, rise."

Rolfe stood, ignoring Duncan, who sat next to the King, his interest open and apparent. Duncan had grown up at court with Rufus. Several other retainers were also within, but immersed in conversation on the other side of the room. Rolfe noticed that Roger Beaufort was not present— apparently he had yet to worm his way back into the King's favor.

"How is your son?" Rufus asked casually. His shrewd eyes belied his tone. Rolfe knew the King's curiosity ate at him.

"Geoffrey is, as always, fine."

"He awaits an audience with me," Rufus commented, taking another sip of wine.

Rolfe was aware of that, just as he was aware of why. "My son is eager to show you his accounts," Rolfe murmured. He and Geoffrey had not discussed the issue, in fact, but Rolfe could not say otherwise.

"If he is eager to open his books to me, then he has surely transformed himself into a man I have yet to meet," William Rufus remarked dryly.

Rolfe smiled. "The archdeacon is your loyal vassal, sire."

"He is loyal only because he cannot best me," Rufus said.

Rolfe decided not to respond.

He had known William Rufus since he was a child. When Rolfe had fought at Hastings at William the Conqueror's side, Rufus had been ten and already the physical image of his father, of whom he was the favorite. There had been the promise that he might be like his father in substance, as well. Now it was clear Rufus would never be the all-powerful man his father had been. Yes, he was as ruthless, and as fearsome in battle, as shrewd in politics, but in many other ways he was lacking.

The bullying boy had become a bullying King. He bullied his nobles, he bullied the common people. His laws and justice were harsh and unreasonable, fomenting intense discontent and opposition. His taxes, which he levied at whim to support all his wars—and there were many—were oppressive. Already there had been one major rebellion in 1088 in the east of England soon after Rufus ascended the throne. He had broken the back of the rebellion with brutal military repression and many promises of good government and relief from his severe taxation and the harsh forest laws. His victory had been quick, the offenders banished forever, their lands forfeit. One of the rebels had been the first Earl of Kent, and much of his lands had been awarded to Roger Beaufort, along with his title, for Beaufort had played a strong role in crushing the rebellion, as had Northumberland. But it had not been long before it was clear that Rufus's promises were false and conditions throughout the country remained the same.

Rolfe had sympathized with the rebels, but he had always been the King's man. First for Rufus's father, William I, now for Rufus, and should he live to see the day, for Rufus's son. But his loyalty was sown from much greater reasons than his strict code of honor and sense of duty.

William Rufus needed Rolfe's sincere guidance. Rolfe never stopped trying to steer the King onto the path of a more just and equitable administration of his subjects and realm. Indeed, in the past four years since the good Archbishop Lanfranc had died, Rufus's penchant for arbitrariness and decadence had worsened. Lanfranc, like Rolfe, had sought to morally guide the King while he was alive. Rolfe knew that should he leave the King's side, Rufus would be influenced only by his cronies, men with the same—or worse—shortcomings as he.

And of course, always, Rolfe protected the interests of his family and Northumberland.

Now he intended to further those interests as never before.

Rufus had dismissed Duncan as well as several other retainers. As they paraded out, not a man among them could conceal their curiosity; each and every one was determined to learn, as quickly as possible, what the King and Rolfe de Warenne deemed important enough to discuss so privily.

As he left, Duncan shot Rolfe a piercing glance. Rolfe wondered what he would think had he known that Mary was hostage at Alnwick. For he was Mary's half-brother.

When they were gone, the door firmly closed behind them, Rufus chuckled. "Jealous vultures, aren't they? They all pant to know what news you bring; each and every man fears that you shall ingratiate yourself further with me and be awarded some priceless boon. And poor, dear Duncan is near frenzy, for of them all, he must know what passes so close to his birthright." His gaze turned sharp. "So tell me, Rolfe, why are we closeted thus? What intrigue brews?"

"Stephen has taken Malcolm Canmore's daughter hostage, Sire."

Rufus choked on the sip of wine he had just taken. "God's blood!"

Rolfe let the King absorb this momentous information.

Rufus began to smile. He rubbed his hands together greedily. His face was redder than ever, a ludicrous combination with his orange hair. "What luck. Ahh, Stephen, how well you have done. What shall we demand? Oh, he shall pay now!" He chortled. "And I shall find a way to reward your son."

Rolfe said nothing.

"So what shall we demand?"

"A dowry."

Rufus stared. "And who shall the lucky groom be?"

Rolfe stared back. "If Stephen marries Canmore's daughter, a real and lasting peace if possible. What better way to reward my son? And if there is peace in the North, you can devote yourself completely to Normandy."

Rufus smiled without mirth. "You want peace, Rolfe, or more power? Is not an earldom enough?"

"Have I ever betrayed you? Have I not supported you in your time of greatest need?"

"Have I not given you more than I have given anyone else?" Rufus replied.

"I seek to protect England and you, Sire."

Rufus's smile was bitter and even self-mocking. "I know you well, Rolfe, and never have you misled me like so many others. As *much* as I can trust anybody, I trust you. In this quagmire we call a Court, amongst all the greed and ambition, you seek only to protect my *father's* legacy—do you not?"

"I seek to protect England and you, Sire; never doubt that," Rolfe repeated firmly.

"Dammit," Rufus said irritably. "I would have loved to rub his face in the muck!"

"His face is in the muck, Sire. He cannot be very pleased about this turn of events."

"Stephen is betrothed to Beaufort's sister," Rufus said pointedly.

"Betrothals can be broken," Rolfe said quietly.

"And when Malcolm dies?"

"When Malcolm dies, Northumberland supports England, as always."

"And when you die?"

"My pledge is Stephen's pledge."

"So we are back to Stephen," Rufus murmured. "We grew up together, as you know, but there is no great fondness between us," he said grimly.

"Fondness means nothing; honor means everything. Are you impugning my son's honor?"

"No!" Rufus heaved himself to his feet. "No, I am not. No man would be so stupid as to question Stephen's honor. Is there a man in existence with more? I doubt it."

Rolfe watched him. When he spoke again, his voice was soft and hypnotic. "I have ever been loyal to you, Your Grace, just as I was loyal to your father. Yes, I confess that I want a lasting peace on the border. I confess that I want this princess bride for my eldest son. But you, you must have Normandy."

William Rufus fell still, silent.

"What happened five years ago will happen again," Rolfe continued in the same seductive tone. "You have too many vassals with landed interests in Normandy, vassals who belong not to you alone, but to your brother Robert as well. Like Odo of Bayeux and Robert of Mortain, they are pulled in two opposite directions constantly. It is an insufferable situation. These magnates want one liege lord, not two. They must have one, and it must be you."

Rufus's gaze burned. "You think I do not know well what you speak of? There are many who connive even now to put my brother Robert on my throne."

"And there are many who know he is too weak to be King of England. Robert could not possibly unite England with her sister land."

They stared at each other. Many minutes passed. Rufus finally sat down and leaned back in his chair. His face was hard and grim. There was no mistaking the magnitude of power the proposed alliance would bring to Northumberland, or the potential that existed for disaster should the de Warennes become too friendly with Scotland. There was also no doubt that Rolfe spoke the truth. He must be free to devote himself to regaining Normandy—if he wished to remain England's King.

"Tell me," Rufus suddenly said, "is she fair?"

Rolfe was startled. "The princess?" The King's question was bizarre.

"Yes, Canmore's daughter. Is she fair?"

"I do not know," Rolfe said slowly, wondering where Rufus could be leading.

Rufus suddenly shrugged. "There is no woman more beautiful than Adele Beaufort, I suppose. And he was not taken with her."

Rolfe said nothing. There was nothing to say. Whether Stephen might find his bride fair or not was more than irrelevant.

Rufus smiled, and it was mocking. "Enough. The idea is entertaining—and I will entertain it."

Rolfe nodded and bowed slightly. "That is all I can ask, Sire." But when he left the chamber he was smiling. And some time later he had sent a messenger north, riding hell-bent to Malcolm Canmore.

Chapter 10

*I*t was a trick.

Mary knew it was a trick. When she had finally calmed down, she had thought very carefully about the situation. Malcolm loved her, and while she did not think he would ever allow her to be stigmatized with a bastard, she was also certain that he would not hand her over to the enemy before he even knew whether she was with child or not. He hated the Normans too much.

The words she had overheard, the apparent bargain being made, had been a part of his very clever ruse.

Mary hugged herself. The night was cool, but there was also a terrible chill in her heart. Despite her certainty.

The moon rose, full and white. She watched its ascent, watched it part pearly gray skies. A thousand stars unfolded in accompaniment, and silvery moonlight danced within the chamber. She stood at the window slit, staring unseeing into the night. Isobel slept soundly and peacefully on the bed they shared behind her. The stars seemed to blur, losing their brilliance.

If only she had had a chance to speak with her father alone. If only he had taken her aside, if only he had comforted her, if only he had told her of his love and explained this ruse!

But he had not. He trusted her, knowing her to be loyal and clever, just as she trusted him to outwit the Normans in the end. And no one was more adept at outwitting the Normans than her father. He had been fighting them nigh on twenty years, fighting them tooth and nail, deceiving them as he must in order to survive and safeguard Scotland. As he now outwitted Stephen de Warenne.

For that was the only explanation why Stephen truly believed their marriage to be based upon some kind of political alliance. He had been duped.

Mary collected herself, wiping a teardrop away with her sleeve. There was no earthly reason for her tears. She must be strong, she must survive each and every day to the best of her ability, with pride and fortitude, and she must not conceive his child.

It was late, but her captor was still downstairs. That evening the hall had been unusually festive, much to Mary's dismay. The men had caroused in an obvious celebration of their lord's apparent success. As the hours passed, their voices grew more slurred. Now the hall below was silent; all had gone to bed.

Except Stephen. Mary could not imagine him drunk, but after this past night, he must be deep into his cups. She was being handed a golden opportunity. Stephen's wits would be dimmed. Would there ever be a better occasion to confront him? To demand the details of all that had transpired between him and her father? To reassure herself of what must be the truth?

Mary did not hesitate. But as she hurried from the solar, her heart thumped. He found her desirable. Did not the bards tell tales of men who lost their wits to dangerous seductresses? Would it not be better to be a seductress than a firebrand? Dare she take on such a role?

Mary tried to ignore the warmth of her cheeks and the too rapid fluttering in her breast as she entered the hall. As she paused on the threshold, it occurred to her that she played a dangerous game. That she very well might wind up on her backside with her skirts about her ears.

She glanced around, trembling. The dying fire in the hearth still glowed, and she could see that the retainers within were all asleep. Occasional snores and moans sounded.

Her gaze shot to the dais; she expected to see Stephen there. No one graced the platform. She felt distinctly uneasy, disbelief welling up in her. She approached the two thronelike chairs in front of the fire from behind, thinking that perhaps he sat in one. But both chairs were vacant. Mary wrung her hands.

He was not upstairs abed and he was not in the hall carousing. She knew damn well what he was about. It was what all men were about at this ungodly hour, assuaging the stiff prick between their legs. Mary could not move, consumed with sudden fury.

Abruptly she turned. Her anger was misplaced. She did not care what the bastard did—no woman could expect fidelity from her lord, and he was barely that now and would never be that in the future.

Mary turned and marched back upstairs.

Stephen was not drunk. Far from it, for he was not a man inclined to overindulgence. He set the candle holder carefully aside. He had no intention of burning his own stable down.

"My lord?" the maid asked, breathless and unmoving.

Stephen was not exactly pleased. She was not to his taste. Her breasts were huge, her hips abundant. Once her softness might have pleased him. At the very least, he liked her hair. It was pale blond.

His lust was huge. This night, like the night before, he was unable to sleep, his manhood swollen and distended. Despite his better intentions, he had found himself fantasizing about his bride like an adolescent boy. He was a man used to assuaging his appetite when it was raised. He had never spent a moment in fantasy before, even as a lad. And he knew he could not spend another night like the one just passed.

And taking Mary to bed now was out of the question. She was his betrothed for all intents and purposes even if the betrothal had yet to formally take place. Such callous use of her would be the height of disrespect. She was no laird's by-blow, no villein. She was of royal stock and blood, and she was his bride. He could not treat her in the manner he would a leman, not anymore. There was no privacy in any keep, much less Alnwick. Unless he tumbled her in the stables in the dead of night, one and all would know of their shared intimacy. The former was out of the question, the latter another kind of abuse he could not inflict upon her. One day she would be his countess; if he treated her with disdain, an example would be set.

Now he eyed the maid standing breathlessly before him. She was a poor substitute for the woman he desired. It did not matter. For it would be absurd to continue this way for a full month until he married Mary. What mattered was the fact that he was in great pain. When she had sat upon his lap in the great hall not too many moments ago, his shaft had raised itself against her buttocks like a pillar cleaving the sky.

Stephen motioned to her. A moment later he had her on her knees, and she was taking care of his huge pain.

Mary did not fall asleep until after dawn. She no longer brooded upon the dangerous game of war and treachery in which she was the most prominent pawn. She was furious and she was hurt, two emotions she had no right to. She could not stop herself from imagining Stephen with some faceless lowborn servant. She should not care what he did and with whom—but God help her, she did.

As the morning grayed, Isobel still blessedly asleep, Mary found herself faced with brutal facts. She had thought about this man numerous times since she had first seen him at Abernathy. It had been impossible not to recall him, stricken then as she was by his virility and his power. Despite the fact that he was her enemy, the attraction had been there from the first.

Mary decided it did not matter. Abernathy was long past. Tonight he had proved the depth of *his* passion for *her*. His passion for her was political. Mary promised herself that she would never forget it.

Mary slid from the bed. Even if he had complete mastery

over her body, he must not ever have any mastery over her will. Never must she allow him to enslave her mind. Her body she now consigned to the realm of irrelevance. After all, as her mother would say, 'twas only flesh and blood. Her soul was another matter indeed.

Anger, both hot and bitter, remained. Mary wanted to strike back. There was one obvious way to use the current circumstances to her advantage. Had he not once accused her of spying? The time had come to take on that very role.

Determinedly Mary began her ablutions, thinking of how proud of her Malcolm would be. Mary finished washing and was leaving the chamber when Isobel was summarily awakened by her nurse. It was not yet prime; Mary slipped out as Isobel began impiously protesting that she had no wish to go to mass that morn.

She saw him the precise instant that she entered the hall. And he was bright-eyed, as if he had not been spending himself last night on another woman. Mary's ire renewed itself. So did the unwelcome hurt.

Mary managed to ignore him, no easy task. Because the morning was chill, she went to the fire, not even greeting him, as if he did not exist. She wondered which woman he had lain with. She wondered when she would be presented with an opportunity to spy.

"If you hold your hands any closer, you will get burned," he said softly, coming to stand directly behind her.

She stiffened. Like all maidens, she wore her hair unbound, and now he lifted the heavy mass, weaving it through his hands. "You have beautiful hair, mademoiselle," he murmured. His tone was magically soft, mesmerizing.

She did not move, every sense she possessed scathingly aware of the heat of his body and the power of him behind her. She recalled his treachery last night.

His fingers brushed her nape. "Did you sleep well, mademoiselle?"

Mary jerked away to face him. "Do not touch me. And yes, I slept very well indeed," she lied. She had barely slept at all.

He studied her. "Why are you so angry?"

"Angry? I?"

"Have I somehow offended you?"

Mary responded with her own burning question. "Did *you* sleep well last night, my lord?"

His gaze locked with hers. "In truth, no. And I am sure you can think why."

"Oh, I know why!" He traced her cheek with one strong forefinger, and Mary batted his hand away.

His eyes glowed seductively. "Then you know that the only way in which I will sleep well, mademoiselle, is if you are in my bed with me, and we have both exhausted ourselves."

That he should be so blunt made Mary speechless.

"You are so angry, Mary. Why? Because I did not do as I pleased last night?"

"But you did do as you pleased, did you not?" she heard herself accusing him.

He was mildly nonplussed. "I most certainly did not. Had I done so, you would not be up and about at this hour, mademoiselle, for you would be unable to leave our bed."

She went red. For just an instant she imagined him taking her so completely, so thoroughly, that she would have to rest abed all day. Then she recalled that today there was a maid somewhere about Alnwick in just those circumstances. She was so livid, words escaped her.

"Soon," he said softly, "after we are wed, neither one of us will suffer from restless nights again."

"You are a hypocrite," Mary cried, unable to restrain herself and throwing all caution aside.

His expression lost some of its softness. "Indeed?"

"Indeed!" She saw that he was growing angry but did not care. "I came downstairs last night just before matins." She stopped. His anger was gone—he was smiling, pleased.

"So you came looking for me," he said, taking her hands in his.

Mary tried to pull them free and failed. "Not for the reason you are thinking!"

He was amused and skeptical. "Come, *chère*, do not tell me that you sought me out at the midnight hour in order to converse?"

It sounded ludicrous. Mary flushed again. "I did!"

Suddenly his smile vanished. "Ahh, now I begin to understand where you have been leading."

Again Mary tried to pull her palms free of his, but it was hopeless.

"You are indeed angry this morn, Mary," he said, whisper-soft. "You came looking for me, but I was nowhere to be seen."

Mary no longer struggled. Her small bosom heaved. "And we both know why, so do not deny it!"

He stared. "I do not deny it. But what would you have me do? My body was hot and hard—for you."

"Please!" Again she tried to struggle free; again it was futile. His words drummed up vivid images of him, fully aroused, that she did not wish to entertain. "I am sure you did not spare me a single thought while you spent yourself on your winsome friend!"

"She was barely winsome, and if you must know, I thought of nothing but you—even while I spent myself on her."

Mary was frozen. He was a sorcerer. Because as angry, hurt, and jealous as she was, she was also warm, too warm, her pulse pounding insistently, disturbingly. How could he do this to her under these circumstances? "I was but upstairs," she finally said, and she heard how wounded she sounded.

His eyes widened. "Mademoiselle, you are to be my wife. 'Tis out of the question that I would use you as I would my leman."

Mary almost gaped.

His voice was low, firm, even urgent. "Do you not think I considered it? Do you really think some overripe villein can compare to one such as you? Do you know how many times I almost went up those stairs in spite of myself? But my will is stronger than that." Suddenly he released her hands to cup her face. Mary was incapable of movement. "I was discreet. Every single man in this hall was asleep. I did not intend you to know. Still, I am glad you are jealous."

She opened her mouth, to deny it, but not a single sound came out.

His expression was harsh. "You ask the impossible, mademoiselle, but I will do as you ask."

She blinked. She was feeling very warm and very dazed. "Wh-What is that?" Her whisper was a croak.

"I will deny myself until our wedding night, as it upsets you so."

Mary reeled. He caught her, and she was in his arms. "Did you understand what I just said?" he suddenly demanded. Mary was hardly shocked to realize that he was impassioned, too. She put her hands on his chest, but whether to push him away or cling, she did not know. As it turned out, she gripped him. "Y-Yes, I-I understand."

His expression was almost savage. "Are you pleased?"

Mary stared, still stunned by the swift pace and unbelievable conclusion of their dialogue. She began to nod.

"Good! I would have you pleased—always, by me." Abruptly he lowered his head, his mouth taking hers.

Mary's mind was chanting an incredible refrain. This man had just promised to practice celibacy until their wedding. In fact, he had promised her fidelity. Celibacy . . . fidelity . . . The refrain lingered as her mouth opened, as he sucked her lips and then plumbed her warm depths, as their tongues finally touched. Stephen drew back, panting. "But I shall undoubtedly lose my head every time you come near," he warned. Then he smiled. It lit up his dark eyes.

In another era, Mary thought with sudden desperation, such a marriage would have been successful. Or even in this era, given different circumstances. But it could not be. For there would be no marriage—the betrothal was a ruse. But . . . Stephen seemed so certain, and he was not the kind of man to be easily duped. "What were the terms of this marriage?" she heard herself ask in a low, strained voice.

Stephen started. His smile was gone. " 'Tis not enough for you to know that your father and I found cause to unite our families?"

"No. I must know the terms, I must."

Stephen stared at her. Carefully he said, "Do you not remember that we discussed this yesterday?"

Mary had to fight for words, she had to fight to steady her voice. "Please, my lord, I would know what my father gains in giving my hand to you—other than—" she swallowed "—our child."

Stephen was silent. Their gazes were locked, his dark and somber, hers glazed with unshed tears. Finally, gravely, he said, "Mademoiselle, you ask about matters politic."

"This is very important to me."

"I know, Mary. I know far more than you think. Trust me. I shall soon be your husband; I will take care of you from this day forth, I and no one else. Malcolm has agreed to the alliance; leave it at that."

"I cannot," she whispered. "I must know exactly what was said."

Stephen regarded her. Very quietly he asked, "Will you by my loyal wife, Mary?"

Mary froze. She knew she must tell him one word, yes. Her heart beat with frightening intensity. She had never been one to lie, and found she could not do so now. Not about this, not to him.

She said nothing.

His face was dark, his words bitter. "I have just promised you fidelity. I have promised to take care of you. But you do not reconcile yourself to your duty. You do not reconcile yourself to me."

She was torn. There was something in Stephen's manner, in his eyes, that made her want to promise him all that he demanded, but surely that was insane. Surely he was enslaving her mind, as she had sworn he must not do. Because in the end there would not be a marriage—she was certain of it.

He gripped her chin, lifting it. "You will wed me, warm my bed, bear my sons, keep my household, and tend my people when they are sick? You will give me succor and comfort? *You will give me loyalty?*"

Mary whimpered. Faced with him now, like this, Mary was suddenly not sure of her own answer. But how could that be? Where her loyalty lay was clear—it had not changed.

His eyes flashed. *"I must know!"*

She shook her head, her eyes beginning to sting.

"Swear to me upon what you hold dear, swear to me upon the life of your father, that you shall do your duty towards me as I have stated," Stephen commanded. "Swear it now!"

Mary inhaled. "I—I cannot."

He released her. She realized he trembled. "You cannot give me your word, or will not?"

"No," Mary said. "I c-cannot."

"And you dare to ask me of politic secrets," he said coldly. "You have one last chance, demoiselle." A vein throbbed in his temple. *"Will you be loyal to me, first and last, above all others?"*

She dared not answer. But she said, "No."

His eyes widened.

"I am loyal to Scotland," Mary whispered, and she became aware that she was crying. The most recent image of her father's hate-filled face came to her mind. How proud of her he would be. While she, she was repulsed.

"Even after we are wed?"

Mary prayed that they would not be wed. "Yes, even after we are wed."

The Earl and Countess of Northumberland arrived later that day.

Mary was in the women's solar when she became aware of their arrival. The women there rushed out to greet Alnwick's mistress, Isobel leading the charge, crying out with delight. Mary made no move to follow, her absence unremarked. She was alone in the solar, a feeling of dismay rising in her breast. She had no wish to meet Stephen's parents, not now, not ever. Especially she had no wish to meet the earl, a very personal enemy of her father's.

But she had no choice in the matter. Some time later, when the pandemonium in the hall had ceased, a woman appeared in the doorway. Mary had not a single doubt that she was the countess. Automatically she rose to her feet.

Stephen's mother was a tall woman of indeterminate age, still possessed of a fine figure and still quite handsome. Her yellow velvet surcote was magnificent, elaborately embroidered along the hem and sleeves with multicolored threads, a gold girdle encasing her narrow waist, heavily encrusted with jewels. Her veil was the finest of silks, in shades of crimson and gold. A strand of red rubies on a gold circlet kept it in place, the stones winking on her forehead. She was one of the most imposing women Mary had ever remarked, but not because of her dress. There was strength to be found in her countenance, and her eyes were filled with razor-sharp intelligence. She regarded Mary intently.

Mary wondered if she hated her and was dismayed because of the alliance. "Madame," Mary murmured.

The countess lifted a brow. Mary was conscious of being studied from the top of her golden head to the tips of the blue slippers she wore. Behind Lady Ceidre, half a dozen ladies, the countess's entourage, also regarded her with open curiosity and tittering excitement. "Come forward, Princess," the countess said. It was a command, said softly but imperiously.

Mary did as she was asked.

"I wish to welcome you into our family," the countess said, her tone softening as she took both of Mary's hands.

Mary realized she approved. "Thank you." She spoke stiffly.

"I wish to be alone with my son's bride," the countess said. Her ladies, smiling and whispering, disappeared.

"Come, let us sit and get acquainted," Lady Ceidre said. She took Mary's arm and led her to a pair of chairs. "You need not be afraid of me."

"I am not," Mary replied as they took their seats. In truth, she was uneasy. But not because the countess was formidable, but because she had the insane wish that they could be as a real mother-in-law and bride.

"I hope Stephen has treated you well."

Mary lowered her eyes, aware of the countess's unwavering regard.

"Both he and his brothers are so like their father. I am sorry if his lust overruled him when you first met." Mary's color heightened. "Still, they all know well enough how to treat a lady. I hope he has played the gentleman since then."

Mary thought of his astonishing promise to remain celibate. Something twisted inside her. "I . . . Yes, he has."

The countess smiled, pleased. "Of course," she continued, "he was raised at Court, a terribly decadent Court, where ambition, intrigue, and desire ruled the day—as it still does. He had to become hard very young." Her tone changed; the sadness was unmistakable. "But do not be fooled. There is a softness within, and I am sure a woman like you can bring it forth."

Mary recalled his soft tone and seductive words of earlier that day. She shifted uncomfortably. "Why do you tell me this?"

"So you might understand my son, the man who is to be your husband. So you can forgive him when he forgets himself."

Mary did not respond. It would be too easy to become intimate with this woman, it would be too easy to like her. She did not want to like her. Her situation was difficult enough.

"When will you know if you are with child?"

Mary's eyes widened. Her face burned. "My monthly time is not always exact."

"That is too bad. If you carry my son's child, you must tell me at once."

Mary pursed her lips.

The countess studied her. "I think we should speak freely with one another, don't you?" She smiled. "I am most pleased with this alliance, Princess. As is my husband, as is my son." Lady Ceidre took her hand. "You are not pleased. You are miserable."

Mary took a deep breath, close to tears, undone by her kind tone. "I . . . Is it so obvious?"

"It is very obvious. Is it Stephen? He does not please you?"

Mary closed her eyes. She must not entertain such a question. Very softly she said, "He is my enemy."

The countess looked at her.

"You are all my enemies, madame," Mary said in the same tone of voice.

"An alliance has been made. You would disobey your father, your King?"

Mary could not answer, for she could not admit that treachery was afoot as she still owed her loyalty to Malcolm. But dear God, the countess was as certain of the alliance as her son, and neither of them were dim-witted fools. Quite the opposite; they were both extraordinarily astute. What if they were both right, while she was wrong? What then?

Dear Jesus, if it came to marriage, if it truly did, what would she do?

Impatiently the Earl of Northumberland waited for his firstborn. Stephen had not been at the keep when the earl arrived. The father knew the son's habits. Until the noon meal, he would sit with his steward and attend to administrative matters. After that he would tend what he must personally, whether it be an inspection of a tenant's holdings or the drilling of his household knights. Rolfe was impatient because he saw Stephen so little. In truth, ever since he had sent him to William I's court as a hostage so many years ago, their paths seemed destined to diverge instead of come together. When Stephen had been at Court, Rolfe had been forced to remain in the North, warring and securing his borders. When Stephen had returned home, Rolfe had been free to go to Court himself, to protect his interests from those who would see them destroyed.

He sighed. He had few regrets, but that he lacked time to spend with his oldest son was one of them.

Stephen strode into the hall.

Rolfe leapt to his feet, smiling. "Little did I think we would meet next on the threshold of your marriage to a princess," Rolfe said in greeting.

Stephen's serious expression vanished. "Rufus has agreed?"

"The King has agreed."

Stephen's smile was brilliant. "I owe you much thanks, Father."

Rolfe felt almost as triumphant. "Rufus had no choice in the end. He must regain Normandy, and he knows it. There were probably many petty factors in his decision, including his current displeasure with Roger Beaufort. Who, by the way, is furious."

"I have little doubt." Stephen gestured and his father sat back down, Stephen beside him. "One and all are undoubtedly appalled and shocked at this alliance—including my little bride." He grimaced slightly.

"A reluctant bride?"

"To say so is to put it mildly."

"And how did you gain Malcolm's consent?"

Stephen looked his father directly in the eye. "He could not refuse, not when I handed him his greatest desire. I pledged to see his eldest son upon his throne."

Rolfe looked at Stephen. "And when I am dead, when Rufus asks you to support him in his quest to place Duncan—whom he has chosen—upon the throne, how will you act?"

"I am ever his loyal vassal," Stephen said coolly. "No matter how I despise him."

It was the first time Stephen had ever openly revealed his antagonistic feelings for their King, and Rolfe was surprised. For many years he had suspected that Stephen's feelings ran deep, and had wondered what could have possibly caused such hostility.

"You will play a difficult game," he warned his son.

"I realize that. But I made no offer that I did not brood carefully upon. Duncan is weak, far too weak to remain for long as Scotland's King, and Edward is young. There will come a ripe time for young Ed. I did as I had to do."

"I do not chastise you," Rolfe said, and then he smiled. "You did well, Stephen."

Stephen smiled, apparently pleased with the praise. "Thank you, Father."

Rolfe continued, his tone brisk. "There are several minor conditions. Rufus has declared that the wedding must take place at Court."

Stephen stilled. "What game is this?"

"He obviously wishes to humiliate Malcolm by having the nuptials take place there. However, the betrothal can take place here upon the morrow."

Stephen nodded; briefly his eyes flashed with satisfaction. Then he said, "Rufus will undoubtedly try to provoke Malcolm by reminding him that he has sworn fealty to him on bended knee. And Malcolm's temper is hot."

"Do not fret. We shall make certain that Malcolm and William Rufus do not come to blows—nothing is to interfere with this union. Rufus has also stated that Mary is to be his guest at Court until the wedding."

"Why?" Stephen asked harshly. "What does he think to

gain, to prove? Does he think to hold her captive until we are wed?" Stephen was on his feet, and his eyes were wild.

"Do not agitate yourself," Rolfe said as Stephen began to pace.

"Or does he intend treachery?" Stephen demanded. "What game does he play now with me and mine?"

Rolfe hesitated. The question burned. A question he had wanted to ask for the past ten years, one he had not dared ask, afraid as he was of the answer.

But Stephen was about to wed. Private times between them were so rare. He might never have this chance again. "Stephen. For many years I have wondered why you dislike Rufus so."

Stephen just looked at him, his thoughts unreadable. The brief moment of wildness had been locked away.

"Is there something I should know about, something that occurred, perhaps, when you were a fosterling in his father's household?"

"No, Father, there is nothing you should know about."

Stephen's tone was quiet but firm, yet Rolfe felt as if he had been soundly slapped. Immediately he withdrew, for Stephen was a man, and he had every right to his privacy. Still, Rolfe could not help but wonder if, had the past been different, had there been more time, Stephen would have confided in him.

"I will never let her sojourn there alone," Stephen said firmly. "I will remain at Court with her."

Rolfe also knew that Stephen despised the Court. Not that he blamed him; a man could only be on his guard for so long without respite. "I am glad you wish to accompany her. You and Mary can leave for Court immediately after the betrothal tomorrow. I will join you once I have met with Malcolm to finalize the details of this marriage."

"Have no fear, Father. Until we are wed, I intend to remain alert. Too many will try to wreck this alliance otherwise."

Rolfe laid his hand upon Stephen's arm. His voice low, he said, "It might be politic to get her with child as swiftly as possible, just in case problems do arise."

Stephen stared. Then, very firmly, he said, "I shall deal

with any problems as they come. But Mary will not share my bed until after we have wed."

Rolfe was startled. Then, wisely, he said no more. There was far more here than met the eye. He had never dreamed to see his son enamored of his bride. He turned away, hiding his pleasure.

Chapter 11

" *'T*is your brother, Sire, Prince Henry. He requests an audience with you," the sergeant said.

Rufus scowled. He was alone with his squire in his private chamber, in the midst of completing a change of habit for a royal hunt that would take place that afternoon. "Balk him. I am in no mood for my brother now."

The door to the royal chamber burst open. Prince Henry stood on the threshold, his face strained with anger, his eyes blazing. Behind him two other sergeants were ashen at having their Majesty so interrupted.

Rufus glared at his brother. "What display is this? I am not available, dear little brother."

"Then make yourself available, Sire," Henry almost snarled, striding into the room. He was tall and muscular as their father had been, topping his older brother by more than a hand. Unlike his brother, now clad in a vivid red surcote trimmed in ermine and matching ankle boots, he wore muted shades of gray and blue, his tunic and mantle spotted with mud from a long, hard ride. "I have heard a rumor that could not possibly be true."

Rufus sighed, and snapped his fingers. Instantly the three sergeants were gone, the door closed behind them. He faced his page. "Bring me the crimson mantle, the one lined in sable, and my crimson and gold hat."

The young, pretty page scurried across the room to obey.

"Tell me it is not true," Henry said, his handsome face contorted. "Tell me you have not allowed a betrothal between Stephen de Warenne and Malcolm Canmore's daughter!"

Rufus smiled. "Jealous?"

Henry inhaled, his fists clenched at his sides. "Are you daft? Have you completely lost your wits? To give Northumberland such power?"

"Power that belongs irrevocably to me," Rufus countered, no longer smiling. He locked stares with his brother. "De Warenne is beholden to me more than ever before."

"Rolfe, yes. But the son? We all know how fond he is of you, brother." And now Henry was mocking, knowing as he did his brother's darkest dreams.

Rufus's ruddy face gorged with blood. "Do not think that I would be soft upon Stephen de Warenne. Should he prove a traitor, he will suffer the same as anyone. And he has everything to lose, unlike you, who has nothing."

Henry made an effort to control his rage, having an infamous temper exactly like that of their sire, William the Conqueror. "You jump ahead of my meaning," he finally managed. "Who spoke of treason?" And he shrugged.

Rufus smiled, pleased at winning that battle.

"Sire," Henry continued coldly, "You must think on what you do. 'Tis exceeding folly to give Northumberland such power. Especially as the land concerned is all in the North. Soon Stephen will rule in his father's stead. What if he allies himself with Scotland against you?"

Rufus's face was bloodred again. "Oh? So now you think to protect my interests?" But he began to wonder if he had made a mistake.

"I do."

"Hah!" Rufus was barely amused, for while they both knew that Henry was indeed a formidable knight and commander, his loyalty was questionable. On more than one occasion he had allied himself with their oldest brother,

Robert, the Duke of Normandy, against William Rufus. By playing brother against brother, he had succeeded in gaining a territorial base for himself in the fortress town of Domfront, and was a count in the Cotentin. His growing might was both a help and a hindrance to Rufus, for Henry could be seduced into loyalty if the price paid was high enough, but likewise, he could be pried away in exactly the same manner. Rufus was no fool. He understood his brother's ambitions exactly, and coin was not the issue.

Rufus accepted his mantle from his page, allowing the lad to help him slip it on. "Fetch me the ruby brooch," he ordered. He turned to his brother. "And I value your loyalty," Rufus finally said.

Henry was silent.

Rufus smiled. "In truth, I thought a bit about marrying her myself; after all, eventually I must wed. But—" he sighed dramatically "—apparently Stephen could not restrain himself. She might be with his child."

Henry was grim.

"Of course, this fact prevents me from even considering wedding with her, for my heir must be mine." He studied his brother. "Come now, be honest, Henry. You are distraught. But is it the thought of my unborn heir that upsets you now or your friend's betrothal? Did you not come here to beg me to give *you* the princess?"

Henry said nothing.

"It did cross my mind," Rufus said. "After all, you are my brother. A prince and a princess make a perfect match, do they not? Still, I decided I prefer Northumberland. Him I know."

Henry said, "But I am your brother. You can trust me."

Rufus raised a brow, and was unable to resist another jab. "Perhaps I will give you FitzAlbert's daughter."

Henry's face grew even darker. "She is a baron's daughter, with naught but a lowly manor or two."

Rufus laughed softly. "As you have naught but a petty estate or two, then aren't you both equally, perfectly matched as well?"

Henry could not contain himself any longer. "You are going to regret this, brother."

Despite himself, Rufus felt a twinge of fear. For he did not trust Henry for an instant. He was too much like their father. The time had come to placate him. "There is another sister, one unsoiled, in the convent, actually, and as yet too young to wed."

Henry's interest was immediate. "Malcolm will never marry both of his daughters to Normans."

"But Malcolm will not live forever. And when he is gone, his realm shall be ripe for the plucking, as shall be his daughter, Maude."

Henry stared, unsmiling. And Rufus felt a moment of intense regret for offering something so great to his brother—who was sometimes his greatest ally and always his deadliest enemy.

The Earl of Kent kept a manor on the south side of London on the banks of the Thames. It spoke of the wealth of Kent. It was freshly whitewashed, the great front door mahogany and engraved with the family's crest. It boasted not one but two Great Halls and many chambers, a luxurious chapel, and separate buildings for the kitchens, buttery, and alehouse. Within, downstairs, the table and benches were of the finest wood, intricately carved, the thronelike chair reserved solely for the earl upholstered in crimson velvet. Upstairs, in the private rooms, exotically designed carpets from Persia covered the floors, and the walls were hung with bright, vivid tapestries.

Roger Beaufort sat negligently in another thronelike chair in his private bedchamber, sipping a fine wine from Normandy. Adele Beaufort paced in front of him, back and forth across one singularly bold red carpet, the fire in the hearth casting her form into long, misshapen shadows. There was nothing restless about her movements; rather, they were volatile and filled with fury.

She stopped, hands on her hips, her beautiful breasts heaving. "Have you nothing to say? Nothing at all?"

"Do not screech," he said. Despite the fact that he was convinced her misfortune was due to the King's current annoyance with him—and her misfortune was his—he was enjoying her rage. Rarely did one best Adele.

"God, how I hate you! I am cast aside like some worthless doxy, and you do nothing, nothing!"

He decided to dig the barb in deeper. "There have been a half dozen offers for you since the betrothal was broken a sennight ago. Henry of Ferrars was most persistent. You will not die a spinster, darling."

"You jest! He is a nobody, a nobody!"

"I do not jest."

"Whom," she spat, "whom could he be intending to wed? Whom could he want more than me? *Who is she!*" she screamed.

Roger's smile was lazy as he eyed his stepsister with interest. "You should not be in here, Adele, and now you shout to bring the household down."

She stared, panting from her rage, flinging back her long black hair, which was unbound. "You know. You know who it is! You have found out!"

He smiled again, taking another slow sip of wine.

"You bastard!" she cried, and she smacked the wine out of his hand.

It spilled on his crimson hose and the embroidered hem of his velvet tunic. He leapt to his feet, grabbing her wrist and yanking her painfully against him. He slapped her hard across the face.

Adele screamed in fury, struggling to break free. He hit her once more, just to teach her her place. Then he released her. Enraged, she backed away, her bosom heaving heavily. He noticed that her nipples were taut. But then, he was taut, too.

"Who is it!" she demanded, her cheek a fierce pink from the blows.

" 'Tis Malcolm Canmore's daughter," he said, with real satisfaction.

She gasped, stunned. "He weds a King's daughter?"

"He weds a princess," he smirked.

Adele made a strangled sound and turned away, shaking, to face the fire. He came up behind her, touching her shoulders, so close that his full groin brushed her buttocks. "Even you cannot rival a princess, dear heart, and they say she is a beauty."

She wrenched away from him. She said nothing—there was nothing to say.

Mary rode beside Stephen on a dainty white palfrey, he on his massive brown destrier. Two dozen knights trailed them, and just behind them, one retainer held the Northumberland flag. The crimson rose on the black, white, and gold field waved above them, proclaiming their arrival into Londontown.

Tolling bells from the royal chapel announced their arrival as they rode sedately towards the drawbridge being lowered to accommodate them. At another time, perhaps, Mary might have been interested by the sight of this palace. Begun by the Conqueror—constructed upon an old Roman site, ancient Roman walls actually a part of the fortifications—it was comprised of the whitewashed tower, four stories high, its battlements crenellated, and a large bailey with curtained walls, and the surrounding wharves. Watchmen paced the towers, and archers guarded the walls. The wharf was quiet now, with many barges and smaller vessels placidly at anchor, including some obviously of exotic origin.

Mary saw nothing but the walls and the Tower. Her stomach was in knots. As it had been ever since she had knelt in the chapel at Alnwick and been formally betrothed yesterday.

The betrothal was official. The betrothal had been real. It was no trick. And now she was within moments of entering the Tower. Seeing the immense fortress now, one still not complete, Mary was stricken with the realization that Malcolm could not possibly free her once she was within those unbreachable walls.

Mary began to shake.

The betrothal was official, there had been no rescue from Alnwick or since leaving it, and there would be no rescue now or in the future. To think so, to hope so, was sheer insanity. Dear Lord, there was no trick.

There was no trick. Her father had handed her over to Stephen de Warenne without even a fare-thee-well. She was nothing but a political sacrifice.

The pain began to rise up in her, and Mary had to shut off her thoughts. If she did not, she might very well enter the King's household in a tearful fit.

They trotted over the drawbridge, beneath the black fangs of the portcullis, and into the bailey. Once inside, they were instantly surrounded by armed knights wearing the King's colors in a fashion that was far from reassuring. Mary could not move. Stephen slid from his destrier. His strong hands closed around her waist, and his eyes met hers. "Do not fear," he breathed. " 'Tis but a show."

He pulled her down from the palfrey and into his arms. Mary was trembling and panting. The moment she realized that she was in his embrace—and he was Stephen de Warenne, the man she would truly wed, the man her father had coldly given her to—she twisted free abruptly. The many royal knights circled them, cutting them off from Stephen's own men. "Why have the King's men surrounded us?" she cried.

In a near panic it blazed through her mind that she would be taken from Stephen, becoming not his wife but the King's prisoner. As much as she hated being Northumberland's bride, it was nothing compared to the thought of being torn from him and thrown in the Tower's dungeons.

Stephen put his arm around her comfortingly, but his face was drawn tightly, his gaze cold and dangerous, belying his gesture and his tone. " 'Tis a show, Mary, a show for me and for my enemies. You are to be my wife. Rufus knows better than to go back on his word. He would never infuriate my family so—he needs us far too much."

Mary was not calmed. How could she be? She was surrounded by the enemy, *he* was the enemy, and no matter what Stephen said, she was obviously to be detained. Besides, she did not believe that he had confidence in his own avowals, for he was rigid with tension and anger, too. Mary was overwhelmed. Emotions she was determined to crush threatened to overpower her. She was truly betrothed to Stephen de Warenne; in a matter of weeks, she would be his wife, and in another minute she would enter the Tower as the King's "guest," and dear, sweet, merciful Jesus, her father had not even waited to see if she was with child before handing her over to his greatest enemy!

Mary had to close her eyes and take a breath, feeling faint. She realized that she clutched Stephen's hand.

It occurred to her that despite the betrayal, he was her anchor in this storm-tossed sea. Furious with herself, with him, with everyone and everything, she wrenched her hand free.

A man detached himself from the dozen knights ringing them, a winsome smile on his bold features. "I have come to greet you, Stephen, in the name of my brother, the King."

Stephen placed his arm around Mary's stiff shoulders, turning towards Prince Henry. "I am honored, Henry."

Henry grinned at him, then focused on Mary. She stared at him as if he had two heads.

She had seen the prince at Abernathy as well, and as he was of the royal household—when it suited him—she knew of him. His reputation as a prolific ladies' man was renowned. 'Twas said he had sired more than a half dozen bastards already, but the look he gave her now was not quite as lustful as it was intense. Her wits were too scrambled for her to fully decipher it. Regardless, he unnerved her, and she flushed.

"Welcome to the Tower, Princess," he said amiably.

Mary knew her manners, and as much as she did not like it, she curtsied. Stephen was forced to drop his arm from her shoulders.

Henry put his hands on hers, raising her to her feet. He was slow to remove them. "A real beauty, more beautiful even than Adele Beaufort." He was amused, imagining she knew not what.

Mary had not forgotten that hated name. She did not actually believe the prince, and found herself wondering if the Essex heiress might even now be within the Court.

Stephen said nothing, but he took Mary's arm, entwining it with his, the gesture possessive, his hard gaze on the prince.

Henry raised a brow, then laughed. "Do not fear me. Are we not longtime allies? I will not trespass, dear Stephen."

Stephen's smile was winter-bare. "Then you have changed since we last met, *mon ami*, for you have enjoyed trespassing upon other men's properties for as long as I can remember."

Henry shrugged. "But not without invitation," he said. "Never without an invitation."

"There will be no invitation here," Stephen rejoined without rancor. He spoke as if stating a fact.

"Do you grow soft?" Henry appeared amused once again, and incredulous. When Stephen only smiled, he shrugged. "Come," he said, with an expansive sweep of one arm, "it is chill and your bride shivers. From the cold, of course."

"Of course," Stephen said, molding her arm to his body.

Mary could barely breathe. She sensed a firm friendship between the two men, but she also sensed a strange rivalry. Surely they were not arguing over her! She almost whimpered as her temples began to pound with splitting intensity. She had the unparalleled urge to climb into bed and pull the covers up over her head.

They climbed up the wooden front steps of the keep and entered the second-story hall. Officially it belonged to the Constable of the Tower and was filled to overflowing with ladies in their finest gowns and jewels, with noblemen in brightly colored tunics and hose, and others looking as if they had ridden for many days, so mud-spattered and begrimed were they. Because there were so many within the four walls, it was hot and suffocating. There was no hint of the evening's air or fall's advent there. And the noise! Mary would have had to shout to make herself heard to Stephen if she had any desire at all to speak with him, which she did not. He, meanwhile, had to shove his way rudely through the crowd, guiding her across the hall and to the next set of stairs. To her surprise, Henry left them there, giving her another sardonic look along with a courtly bow.

On the landing it was quieter. Mary's heart began to slow its pounding, so relieved was she for this moment of respite. She massaged her throbbing temples. "Where are we going?" she asked.

"To greet the King, of course."

Her heart slammed again. Sick dread welled up in her.

On the landing above they encountered a group of descending noblewomen, a flurry of rich silks and bright brocades, heady with perfumes and painted with powders. Stephen politely stepped aside, still gripping Mary's elbow. The ladies passed them with many covetous looks at her captor and wide-eyed glances at her. One woman paused. She faced them, making Mary's stomach coil up into even tighter knots of apprehension. The woman ignored her, having sultry eyes only for Stephen. "My lord," she said, her voice husky and low, and she sank into a deep curtsy.

"There is no need for that, my lady," Stephen said.

She straightened, barely condescending to notice Mary. She was strikingly beautiful, tall and voluptuous, her hair blacker than midnight, her eyes as dark and beguiling. Mary had not a doubt that this was one of his mistresses, so seductive was she.

"I want to wish you felicitations, my lord," the temptress said softly.

"That is very generous of you."

Her lashes swept down, long and black, then she gave him a look, one that scandalized Mary. "I hope we can still be friends." Her tone was even more promising, and Mary was certain he was intimate with this woman.

Stephen's mouth curled in what appeared to be a smile: "As you wish, my lady," he said, bowing abruptly. Then he pulled Mary with him, leaving the woman standing there on the landing.

Mary hated the other woman. The hatred filled her with such force that it left her heart thundering and her lungs breathless. She had understood their wordplay too well! His mistress intended to continue their relations in spite of his marriage to Mary.

"You are shaking anew," he commented, eyeing her.

"You promised me . . ." She could not get the word out. And even as she spoke, she knew with her brain that she should not care—but she did. God help her, she did.

His dark, intense gaze locked with hers. "Fidelity? So I have, Mary, and you can rest assured."

Some of her anger—and her incredible jealousy—dimmed. He might be a treacherous Norman, but Mary thought him a man of his word. Whatever had been between him and the other woman was now over.

"You must trust me, Mary," Stephen murmured.

His kind words, intended to soothe, brought forth the overpowering urge to weep. She was seriously overwrought.

They had entered another hall, this one high-ceilinged and vast, far grander than the one below, obviously a part of the royal suite. Here only a dozen men or so, and as many women, waited and were engaged in conversation that was much less animated than that downstairs. Mary's heart pumped fiercely now. She tried to convince herself that she had no real cause for fear.

"The King's chambers are over there." Stephen nodded across the room where two sergeants stood guarding massive, closed oak doors.

Mary hated herself for her cowardice and followed Stephen, glad now for his grip upon her arm. He spoke briefly to the sergeants, and one disappeared within. A moment later the man returned and stepped aside so they could enter, escorted by two ushers.

The King stood in the center of the chamber while a cleric droned on, reading from scrolls, an account that sounded to Mary like an inventory of an estate. The King was not listening. He was staring in their direction with a look of great expectation.

For a moment Mary saw nobody else in the room, so colorful was William Rufus.

His long undertunic was a startling silver, his surcote the brightest purple Mary had ever seen, both gowns heavily embroidered in silver and gold thread. His gold girdle was several handspans wide and blinding in its brightness, encrusted with rubies and sapphires. His shoes were gilt, and upon the pointy toes were tassels strewn with more gems. He wore several heavy necklaces, many large rings, and of course, the crown of England.

Three courtiers lounged on chairs behind the King, listening to the cleric. All attention focused instantly upon the two of them as they entered the room. The cleric finally realized no one was paying him any mind, and his voice trailed off. Stephen led Mary across a silent chamber.

William Rufus smiled. To Mary's surprise, he did not look at her, staring instead at Stephen. Mary did not understand. She glanced up at Stephen and saw that his expression was immobile and unreadable, as if carved in stone. When she turned again toward the King, he was finally remarking her, coldly and intensely, and somehow, he seemed displeased.

She knew she should not stare back, but she could not help herself, having never seen this man before, a man whom she had been taught to hate ever since she had been born.

She had heard he was a peacock as well as a sodomite, and that he spent lavish amounts of silver upon his wardrobe; still, his appearance surprised her. He exuded enough power that it stopped just short of being comical. He was of average height, florid, and just going to fat. Once he might have been attractive, but not anymore. His eyes were a bit small but unmistakably shrewd, and when he finally smiled, with real warmth, she saw that he was missing one tooth. He smiled only at Stephen.

"Welcome, Stephen, welcome. We did not expect you, only your bride."

"Indeed?" Stephen said, his tone silky-soft. Mary realized in the instant that he spoke that he disliked this man immensely. His eyes were dark, his mouth tight, and there was the faintest hint of mockery in his tone. "You thought I would send my bride to you alone?"

Rufus shrugged. "But we are pleased to see you after such a lapse on your part. It has been too long since last you visited. We have much to discuss, you and I." Rufus held out his hand. "You will dine with us tonight."

Stephen bent on one knee and took the King's hand, kissing the air above it. His movement was graceful, yet somehow lacking, for there was something disdainful in the set of his shoulders and his head. Rufus finally turned to Mary, who came forward until she stood beside Stephen. She curtsied deeply, and remained so until he told her to rise.

"So you are Malcolm's daughter," he mused. "Why has he waited so long to wed you? And how old are you? You appear more of a child than a woman."

Mary bristled. She could not care for his condescension. As she raised her eyes, she was aware that she had the attention of every man in the room. She should not defy this man, England's King, but she was loath to answer him. Finally, reluctantly, she answered one of his questions. "I am sixteen."

Rufus's regard had long since wandered to Stephen, who stood unmoving at Mary's side. "Does she please you, Stephen?"

Mary gasped. What kind of question was this?

The King continued blandly—as if she were not present. "She is nothing like Adele, so small and pale—she could pass for a boy if it were not for her hair."

Mary was enraged. She was also incredulous, that he would insult her so. She turned to Stephen, expecting a defense.

But Stephen shrugged. His mouth was tight. "You know I do not like boys."

Rufus began to smile. "No—your women have always been fleshy and ripe."

His tone as bland as the King's, Stephen agreed with him.

"So she does not please you?" Rufus's eyes gleamed now.

"She is Malcolm's daughter. *That* pleases me, Sire."

Mary was sick. It was the final, fatal blow. She clenched her fists, her own nails cutting her palms, nearly causing them to bleed. She told herself she would not throw up her noon meal, not now, not here, in front of everyone.

In the short silence that followed, Stephen gripped her arm, steadying her, for she was shaking again. Furiously Mary tried to jerk free. His hold was so tight, she was immobilized, and she quickly gave up. To her horror, her lids began to sting.

But Rufus had changed the topic. He began to ask Stephen if all was well in Northumberland. Mary did not listen, too devastated now to comprehend their words. She only wanted to get out of the royal chamber as quickly as possible, away from the horrible King, away from Stephen, away from the realizations that danced in her head.

But suddenly Rufus was addressing her. "How is your father?"

As Mary had been trying with all of her will not to think of Malcolm, she could not respond, not even when Stephen poked her. She blinked at the King, determined not to cry. Not here, not now, please, dear God.

"Your father, Princess," Rufus repeated as if to an idiot. "How is your father? You do speak French?"

Mary tried to speak. But if she opened her mouth, she would sob or scream.

Rufus turned to Stephen. "Is she a dimwit? Is her mind sound? I would not marry you to one who would breed you fools."

"She is of sound mind, Sire, she is just overtired and, I think, distraught."

Mary dared not look anywhere but at the floor. A few tears had managed to spill down her cheeks.

"I must trust your judgment, then, for always it is sound. Get rid of her. Send her to the chamber she shall share with some of the other ladies who sojourn here. We must talk. We have much to discuss after so many years."

Stephen bowed, still gripping Mary's arm firmly. "Sire."

They moved away. Mary was barely aware of being marched across the hall and from the room. She moved like the dimwit she had been accused of being. Once outside the chamber doors, Mary gulped the air.

Stephen spoke quietly with a man-at-arms. Mary's vision cleared. Her breasts began to rise and fall more rapidly than usual. She did not protest when Stephen again took her hand, and she ignored him when he gave her a long, searching look as they followed the soldier upstairs. "Mademoiselle?"

Her jaw clenched, she did not speak. She no longer breathed.

Stephen also fell silent. The guard cheerfully told them that this was her chamber, flinging open a door. Mary shrugged off Stephen, who let her go, and marched inside. He followed her, as she had known he would do, and then the guard was gone.

They were finally alone. "Mary," Stephen began.

Mary screamed. As she screamed, and screamed and screamed, a scream of rage and agony, she raised her arm and open-handedly lashed him with all her might across his face. The sound of flesh cracking against flesh actually echoed. "Get away!" Mary cried. "Get away from me this instant!"

Chapter 12

*F*or a moment, Stephen was frozen.

So was Mary.

And the sound of her hand cracking across his flesh seemed to linger in the stone chamber.

His disbelief coalesced into anger. "Mary," Stephen said grimly. He took a step towards her.

"No!" she cried, raising her hands as if to ward him off. And the denial released a harsh sob.

He halted. He had sensed her nervousness as they entered the King's bailey, had watched it grow ever since. He sorely regretted having to act as he had in front of the King, but he'd had no choice, knowing Rufus as he did. He did not blame her for slapping him after all. "Mary, I must explain to you my behavior in the King's chamber."

"No!" She backed away from him until her legs hit one of the room's three beds. Instantly she jumped aside and backed into the wall—which was as far from him as she could possibly go.

"Mary," Stephen said, forcing himself to remain calm, speaking as he might to an invalid, or someone deranged, "I could not let the King see how pleased I am with our forthcoming union. You must trust me. In time I will explain more fully, when you are reconciled to our union, when you are loyal."

"I will never be reconciled—I will never be loyal!"

Stephen flinched.

"How I hate you!" Mary cried, choking on another huge sob. "Dear Lord God, we are truly to be wed!"

Stephen started, wondering if she was going insane. "Of course we are truly to be wed. 'Twas decided days ago."

She moaned.

He felt helpless then, not understanding this at all. "You are distraught. When you are calmer—"

Her wild laughter cut him off, choked with tears. "Of course I am distraught! Can you blame me, Sir Norman? How would you like to be imprisoned here?!"

He stood unmoving, expressionless, except for the tightness of his jaw. A long pause ensued, in which he did not speak, his eyes pitch black, while she wept, almost silently. "You are not a prisoner, demoiselle," he finally said, his tone harsh. "You are my bride, soon to be my wife."

No sooner had he spoken than she covered her face with her hands, her shoulders shaking. This time her sobs were audible.

Obviously the thought of marriage moved her to this hysteria. He did not understand why she should have this crisis now, instead of earlier, and could only guess that his having humiliated her in front of the King had set it off. Stephen was unmoving, torn with guilt. Guilt not just for the crisis he had provoked, but because he was forcing her against her will to this marriage—a fact he could no longer ignore. Was he any different from William Rufus?

He was as horrified as he had ever been in his life. But Rufus had not been offering him respectability, power, or marriage, he reminded himself. Rufus had wanted to use him, abuse him. Still, the parallels truly frightened him.

Yet he was helpless, too, a prisoner of his own lust and ambition. He could not free her, he would not.

"You are not a prisoner," he repeated, but whether to convince her or himself, he dared not know. "You shall be my wife! Everything that is mine shall be yours."

She dropped her hands, her face glazed with tears, her eyes wild with rage. "There is nothing you have that I want!"

She had goaded him as only a woman can a man. "Do not make me prove the falsehood you have just uttered!" He found himself leaning over her. "In bed you are hardly unwilling!"

She choked. "Not in bed—no—for you are a devil who has ensorcelled me—but otherwise I am only unwilling—and I will never let you forget it!"

He could not move away from her even though he longed to then, transfixed by her hatred. "Unwilling, disloyal, it hardly matters," he said heavily. There would be no turning back. "We will be wed, as your father and I have planned."

"Do not speak to me of Malcolm!" she screamed.

And Stephen had a glimpse of what moved her to such fury, and he was aghast. "Mary, you are angry with Malcolm?"

"I *hate* you!" she screamed. Suddenly she drove herself off the wall, launching herself at him. Stunned, Stephen caught her as he stumbled backwards. She pummeled him with her fists. Stephen fell onto the bed, trying to embrace her even as she beat him. Enraged that she could not hurt him, she curled her fingers into claws. Stephen winced as one of her nails ripped a deep scratch along his cheek. He had no choice then but to throw her on the bed. Standing, he held the stinging scratch and felt the moisture of his blood.

Mary doubled over into a ball, hugging her abdomen, moaning.

Stephen forgot the small wound. How could he not go to her—despite how she felt about him? He sat beside her, taking her into his arms, stroking her hair as she wept openly against his chest. How could he soothe her? God damn Malcolm Canmore to hell! God damn himself!

She stiffened when she realized that he held her, and wrenched free. She leapt from the bed, maniacal. " 'Tis your fault!"

He was motionless, except for the slight tremor that afflicted him. He opened his mouth to defend himself, recalled abducting her and seducing her, and promptly shut it. Even if he dared defend himself, to do so would only cast more blame upon her father, which he was reluctant to do.

Mary pointed a finger at him, unable to keep it steady. "You did this! You came between us! You turned Malcolm from me! *'Tis all your fault!*"

How she hated him. It flashed through his mind that he had secretly anticipated something far more than a marriage of either resignation or hostility. He had envisioned warmth and sweet succor, gentle laughter and genuine loyalty. Pain pierced his breast. For both his bride and himself.

He slowly rose to his feet. His own fists were tightly clenched. With an effort, he relaxed them. "I am sorry you lay the entire blame for this affair at my feet," he said stiffly. "But perhaps you are right. For I do want to wed you—and I will, no matter how you hate me."

Mary choked on a sound of raw despair.

He was grinding his jaw from the tension. His chest ached. Without looking back, he swung open the door and disappeared into the hall.

As soon as he was gone, Mary collapsed on the bed. She realized she could not cry anymore. The pain throbbed on in her. She wanted to beat the bed, claw the sheets, claw herself. She wanted to rave against the injustice of it all. In that moment, she felt like a madwoman, caught in the horror of a madness that defied reality.

Many minutes dragged by, minutes in which she grew calmer and saner, minutes in which she grew unthinking and numb. Gradually a feeling of unease stole over her. Mary felt eyes upon her. Cold, hateful, intent eyes. She realized that she was being watched.

She jerked, for the woman who stood in the shadows of the open doorway, observing her with real pleasure, gloating over her distress, was the very last person Mary wished to see. It was the too beautiful black-haired woman who had confronted Stephen so intimately just an hour ago; it was his Norman mistress.

They stared at each other.

The other woman's gaze swept over Mary with no small amount of contempt. "Do not tell me you are sharing this room!"

Mary drew herself up straight, chin lifted. She was very aware of her vulnerability, of having been caught by this woman, Stephen's beautiful, voluptuous ex-mistress, off guard and in a moment of extreme weakness. "I am indeed," she said quietly, trying not to show her dismay.

The woman entered the room, sauntering around it—and around Mary. "So—they force you to wed Stephen."

"It appears that you know who I am," Mary said tersely, unsmiling. She stood up. "But you have yet to introduce yourself."

The woman smiled, not prettily. "I am Lady Beaufort," she said. "Adele Beaufort. The woman Stephen was to wed."

Mary could not contain her shock. She had assumed, so wrongly, that this woman was his mistress. She was not his leman, she was one of England's greatest heiresses. Mary's dismay increased. She had assumed Adele to be his consort because her actions—and Stephen's—had indicated that they were intimate with each other. Knowing that, and knowing now that Adele was a noblewoman and a great heiress, somehow deflated Mary. She told herself that it did not matter, for Mary far outranked her, and regardless, they were not rivals. But Mary felt as if they were rivals—as if they were great and bitter rivals.

"He only marries you because of the alliance you bring him," Adele said with narrowed eyes. She had closed the door; now she smoothed a hand over her stunning turquoise gown, over her voluptuous hip. Her stance was provocative, and Mary knew she flaunted her curves deliberately in the face of Mary's own slender, boyish body.

"Just as he intended to marry you for your wealth," she retorted. But her tone was weak. This woman was ripe in the way all men preferred, and Mary could recall too well Stephen's words to the King just a few minutes ago. Perhaps the King had even been referring to Adele Beaufort when he had said Stephen had always liked fleshy women. Of course, she did not care. She hated him for all that he had done.

"For my wealth, yes, and for so much more," Adele said in husky tones.

Mary could imagine them in a torrid embrace, and found herself hating this woman again. How could that be? As Adele had said, she was being forced to wed Stephen, and he had not just insulted her but failed to defend her in public, and worse, far worse, she despised him for destroying her relationship with her father, for destroying her life.

Yet in spite of all happenstance, Mary began recalling intimate moments shared by her and Stephen, moments of sublime, uncontrollable passion. Had he touched Adele as he had her?

Adele stepped forward until they stood facing each other. She dwarfed Mary, although Mary was not cowed by her giant size. "I can help you."

Mary started.

Abruptly Adele turned and went to the door, flung it open, and peered out into the corridor. No one spied upon them. She shut the door and leaned against it. Her eyes were brilliant, like onyx drenched by the sun. "I can help you," she said again, her voice low and terse.

"I do not understand," Mary said slowly, but in truth her mind had raced far ahead, and incredulously, she began to comprehend where Adele Beaufort would lead. But surely— she did not dare follow!

"You do not wish to wed him."

Mary nodded, her gaze locked with the other woman's.

Slowly Adele smiled the smile of a temptress. "Do you wish to escape?"

Mary hesitated. Two competing images flashed before her eyes: her father's face, at once hate-filled, and Stephen's, seductive with promise. She shook herself free of the snare. "Yes."

"Then I will arrange it."

Stephen left Mary in the chamber she was to share and walked downstairs. He refused to make eye contact with anyone, not wanting to be drawn into a conversation. He desperately needed some fresh air. He desperately needed to think.

"Stephen!"

His brother's voice brought him to a halt. Stephen turned and saw Geoffrey crossing the Great Hall, apparently just having left the King's chambers. As he came closer, Stephen saw that his jaw was clenched so tightly, a muscle ticked just above it.

Geoffrey drew abreast of him. "I heard you had arrived with the princess," he said.

Stephen did not want to talk about Mary, not now, not after she had revealed the extent of her feelings for him. "Yes."

"Where do you go?"

"Anywhere but here. Perhaps for a ride. Do you wish to join me?"

Geoffrey's laugh was short and hard and angry. "Like yourself, I have no wish to linger here!" But as Stephen made to go, he gripped his arm, halting him. "You have left someone to guard her?"

There was no question of whom he spoke. Stephen flushed. It was not like him to be so thoughtless. "No."

Geoffrey's voice was an urgent whisper. "Your marriage is the talk of the Tower. Many are displeased. Many are afraid. Especially Beaufort, Montgomery, and Duncan. You can not leave her here alone and unguarded. I have not a doubt that one of the parties will seek to end the alliance—and what easier way than to harm Mary?"

Stephen was furious with himself. "Or kill her," he said grimly. "God's blood, she has upset me so, I was running out without a thought to her welfare—and I know well of what you speak. I did not come with her to court for my amusement, Geoff."

"Come." Geoffrey took his arm. "I saw Brand downstairs when I came in; he can take over guard duty until you send someone else."

They went down the narrow stairs and found Brand waiting in the hall below with several other household knights, whiling away the time as he was wont to do when he was not off in the countryside squelching rebellions and in other ways fighting for his King. His face brightened when he saw them, then sobered when Stephen made his request.

"Have no fear," he assured his oldest brother. "I will stand outside her door until you return. In truth, I hate loitering at court—I much prefer battle."

Stephen and Geoffrey left the keep. "He is still young," Stephen commented. "In a few years he will find war tiresome."

Geoffrey's face darkened. "It seems my battles have just begun."

They paused in the open space in front of the keep, ignoring servants, knights, and courtiers coming and going around them. "What has passed?"

"Rufus demanded my presence here, as you know—then once I arrived, he failed to summon me for three entire days." Geoffrey's blue eyes flashed with hard sapphire brilliance. "He enjoys toying with his subjects, he enjoys abusing his power!"

"Did you meet with him at last?"

"I have just left him." Geoffrey faced Stephen, intense. "He spent half an hour ranting to me about Archbishop Anselm. It appears, now that Rufus has recovered from his brush with death, that they have had an abrupt falling out. I suspected Anselm of being a zealot, and his actions this week have proved my suspicions correct."

"Dare I ask what they fight over?"

Geoffrey barked with mirthless laughter. "They argue over a minor part in the ordination ceremony, a part the King demands to be his right, which, of course, the Church is claiming."

"And after he finished raving about Anselm?"

"As I anticipated, he wanted to know exactly how many knights the see owes the Crown."

"Did he say why?"

"No, but he hinted that he would be demanding his vassals. shortly." Geoffrey grimaced, his gaze piercing. "Rufus has told me that, should Anselm refuse to field the knights, he expects me to do so."

Stephen stared as the immensity of his brother's predicament dawned upon him. Finally he said, "Tell me, Geoff.

Whom would you defy? Your archbishop or your King?"

Geoffrey turned his blazing blue eyes towards the distant horizon, as if seeking the answer from God. "I do not know."

Stephen was silent, commiserating with his brother, whose battles were as great and as endless as his own.

Geoffrey hesitated. "Stephen, he cannot be thinking of going to Normandy now."

Stephen started. A very alien feeling of dread swept through him, chilling him to the bone.

"His relations with his brother Robert are peaceable at this moment. I have a feeling, brother, that despite your marriage to the Scot princess, Rufus intends treachery. I think he still might invade Carlisle." Geoffrey clapped his hand upon his shoulder. "Should he do so, it will not be easy for you and Mary, I know," he said with sympathy.

Stephen could not speak. His brother's words were a vast understatement. Should Rufus summon his vassals to invade Carlisle, Stephen would be summoned, too. Already Mary hated him. Already his marriage had little chance in hell of being more than a truce seething with hostility. If England invaded Carlisle, any chance they might have for happiness would surely disintegrate with the first sword blow.

Mary knew that she must not be a coward. Rufus's open scorn had taken her by surprise. Now that she knew how he felt about her, and having had time to think about it, she guessed it had to do with his dislike for her father and his preference for boys. Now she was prepared, and she would not appear the dimwit this time.

Stephen arrived in order to escort her down to a late supper. They barely exchanged civilities. Just before they arrived on the landing below, some of Mary's courage evaporated. She could hear loud masculine voices raised in drunken conversation and rough laughter, and every tale she had ever heard about the decadence of Rufus's Court came swiftly to mind. Drinking and debauchery ruled the day. Mary was aware of feeling terribly alone.

She did not realize that she had paused. She jumped slightly when Stephen placed his hand upon her waist. Briefly she met his searching gaze, then quickly looked away. She wondered what he would do if he knew of her plan to escape with the help of Adele Beaufort.

Perhaps a hundred lords and ladies were present at the table, dining with their King. Already the table was heavily laden with food and drink, and behind the diners, clowns caroused and a minstrel sang. Stephen guided her past the low end of the table, towards the dais where King Rufus sat.

Rufus had been laughing; now his smile died and he stared. Not at her, but at Stephen. Mary felt compelled to glance up at Stephen's face. It was bland, impossible to read.

"Come, come, sit with me!" Rufus cried with a smile. "We have yet to finish our discussion, dear Stephen."

They took their seats, as guests of honor, upon the dais. The King was on Mary's left. Mary so hated him that she was rigid with tension, although she knew she must disguise her emotions. The last thing she should do was anger the King of England while a virtual prisoner in his keep.

Stephen sat upon her other side. He had said nothing to her since escorting her to the meal, and now he began to respond to the King's amiable questions. He sat uncomfortably close to her—their thighs pressed from knee to hip. Mary wanted nothing to do with him, but the table was overcrowded and there would be no relief from Stephen's proximity until the meal had ended.

Mary became aware of the many avid and curious glances directed her way. She was on display.

Her cheeks grew hot. She was no guest of honor, and everyone knew it, she thought bitterly. She was a prisoner and a heathen Scot. The Norman lords and ladies were staring at her as if she had scales and breathed fire.

Then Mary noticed Adele Beaufort. She sat just below the dais, ignoring Mary, although frequently she cast her sultry gaze upon Stephen. Reminded of their plan, the details of which had yet to be formed, Mary grew uncomfortable, for if all went well, Adele would one day become Stephen's wife.

The Essex heiress sat between two men Mary recalled from earlier that day. They had been present in the King's private chamber when she had suffered through the humiliating interview. One of the men was tall and auburn-haired, and for some reason, he seemed strangely familiar to Mary, but she was certain they had never met.

Still Stephen did not speak to her. The King was expounding upon some difficulties he was having in Kent. Mary did not listen. Mary could hardly care. Stephen, while attentive to Rufus, was offering her his wine.

Mary could not drink. How she wished to be anywhere but there, how she wished the meal were over.

"Does my brother's court not please you, Princess?"

Mary's attention was diverted to Prince Henry, who sat on Rufus's other side. He smiled at her. He reminded her of a lazing wolf, one that would soon spring upon its hapless victim. "Of course it pleases me, Sir Prince," Mary said, somehow smiling. "How could it not? I mean, I am here with my *beloved*, and we are honored by his *great* King. Indeed, I am overwhelmed." Her tone was mostly innocent, but her eyes sparked.

Prince Henry stared at her, no longer smiling. He guessed at her sarcasm, which Mary intended for him to do. Unfortunately, Stephen had not been as engrossed in conversation with the King as she had thought, and he had heard her, too. For him, her facetious meaning was crystal-clear. Now he placed a warning hand upon hers. In turn, Mary gave him cow eyes and a brittle smile.

"And what do you think of London?" Henry asked, slouching now. But his gaze was sharp.

"Such a big city, how could I not be impressed? Indeed, you Normans are most impressive. Your deeds inspire awe. *All* of them." Mary could not stop herself. "After all, it takes great courage for you Normans to force a captive Scotswoman to the altar—does it not?"

Stephen froze—as had Henry. Mary trembled, for she had succeeded in infuriating Stephen, although Henry was amused.

"I imagine courage has little to do with it." Henry's lids lowered. When they lifted, he was smiling again, and Mary found herself tensing. "Do you not want to meet your dear brother, Princess?" he drawled.

"My brother?" In an instant he had shattered her composure.

"Pardon me, what a slip of the tongue! Your half brother, *my* brother's dear friend, Duncan," Henry laughed, gesturing towards the auburn-haired man who sat beside Adele, the man who had somehow seemed so familiar to her.

Mary started. Of course Duncan was here at court, for he had come here as a child hostage almost twenty years ago! He was her father's eldest child, from his first marriage. In fact, he was close to the same age as Rufus and had undoubtedly grown up with him, which would explain how they had come to be such friends. And if they were such friends, it would explain why he had been one of the three courtiers closeted in such intimacy with the King that afternoon. Excitement rushed over Mary. She was no longer alone.

Duncan slowly stood, bowing slightly. "At long last," he said, "we meet. I am overcome with this event, sister."

Now Mary recognized him. His coloring was their father's, as were his eyes. Although his words and tone were somewhat wry, his smile was warm. Mary smiled back. She had a real ally here at court, one real ally among so many enemies, her nearly forgotten half brother.

"Come, sister," he said, holding out his hands and walking to the dais. "A kiss between long-lost siblings."

He watched her.

Mary had been given the seat of honor on the dais directly beside the King, and Stephen de Warenne sat on her other side. Unlike that afternoon, when she had appeared bedraggled from the long ride, today she wore her finery in a blatant display of royalty and riches. The gold surcote with teal embroidery at the hem and sleeves set off her complexion in a dazzling manner, while a heavily bejeweled gold girdle and a circlet winking with sapphires proclaimed her status and wealth. Today there was no mistaking her for anyone other than a princess.

He watched her. She appeared to hate her groom, to hate her sojourn there in the Tower. She could not hide her displeasure, and Stephen de Warenne was hardly pleased. Her wit was obvious, as was her foolhardy courage. Yes, she was Malcolm's daughter, in manner but not in appearance. There she was every bit Queen Margaret's.

Rufus had called her boyish. She was small but hardly boyish; no woman so beautiful could be considered boyish. He doubted that her groom thought of her that way.

He looked at Stephen de Warenne. All evening de Warenne had listened to the King, speaking when it was necessary. He had not smiled even once. But Rufus did not care. He was animated as never before; his spirits had never been higher. And he was hardly drunk.

Stephen de Warenne met his gaze. Duncan looked away, feeling a frisson of fear. He had always disliked de Warenne. They had known each other for many years; although a decade separated them in age, they knew each other too well. Duncan had always been jealous of de Warenne's manhood. Now, watching him in the seat that Duncan usually took upon the dais, he was more than jealous. He felt threatened. He told himself that Stephen de Warenne would not remain for long at Court, but he was not soothed.

Far from it. Three weeks remained until the nuptials, and three weeks was a dangerously long time.

Duncan was also peeved on another score. De Warenne had never tried to hide the contempt he felt for Duncan. To this day, Duncan did not know if that contempt was based upon the fact that he shared Rufus's sexual preferences, or his political conniving. He had always suspected that de Warenne knew the truth about him—that he always did what he had to do in order to further his far-flung ambitions.

Now the fear de Warenne raised in him increased his ire. How Duncan despised him. But he did not hate him as much as he hated de Warenne's bride, for Mary was his own flesh and blood.

Duncan could not help but turn his gaze onto Mary again. She had grown up in the bosom of their family, as he should have. He could not look at her without thinking of their father, whom he despised more than he despised anyone.

The illustrious Malcolm Canmore. The heroic Scot King. The father who had given over his eldest son as a hostage to William the Conqueror for his own good behavior—then proceeded to violate his oath again and again, careless of how he endangered his son. The fact that Duncan survived was due solely to his own shrewdness, even as a boy.

Malcolm's days of glory were numbered. He was old and one day soon, Duncan hoped, he would underestimate one of his enemies and succumb to a fatal blow. Then the throne of Scotland would be ripe for the plucking, and Duncan intended to be the one who plucked it.

Duncan would not let anyone stand in his way, certainly not his sister and her husband. While Northumberland had always remained loyal to the Crown, while it had always been instrumental in crushing rebellions, Northumberland had never before been allied to its enemy, Scotland. Duncan was shrewd enough to glimpse possibilities that boded ill for his ambitions. Northumberland might remain firm in its support for William Rufus—and thus for him—but what if it did not? The frightening ambition of the de Warennes was well known. What if they chose to support Malcolm's choice of successor, his eldest, Edward, or attempted to thrust one of their own upon the throne? Mary's unborn son had as much a claim to Scotland as anyone.

There was no question that this marriage was going to take place in three weeks time. Unless, of course, there was an accident . . .

Chapter 13

Stephen wandered among the stalls and vendors at Cheapside. Repeatedly he was waylaid by the merchants, all of whom recognized a wealthy lord and prospective buyer when they saw one.

Several days had passed since he and Mary had arrived at Court, but little had changed. She made no secret of her hostility to him, their marriage, and the King. His sympathy for her distress had long since evaporated; his annoyance threatened to bloom into full-fledged anger. What woman refused to resign herself to her fate? Only Mary could be so bold and so determined.

Their union was still the talk of the Tower. Now speculation ran rampant. Stephen knew the lords and ladies of the Court expected him to bring Mary to heel, and soon, even if it meant beating her soundly for her defiance. They were beginning to snicker about his unwieldy relationship with his bride.

Stephen had no intention of beating her. No matter how much trepidation she raised within him, her astounding sense of honor was admirable. If ever he might come to own her loyalty, he would be a very lucky man, indeed.

But he did not fool himself with misplaced hope. He thought it unlikely that he would ever see that day.

And for a bare moment, he was bitter. A woman like Mary could so ease his life. Why did the image of Mary with her arms outstretched, a smile on her face, awaiting him on the steps of Alnwick, continue to haunt him?

He told himself that he was becoming a soft and weak fool. He was a battle-hardened knight; one day he would be a ranking earl, one of the greatest lords in the realm. He had relied on himself since he was six; he could rely on himself until he was sixty. If his wife refused to give him succor, he should not even dwell on the lack thereof.

He did not want to become softhearted. In this world, only the strong survived. It did no good to crave her in such a manner. He had not thought about Adele Beaufort so foolishly when they had been betrothed. Indeed, he had not thought about her at all, just about her dowry.

Nor had Adele Beaufort created the kind of lust he was constantly afflicted with. Mary's mere presence seemed to generate a heavy pulse between his legs. It was no easy thing. But tonight, and tomorrow, and for many days to come, even now, he would continue to ignore it.

He could look forward to one thing. Once married, his wife might be of little comfort to him outside of bed, but within it, she exceeded his wildest expectations.

. No, he would not beat her. As he would tame a wild falcon, he would woo her with gentleness. Today he would buy her a gift and bring her a peace offering. This dispute had gone on long enough.

As he ventured among the merchants, he had the impulse to buy several items for his bride, especially a delicately carved wooden box so small it was almost useless except as an object to be looked upon, a brooch set with one large garnet in what was almost the shape of a heart, and a yard of fine Flanders wool in a brilliant hue of scarlet. Practicality ruled and he chose the wool, envisioning Mary clad in it.

But when it came time to leave, instead of mounting his horse, he turned around, went back, and bought the box and the brooch as well.

By the time Stephen returned to the Tower, it was almost nonce; he had spent several hours among the merchants, making his decisions. He hurried up the stairs to the chamber Mary shared with several other women, beginning to anticipate her surprise—and her delight—when he gave her the fine gifts.

Rufus had one of his sergeants guarding Mary day and night—but so did Stephen. He nodded to both men and rapped sharply on the door. Mary opened the door herself. Stephen was surprised to see that she was with Adele Beaufort, who sat upon one of the chamber's three beds. Mary flushed with guilt when she saw him. What scheme was she up to now? Or was it distress he read in her green gaze?

"You seem dismayed to see me, demoiselle."

"Of course I am dismayed," she said, seeking as she did so often these days to annoy him. "How I have enjoyed being rid of my shadow."

Since they had come to Court, he had hardly let her out of his sight; in fact, at night he slept upon a straw pallet in the corridor not far from her door. "Well can I imagine your joy." He took her arm. She tensed, inhaling. The contact jolted him as well; already he grew stiff with lust he would not assuage until their wedding night. "What are you hiding, Mary?"

She refused to look at him. "Nothing. I . . . I am tired. Please—"

Adele came forward, her stride sinuous, hips swaying provocatively. "Good day, my lord," she murmured in her husky voice.

Stephen did not return her smile. God's blood, but was it possible that these two conspired against him? Every instinct he had said it was so.

Adele boldly touched his sleeve, and let her hand linger. "I have been explaining to your bride the order of the ceremony. She is not familiar with our Norman ways."

Stephen stared at Adele, whose regard was decidedly seductive. "How very generous you are, Lady Beaufort, again."

Adele shrugged, finally dropping her hand, turning to

Mary. "I can see that Lord Stephen wishes a moment of privacy with you, Princess. Perhaps we can conclude our discussion another time."

Mary looked from Stephen to Adele and back again. "Yes. Thank you."

Adele swept from the room, brushing past Stephen as she did so. When he looked at Mary, he saw that she was very unhappy—even irate. "How interesting. The two of you have become such fast friends."

Mary blanched, then found her tongue. "But we are hardly as friendly as you and she!"

Stephen took her hand, gripping it far harder than he intended. "Jealous, *chère*?"

"Of course not!" She tried to jerk free of him and failed.

Stephen was a heartbeat away from pulling her even closer, so she might understand the full extent of his frustration. But her glance was flickering over his obviously swollen loins, which his tunic could not hide, and that aroused him even further. He released her. He had no desire to torture himself now with what he could not have for another three weeks.

"What do you hide from me, demoiselle?"

She paled again. "I am not hiding anything from you! Adele spoke the truth! She has so kindly offered to help me prepare for the nuptials!" Tears had gathered in his bride's eyes.

"I lived in the King's household for nigh on ten years," he told her. "I recognize intrigue easily enough when confronted with it. Adele Beaufort is like most of the ladies here, vain, selfish, and ambitious in the extreme. What do the two of you scheme, Mary?"

Mary said nothing, tight-lipped. He could see her mind racing. When she spoke, he knew she lied, and although he had expected it, his disappointment left a bilious taste in his mouth. "I have been imprisoned in this airless tomb for almost a week! A single Scotswoman amongst a hundred Normans. Yet you begrudge me my single friend. You cannot keep us apart."

"She has not a generous nature, demoiselle. She befriends no one unless it furthers her own cause. Mark my words,

Mary. If you believe her to be your friend, you are mistaken. In fact, there is no such thing as friends in a life such as this."

She eyed him, defiant, frightened, trembling.

"Whatever you are planning," he said abruptly, "I suggest you end it, now."

"Your imagination runs wild," she said through stiff lips. "There is no scheme between us."

"We shall soon see, I suspect," he said flatly. "Are you interested in joining me for the noon meal?"

"No," she said. "No, I have a terrible headache, I cannot."

There was nothing graceful about his acceptance of her words; irritation and anger hardened his features one by one. Mary ducked her head away from him and turned to leave him. He stopped her, gripping her shoulder. "Wait." He gestured to one of his men, who had followed him up the stairs, who now came forward with the bolt of Flanders wool, carefully wrapped in cheap colorless linen. His mouth turned down. There was no pleasure in the giving, none at all.

"What is this?" Mary whispered, her eyes huge.

"For you, mademoiselle," Stephen said curtly. He nodded in parting. "I hope your megrim soon eases." He found he could not give her the rest of her gifts. Apparently the war was not over yet.

Geoffrey strode through the great hall. His golden face was flushed with anger, anger he must at all costs hide. For the third time in as many weeks, he had received a royal summons. But this time he was not being made to wait. This time the summons had been delivered by the King's own men, who had escorted him posthaste back to London, who even now accompanied him to the King.

The sergeants who stood at attention outside the royal chamber stiffened and stepped aside. Geoffrey was ushered within immediately, and only then did the two knights leave his side.

Geoffrey almost faltered as he came across the room, approaching Rufus, who sat upon a throne that was the exact replica of the one in the hall outside. For three men were present with him, Duncan, Montgomery, and his father, Rolfe de Warenne.

The Earl of Northumberland's eyes flashed to his, with warning.

"How pleased We are, dear Geoffrey, to see that you have come to Us so swiftly," Rufus said.

Geoffrey's mind whirled. He could think of no reason for this summons other than to be put to the test—the King would demand the knights owed him.

Geoffrey knelt briefly on one knee and rose at the King's bidding. "Sire?"

"The time has come for you to make your choice," Rufus said, smiling as if he had just asked Geoffrey about the weather.

Geoffrey's heart skidded wildly, then resumed its steady beat.

"Will you swear fealty to your King, Archdeacon? In front of these three men, with God also as Our witness?"

Geoffrey blanched. He had been wrong. The King was not demanding mere service after all.

He was demanding far more: that Geoffrey swear homage to him in front of witnesses. Recently some churchmen claimed that no cleric should ever swear fealty to their King, that their real allegiance was only to God, and therefore, the Pope. These reformers refused upon investiture to make such vows, and their refusal was encouraged by Rome. These prelates also disputed the King's power to appoint and invest clerics. So far, Rufus continued to follow in the footsteps of his father, demanding and exercising his rights over the Church when it was necessary, such as when he had appointed Anselm Canterbury's archbishop. He was demanding those rights now, from Geoffrey.

"And when would this act take place?" Geoffrey asked. His mouth was dry; he wet his lips. He was sweating.

"Today. Here. Now."

Geoffrey forced his stunned mind to think. There was no time to maneuver himself out of this new dilemma. The King demanded homage now. Normally an archdeacon was hardly a significant prelate. In fact, having run Canterbury ever since Lanfranc's death, Geoffrey had risen to an unprecedented position of power and preeminence. For the past four years, in the absence of an archbishop, he had battled the Crown head-on as he ruled Canterbury. Rufus was pushing their ongoing battle to its final conclusion. For Geoffrey had two choices, yea or nay, and he had little doubt that refusal would precipitate his direct descent to the dungeons below. Rufus had done far worse to those who defied him.

"You hesitate," Rufus said, his smile no longer pleasant. "Are you a fanatic then?"

His jaw clenched; a muscle ticked there. "I am no fanatic." Geoffrey forced himself to smile. "As you wish, Your Majesty." And he dropped to his knees.

Someone gasped, perhaps Montgomery.

Geoffrey was not a fanatic, yet his cause was the Church. He supported most of the suggested reforms, he supported the rights of the Church against the claims of the King, and he would continue to do so. But the past four years had proved that he could not best the King in open war. To what good had all his efforts so far been? The King's last accounting had resulted in another rape of the see to the tune of several thousand pounds.

The time had come to change his tactics. Could he not become an ally of the Crown, yet surreptitiously continue to further the interest of the Church and God?

"How wisely you have chosen," Rufus murmured. Then his voice turned sharp. "Let us be done with it!"

Before the gathered witnesses, Geoffrey swore to uphold and obey his liege lord, King William of England, in all manner and for all time. In turn, Rufus surprised him by granting him a small but exceedingly rich manor farther in the south. Geoffrey kissed the King's knee and was allowed to rise.

Their gazes met. There was no mistaking Rufus's satisfaction. "Prove that you are worthy of the trust I place in you, and you shall go far," Rufus said.

Geoffrey could not mistake his meaning. The test was not done yet. And should he continue to submit to the King's will, there would be more for him personally to gain. As he was only an archdeacon, Rufus very obviously referred to a more significant appointment. Geoffrey did not feel elated.

Instead, his insides constricted painfully. Instead, he felt a
moment of frightening despair.

The choice he had just made would be nothing like the
choice he must soon make, if the King spoke true.

Rolfe came over and gripped his arm, his smile reassuring
but not overly bright. As he prepared to leave, the King
called out. "Wait, dear archdeacon, wait."

Slowly Geoffrey turned.

Rufus smiled. "I am afraid your work has hardly begun.
You see, just this morning Anselm has refused me. He will
not muster the knights owed to me. He refuses to use the
power of Canterbury, he says, to further my own bloody
ambition." Rufus stared. His next words rang like a question.
"You, of course, will bring me the vassals owed."

It was the first test. Geoffrey did not pause. Regardless
of what might eventually come. "When—and where?"

"In two weeks time we advance upon Carlisle."

Geoffrey reeled. Beside him, his father stared at the King
in shock. Then the father and son who were such exact
replicas of each other exchanged glances, alarm mirrored
equally in both of their eyes.

Rufus smiled and rubbed his hands together gleefully.
"Malcolm will never suspect our plans, coming as they do
just days before the union of his dear daughter and our dear
Stephen." Rufus crowed. "We cannot possibly fail! The Scot
is finally doomed!"

Mary could not sleep. At supper Adele had given her the
"yes" signal that they had agreed upon. She was filled with
despair. If she dared to analyze her thoughts more closely,
she might very well learn that she had no real wish to escape
her betrothed.

But she must. She must flee this hateful marriage. How
could she wed him now, after all that had passed?

Had he not destroyed her life?

She rolled onto her side. The bell had tolled lauds and
soon the sky would gray, soon she must begin her attempt
to flee all that was abhorrent to her. For some wild reason,
a sob seemed to be working its way up from her chest. She
gulped it down. An image of the gorgeous red wool, the gift

Stephen had brought her, filled her mind yet again.

His page had made sure she knew that his lord had ridden all the way to Cheapside to do the picking himself.

Mary turned onto her stomach, feeling lost. She could not fathom why he had brought her the present that he had after she had flung her hatred of him in his face. It was making her feel miserable. For tonight she would repay him with treachery.

His dark image swam before her. His even darker words as he told her that she should be wary of Adele, that friends did not exist. He was a lonely man. How clearly she recognized that now. He most certainly needed a friend, a helpmeet, a wife.

But it would not be her. He had ruined her life. He had, and Mary knew she would never be able to forgive him for it.

Her temples throbbed as they so often did since she had arrived at Court and learned the obvious truth, that her father intended no ruse, but a real alliance. Mary closed her eyes. Still, tears seeped. Although she intended escape, what would happen to her once she reached her home? Would Malcom welcome her—or send her back?

If he was the man she thought he was, he would welcome her with open arms, and he would be proud of how she had deceived the Norman enemy. Surely he had been coerced into forsaking her. Mary had thought long and hard and had yet to find a single advantage that her marriage would bring to Scotland, other than peace. And Malcolm scoffed at peace, bent as he was on extending his borders until Scotland was as it had once been.

Mary was not sure she could go through with it. She kept recalling Malcolm's words that day upon the moors. "Mackinnon brings me vast support. What do you bring me?" And she kept seeing Stephen as she had last seen him that afternoon, his face dark with disappointment when she failed to thank him for his gift.

"Mary," Adele whispered in her ear. " 'Tis time, you must go!"

Now was not the time to have second thoughts. Mary slipped from the bed, trembling. Her gaze met Adele's. The heiress's black eyes glittered with triumph. Soon she would have Stephen to herself—as she planned.

Stephen de Warenne poised the largest threat to the scheme Adele had designed. He was too shrewd, suspecting what was afoot. That night, at supper, Mary had followed Adele's suggestion and put several drops of poppy into his wine. Stephen had downed several glasses of the narcotic-laced burgundy, and Mary had watched him growing sleepier and sleepier. When she had left him at her chamber door, he had been blinking at her, bleary-eyed. She had not a doubt that right now he was sound asleep, and would sleep that way for many hours more.

Adele gave Mary a shove. Mary could delay no longer. Outside the narrow window, through the costly colored glass, the night was no longer ink-black. Quickly Mary slipped on the clothes she had left within easy reach. Adele crept back to bed but watched her like a cat. None of the other women in the chamber stirred, and it was so quiet, she could hear her own slightly uneven breathing. She hurriedly pulled on her slippers, and feeling very much like a thief, she stole one of the lady's cloaks.

Adele waved at her furiously to hurry and go.

The first gray light of dawn began to filter into the room as Mary let herself out. The guards questioned her while she explained that she needed to use the garderobe, shivering as if with cold, an explanation for the cloak. Her gaze drifted over Stephen. It was very dark in the corner where he'd made his pallet, and it was impossible to see him clearly, but he did not even snore. At least she need not worry about him; he would still be under the influence of the poppy. Her nerves fluttering, Mary followed one guard down the dark, empty corridor.

She slipped into the garderobe, ignoring the foul smells, waiting. It struck her then that she would never see Stephen again—unless Malcolm sent her back. Jesu, what was she doing!

Mary jumped, hearing a loud thump. She dared to slip out. The guard lay upon the floor as if dead, while another man stood over him, his face masked. He gestured at her angrily and then fled before her down the back stairs.

Mary dared not pause, just as she dared not think, other than to pray that the guard had not been killed on her account. She saw no one who was awake as she flew down the back stairs in the wake of the man hired by Adele.

Mary exited through the kitchens. By now she had her cloak pulled up over her head, shadowing her face. Once outside, she began to run.

If anyone saw her as she darted across the open courtyard to the stable she had been directed to, no one called out. She did not expect anyone to. With her mantle pulled up over her head, she could be any woman, and no doubt these guards had seen more females furtively crossing the bailey for their assignations than not. Mary rounded the stable and hurried through a door in the thick outer wall, down steep stone steps, across a narrow corridor, and out another door. She was outside and beneath the castle walls, on the wharf. She had made it.

Why did she not feel triumph?

The day was growing light. The rising sun appeared as a fuzzy apricot ball on the smoky horizon. It was fiercely cold, and for a moment, as Mary stood there searching for the oarsman, she was strangely elated, thinking he had not come. Then she saw a small boat being rowed towards the dock, and her heart hammered wildly. This was it. If she wished to leave, she must do so now.

She paused on the edge of the dock, trembling with the awesome decision she must make—a decision she had thought firmly made. It was hardly that, she realized, for she was filled with hesitation, with reluctance. She edged closer to the landing's edge, fists clenched, praying for guidance. Stephen's image haunted her.

She was suddenly loath to leave. In the span of a fortnight, he had become the focus of her life.

Slowly the rowboat approached. Mary began to cry. At first she was not aware of it, but then she felt the wetness on her cheeks. Was he really to blame for all that had passed?

She shoved a fist against her mouth so she would not make any sound and alert the guards upon the watchtower. She was the one who had slipped from Liddel in disguise against all better judgment in order to rendezvous with

Doug. She was the one who had refused to yield her identity to Stephen, yielding instead her virtue. And dear, sweet Lord, Malcolm was the one who had handed her over to Stephen, without even giving her a single word of comfort, without even waiting to see if she was really with child.

Stephen hardly deserved the blame she had cast upon him. It was easier to blame Stephen than to blame herself, or worse, to blame Malcolm.

Mary covered her face with her hands. Her thoughts were terrible, terrifying. *She was nothing but a political sacrifice.* She realized with startling clarity that she might escape, but she could not go home. She could never go home again. She had no home.

Consumed with grief, she never heard the man approaching her from behind. And just as the sun slid past the murky horizon, vivid and yellow, she felt someone's hand upon her shoulder.

For the briefest of instants she thought it was Stephen, that he was not still drugged after all, that he had followed her from the keep and now prevented her escape. She turned, not to protest her innocence—but with open arms, with relief.

A masked man pushed her violently backwards.

Mary screamed as she fell. Time seemed to stand still as she floated through the air. In that endless moment as she fell backwards, Mary realized with horror that she had been pushed into the Thames, and that she was likely to drown.

She hit the water with a splash and went under. At first Mary could not move. The water was freezing cold, stunning her. An intense desire to survive brought her out of her stunned state, but her cloak and skirts were tangled about her limbs, trapping her as she sank rapidly through the blackness. Panic exploded in her as she began to feel the effects of holding her breath. Mary began to thrash, but only became more coiled in her clothing, sinking even deeper.

Dear Lord, she was going to die.

She was going to die without ever seeing those she loved again, without ever saying good-bye. Dear, cherished faces flashed through her mind, her mother, her brothers, her young sister, Maude. Malcolm. Regret swelled in her heart.

And Stephen, she thought of Stephen, whom she had so grievously betrayed.

Mary did not want to die. She was too young to die. She had not lived yet. She realized that she had been upon the precipice of a whole new life, as Stephen's wife, and suddenly, fervently, she knew she must live in order to explore it.

But she sank deeper and deeper. She began to cough. Water flooded her lungs, and she began to choke. Her body throbbed painfully from the pressure of the river pushing in upon her, and her lungs felt as if they were about to explode.

Shards of light splintered in her brain, and just before the blackness, Mary knew it was too late.

Chapter 14

Stephen saw the masked man as he pushed Mary into the River Thames.

He had never imbibed any of the drugged wine. Having been suspicious of his bride's intentions to begin with, he had seen her furtively slip the contents of a vial into his wine that evening. He only pretended to drink several glasses of the burgundy, recognizing quickly enough the odor that tinged it. A small portion of his fury was mitigated when it became obvious that she did not intend to kill him, merely to drug him.

He had feigned the effects of the drug, waiting for her next move. Soon it became clear that she thought to escape. When she left the Tower, he followed, finally hiding in the shadowed doorway of the keep's outer wall. He could hardly believe the extent of her defiance.

Now all fury fled. With a roar, Stephen catapulted from the doorway as the black river sucked Mary under.

At the dock he halted, wrenching off his sword belt while he scanned the rippling surface of the water, hoping to see her rise once more. He tore off his tunics in frantic haste, then his boots. There was no trace of Mary. The water had become smooth and unblemished where she had fallen in.

His heart pumping painfully, Stephen dove in after her.

Less than a half a minute had gone by since she had disappeared beneath the water's surface. But as he plummeted through the dark depths, completely blinded by the blackness, he could not find her.

The momentum of his dive ended. Stephen swam with furious intention now. He thrashed through the water, churning his arms madly. His lungs began to ache, began to burn. Where was she?

He refused to give up. He could not give up. If he did, she would die.

Pain began to distract him, threatening to overwhelm him. Stephen forced his mind to function—he must not lose sight of his goal, he must find Mary! He thrashed about in a circle, forcing his body even deeper, lights beginning to explode in his brain. Panic started to sear him, an animal panic that had no logic. The instinct for survival, the instinct that screamed at him to cease this madness and swim for the surface, *now*, warred with his determination to find her. But he *must* find her. *He could not live without her. How he needed her. It was all so very clear.*

He could no longer breathe.

Apparently he would die with her this day.

Brilliant white light consumed his brain, and with it, pain. His fingers brushed fabric.

Stephen began to choke. But he had already grabbed a fistful of silk tunic. A moment later he had her in one of his arms. Kicking furiously, pawing the water with his one free arm, he forced them both upwards, upwards and upwards, through the thick, heavy, punishing torrents of water. He vowed that they would make it.

His head broke the surface of the river first. He gulped air into his burning lungs, hazily aware of men shouting from the dock, their images blurred and out of focus. Mary floated loosely in his arms. His vision sharpened. Horror seized him. Her face was pinched blue, lifeless.

"Stephen," someone shouted. It was Brand. A second later

his brother was beside him in the water, taking Mary from him and swimming with her to the shore. Stephen followed. Many arms reached for him, pulling him onto the wooden dock.

Stephen shrugged off the men. He crawled to Mary, who lay on her back. She was not breathing.

"Stephen," Brand panted, gripping his arm. There was commiseration in his tone.

Violently Stephen flung him off. He flipped Mary onto her stomach. He smacked her hard on the back. She spewed up gallons of water. He smacked her there again, and more water came from her in a rush like a geyser.

He flipped her onto her back. "Breathe!" he cried. "Breathe, Mary, please!"

She was unmoving, a corpse.

Brand gripped him again from behind. "Stephen . . . she is dead."

"No!" he cried. In that moment he knew nothing other than that no one, not even God, would cheat him of his wife. She needed air. He would give her his.

He bent over her, touching his lips to hers. He forced open her mouth. He forced his own life breath into her. Again and again. He thought that her body quivered ever so slightly—and savage hope seared him.

"Stephen, stop," Brand finally said from somewhere above him, agonized.

Stephen did not hear him. His hands found her narrow rib cage. He pushed it in as he pumped more of his own air into her lungs. He found a rhythm not unlike that of his own natural breathing.

Mary seemed to grow warm beneath his cheek.

He paused, grabbing her face in his hands, staring down at her. She seemed less blue, she seemed to move . . . Dear God, she was breathing!

With a cry that sounded like a sob, Stephen collapsed beside her on the dock.

"She's breathing!" someone exclaimed. "De Warenne's given her back her life!"

Stephen flung his arm over his eyes so no one would see him crying. He could not stop the flood of tears. He had not cried in seventeen years. It was amazing, for he had thought that he had forgotten how.

"Get a physic and furs," Brand was ordering. A moment later Stephen was aware of his brother wrapping a tunic around his mostly naked body. He had been clad in nothing but braies and hose. He began to shiver. But he threw off the tunic, ignoring Brand's protest, sitting up. Mary had been covered as well. He pulled her into his arms and rose to his feet with his brother's aid. Mary was alive; nevertheless, she was barely breathing and as pale as any ghost. His gaze met Brand's.

"Bring me a horse," he said. "Then send the physic to Graystone."

Stephen laid Mary on his bed, quickly and efficiently stripped her of her sodden clothing, and wrapped her in several woolen blankets and a heavy fox fur. She was still a deathly shade of white, and from time to time a shudder swept her. She was unconscious.

Without hesitation, Stephen stripped off his own wet underclothes and crawled into the bed with her. He pulled her into his arms and between his legs. He began to massage her icelike hands.

Not for the first time Stephen looked at Mary, his face a mask of bitterness, anger, and fear. How, he despaired, how could she hate him so much? Had he not known Mary, he would think this all a bad dream. It was incredible that a woman would go to such lengths to avoid wedlock. And who, who had dared to try and take her life? Who was behind the masked assassin?

"She was trying to escape," Stephen said some time later in the hall below. All the de Warenne men were gathered there, even Geoffrey, who had spent the night and had been planning to adjourn to Canterbury that morning. "But alas, her plans went awry. For as she waited for the boat, a masked man came upon her from behind, and pushed her into the River Thames."

A grim silence followed his words. Finally Rolfe spoke. "We shall have to watch her carefully to make certain she does not try such foolishness again. And of course, as the attempt of murder failed, we must be on guard to see that the murderers do not practice such treachery another time."

Very weary, Stephen sat down at the long trestle table, his head in his hands. "I think Adele Beaufort was involved in the plan to escape."

"Adele Beaufort?" Geoffrey said, his brows raised, his skin white. "Do you really think she could be involved?"

"She cannot be pleased that I wed with Mary," Stephen said, looking up.

Geoffrey said nothing.

Brand coughed. "I hate to remark this, but she was there this morning."

"What?"

"I was returning to the Tower after a night of, er, well, sport. I heard the cries and came to investigate. I was shocked when I was told that you had dived into the Thames—many minutes ago. As I waited for you to come up, I saw Adele from the corner of my eye. She appeared as shocked as anyone else, I think. She was hiding in the shadows by the walls. When she saw me, she turned and fled."

"Surely she is no murderess," Geoffrey said tightly.

"There are other parties who might have had a hand in the deed, as well," Rolfe pointed out. "Duncan, Montgomery, and Roger Beaufort all are most displeased with the forthcoming union. Speculation leads us nowhere. We must seek to ferret out hard information, cold fact. If we can find one of the hirelings, undoubtedly he can be coaxed to speak."

"Any hirelings are by now mid-Channel, bound for France," Brand said. "If they are wise."

"Hirelings tend to lack wit," Rolfe said wryly. "Let us conclude the business at hand. Nasty rumors will soon fly. They must be nipped in the bud. I will put out word that Mary was abducted and thrown into the river. I will make clear the displeasure of Northumberland. Any would-be assassins will think twice, I promise, before striking again."

"She will not leave Graystone until we are wed," Stephen suddenly said. His tone was hard, his eyes ice. "And if the King attempts to take Mary from this threshold, I will meet him and his men personally with my sword."

For just a moment, everyone in the hall stared at Stephen. For such defiance, if it came to that, would be nothing short of treason.

Rolfe walked to his firstborn son and put his arm around his shoulder. "You are distraught. We can move the King to our cause far more easily with seduction than with swords. Come, Stephen—"

Stephen stood. "She does not leave the manor, Father." It was a challenge.

Father and son stared at each other. Rolfe finally spoke. "I am in agreement with you, Stephen—we are allies, not enemies. I, too, wish for her to remain here until you have wed with her. Let me speak on this to the King. I shall also gain his consent to hasten the nuptials."

"And how will you do that?" Stephen was sarcastic. "After all, now that Rufus has revealed his plans to invade Carlisle, I doubt he thinks the wedding will ever take place!"

"Unfortunately, Rufus is often impossible to second-guess. However, as he dearly loves to goad his foes, I can impress upon him that Malcolm will be doubly goaded if his daughter is wed to you *before* we take Carlisle."

Stephen's jaw was clenched. "He is a lackwit! This union promises peace—but he will undo all we have so far achieved, and for what? For what? For an extra piece of land? To lord over a few more warring clans? To harden Malcolm into an even more bitter enemy?"

Rolfe touched his shoulder. "Do not fear. A day will not go by that I will not whisper in his ear, softly wooing him away from his bloody scheme." He gripped his son reassuringly, then turned to Brand. "Come, we will return to Court. I will inform Rufus of all that has passed and begin to press for a more timely wedding."

After they had left, Stephen began to pace in silence, casting frequent glances towards the stairs. "What keeps the physic? He has been up there for a quarter hour."

Geoffrey went over to him. "I am sure all is well, Stephen."

Stephen stared at his brother. Briefly he revealed his torment. *"She almost died."*

"But she did not. Brand told us what happened. You gave

her back her life, brother." Geoffrey hesitated. "One day, I am sure, she will be grateful."

"I do not want her gratitude," Stephen said without thinking. Then he blushed furiously. "What a fool I am! There is no hope! She despises me, and after we are wed—if we are wed—she will hate me even more for warring upon her land and her kin!"

Geoffrey hesitated, grave, for any response he might make could hardly suffice. "I will pray for you both, Stephen. Maybe, in time, there will be peace, both for the border and for you and your bride."

Stephen's expression was dubious.

Both men turned at the sound of the physic's voice. "My lords, I have good news indeed," he said, entering the hall.

"She is well?"

"She has suffered greatly, but I can find little wrong with her other than an extreme weakness, which is understandable. I prescribe a diet of raw eggs and ox blood, known to be particularly fortuitous in restoring the heart. In a day or two I expect that most of her humors will be restored to their natural state—if you follow my advice."

Geoffrey nodded. Stephen said tersely, "How is she now?"

"She sleeps, but it is a healing sleep. And may I suggest, my lord, that you rest, too?"

Stephen nodded, thanking the physic. He turned and slowly went up the stairs, finally allowing himself to feel the full extent of his exhaustion. His jaw hardened. Mary was alive, she had not died . . . thank God . . . and if Rolfe continued to exercise the influence he was wont to have, they would be wed, not in three weeks, but in mere days.

But then what?

Geoffrey wondered what it was like to love a woman so much that he would willingly give up his own life in order to save hers. Briefly, oh so briefly, he succumbed to temptation, and could imagine the passion, the love, the friendship, and the dreams.

The sound of riders approaching at a gallop broke into his thoughts. Geoffrey became still, listening. The hour was not even seven. Rolfe and Brand had left only moments ago, and he wondered if it was possible that Rufus had learned of Mary's whereabouts so soon.

He strode to the windows and saw five riders clattering into the courtyard, showing off the bold blue and gold colors of Essex. Geoffrey tensed. In their midst was Adele Beaufort.

At her knock, Geoffrey let her in. She was wrapped in a fur-lined cloak, her cheeks red from the wind. She stared at Geoffrey for a brief moment; he in turn was as unsmiling. He remembered too well their single encounter. The moment stretched out between them.

"What brings you to Graystone, Lady Beaufort?" he at last asked. "Surely not the need for morning exercise?"

She pulled her hood from her head, lifting her raven tresses and letting them flow free to tease the back of her thighs. "Whatever could you mean, Lord de Warenne?" she said coolly, then she ignored him, moving briskly past him into the hall. He was aware of her thigh brushing his hip.

He followed. He watched her pause in the center of the hall, facing the stairs. He folded his arms. She tore her gaze from the stairwell. "Well? Is Stephen here?"

"He sleeps."

She hesitated, her eyes searching his face. "And Mary?"

Geoffrey's smile was wry and brief. "Ahh, so now we come to the purpose of this visit."

She was stiff. "The whole world knows the princess almost drowned. Is she . . . alive?"

"She is very alive."

Adele turned away, but not before he had seen her dismay.

Geoffrey strode the short distance separating them and gripped her arm, turning her to face him. She cried out. He had never manhandled a woman before, and was inwardly ashamed, but Adele was no ordinary woman. "How distraught you appear, Lady Beaufort!"

She glared but ceased struggling. Her heavy breasts rose and fell, hard.

"Did you hire the assassin?" Geoffrey demanded, giving her a rough shake. "Did you?"

"No!"

"Are you a murderess as well as a temptress?" he demanded, shaking her once again.

"No!"

He believed her. He released her, relieved.

She rubbed her arms, staring at him, her eyes black. "I admit I wish that Mary was gone, but she planned to escape—not to drown!"

"Were you involved in the escape plan?"

Her hesitation was minute. "She asked me to help her. And can you blame me?" she flung. "Can you blame me?"

He stared.

Tears welled in her eyes. "Stephen was mine for two years; for two years the world knew I belonged to Northumberland! And now what? Now what! I am a laughingstock with laughable prospects!"

He softened. "You cannot be at a loss for suitors, Lady Beaufort."

"But none is Stephen de Warenne, heir to the Earl of Northumberland!"

How well he understood her ambition; it was so like his. "I am sure you will make a good match."

"Good, yes." She was bitter. "But great? No."

He did not realize that he had moved closer to her. "Is it the loss of Northumberland that moves you so closely to tears—or the loss of my brother?"

She blinked. "Why do you ask?"

His jaw was tight. So was every inch of the rest of his body, including his loins. "I need to know."

She gazed into his eyes. "You want me, don't you?"

He swallowed. God, he did! "Even mere wanting is wrong."

"No," she breathed, advancing. " 'Tis not wrong—for us, 'tis so right!"

Suddenly he could not help himself, and her face was in his hands. "Did you lust for Stephen as you do for me?"

"No! Never!" she cried. "How I wish you were the eldest! Somehow I would get rid of Mary, for I would never let her have you! And then it would be you I wed, you! And you would not be sorry!"

"You go too far." But he did not release her stunning face. It flashed through his mind that she might be capable of murder. But the thought was brief. For he was overwhelmed with a dark, primal fear, a foreboding.

Adele was not like the widow Tam. Her pull was far greater, and far more dangerous. And with that lure there was the threat of complications, complications he sensed but had yet to understand.

"Admit that you want me," Adele was whispering.

Geoffrey looked at her upturned face, gripped in his large hands. His thumbs moved slightly along her jaw, stroking her silken skin. She was wicked. He wanted to be wicked with her. "I want you."

"I want you, too, dear God, I do! So badly at night that . . ." She trailed off, her full lips parted and quivering, ripe for his kiss.

He was mesmerized. "Tell me," he whispered hoarsely.

She took one of his hands, squeezed it, then brought it down between them. Geoffrey was frozen. She pressed his palm even lower, against the swell of her femininity. He could feel her blood beating against his hand. "At night I touch myself, dreaming that it is you. When I cry out, 'tis your name I speak."

He groaned. Of its own volition, his hand cupped her sex, ignoring the thin silk that sheathed her. He imagined what she did to herself, imagined what he might do to her. For the first time he faced the depth of his lust. He wanted to rut with her in a mindless, animal-like frenzy. The extent of his own carnality shocked him. Just once, he wanted to let go of all thought and allow his body to do as it willed. He wanted to sink into utter depravity with her. Just once.

He was only a man, and a weak one at that. She would not be the first woman he had taken, but she might very well be the last. For if he soon received the kind of appointment the King had hinted at, he must make his final vows, committing himself irrevocably to God. Vows he would never break.

Geoffrey gripped her hand. Her eyes widened. His mouth carved itself into a harsh smile. "Let us fall from grace together, Adele. Today. Now."

She gasped. He was pulling her with him across the hall

and outside. She had to run to keep up with him as they crossed the courtyard, passing the stables. He was aware of nothing and no one other than the woman at his side, and his sinister intent.

"Where are you taking me?" she cried hoarsely.

"To the woods," he said shortly, panting. His uneven breathing had little to do with the rapid pace he had set for them.

Finally they were sheltered by thick stands of trees. Geoffrey turned to face Adele, already pulling at his braided belt. It dropped to the ground, the gold cross that hanged from it glinting dully in the daylight amidst fall's crimson leaves. He did not take his eyes from her face. She appeared mesmerized. He stripped off his robes. She whimpered when she saw his straining phallus.

"Lady Beaufort?" he queried, restraining his impatience with a superhuman effort. "Your clothing. I want you naked."

She came to life. Her laughter rang out wickedly as she pulled off her cote and surcote. Geoffrey started when he saw she wore no chemise. She laughed again, displaying herself proudly, standing broad-shouldered and full-breasted, her black hair waving in the wind. She preened without shame.

Adele held her arms out to him. "Come," she whispered. "We have only just begun, you and I. I have never been more sure of anything. You are hard, hurting. Come to me, my lord. Let me ease the pain."

He pulled her against him. Their mouths met in a wild fusion. She tore her lips away. Before he could protest, she was slithering down his body. On her knees, she nibbled his navel, rubbing her breasts against his sex. Then her head descended, and with her tongue, she began to lick him in slow, sure strokes. Finally she took him deep into her mouth.

Geoffrey was unthinking, at last. With a groan of pure pleasure, he pushed her down on her back. "My turn," he rasped, laughing deep in his throat.

He spread her thighs wide, spread her hot, wet lips. As she had done to him, he licked her throbbing flesh. She screamed, clenching fistfuls of his hair. He laved her mercilessly. He licked every recess, every fold. He sucked and teased. He had one goal now, and that was to be a slave to animal desire—and to enslave her with him.

When he rose up over her, she was sobbing. With a savage cry he thrust into her. She screamed again, her nails raking down his back.

A long time later they were both spent. The sun had risen high into the sky and was just beginning its descent. They lay in sheer exhaustion, in the dirt and leaves, unmoving.

Adele finally stirred, raising herself up on one elbow. Greedily she inspected every inch of his perfect body with her eyes. He had one arm flung over his face, so she could not determine if he slept or merely rested. She sighed. No man had ever taken her to such heights of ecstasy before.

She began to smile. This was only the beginning. She was as certain of that as she had ever been of anything in her entire life. This was only the beginning for them both. Now, now she could be glad that he was of the Church. For even after she one day married as she must, he would never belong to another woman. He would only belong to her. It was a promise she made to them both.

Chapter 15

Duncan's mood was extremely foul. Who had beaten him in wielding the blow against Mary, only to so badly bungle the attempt upon her life?

Gossip blazed among the lords and ladies of the Court already, as it had ever since sunrise. Some said that the princess had attempted an escape from the Tower, others said she had been abducted, but no matter the reason she was outside the walls, all agreed that no one fell into the River Thames without a solid push.

Though apparently, no one had seen that event. Duncan had been discreetly interviewing the watchmen, but they had only witnessed Stephen's determined rescue of the princess from the river's murky depths, and the incredible manner in which he had summoned her back from her death.

Duncan was livid. Was de Warenne always in the right place at the right time? If the bastard heir had not been about the wharves at dawn, Mary would now be dead, and he, Duncan, would be innocent of the bloody deed.

Duncan could guess, like everyone else, who it was who had the largest stake in preventing the union of Scotland and Northumberland easily enough. The next question was, would the other party—or parties—try again, this time successfully?

He doubted it. The de Warennes were on alert. No murderer would be given even half a chance to send Mary into the everafter now. Justifiably he was furious. For he would not be given a chance, either. And Duncan would not be so foolish to try and kill Mary under such circumstance.

No, he must postpone his scheme, at least before the wedding, at least for now. Perhaps he must even change the means. But the end remained the same. He could not allow a union between his little sister and Stephen de Warenne.

Mary first became aware of the voices. Soft murmurs that were so faint as to be inaudible. She thought she was dreaming. Then she realized that the raw hollowness in her lungs was no dream. The voices grew louder, becoming distinct from one another. Suddenly Mary recognized the firm tones of the Countess of Northumberland and the high, childish ones of her daughter, Isobel, and she was fully awake. Comprehension dawned.

She had almost drowned. Mary stiffened, only peripherally aware of people standing over her. Sensations flooded her: being sucked down into wet, black darkness, panic filling her breast, her lungs burning, burning . . . Oh, dear Lord, she had tried to escape, but instead of escaping, she had been pushed into the Thames—she had almost died.

Someone had tried to murder her.

"Mother, Mother, she is awake!" Isobel cried excitedly.

"Can you hear me?" the countess asked softly.

But how was it that she was not dead? With frightening clarity, Mary recalled her last thoughts before losing consciousness.

And then she remembered. The scene was vivid, unshakable. Stephen holding her in his arms in the river, where she floated like a corpse, then Brand taking her to shore. Mary opened her eyes wide. How could she have such a memory? The perspective was all wrong—as if she were far above the ground, looking down upon the players in a singularly strange drama.

But it had been no play. Mary was certain that what she had seen had really happened—for now, like the acts performed by traveling players, the scene unfolded with frightening intensity and startling swiftness. Brand laying her upon the dock, Stephen being hauled from the water. And then he was upon her, pounding her back. Turning her over, begging her to breathe. And then he was breathing the air from his own lungs into hers. The memory grew darker, the images fuzzy. Mary could distinctly hear Brand telling Stephen that she was dead. But then she heard no more, and the recollection had blackened into nothingness.

The countess was smiling. "Hello, Princess. We have been hoping you would waken soon."

Mary blinked at her, trembling. Had she really seen herself on the brink of death? Had her soul, perhaps, been winging its way towards Heaven? Had Stephen somehow called her back?

"You almost died, Lady Mary!" Isobel cried, taking Mary's hands in hers and squeezing them with obvious delight that she was in fact alive.

"I almost died," Mary echoed.

"Isobel, do not distress the princess," Ceidre said sternly.

But Mary was sitting upright, clinging to Isobel's hands. "Did Stephen save me? Did Stephen breathe into my mouth?"

Both the countess and Isobel started. "But—how could you know such a thing?" Ceidre said. "Stephen said you were unconscious, unbreathing, near dead."

Mary sank back onto the mattress, her heart pounding. She squeezed her eyes closed. Hot tears stung her lids.

She had almost died. Stephen had saved her. Stephen had given her back her life.

And as she could not explain to herself the strange memory of watching Stephen minister to her on the dock, she could not explain it to them. One thing was clear. That she lived was a miracle, and she owed Stephen far more than mere thanks.

"Isobel, bring me a chemise and cote," the countess said. Isobel scurried to obey. "Raise your arms, dear; I will help you dress."

Mary obeyed. As Stephen's mother helped her to dress, she thought about how she had tried to drug Stephen. Either he was superhuman or he had known of her scheme. It was easy to feel horrible now for deceiving him, for such treachery. How could she have done such a thing?

"Are you all right, Mary?" the countess asked with concern.

Mary froze, speech escaping her. For standing in the doorway was the man consuming her thoughts.

The wintry light straying through the windows of the chamber was dismal, and Stephen was cloaked in it. His expression was impossible to determine. Mary's heart thundered. She had the urge to cry out to him, in greeting, in gratitude, and in some nameless emotion she dared not identify. But she did not. Instead, she collapsed against the pillows, watching him.

The bedchamber was small, and he crossed it quickly and decisively, pausing at his mother's side. His gaze held hers. "Good day, mademoiselle."

Mary knew she must thank this man and apologize for her horrible betrayal of him. But still she could not speak. Nor could she look away; indeed, she was no longer aware of the countess or Isobel. Finally he said, "We have been waiting for you to awaken."

Mary wet her lips, which were dry.

"Here," Isobel said, instantly handing her a cup of water. The child smiled at her. "Drink this, lady."

The countess straightened. "Come, Isobel, Stephen wishes a moment alone with his bride."

Mary barely heard the countess's words, did not even see as she and her daughter left the chamber, closing the door behind them. They stared at each other. He was grave, she was anxious and mute.

A moment later Stephen was on the bed beside her, and Mary was in his arms.

It was so natural to cling to him. He was strength and safety, power and integrity, he was life. She felt crazed by the intensity of her emotions, by the sum of them. How safe she felt, how secure, how right. The leather of his gambeson was smooth beneath her cheek. For a long moment they both held each other, neither moving or speaking. Until he said, soft and rough, into her ear, "I, for one, am more than glad to see you awake."

Mary slowly turned her head so she could gaze up at him. Could it be? Could this man have some small amount of tendre for her after all they had suffered together? After all she had done? Had he not risked his life for her?

She recalled his desperation, the way he had breathed life back into her body.

And he gazed into her eyes with unwavering intensity, as if he wished to glimpse into her soul.

Mary's chest tightened and she found herself meeting his regard openly. She had the overwhelming urge to open all of herself to him, completely.

"How do you feel?" His tone was not quite steady, unlike the light within his eyes, which was so fierce. Mary thought that she detected a film of moisture there, but she could only assume it was from a speck of dust.

"I am glad to be alive, my lord. I—I must thank you."

She felt his entire body tightening and he moved his mouth even closer to hers. Her body came to life when he spoke, his breath feathering her, tingles sweeping down her spine. "I would have more than thanks from you."

Mary was hoarse. "W-What would you h-have, my lord, of me?"

"Do you truly not know?"

Mary felt dizzy with the possibilities. She was faint, and unsure of what was happening between them. "You—you have more than my thanks," she heard herself say.

His gaze searched hers intently. "Do you bend to me now, finally, Mary?"

Mary trembled. What bond were they forging, what pact? Did he understand her pledge; did she? "You have saved my life. I almost died. If not for you . . ." She cried out, unable to continue.

His own grip upon her tightened. "You have nothing more to fear, mademoiselle," he told her. "No harm will befall you; you have my word."

Mary gripped his leather gambeson. They were upon the verge of some new and great understanding, and she was both afraid and exultant. "Stephen," she whispered, knowing that she had never called him by his given name before, "I am sorry. I am sorry for betraying you. I will never betray you again, my lord," she said with fervor. *"I give you my word."*

He was still for a moment; he did not appear to even breathe. His gaze had become very dark and very fierce. "If you are finally speaking the truth, Mary, I would be well pleased."

"I am," she whispered.

His expression changed, became somehow primitive, and triumphant. "Do you finally come to me willingly as my wife?"

Their regards locked again. Despite her weakened condition, Mary felt the fluttering of desire low in her belly. "Stephen," she whispered faintly. A surge of emotion so intense it almost blacked her out overwhelmed her. Mary was stunned to realize that she loved this man. And then, in the next heartbeat, she was not stunned at all. "Yes," she said softly.

His eyes widened. A moment later he was bending closer and brushing his mouth gently over hers; in the next instant, there was little gentle about his kiss. Mary did not care. She loved him. She kissed him back.

Eagerly their tongues mated. Mary pulled Stephen down on top of her, exulting at the feel of him, at his unmistakable reaction to her invitation. He was disturbingly hard and long against her thigh. Mary whimpered. She had almost died, and now, now she was overwhelmed with the urge to take him deep inside her, to cry out in abandon, in ecstasy, and to coax his seed to life. Nothing had ever been as important.

Stephen was the one to break their kiss. He lifted his head, panting, his brow furrowed, his face grim. "Mary? If we do not stop now—"

"No!" she cried, shifting so the ripe tip of him brushed the apex of her thighs. "No, my lord, you have saved my life—now let me give you life!"

Stephen froze, only for an instant. Then he rolled over her, stroking his hands down her belly, stroking intimately between her thighs. Mary moaned in pure pleasure. She thrashed beneath him, panting.

Her tunic was in the way. With a savage little cry Mary shoved her skirts up to her waist and pressed Stephen's hand hard against her wet heat. He was startled; his eyes blazed. "For you, my lord," Mary whispered, aware of being totally carnal in that instant and unable to help herself. "Only for you, my lord."

He cried out. A moment later he was sliding his huge shaft deep within her, in an act not just of penetration, but of possession.

Mary sobbed her joy. She keened her ecstasy. Stephen gasped, sliding in and out of her, stroking her again and again with his massive manhood, until Mary knew a second, even greater ecstasy than before. With a harsh cry, he finally convulsed deep within her. The sounds of their heartbeats, uneven and rapid, mingled with their harsh, heavy breathing.

Mary sighed.

"I like your smile, mademoiselle," Stephen whispered.

Mary wondered if she looked as love-struck as she felt.

"We shall do more than well, you and I," Stephen said.

Mary tensed. His words had a hard edge to them, as if a challenge, or a vow. She sat up, staring at his dark, handsome face. He was so somber now, as if unsure.

"It will be so," Mary whispered, but suddenly she was wistful and afraid, aware now more than ever of the immense past that loomed between them, one that went much further back than just the few weeks since he had captured her; a past consisting of countless battles in which their fathers had crossed swords with deadly intention, a past in which she herself had committed many acts of treachery against him. How Mary yearned then and there for the kind of relationship he had just alluded to, one far more successful than most, one without complications, one honest and real. A relationship that, for them, history and circumstance conspired against.

And such a conspiracy did not bode well for them. But it was too late. Mary recognized that she had given her heart boldly away and that it would never be hers again. And she was stricken. Not only did the past and present conspire

against them, so did many avid, ruthless players. Even if he
did care about her, and she was truly beginning to believe
that he did, what kind of future could they possibly have?

Mary reached for him. *"Someone tried to kill me."*

"I know."

But before his words were even out, it struck Mary that
Adele Beaufort had engineered the attempt on her life. No
one else had known she would be on the wharves at that
hour, that day.

"What is it?"

She raised her shocked gaze to his. "My lord," she whispered, horrified, "only one person knew of my plans to
escape!"

"Adele Beaufort?"

She was sick. She nodded dumbly.

"Adele had help in arranging your escape. We cannot be
sure that she was behind the attempt on your life. There are
many factions against us, Mary."

Mary had been near tears; now she froze. "Who? Who is
against our union, Stephen?"

"Must you know?"

Her temper flared. "I would know who is my friend and
who is my foe, yes!"

"Adele's brother is furious that she has been cast aside.
Montgomery fears that Northumberland's power outstrips
Shrewsbury. And Duncan—"

"Duncan! Surely he would never try to harm me! He is
my brother!"

"He is your half brother, whom you have only just met,
and he loves only himself and his ambition, Mary."

"Perhaps he has ambition, but that does not mean he
would harm me!" The very idea was ludicrous, frightening.

"His ambition is to rule Scotland, to be her king."

"No! He could not seek to depose my father!"

"He is not such a fool. He hopes to succeed your father.
Why else has he remained at Court here for all these years,
serving Rufus like some heathen slave? And he is Rufus's
choice."

Mary stared. Finally she shook her head, unable to decide
how much to say to this man, her future husband. Aware that

even now, so soon after her discovery of her own true feelings, and perhaps even his, politics threatened them. "No. Edward shall be Scotland's next King. Father has decided, and it must be that way."

Stephen regarded her. "And Malcolm can do no wrong?"

Mary jerked. "Let us not discuss Malcolm," she finally said sharply.

"Why not, Mary? Is he always right?" Suddenly Stephen's tone had changed, suddenly he was angry.

Mary's heart beat too hard; she shook her head, refusing to answer. Unable to answer.

Stephen stood abruptly. "We cannot take any more chances, Mary. Therefore you will remain here at Graystone for the next few days, where you will be safe, until our wedding."

"For the next few days? But our wedding is not for another three weeks!"

"No," Stephen said, leaning over her. "Our wedding date has been changed."

"Changed?"

"The King has agreed. It is most unwise to delay now, in the light of all that has happened. As soon as you are capable of making your vows, we shall be wed."

Mary was wide-eyed. Her heart turned over in real pleasure. She could not help smiling. In a few days they would be wed—in a few days she would be his wife!

It was not until Stephen had left that she realized that his own response had been far different from hers. He had not been smiling when he told her the unexpected news. In truth, he had been grim and uneasy, as if he expected disaster to strike in the very near future.

"As soon as she can make her vows!"

"That's correct, dear brother, as soon as Princess Mary is well enough to stand for the mass and make her vows, they shall be wed." Rufus smiled, not pleasantly. "Is there a reason such haste should upset you, Henry?"

Prince Henry was furious. "You know I am against this union; I have said so from the first. I keep hoping you will see reason, and forbid them to join."

"Why do you think I agreed to the union in the first place?"

"I cannot even begin to fathom why."

"So that Malcolm will be at rest when our armies swoop down upon him." Rufus grinned. "It has occurred to me that he will be even more unsuspecting *after* the wedding."

"You have outdone yourself, brother," Henry said softly, angrily. "What will you do, my lord, if ever the day comes that Northumberland turns to Scotland—against you?"

"That day will never come."

"You are mad! For the sake of some worthless hills you give de Warenne enough power to make or break you!" Henry paced the King's apartment. It was at times like these that he knew—he absolutely knew—that he should be England's monarch. Never would he give a single noble such power. Never would he trust one of his vassals with such power. Given his brother's stupidity, he could not help being sorry that Mary had not drowned. "Who tried to kill her?"

"I do not know. Was it you, Henry?" Rufus asked blandly.

Henry's face reddened with the rush of blood that his renewed fury brought. "If I had been behind the murder attempt, you can be sure she would not be alive this day!"

Rufus stood, walked to the window, and looked out upon London. "I believe you."

"So it was attempted murder?"

"Contrary to some of the gossip now running rampant, it was."

Henry was suddenly smiling. "Was she really running away from de Warenne?"

"You find that amusing?"

"Very amusing." He laughed. "By God, I'll wager Stephen was enraged. That little chit daring to defy him—how I wish I could be privy to at least one of their conversations!"

"Hmm. I imagine you would rather be privy to that little chit."

Henry eyed his brother. "Would such temptation be delivered to me, I would never refuse. And if de Warenne gave you the slightest encouragement, you would jump into his bed as quickly, would you not, Your Majesty?"

Now it was Rufus's turn to be furious. "Perhaps when he was a boy, but now such a man is hardly attractive. Hardly attractive," the King repeated harshly. Yet he was lying, not just to his brother, but to himself. Unrequited lust was a dangerous thing, especially after so many years.

"Perhaps Stephen will be so grateful, he will thank you as you would like," Henry said, striding to the door and laughing. "But I do not think so, Will. I do not think so." With a mocking bow, Henry left.

Rufus stared after his brother, fists clenched. If Henry were not such a valuable military ally, with a host of Norman mercenaries at his beck and call, he would toss him in the dungeons and throw away the key. Sometimes he hated his brother so much that he was truly tempted to do so. But that was not relevant to his cause. So he would use his brother to the best advantage that he could, always taking care to remain one full step ahead of him. For Rufus understood his brother far better than Henry thought. The reason Henry was so furious over an alliance that hardly affected him now was that he dearly coveted England's throne. But that, of course, would never be.

Adele Beaufort lay sprawled flat on her stomach in bed, uncovered, her arms around a pillow, clad only in a short, thin cotton chemise. She was alone in the chamber, all of the other ladies partaking of the day's last meal. Her eyes were closed, but she was not asleep, and her breathing was irregular.

The scene from the other day with Geoffrey de Warenne replayed over and over in her mind, and each time her resolve rose anew. Never had she felt the consuming desire for anyone that she felt for him. These past few days he ignored her, pretending she did not exist, pretending that the afternoon they had shared in such utter abandon had never happened. But it had. And she would have him again, and soon. She must.

She moaned softly, low, clutching the pillow harder, her body on fire. He was here, at the Tower; even now he was downstairs, with everyone else, dining. Adele's knee came up and pressed into the bed, her shift baring her buttocks.

Adele recalled everything he had done to her that afternoon, and everything she had done to him. She moaned softly, the fire creeping up her limbs. After such an encounter, she did not think she would ever be really satisfied by any other man.

She heard footsteps and became still. They were heavy and male and they paused outside the door of her chamber. She did not open her eyes, but the throbbing of her body increased. She imagined Geoffrey entering, running his hands over her back and clasping her buttocks in prelude to impaling her with his massive cock.

The door opened, without a knock. Adele squeezed the pillow harder, knowing he was staring at her.

Slowly he closed the door. "Who has you so hot, you little bitch?"

Adele moaned, the only response she was capable of, unable to stand the agony much longer.

He approached. "Who?" he asked, pausing at the foot of the bed. "Who has you writhing alone in your bed? Do you even need me, Adele?"

"Please," she whispered, hating herself, hating him, fiercely.

She heard the sound of loosening fabric as he undressed.

"Please," she whispered again, begging now.

He laughed. The pallet buckled from his weight as he knelt between her thighs, his hands roaming up them and only stopping when they had grabbed handfuls of her buttocks. Adele spasmed, gasping.

"Who has you like this?" He was getting angry, and he gripped her hard, making her cry out. "Who, dammit!"

Adele spread her legs. "Geoffrey de Warenne," she gasped.

With a cry, he thrust into her. Adele bit her tongue to keep from screaming, instantly swept up into a violent climax. Shortly after, he followed, collapsing on top of her.

She shoved him off, leaping to her feet. In one stride she had reached her tunic and was pulling it on. She looked at the man lounging on her bed. "Get out of here!"

Roger Beaufort sat up indolently. "I locked the door." His smile was taunting. "Is this the gratitude you show me, darling?"

"Get out," she repeated furiously. She hated him, she always had, for it was he who had revealed to them both the depths of her immorality—a long time ago.

Beaufort rose, dressed slowly, and sauntered past her. "You will never change," he said into her ear. "And he only toys with you—for he has virtue—something you do not even remotely understand."

"And you do?" she queried with sarcasm. "Tell me, Roger, just when did you decide to murder Mary? Would it not have been enough for us if she had escaped?"

He paled. Then he shoved his face to hers. "If you betray me, sister dear, I shall implicate you up to your ears. If I fall, you fall as well."

Adele jerked away from him. "Get out!"

His smile was ugly. "Perhaps I shall even speak with the good archdeacon. I do not think even your body would attract him should he believe you capable of murder."

"Get out!"

Chapter 16

Mary was tense. Malcolm and Margaret had arrived in London yesterday; tomorrow she would be wed. Stephen had suggested she visit them at the King's Tower, and as she could not refuse, they were on their way there now. Mary had almost refused. She had wanted to refuse. She did not want to face Malcolm, not now, the day before her wedding.

Three days had passed since her near death, such a brief period of time, but she had been happy. Although Stephen spent much time at Court, he had attended her every day. They did not speak of what had happened the day they had consummated their union again but Mary believed that they had attained a new and wonderful understanding. She trusted him—how could she not? Brand had been a visitor, and he had told her how Stephen had risked his life to pull her from the river. He had risked his life for her and then given her back her life. Oh yes, she trusted him completely.

And she had not dissembled when she had promised him that she would never betray him again. She recalled how moved he had been by her vow, and was certain that he trusted her as well.

She was afraid to visit even briefly with her family. She was afraid of what might happen, of what she might learn.

As they drew closer to the Tower—and to her parents—Mary realized that Stephen thought he did her a great favor by bringing her here for this visit. As Mary did not want to face her own feelings herself, she could not share her reluctance with him. But with every step that brought them closer to the Tower, her heart beat faster, her stomach tied itself into a tighter knot.

She had learned that Malcolm had arrived at the gates of London with a sizable army. He had only been admitted, however, with a few dozen men, and those men had been required to surrender their weapons once inside the bailey of the Tower. William Rufus was taking no chances with his most bitter enemy.

As she traveled across London, Mary worried. She knew her father well. He was undoubtedly furious at being forced to leave his men and weapons behind. She knew how quick he was to strike back when enraged. Would Malcolm disrupt the alliance at this last moment, or even disrupt the wedding itself? Mary was afraid. How she had changed. She did not want anything to interfere with their wedding, not even Malcolm. He was so ruthless with his enemies, and there was no doubt that he still hated Northumberland—and Stephen.

The King's Tower came into sight. It soared above the walls of the bailey and reflected upon the smooth surface of the Thames. Mary had kept the curtains of the litter open. She began to tremble. Stephen rode ahead of her on his brown destrier, behind his standard bearer and the red rose of Northumberland. A score of heavily armed knights escorted them.

From the moment they crossed the drawbridge and entered the bailey, they were given a royal armed escort into the keep. Stephen helped her from the litter, surrounded not by his own knights now, but by the King's men. Mary had been in the exact same situation before, and again she felt fearful and powerless. She did not release Stephen's hand, and he gave hers a reassuring squeeze. Of course, the King himself would never disrupt their marriage now, he would not dare.

As they climbed the steps to the keep with their escort, Mary wondered if she would always fear and dislike the English Court, if she would always feel like an alien among the enemy. It was another sobering thought when she wanted to feel nothing but bridal jitters and real gaiety on the eve of her wedding.

Their party entered the Great Hall. Conversation dimmed and ceased. Every lord and lady they passed turned to regard their group, eyes bright with speculation. Mary regretted ever having attempted to escape. Stephen could not be pleased that her defiance had been so publicly aired. She had little doubt that many of the jealous lords here had been thrilled with Stephen's brief humiliation.

As they crossed the hall, Mary glanced at him. His head was high, his gaze trained ahead, his expression unreadable. She thought she heard someone snicker and mention Stephen in the same breath as they passed, but when her gaze flew to the crowd, she could not find the culprit.

In time, she thought vehemently, the whole world would know of her love for Stephen and her loyalty. She would make it up to him.

They went directly to the King's private rooms on the third floor. As soon as they entered, Mary saw that Malcolm and Margaret and three of her brothers were already within, her parents conversing rather stiffly with the Earl and Countess of Northumberland, near the dais where Rufus sat upon his throne. Mary was very surprised to see Doug Mackinnon standing between Edward and Edgar, and when he caught her eye, she quickly looked away.

She was horrified that he was here. She could not imagine why he had accompanied her parents. Also, she was struck by the knowledge that since the day she had first been captured by Stephen, she had hardly spared him a single thought. How could she have ever thought herself to be in love with him? And how would she ever face him now?

Mary peeked at Stephen, but he was expressionless. She realized he did not know who Doug was, and she found herself inordinately relieved. She knew him well enough now to be certain that he would not be pleased to make Doug's acquaintance.

Her parents saw her. Mary was frozen, unable to move.
She had avoided looking at her father except for a single first
glance. She managed to smile at her mother, who appeared
close to tears. She ignored Malcolm. She could not look
at him.

Stephen and Mary greeted the King.

"I am glad to see you so well, Princess," Rufus said
expansively, red-cheeked and smelling of wine. There was
a gloating look about him. "You do not look as if you have
suffered from your near-death."

"I am recovered, Sire."

"How glad We are." But Rufus was hardly interested in
her. He was smiling at Stephen.

Stephen did not smile back. "Sire," was all he said.

Mary looked at the man she loved, then at the King.
Stephen's face was unreadable, but the King's expression
was animated, his eyes sparkling. Mary could not move,
could not even drop her gaze from William Rufus's countenance. How well she recognized such an expression now.
Dear God, the King is in love with Stephen!

Rufus finally looked at her, catching her staring, his smile
vanishing, his gaze becoming cold. "Your father waits to
greet you, Princess."

Immediately Mary turned away, but she was still shocked
with what she had discovered—for she had not a single
doubt that it was true.

She had no choice but to look up at Malcolm. He was
smiling at her as he always had, and her heart twisted
painfully. Tears formed in her eyes. His gaze was warm,
affectionate. It was as if that horrid moment upon the moors
had never happened, as if there had been no negotiation over
her as if she were mere chattel, and unloved at that. It was
as if he was glad to see her. "F-Father," she managed.

"Daughter! How pretty you are, as always! Are you well?"

Mary nodded, trembling. She stared at her father, wishing
desperately that he might take her in his arms. Of course,
Malcolm had never been one to show such exuberant affection. She did not expect him to do so now.

But in that blink of an eye, Mary knew she loved her
father and she always would. She knew he loved her as

well. He had given her to Stephen for politics, but that was every bride's end. She had never expected to marry for love—yet through an incredible twist of fate, she was. Her feelings of betrayal had been generated by mere appearances that day upon the moors. But 'twas only that, appearances. Malcolm had seemed harsh and singularly unconcerned for her welfare, and there was no explanation, not when faced with his warmth now. Perhaps he had been so hard because he was dealing with the enemy, and not just his enemy but the man who had abducted and ruined his daughter. Mary could not know. It did not matter. She loved him, and she forgave him with all her heart.

Mary turned to her mother, who stretched out her arms. Mary released a harsh sob, rushing into her dear and familiar and oh so comforting embrace. Margaret rocked her as if she were in swaddling. When the embrace ended, Mary smiled up at her mother through her tears, and saw that Margaret was crying, too.

"You are finally to be wed," Margaret whispered. "My little minx is finally to be wed."

"I am happy, Mother."

"Oh, thank God!"

They hugged each other again. Then Edgar swooped down upon her, demanding after her welfare. Because they were so close in age, they had been nearly inseparable as children, and of all her brothers, Mary was closest to him. He was grim, clearly unhappy with her betrothal and worried about her, reminding Mary once again of the political realities. She glanced at Edward, the oldest brother, and the most practical. Mary was used to turning to him for wisdom and advice. So often he had rescued her from her mischievous deeds, calming her when distraught, defending her when accused. He, too, was somber. And Edmund was openly displeased.

Mary was dismayed. And suddenly she became aware of tension seething at her back. She turned from her brothers to witness Malcolm and Stephen exchanging terse, barely civil, greetings. Mary's heart sank.

How they despised each other. There was no amiability between her father and her betrothed, just cold, hard-edged, hate-filled politeness—if that.

The memory flashed through her mind. The winter-white day, cold and bleak, the bare, gaunt trees, the freezing wind. Stephen, hard and proud, standing behind Rufus at Abernathy, while Malcolm pledged his fealty to the King of England on bended knee. Malcolm's face had been a mask of hatred and fury.

Nothing had changed, except that Stephen appeared to detest Malcolm with an equal fervor.

Mary told herself that she could bring Stephen and Malcolm together—she could. Once upon a time she would have never considered such a possibility. Now she must do more than consider it, she must breathe life into the event of peace. Surely one and all could see the logic of an alliance between her family and Stephen's. There had been so much bloodshed over the past two generations; was it not time for a lasting peace?

Mary was determined. For she had the horrible feeling that she would be the one to pay the price of war, she and Stephen.

Margaret smiled and touched her cheek, breaking into her thoughts. "Come. We have permission to adjourn to the next room."

Surprised, Mary glanced at Stephen, to see him nod. Then she realized that it would only be her mother and herself enjoying a private moment; undoubtedly her mother thought she must impart some maternal advice to her daughter on the eve of her wedding.

Mary made sure not to glance at Doug as she passed him, following her mother behind one of the oak partitions. But she sensed that he was both determined and desperate, and she was filled with trepidation. Was her plate not full enough already? She could not handle anything more, not today!

Margaret did not waste time. "Are you all right, dear?"

"I am fine, Mother."

"Are you with child?"

Mary blushed and was ashamed. "I do not know yet. Mother—forgive me."

Margaret's smile was tender and forgiving, but she said, "I cannot do that, my dearest. Only God can forgive you— God and yourself."

"I love him, Mother," Mary said almost shyly.

Margaret burst into tears, taking Mary's hands. "How happy I am! Oh,'tis so rare to marry and find love, too!"

"You love Father."

"Aye, I do." Margaret cupped her chin. "Need I remind you of your duties? As a good, Christian wife?"

"I promise to be obedient, Mother. To Stephen and to God."

"Do not forget your duties to those who depend upon you, Mary. Do not forget that you shall be responsible for all those who toil for your lord, both vassals and villeins. And do not neglect the poor and the sick, my dear."

"I won't, Mother."

Margaret softened. "From what I can see, Stephen de Warenne is a good man."

Mary was relieved. "He is! Mother—if only you could persuade Father that Stephen is not the Devil's own, and that our families are now allies—not enemies!"

" 'Tis hard to persuade Malcolm in matters of state, dear," Margaret said gently. "You know I do not like to interfere. But I shall try."

"Thank you," Mary said fervently.

They spoke for a few more minutes, then together they returned to the other chamber. Mary was disappointed when she realized that Stephen had left. She turned to her brothers, glad to have a moment to converse with them, unsure of how many more moments there would be after her wedding.

But Edmund said, in her ear, "Do you carry his brat yet, little sister?"

She drew away.

" 'Tis an honest question, an important one," Edmund continued, his eyes holding hers.

"Go to hell," she whispered furiously, turning her back on him.

Edward grabbed him, spinning him around. "You oaf! Can you not at least ask if she is well?"

"I can see that she is well!" Edmund retorted.

"Do not start, not now, not here," Mary whispered angrily. She had played the peacemaker often with her brothers, and under her unrelenting stare, they finally relaxed.

"Mary?"

Mary froze, recognizing the voice behind her, a voice with an urgent tone. Reluctantly she turned to face Doug, whom she had hoped to avoid. As if they were alone, Doug gripped her arms. Mary stiffened. "Doug—"

"We must speak!"

She was stunned. His expression was intense and strained, and there was no mistaking the wild, desperate light in his eyes. "What is it? What is wrong?" Even as she spoke, she glanced quickly around, to reassure herself that Stephen had not returned to witness Doug touching her in such a manner. Relieved, she shrugged free of Doug's grasp.

"I had to beg your father to let me accompany him, Mary," Doug said, low.

"I do not understand why you have come."

He appeared confused. "Why I have come? To see you, of course!"

Mary's eyes widened. Was it possible that Doug still cared for her?

"Mary—are you all right?"

"I am fine."

"Has he hurt you?" Doug demanded.

Mary wondered if he was asking her if Stephen had used her. "No, he has not hurt me."

Doug flushed. He gripped her arms again, bending over her. Mary grew nervous. "Are you with his child, Mary?"

She wet her lips. "I do not know." She was scarlet.

He grimaced.

Mary waited for him to berate her, but he did not.

"I do not care," he finally said. "If you bear his child, I do not care."

Mary was too surprised to respond.

He said urgently, "Do you still love me?"

"Doug!"

"Mary—we can run away. We can run away tonight, to France. We can still be married, and I will rear the child as my own. 'Tis not too late."

Mary stared.

"Just say yes," Doug cried, "and I will get word to you this night. I have a plan, Mary, and we can succeed."

"Doug," Mary whispered, aghast. He still loved her enough to forgive her for her loss of virtue and to accept another man's child, which was overwhelming enough, but the suggestion itself was even more shocking. "You must be mad! I cannot run away with you, I cannot!"

"Mary—think about it."

"I do not have to think about it. It has been agreed, I am to wed with Stephen."

Doug paled.

Mary knew, and she whirled.

Stephen smiled at them both, coldly.

Chapter 17

To Doug's credit, he did not flinch despite the unwavering stare Stephen subjected him to.

Stephen said, "Do you subvert my bride, Mackinnon?"

Doug squared his shoulders. "She would not be your bride, de Warenne, had you not abducted her and raped her."

Mary winced, as pale as Doug now, expecting Stephen to cruelly expose the truth of her participation in his seduction.

Stephen smiled again, unpleasantly. "But that is all the past, is it not? And tomorrow she will be my wife. So cleanse your mind, Mackinnon. Mary will have no suitors other than myself."

Mary was terribly relieved that Stephen had spared her such humiliation. She dared not intervene, though. But that immediately proved to be a mistake.

Doug's amber eyes flashed. "You can marry her, de Warenne, but you cannot take away what we share, she and I."

Stephen was still. His eyes had become black. "And just what is that, Mackinnon?"

Doug smiled, and it was his turn to be cold, even triumphant. "Love."

Mary closed her eyes, choking off a moan. Her heart twisted for Doug. He still loved her, and he thought that she still loved him. She was dismayed. She should have told him forthrightly that her heart now belonged to another. And she dreaded Stephen's response, sure he would be frightening in his fury.

But he only laughed and shrugged. "Love is for fools like you, lad, not for a man like me." He turned to Mary, his regard chilling her. " 'Tis time for us to return to Graystone, demoiselle."

Mary knew he was angry with her, without cause. Tears glinted in her eyes, as much for the unjustice as for poor Doug, and she touched Doug's arm. "Tomorrow Stephen and I shall be wed, Doug, as our fathers have agreed. Please, please give us your blessing."

Doug stared into her eyes, communicating silently with her, pleading with her. Mary's heart sank. He still thought to persuade her to agree to his mad scheme to run away and elope. "Doug?"

"Do not ask the impossible of me, Mary," he said stiffly. Clenching his fists, he turned and stalked away.

Stephen gripped her arm. "You surely must be overwrought by now."

"Stephen . . ." Mary balked, facing him.

His smile was sardonic. "What are you going to say now, Mary, in order to appease me? That you do not love him? Do not delude yourself—you may love him. I do not care— not as long as it is *my* keep you inhabit, *my* bed you warm, and *my* children that you bear."

Mary wanted to cry. He did not understand her at all.

It was a fine day to be wed.

The skies had cleared, giving way to a winter sun, and the previous week's chill had relented; the day was sunny and warm. Mary barely noticed. She was consumed with nervousness as she had been all that night before, for soon she would wear Stephen de Warenne's ring, soon she would be his lawful wife. She was eager, but she could not help feeling fear. She was about to wed a stranger, to join with him for the rest of her lifetime; she was about to marry her family's archenemy. Once joined, their union could not be breached; they would remain man and wife until death parted them, despite any and all circumstance. If in the future there was war, how would she survive?

Her knees hurt. The mass was endless, but Mary, so familiar with the ceremony, was barely aware of Archbishop Anselm as he led the congregation. She knelt beside Stephen. He was as still as a statue; he had not moved once since sinking down onto his knees on the floor. Even now, as Mary tilted her head slightly so she could see his hard profile as he bowed his head, he did not even shift. He had not looked at her since she had come up the aisle, escorted by her father.

He was still angry with her for the conversation she had had with Doug, although, had he overheard it all, he would know that she had refused to elope with the Scot. He had barely spoken to her since escorting her from the Tower yesterday. Mary's stomach was in knots. They would get past this small moment of conflict, of course, but it was a rude way to begin one's married life, with a coldly distant groom and the threat of never-ending war.

The archbishop bid them rise and join hands. Mary was jerked back to the present. Her knees were stiff, and Stephen's strength as he helped her up was welcome. She tried to meet his eyes, and was finally rewarded. Their glances held. No matter what ill-placed jealousy he might be feeling, when their gazes collided, something vibrant and powerful sparked between them, something potent and exciting.

Mary was stricken with the urge to tell him many things, to tell him that she would be a good, dutiful, and loyal wife, to tell him that he could trust her, to tell him that she would do her best to ease his life. His gaze was assessing. Mary's heart wrenched. She would give her right hand to have him trust her wholly and love her in such an unyielding manner.

Vows were made, and finally Stephen placed his ring upon her third finger. The archbishop blessed them, smiling, and Stephen leaned forward to kiss the bride.

Mary strained towards him, dazed, as his lips brushed hers. Stephen moved away, obviously intending only a ceremonial kiss. Mary, on her toes and leaning forward, stumbled against him.

Stephen steadied her. Mary blushed hotly. His eyes were unmistakably warm now. "I am glad you like my kisses so much, madame," he murmured. "There will be many more, far more bold, in the course of our lifetime."

Mary held his regard, her pulses skittering, her wits scattered, thrilled.

He escorted her down the long aisle. The crowd, all the greatest Norman and English nobles of the land, cheered. As they exited the church, rye seeds rained down upon them. Mary laughed exultantly. To her surprise, as the rain of seeds became a torrent, Stephen also chuckled.

"With so many seeds, I imagine our union cannot be anything but fecund," he said.

He still gripped her hand. Mary's laughter died. His genuine pleasure had lit up his saturnine face, causing her heart to leap uncontrollably. "I hope so, my lord," she said earnestly.

His own smile died.

Mary's expression became impish. "After all, my mother had six sons and two daughters. Would that not be enough for you?"

But Stephen was solemn. "Give me one son, Mary, just one son, and I will give you your heart's fondest desire."

The wedding celebration was at the Tower in the Great Hall. The hall was overflowing with nobles, overcrowded and stifling warm. Mary and Stephen sat upon the raised dais alone, with King Rufus just below them on one side of the long trestle table, Northumberland on the other. Malcolm was seated after the de Warennes. It was a deliberate insult.

Geoffrey had no appetite. He wondered at his King for humiliating the bride's father so deliberately, for his never-ending provocation of Malcolm. Fortunately, Malcolm carried no weapons and would not dare to strike out now in his anger, and it was too late for the union to be destroyed. But not too late for the alliance to suffer, he thought grimly, knowing that in a few days they would strike Carlisle.

Geoffrey abruptly rose from his seat, ignoring his father's inquiring glance. He did not want to watch the bride and groom any longer as they fed each other and gazed cow-eyed at each other. He was not jealous, but he was envious—and he had no right to such an emotion.

Hadn't he made his choice deliberately?

Geoffrey walked through the performing clowns, passed the dancing girls, and almost stepped upon a small trick dog. He found an empty corner somewhat removed from the press of humanity. He leaned his shoulder against the wall, and unable to help himself, his regard wandered back to the bridal couple upon the dais. Stephen whispered in Mary's ear. She pinkened and gave her husband an exceedingly bold look.

Geoffrey's chest ached.

What would it be like, to have such a wife?

He tore his gaze away, angry with himself, and watched the dancing girls. They sought to tease and provoke. He found them attractive, as any man would; they were barely clad, dark-skinned and exotic. Then he saw Adele Beaufort suddenly rise from her seat. His interest in the dancing girls waned. As Adele walked into the crowd of dancing revelers, he lost sight of her briefly.

One single afternoon could not make up for many months of abstinence. But if he dared to identify some of the anguish he carried, he might realize that the gaping wound left behind by his rendezvous could never be healed by sexual indulgence.

Geoffrey did not hate himself. But he despaired. His worldly inclinations were still more powerful than his holy ones. But hadn't it always been that way?

He had been cloistered with monks at St. Augustine's from the age of thirteen for three long years, and as a novitiate he had taken vows of chastity, among many others. But he had been young, his blood hot, and he had been unable to uphold his vows—unwilling to uphold them. Fortunately there were no opportunities to chase the fairer sex in a monastery, but at night, alone and in bed, he had engaged in the loneliest, lowest sexual act a man could. The few times he had left the cloister on Church affairs, always with Lanfranc, he had stolen away in the night and lifted whatever skirts he could find. Guilt had been a heavy cross to bear, and Geoffrey had been certain that his mentor always knew of his midnight excursions. But Lanfranc had never lost faith in him. Somehow Geoffrey kept faith in himself, too.

His will was now a man's and far stronger than that of an adolescent boy's. He abstained for long periods of time. Until the yearning of his flesh overrode all his holy intentions. But—he was not ordained. Most archdeacons were ordained priests. Certainly all bishops were—even if the ordination was merely a ceremonial show.

If such an appointment came, he would have achieved a lifelong ambition.

If such an appointment came, there would be no turning back.

He had avoided ordination because he knew that if he made the required vows to God, if he became one of God's representatives on earth, he could never forsake those vows. Unlike other clerics, who made vows and broke them, sometimes in the same breath, he could not—he would not.

He was not ready for that final step, for that final commitment. Maybe he would never be ready. Or maybe he was afraid to make such vows, afraid that ultimately he would fail both God and himself.

And Geoffrey, like all the de Warennes, could not tolerate failure. It was unacceptable, impossible.

Geoffrey realized that Adele was leaving the hall. He ordered himself to go back to the table. Where she was going—even to whom—was not his concern.

But he was aching, an ache in his chest that he wanted to confuse with the ache in his loins. He followed her.

He did not have far to go. On the landing below the hall he found her staring out of the window, her back to him. Her shoulders were shaking. Geoffrey was startled when he realized she wept. He walked closer, almost touching her. "Lady Beaufort?"

She jumped. She saw him and batted her thick black lashes furiously. He was surprised to see her features ravaged by her tears. "You have startled me!"

"That was not my intention." He almost touched his finger to her damp cheek. She pulled back before he could make contact, squaring her shoulders. "Why do you cry?" Geoffrey asked. How well he understood her. She hated him seeing her in a moment of weakness.

"The King gives me to Henry Ferrars!" she cried, then she wept again.

Geoffrey hesitated, then, as her distress was real, he took her into his arms. He was well aware that Ferrars was not comparable to Stephen. The knight had been awarded a huge estate at Tutberry for his loyalty, and he was a great soldier, but of humble origin. "He is a good man, Adele. I imagine he is in love with you—or he soon will be." He held her almost gingerly. This was a role he was not used to.

Adele pushed back to gaze at him, startled. Then her nostrils flared. "I care not what he feels! The King has insulted me—and all because of my damned brother, Roger! And Stephen and Mary, even now, they make a fool of me with their open show of love and lust!"

"Lady Beaufort," Geoffrey said, trying very hard not to shake, his body impossibly aware of her, "no one would ever laugh at you."

She did not move. In that instant her attention shifted; he knew she became aware of him and his growing lust. "You have avoided me," she whispered, placing her hands on his shoulders.

"Yes. I have."

"Why?"

"You would not understand." And Geoffrey regretted touching her, knowing he was poised on the brink of surrender to his lust—and simultaneously he did not regret it at all. How could he survive this battle he was forever waging, one far more important than any other, the battle he waged for control of his own soul? If he had an ounce of holiness in him, he would back away. He did not move.

Adele gripped his shoulders tightly. "Why are you being so kind to me?"

"You were distressed."

She blinked as more tears seemed to fill her eyes. "No

one has ever been kind to me, not once in my entire life. Is that not amusing?"

"You exaggerate, Lady Beaufort."

"No." She shook her head wildly. "My parents were indifferent as I was not the boy they so greatly desired. Then my father died when I was still in swaddling and my mother was given to William Beaufort. When I was ten I was orphaned—you did not know? Beaufort and my mother were killed in an ambush by rebels in the North. My step*brother*—" she spat the word "—did not even come to see me for two long years—and he was my guardian. Then, then he only wanted one thing." Her mouth formed into an ugly line. "Do not speak of what you do not know! I do not exaggerate!"

"I am sorry," he said, and he pulled her up against his body, kissing her as he might a lover, with thorough gentleness.

The kiss meandered lazily, then abruptly changed course. Their tongues thrust deep, mating. Adele withdrew, gasping. "I thought you hard and dangerous. I did not think you kind."

"I do not feel kind right now, Lady Beaufort." His blue eyes blazed.

She stared into his eyes. "I do not want your kindness just now, my lord."

"Then let us celebrate the nuptials together," Geoffrey said. But even as he took her mouth with his, he knew that he could only assuage the ache in his loins, not in his chest. He knew that afterwards the emptiness inside him would be far greater than before.

Stephen attended Mary as if she were his lover. They shared the bride-ale, and every morsel that passed through Mary's lips was chosen carefully for her by her husband and fed to her by him as well. It was not a time for words; indeed, Mary could not have found her tongue if she tried. It was a time of acute awareness and long, deliberate looks. Mary knew Stephen was thinking about the night to come, too.

Hours must have passed before the twelve-course meal was finished, but it seemed like minutes. There had been entertainment throughout—dancing, clowns, jongleurs, trick dogs, minstrels, and a monkey man. Now the crowd was frenzied in pursuit of their pleasure, in their dancing, in the last sweatmeats, in the mead and wine. Stephen gave her a look that was so blatant, so sexual, that Mary trembled. Surely they could leave now.

"Might I speak with my daughter and wish her well?"

Mary looked up to see Malcolm smiling at both her and Stephen, standing beside them on the dais. Stephen stood, unperturbed, even smiling himself. "Of course." His glance stroked Mary. "I will be back in a few minutes, madame."

Mary's chest was tight, her heart pounding. He kissed her hand, his mouth lingering, his breath feathering her flesh.

As Stephen stepped off of the dais, instantly surrounded by well-wishing, raucous males, Malcolm slipped into his seat. He put his arm around Mary. Mary firmly shoved her ungenteel thoughts out of her mind. She was thrilled that her father had come to sit beside her and wish her well.

"You seem very pleased, daughter, with this union."

"Oh, Father, I am. Although at first I fought it and was disappointed with the union, I have now accepted Stephen with all my heart."

" 'Tis a good thing for you to accept what must be, Mary," Malcolm said, no longer smiling. He studied her closely.

Mary tensed, touched with a finger of foreboding. She did not care for the look in her father's eye. "Father? Is it possible that now that Stephen and I are wed, there might truly be peace upon the border?"

His expression was impossibly hard. "How quickly you forget!"

"Forget what?" she asked. "Blood and death?"

"How quickly you forget who you are, Mary."

"Am I not Stephen's wife?"

"You are my daughter. You will always be my daughter, and that can never change."

Had his exact words been spoken in a different context, in a different manner, Mary would have been thrilled. Instead, she was held in the grip of gut-wrenching tension. "Of course, Father. That will never change."

"You are still Scotland's daughter."

Mary gripped the table, finding it difficult to breathe. "Yes, I am that, too."

Malcolm smiled, but it did not reach his eyes. "I am depending on you, Mary."

"Depending on me?" she echoed, a hollowness forming in her heart and in her very soul.

"I am depending on your loyalty."

"What are you saying?" she cried, on her feet.

Malcolm stood, too. "What I am saying is that you belong to Scotland before you belong to de Warenne."

Mary's nails clawed into the wooden table. This could not be happening, it could not! Her father could not be saying such a thing—and surely he would not continue in such a vein!

"You must, of course, be a good wife, a dutiful wife. But you must not forsake me, you must not forsake Scotland."

Tears were blurring her vision. She could not speak, not even in denial, so filled with despair, with horror, was she.

"You must spy for me, Mary," Malcolm said. His eyes were brilliant.

Mary felt faintness come over her. She clutched the table. "You ask me to spy? You ask me to spy upon my husband and his people?"

"You must! For nothing has changed. The Normans hate me, and I, them. Northumberland still encroaches upon me, Rufus still seeks Scottish soil. You must remember who you are. You are a princess of Scotland first, de Warenne's wife second. No opportunity could be more perfect. Why do you think I allowed you to marry him in the first place?"

Mary could not look at her father another moment. And not because of the tears that blinded her. "This is my wedding," she whispered.

"And you are a beautiful bride," Malcolm said, patting her shoulder. "Wipe your tears, your groom approaches. Remember, Mary, who you are and where your duties lie."

Part Three

Into the
Darkness

Chapter 18

*T*hree days later they returned to Alnwick.

The past few days had passed too quickly, in a haze of torrid lovemaking and sated bliss. The newlyweds had not left their bedchamber. Mary had no time to think or reflect—nor had she wanted to. Stephen was a demanding lover, voracious and insatiable, but never selfish or cruel, and Mary found herself his equal when it came to the passion he aroused in her. She had no will to deny him anything, and quickly learned how to entice him. If she was not pregnant before, she imagined that after these two days, she must certainly be carrying his child.

Alnwick loomed ahead of them. The daylong journey had brought with it the unwelcome intrusion of cold, frightening reality. Under normal circumstances, if Stephen were not a de Warenne and if she were not a Scott princess, she would be thrilled to be adjourning to her new home and to her new life as Stephen's wife. If circumstances were different, she would be filled with eagerness and excitement, the future beckoning bright and full of promise. But the circumstances were what they were—her husband was Northumberland's heir, she was Malcolm's daughter—and instead, Mary was torn with foreboding.

How she wanted to begin the lifetime that now belonged to her and Stephen; how afraid she was of what the future might bring. Now, in the light of a new day, Malcolm's words haunted her, a terrible reminder of the reality that their marriage was doomed by who they were.

She had not had a single moment to dwell upon what her father had asked of her at her wedding feast. Today's long journey encouraged a reflection and remembrance she was desperate to avoid. Yet she could not. Not now, and no longer. *Malcolm had asked her to spy for him. To spy upon her husband.* Mary was in shock.

The whole reason he had arranged the marriage to begin with was to plant her as a spy in Northumberland's midst.

Mary was not just shocked, she was devastated, and she was furious.

Was this the man she had loved and worshiped her entire life? The man who had laughed at her boyish antics while her mother scolded? The man who had been so proud of her wit and beauty as she grew older? Was this the great Scot King?

How could he do this to her?

For there was no question that she still loved her country and her kin—her marriage did not, could not, change that. There was no question that she wished to see Scotland remain whole and independent. She could not, would not, wish to see Northumberland make further inroads across the treacherous borders.

But there was also no question that she would refuse to do as her father wished. She had made her vows before God, and she had meant them. Her duty was to her husband first, before anyone or anything else—even before her duty to her father or her country. But sweet, merciful Jesus, now that she fully understood Malcolm's intentions, now that she understood that there was no alliance, how would she survive? How would her marriage survive?

Obviously Malcolm intended treachery against Northumberland—against her husband. It was only a matter of time before the fragile peace was broken. Despite having given her allegiance to Stephen, how would she feel when he rode forth to battle her father? Oh, why could there not be peace!

Mary was heartsick. Bile left a sickening aftertaste in her mouth. Malcolm's horrible demands remained with her, echoing in her mind. How could he think to use her so, and in so doing, to destroy any chance she had for happiness?

"We are home, Mary," Stephen said quietly, breaking into her thoughts.

Although Mary had been thoroughly absorbed by her own thoughts, she had been peripherally aware of Stephen's presence all that day. He had ridden by her side, but he said little. He had appeared as grim as she, as if he knew the crazy circles her mind ran in, as if he knew what Malcolm had asked of her.

She looked at him and compelled herself to recall the wondrous splendor of the past few days. Although she had probably engaged in a dozen different intimate acts, although she had slept in his arms repeatedly, he was still a stranger. She forced a smile to her lips. She must not let him see that she was disturbed, she did not want him to know of the turmoil she was in. And God forbid he should ever find out what Malcolm had asked of her. "Home," she echoed, pain overshadowing any joy she might have been feeling otherwise. She turned to her husband, strong, urgent feelings washing over her. "I am going to be a good wife to you, Stephen. I promise you." She was trembling.

His gaze searched hers carefully, as if he sensed that a different substance lay behind her words, a substance he wished to find. "Is something bothering you, Mary?"

Mary shook her head in denial, unable to speak further, and turned to gaze upon the impenetrable fortress of Alnwick. It was a gray day, and the heavy shadows overhead made the dark stones of the walls and keep appear black and depressing. Mary knew that it was only her own thoughts, really, that cast her new home in such a forbidding light. It was not an omen, foretelling a bleak, tragic future.

* * *

The moment they arrived in the bailey, Stephen was met by Neale Baldwin and quickly engaged in a conversation involving Alnwick's current affairs. Mary excused herself, aware of Stephen's glance lingering upon her even as Neale carried on about the sickness killing dozens of sheep, and she fled up the steps and into the keep, servants rushing to follow after her. Mary raced upstairs to the chamber they would use while the earl and countess remained in London. She immediately ordered Stephen's belongings unpacked, had a fire stoked, and sent for spiced wine. She asked that a bath be drawn for him as well, then she flew downstairs to see what preparations were being made in the kitchens for their meal. It was chaos, of course, due to Stephen's sudden arrival at such a late hour. Mary calmed the distraught master cook, and quickly they arrived at a simple but pleasing dinner menu. As she rushed from the kitchens, Mary caught the arm of a servant girl and instructed her to add fresh herbs to the rushes in the hall. Then, her skirts in hand, she flew back up the stairs.

She was out of breath. The bath, a big copper tub, was being filled with steaming hot water, carried up pailful by pailful by two brawny lads. Mary glanced around the room, saw that the fire was in full blaze, that the wine sat upon the chest, and that fresh clothes had been laid out for her husband. She smiled, pleased with herself. Being a wife was no easy thing, and it was not a role she had ever yearned after, or even studied, but now she was glad to have had her mother's behavior to emulate. She wondered what else she might do to please her husband, then saw that he stood in the doorway, looking somewhat bemused.

His warm regard, the soft, slight tilting of his mouth which suggested a smile, and his powerful presence all made Mary flush. She curtsied slightly in response to him, aware of the quickening of her heart. She imagined she appeared a mess, after the long journey and her rush to see to his comfort, not at all like a princess but more like one of the serving women below. Hastily Mary tried to tuck the errant strands of her hair back in her wimple. Stephen strode forward, unbuckling his sword belt. Mary leaped to take it from him.

His smile broadened and reached his eyes. "You cannot handle my sword, madame, not one as small as you." He placed the long, heavy, scarred weapon on a chest within easy reach of the bed.

"Can I not, my lord?"

His gaze swung to her, wide with surprise.

Mary could not believe what she had said, but she held his regard, and added huskily, "*Have* I not, my lord?"

"Yes, madame, you have, and adeptly, I might add."

Mary was breathless. "You have taught me boldness, I fear."

"I like your boldness, madame, at least the boldness we are now discussing." His glance left her, moved around the room, no longer chill and dark, then over Mary, slowly and warmly. "Perhaps I should have taken you to wife sooner."

Mary smiled in real pleasure. "I am glad if you are pleased, my lord."

"I am more than pleased, Mary."

She could not mistake his meaning, for the gleam in his eyes was overly familiar to her now. Her tone had grown husky. "Is there naught else I can get you, my lord? Or do for you?"

His look was piercing. "You may help me disrobe," Stephen said, sitting down and taking off his muddy boots.

Although Mary had just spent two long days and three even longer nights in bed with her husband, pleasing him in every way that he might think of and then in some she had thought of, she was overcome with a strange combination of both nervousness and pleasure at being able to perform such a simple wifely task as helping him unclothe and take his bath. Of course, she had a very good idea of exactly how his bath would end, and was breathless with the anticipation.

Quickly she went to him and helped him shed his belts and tunics. Her pulse quickened as her hands moved over him; she would never become indifferent to the feel of him, to the sight of him. His broad shoulders, wide, hard chest, and flat abdomen were bared to her possessive gaze; when he moved, thick muscle flexed and long sinew rippled. "You are a fine man, mylord," she heard herself say.

Stephen, clad only in braies, hose, and cross-garters, swiveled to meet her eyes. "I am glad you think so, madame."

Mary's heart beat harder. She knelt beside him and fumbled with the garters. It was impossible not to be aware of her husband's aroused state. His hose and braies slid to the floor.

Kneeling, Mary looked up at him. He regarded her back steadily, then held out his hand to her. Mary stood and found herself held loosely in his arms. "You also please me, madame wife," he said low.

She flushed with delight. "Do you not want your bath?" she asked as levelly as she could.

"My bath, and you." Stephen sighed. "I do not know how you can keep me so excited, madame, but you do. A man my age should have been long since worn out. Have you given me a potion I do not know of?"

"No," Mary said, smiling. "A love potion would undoubtedly kill us both."

Stephen grinned, humored, and the effect was dazzling, taking Mary's breath away. Stephen had a hard, serious look about him usually, but his smile bathed his face in soft, masculine beauty.

He stepped into the tub and settled himself in it. Mary picked up the washcloth and looked at him. Her hand shook slightly. "Do as you will," Stephen murmured.

Trying hard to think about giving her husband a bath, and not taking his invitation as literally as she would like to, Mary began washing his back. Stephen sighed in pleasure. When she had finished soaping and rinsing the hard expanse of muscle, flesh, and bone, Stephen turned slightly, his eyes glittering like jet. Mary tried not to tremble. And she tried to keep her eyes off of the water swirling about his hips and the part of his body that beckoned her so stubbornly. Stephen's mouth had a hard line to it now. He leaned back. Mary knelt beside him, and dropping the rag, she used her hands to lather his chest with soap. Her palms slid over hard muscle and silken skin. Her husband was tense and unmoving. When her hand slid down his hard, flat belly, stroking in circular motions, Stephen closed his eyes. His jaw was tight, his neck tightly corded, his expression strained. Mary looked down, then let go of her restraint. She plunged her hand into the water. She lathered his heavily distended penis.

Stephen groaned.

Mary did not remove her hand. Her mouth was close to his ear. "Is there aught else you wish from me, my lord?"

His laughter was low and rough. Before she knew it, he had lunged to his feet, sending water splashing all about them. A scant instant later Mary was flat on her back on the bed. And he straddled her, her skirts up to her waist, his hot, slick member pressing against her swollen skin. "Who teases whom, madame?" he murmured.

Mary was incapable of speech, incapable now of responding. She clutched his shoulders, her nails digging into his skin, free now to act as she would, to give up all pretense at proper wifely behavior, to be the carnally insatiable wanton he had taught her to be, and she panted beneath him, spread and desperate. Stephen laughed in male exultation and thrust into her. Mary shouted her pleasure. Within moments they were thrashing together in hot, mindless abandon.

Although Mary came down late to the dinner, it was a success.

The moment she arrived in the hall she saw that Stephen was relaxed and in good humor; upon seeing her, he sent her a very warm look. Mary blushed, and a quick glance around told her that the men-at-arms below the dais regarded them with knowing gazes and tolerant amusement. Mary imagined that they understood exactly why the lady had been late to dinner, for Stephen's replete and satiated air could not be mistaken for anything other than what it was. Mary hoped her own appearance was more circumspect.

But if it was not, if the glowing love she was feeling from the top of her head to the tip of her toes showed, she did not care. She would no longer dwell on her morose thoughts, on Malcolm and his demands. There was no point. She had made her decision, and the right one it was, too. And then, as she came to take her seat beside Stephen, had she needed any further proof, it was there before her on the table.

A single crimson rose in full bloom.

Mary paused, stunned. Dazed, she looked at Stephen, who smiled at her lazily. There was a promise in his eyes that was far more than sexual. "How did you find this?" She whispered the first words to pop into her head.

" 'Tis a strange phenomenon, is it not? A rose in winter. 'Tis for you, madame, a gift from me."

Mary felt like crying. She took her seat, but did not touch the rose. He had clipped the stem short, and it resembled the rose upon his shield exactly, right down to the thick, spikelike thorns.

"Actually, my mother grows roses, and I can only guess that last week's warm weather fooled the plants into an early showing."

Mary did not want to cry foolishly. What did this mean? She faced Stephen, seized with determination. She would decipher precisely what he meant by this profoundly romantic gesture, a gesture she would have never dreamed of being possible from him. "Stephen, you have cut the stem. This rose—it looks exactly like the one upon your arms."

His smile was pleased. "I am in agreement, madame. I had hoped you would notice."

"What does it mean? Your coat of arms."

He leaned towards her, his gaze stroking her face. His tone was intense. "The sinister black field which all else rests upon is power, Mary, and a warning to all those who might war with us."

Mary shivered.

"The white field above 'tis for purity, the gold for nobility."

"And—the rose?"

"The red rose signifies passion, madame. I am surprised you should ask."

Mary blushed. Her heart beat wildly. Power, purity, nobility—passion.

"The de Warennes are known for their power, their honor, their nobility, and their extreme passion for all causes dear to them," Stephen said in a strained, low tone. His gaze held hers.

Mary was mesmerized. She knew she did not mistake what he said—or why he had given her the rose. He was giving her himself. "Stephen . . . thank you."

Stephen stared. Mary could not look away for a long moment, his gaze was so intense. Then she reached for the rose. Quickly he reached out to restrain her. "But you must have a care," he murmured, "that you do not harm yourself on the thorns."

Most mornings Stephen immersed himself in administrative matters with his steward in the hall, but not this day. He stood, staring unseeing into the hearth. Mary was occupied with her responsibilities as chatelaine; he knew she was in the pantries with the pantler. His retainers were all about their duties, as well. He had a rare moment, for he was completely alone.

There was a persistent pain in the back of his head. A throbbing he was not unfamiliar with. For many years now he had recognized that the megrim came during times of distress.

He had been married for four days. Four perfect days beyond his greatest expectations. If he did not know himself better, he would think himself a romantic fool, so pleased was he with his bride, so besotted. He could hardly believe he had found and given her a red rose, but he had. She had understood its meaning perfectly. She had been well pleased—he had seen it in her eyes.

He should have been completely happy. But he had the worst megrim he had yet to have, instead.

For the terrible question remained. Had Rolfe succeeded in turning the King from his plans to betray Malcolm and invade Carlisle? Or was he about to ride forth to war upon his bride's home and family?

Jesu, how would she react if he went to battle with Malcolm? Would she understand that he did his duty to his King, as always? Would she support him, as was *her* duty?

She was his wife. Their relationship had changed since she had awakened after her near-drowning. There was no question that she had accepted her fate, had come to him willingly as his wife on the day of their wedding. She was performing her duties at Alnwick with enthusiasm, and he was acutely aware that she sought to please him. God, but he was pleased. But did he have her loyalty first and foremost as he must have?

Mary was one of the proudest, most determined human beings he had ever met. Could the minx who had fought and defied him at every turn up until someone had tried to murder her actually change her loyalty and allegiance so swiftly and completely? Was she his wife in her heart as he was now her husband with his? Was she?

He did not know.

He was afraid to know.

And he was afraid of what the next few days would bring.

The Earl and Countess of Northumberland arrived at Alnwick the following afternoon. Isobel was with them, and so was Geoffrey. Stephen was not at the keep when they arrived, so Mary went into the bailey to greet her parents-in-law properly. Warm, heartfelt greetings were exchanged by everyone. Mary was absurdly pleased to realize that she was not merely accepted by her husband's family, but loved by them as well.

Mary then rushed upstairs to supervise the removal of her and Stephen's belongings from the master's chamber, wishing she had been notified a bit in advance of the earl and countess's arrival. Shouts from the guards on the watchtower, followed by the sound of a small cavalcade drumming over the drawbridge and into the bailey, told her that Stephen was home. With a warm smile, Mary went to the window slit and watched her husband slide from his destrier, handing the reins to his squire. He was up to his knees in mud; the last few days it had rained incessantly. Stephen would need a bath, But Mary was certain that he would not bathe until after dinner, that he would want to enjoy his family's company first.

Some time later, having made sure that the lord's chamber was swept clean and ready for the earl and his wife, Mary went downstairs. As she neared the hall below, it became clear that the earl and his sons were in an intense, yet hushed conversation. She had not heard a single female voice as she descended, so quite naturally she felt as if she were intruding, and her steps slowed. As she rounded the corner she heard Geoffrey making a remark about the fortifications at Carlisle being ancient rubble in need of repair.

Mary had barely assimilated the fact that the topic they were bent on was Carlisle as she entered the hall. The three men seated at the table there instantly fell silent. She paused. Her smile, one reserved for her husband, died, and the greeting that had been on the tip of her tongue was forgotten. The three de Warenne men all turned to look at her. No one was smiling. Obviously she was intruding, and just as obviously they did not want her to overhear their discussion.

Mary stopped in her tracks halfway across the hall. For the first time since she had been wed, she felt like a Scot intruder, instead of the mistress of Alnwick and Stephen's wife. She managed a frozen smile, one directed at her husband. "Good day, my lord."

Stephen rose. Behind him, his father was sipping ale, and Geoffrey was drumming his fingers impatiently upon the table. Stephen came forward, but not to greet her. "My mother is in the solar with Isobel. Why don't you join them?"

Mary's mouth tightened. Her heart beat in hard, painful spurts. He, too, saw her sudden appearance as an unwelcome intrusion; he was dismissing her. Hurt rose hotly, achingly, in her breast as she looked up into her husband's handsome face. He did not trust her.

He did not trust her, and they spoke about Carlisle's defenses.

No, it could not be.

She stared at him for several heartbeats, waiting for a sign, any sign, that this private meeting was not as it appeared. But he only repeated his barely disguised command. "Why do you not join my mother in the solar, madame?"

She had bent herself over backwards these past few days to please him, accommodating his every inclination, offering him every form of comfort, and openly she had sworn

to obey and uphold him, but still he did not trust her.
Mary felt sick. *He did not trust her, and they spoke of
Carlisle!*

With a curt nod, unable to speak and filled with dread,
Mary turned abruptly and fled into the solar.

The countess looked up from the embroidery she held, her
gaze concerned. Isobel raced over to Mary with a glad cry
and began to tell her the latest news from the London Court.
Mary nodded, pretending to listen, not hearing a word the
child said. She tried telling herself that all was not as it
appeared, that she was jumping to conclusions, and that her
husband, in sending her from the room so he could speak
with the men around him, was no different from most other
men. Yet her silent words rang hollowly, and Mary did not
believe them.

Carlisle. What did they plan? Could they be planning war?
Could they?

It was not possible, Mary cried to herself in silence.
For just that dawn Stephen had held her so tenderly after
their lusty lovemaking, and his sleepy smile had spoken of
love. Just yesterday he had given her the rose, his promise
of undying love—or so she had thought. If he loved her,
just a little, he would not make war with her family over
Carlisle.

She had to find out their plans. Yet how could she
eavesdrop without alerting the countess? Mary looked
at Stephen's mother and turned a guilty red, for the
woman was regarding her somberly, making no attempt
to wield her needle and thread, as if she comprehended
what Mary intended. Mary felt like a lowly traitor,
but she reminded herself that she was not about to
betray anyone. She merely wanted to learn if her husband intended to war on her people or not. She had
to know.

He must love me a little, she thought desperately. *Just a
little.* In which case there would be no war—Stephen would
refuse to participate.

"Excuse me, madame," Mary said to the countess, "I am
not feeling very well. I think I shall go upstairs to lie down."
How she hated deceiving her mother-in-law.

"Shall I have some fare sent up to you?" Lady Ceidre asked, standing now and watching Mary too closely, even gravely.

Mary had no appetite, and she declined. Then, nervously, she slipped from the solar.

As the women's chamber opened directly upon the hall, she was once again interrupting the men's conversation. They saw her instantly and all talk ceased. Mary ignored them, although her face burned with humiliation. She hurried from the hall. Only when she was halfway upstairs and she heard their voices resume did she pause, trembling, pressing against the wall.

And even as she did so, she was close to tears. She was newly wed and in love with her husband, but she was about to spy upon him.

She could not hear them well. Mary began inching silently downstairs. When she was on the second landing she could go no farther, for to turn the corner would be to reveal herself. But now she could hear their every word, and they were talking about all that she had feared—treachery against her father—an attack upon Carlisle.

"He summons every knight I can muster," Geoffrey was saying.

"How do you stand with Anselm?" Stephen asked, his voice strangely toneless.

"We are enemies. He is far more zealous than I ever dreamed," Geoffrey said grimly. "But Rufus needs Canterbury now more than ever. My spies say that the prince is so enraged with your wedding, he refuses to spend himself on this cause. While I have beggared myself to muster these men, as Canterbury's treasury is dry."

"Your duty is clear. And though you may be impoverished now, do not forget how close you are to reaping your true reward," Rolfe said firmly. "No price is too dear should you succeed in gaining an appointment from the King."

Geoffrey said nothing in reply.

Rolfe continued. "Do not be fooled. Henry chooses to keep his nose clean now only so he can bloody it another day. Is it not better for all of us to fight as one—and to be weakened as one? Who better to next step into the breach than the ever clever prince?"

"Hopefully Carlisle will fall easily, sparing us too many losses and sparing me unnecessary coin," Geoffrey said wryly after another pause. "And absolving Henry of the need to step into any breach."

Finally Stephen spoke again. "The rain works against us," he said flatly. "We rely on our mounted knights heavily. Horses move with difficulty in the mud."

"I would have preferred such an action a month ago, if action we must take, but we have little choice now," Rolfe said. "The King has made up his mind. There is no moving it."

"Yes," Stephen said, "Rufus made up his mind long ago, and nothing will hold him back from his cause, nothing and no one."

"At least we take Malcolm by surprise," Geoffrey remarked, again wry. "After all, you have just wed his daughter."

"Yes," Stephen said, "we will definitely take Malcolm by surprise."

Mary choked. Stephen had echoed his brother so dispassionately. How could he be objective, so wholly without emotion, when discussing treachery against her country, her kind, her kin? The full import of what she had overheard suddenly hit her. Her marriage was a mockery, she thought bitterly. She was no beloved wife, merely a leman and serving woman combined. He did not care one whit about her after all, or he would at least have expressed some small regret for breaking the alliance he had made with her father! Mary wanted to weep, she wanted to shout and scream. Their marriage meant little or nothing to him beyond its political utility—and undoubtedly she meant even less. She clung to the railing, panting, trying not to weep.

There was no point in lingering, she decided, forcing herself to come to her senses, aware of the silence in the hall below. She had learned what she had come to learn, what she did not want to learn, what she feared to learn. How it hurt. It was so hard not to cry. She imagined each man absorbed now in anticipation of the battle to come.

Damn them all! And God damn Stephen, her husband! Mary turned to go upstairs.

In her agitation, she slipped. She cried out as she slid down several steps. Horrified, certain one and all in the hall below had heard her, she froze on her hands and knees, a scant instant from leaping to her feet and fleeing. But it was too late. Her husband was faster, far faster, than she.

Mary recognized the feel of his hand and the strength of him instantly. He hauled her upright by the scruff of her neck, whirled her around, and released her.

Mary stumbled, as much from the force with which he handled her as from the expression on his face. He was stunned and disbelieving.

In that moment she did not care, in that moment she was too enraged to care. "Damn you," she hissed, then regretted her words immediately. His shock turned to fury. She turned and ran.

The enormity of what she had done struck Mary—eavesdropping on her husband, and worse, being caught at it and thus appearing to be a spy. She cried out as she heard the sound of Stephen pounding up the stairs, closing the gap between them. Terrified now, Mary raced into the chamber they were using, just a step or two ahead of him, and turned to pull the door shut—hoping to lock him out. Too late, he was on the threshold, and he slammed the door back against the wall with one outflung arm as if it were mere beechwood and not heavy, triple-layered oak.

Mary jumped back from him. Tears stained her face.

Stephen towered over her, his eyes wide, his face hard, his body trembling in rage. "You spy upon *me*—your husband?"

"You war upon my people?" Mary cried back.

Stephen stared.

"How could you?" Mary cried, her heart pumping madly. "How could you go to war now?"

"You question *me*?" he asked finally, low and strained. The muscles in his jaw bulged, so tightly was it clenched. "You accuse *me*? I do my duty, madame, just as you do yours."

Mary did not respond. She was shaking.

"Madame," he said, very stiffly, and he was shaking, too. "War is not your concern. You have but one concern, and that is seeing to my comfort."

"Yes, your comfort is my concern," Mary said unsteadily. "But when you war upon my family, my home—then my concern becomes that war! Do not ask me to remain ignorant now!"

"I do not ask you to remain ignorant. But I ask you this— do I have your loyalty, Mary?"

She opened her mouth, and said, "Do you go to war against Scotland, Stephen? Do you?"

"You have not answered me, Mary." His expression, his stance, his tone, had all become dangerous.

"Nor have you answered me," Mary whispered brokenly. Her palms pressed against her breast, against her aching heart.

"Answer me, Mary!" Stephen demanded.

"Yes," Mary said, the way a villein might answer him, with a broken spirit. "Yes."

"Do you lie now?" His tone was higher. His gaze was more wild. "Did you not spy?"

"Yes." She closed her eyes, just for a moment.

"How can you be my loyal wife, madame, if you spy upon me?"

She did not answer.

"Answer me!" he roared. He raised his hand. Mary flinched. He froze in the act of striking her, then grabbed her by her shoulder, shaking her, and Mary was afraid, knowing he was on the brink of brutality. "You spy upon me in my own home! Is that not disloyalty?"

"I hate you," Mary whispered. She realized she was weeping. Just hours ago she had been in his embrace—just hours ago she had been filled to overflowing with love for this man. This man who cared so little about her.

For an instant they were eye to eye as he dragged her up close. "So now we arrive at the truth!"

"The truth," she said, "is that you are no different from my father, marrying me in order to use me, to aid you in your ugly treachery."

He threw her upon the bed. Mary cringed, waiting for his blows. They did not come.

Stephen's hands, rough and hard, forced her onto her back so that she had no choice but to look up at him. He leaned over her. "My treachery? My treachery? Still you dare to accuse me? I wish you to explain your treachery, madame wife! Explain yourself now!"

Mary could not think of a single thing to say in her own self-defense; in truth, she had no desire to defend herself, not to him, not now.

"Where is that clever, cunning wit now? Do you not at least deny the accusation?"

Mary swiped her eyes with the back of her hand, fiercely mute.

Stephen pressed her into the bed. "You are my wife, madame, *my wife*. Our vows were made before God. *What of your vows, madame?*"

She had no choice but to answer, he was so enraged. "You will not believe me if I tell you the truth."

"Oh ho! And what truth are you going to foist upon me now, Mary?" He straightened, looming over her. "That you love me? That you would never betray me?" He was shouting.

Mary trembled, for it did not seem possible that she had thought herself in love with this man such a brief time ago. She sat up, clutching the blanket beneath her in her fists.

"Why did you spy?" He ground out the words.

"To learn your intentions!" Tears filled her eyes again. "And how vile your intentions are!"

"To learn my intentions." Stephen's mirthless laugh was harsh and grating. "And to warn Malcolm. To warn Malcolm against me. To betray me."

"No!"

For an instant he did not speak, he only stared at her. "Give me cause, Mary. Give me cause to believe you."

Mary was panting. "Have I not given you cause, these past few days, to trust me?"

"You expect me to trust you!" Stephen was momentarily in disbelief. "From the moment we first met, you have sought to deceive me. Repeatedly. It would take more than a few days of shared lust, Mary, for me to come to trust you, or do you perceive me to be a weak, besotted fool?"

Mary flinched. How hurtful his words were. She had seen these past few days as more than "shared lust"; she had seen them as the beginning of a shared lifetime. More tears swelled and fell. Her husband was an unfeeling brute—how could she have ever thought otherwise?

Finally she met his cold, unwavering stare, and when she spoke, her tone was bitter. "Treachery suspects treachery, does it not?"

Stephen moved so quickly that Mary had no time to react. He hauled her to her knees and up against his body. "I am so angry that if you continue in this vein, I will lose all control, Mary. You do not want to be near me when that happens. You would not survive should that happen."

Mary did not doubt it. She could feel him shaking with his fury. They were almost nose to nose and eye to eye. His gaze was black, livid. He was terrifying under these circumstances. His grip hurt her tender flesh, too, but in a way, she welcomed the physical pain, for it was easier to bear than the other. She choked on the pain in her heart. "If you cared for me at all, you would not do this."

"If I cared for you, Mary, all that is dear to me would be lost. How clear that is! And even if I cared for you, you could not sway me from my duty to my King." His jaw tightened, their gazes held. "Never could I love an unfaithful wife."

Mary was still. The way he stared at her made her want to tell him that she was not unfaithful, to insist again that she had not been ready to betray him. He almost seemed to be waiting for such a denial, but surely she was wrong. Surely there was no hint that he might love her if she were loyal to him. His manner, his words of the day before when he had given her the red rose, swept through her with stunning force. She began to cry. "Stephen—"

His smile was twisted and he held up his hand, halting her before she could begin she knew not what. "Enough. Cease your tears, cease them now. Your actions have proven your guilt more than any words—or tears—can ever prove your innocence."

"No," Mary whispered, aware of the crushing pain of heartbreak. It flashed through her mind that nothing but a future of misery could await her now—as she had foreseen. Unless they stopped this now. But, dear God, how?

He turned away from her abruptly. He was leaving, and their marriage had been shredded, her love trampled into dust. She raised herself up onto her hands, staring after him. She was almost compelled to run after him. She should not let him leave her upon this note. But then Mary thought about what he intended, and was choked with bitterness, unable to go after him, unable to call out.

He paused abruptly in the doorway, standing with his back rigidly to her. He appeared to be waiting. Mary told herself to speak before it was too late, before their marriage was forever destroyed. She opened her mouth but only sucked air.

His shoulders stiffened. "I am a fool," he said harshly—and then he was gone.

"No!" Mary cried. It struck her then that despite his treachery and his betrayal, it could not end like this. She lunged to her feet and ran after him, out into the hall. "Stephen! Stephen!"

But it was too late. There was no response—he was gone. Mary sank down on the floor, awash freely now in bitter tears and heartache.

Chapter 19

Mary had been confined to her chamber as punishment for her treachery. She had not cared at the time, but she quickly lost her indifference. When her tears finally subsided, she realized that it had grown dark outside, that the stone floor beneath her body was terribly cold, and that she was chilled to the bone herself. She was shivering. Although exhausted from the fight and the emotional upheaval that had accompanied it, she got to her feet.

Her glance took in the small chamber, lost in the night's dark shadows. No fire burned upon the hearth, no tapers were lit, and although she was not hungry, she was thirsty, but no pitcher of water was present. Most of all, she would love to drown her sorrow in a cup of spiced wine. But she might as well ask for Stephen to return to her now, on bended knee, begging her forgiveness.

Mary moved to the bed, suddenly realizing just what her confinement meant. Her husband might very well make her suffer with the cold and with the lack of the usual comforts of food and water, but she could survive that. She wondered, though, if she could survive the humiliation of her punishment. Everyone at Alnwick would soon know of it. By now Stephen's family and retainers certainly knew she was in a forced confinement. Her absence at the dinner table had surely been remarked, and Mary did not doubt that Stephen would explain just why she had failed to appear. He had no reason to dissemble. He was not the kind of man to dissemble in this instance. Mary's cheeks flushed.

She was not the first wife to be so shamed, but that did not matter. She had never expected her marriage to Stephen to come to this! By tomorrow, when Stephen left to make war upon Scotland, all of Alnwick would know that its new mistress was in her chamber in confinement. Mary folded her arms and hugged herself, wondering how she would face his family once she was able to do so, how she would face the lowest of servants.

It was not fair. She had spied, and perhaps that was wrong, but she had never intended to betray him. While he, he had betrayed her, marrying her while intending to war upon her family. Nevertheless she had taken vows, vows to honor and obey him, vows she would keep. They might never recover from this terrible time, they might never recapture the brief joy they had known, but she was his wife regardless of any and all circumstance until God saw fit to part them.

Slowly she adjourned to the bed. She moved like an old woman, but not because of her aching body; because of her aching heart.

Mary had a blanket and a fur with which to ward off the night's chill, fortunately. She curled up beneath the covers. Sleep refused to come, although the oblivion it brought would be so welcome. She wanted to escape her grief—oh, how she wanted to escape—but the argument she had just had with her husband replayed itself over and over again in her mind. She had little strength left in her exhausted state, not enough with which to remain hot and angry, and there was only despair and sorrow vying for her heart instead. And pain.

Sounds began to drift to her, piercing her painful thoughts. She could hear the rumble of deep male voices from the ramparts outside as Alnwick's retainers engaged in some form of unusual nocturnal activity. She dared not imagine what it might be. She was too tired. But she found herself trying to distinguish her husband's voice from the lot. It was probably better that she could not. Look at what her prior lapse into eavesdropping had done. Yet she found herself wondering if he felt any remorse at all for the death of their relationship, if he felt any of the pain.

Mary awoke at dawn. She had slept so heavily that for a moment she was confused, searching for Stephen's big, warm body in bed beside her. However, the sounds that had awoken her, sounds from the bailey below, quickly became recognizable. Mary sat up, fully awake. Stephen was not beside her; last night he had accused her of treachery, and she was in solitary confinement as punishment for her crimes. Mary's stomach wrenched with dismay, his furious image coming quickly to her mind. Last night he had revealed his own treachery. And outside, outside she could hear the ebullient chatter of many men and the stamping hooves and snorts of many mounts, along with the jangle of spurs and bits and bridles, the creaking of leather and the clang of metal weapons.

War. Did they ride to war today—to war upon her people?

Mary slid from the bed, shivering when her bare feet touched the cold stone floor, and rushed to the window. She peered out. Her heart immediately sank.

Perhaps fifty knights, all fully armed with mace and shield, sword and lance, and in complete armor, were mounting up. In their midst the standard bearer already waved the tricolored banner with the oversized bloodred rose in its center. Mary shuddered, her body's reaction having little to do with the cold. She knew that the force that she gazed upon was nothing in comparison to the one the de Warennes would ultimately cast upon the battlefield. Northumberland had hundreds of vassals. If the earl chose, he could field close to four hundred men—Mary knew it for a fact because Malcolm had told her so.

She looked down on the small force assembled below her and wanted to cry. Despair shredded her already broken heart. She was watching an army that was about to make war upon her own people. How could he do this?

It occurred to her that this marriage had been insanity, doomed from the start.

Yet her mind dared to recall the last few days, Stephen's warm glances, his slight smile, and the way he looked at her when his intentions were wicked. She recalled when he had given her the rose.

Mary choked. Her glance slid across the throng below, at first unconsciously and then deliberately searching for her husband. She found him quickly, for he towered above those around him with his great height despite being still on foot. A tear seeped. He was riding off to war on her people; perhaps he would even cross swords with her own kin. Mary hugged herself, filled with anguish. She wondered if she would ever want to forgive him.

Yet she could not take her eyes from him. He had not donned his helmet, so his face was completely revealed, but from this distance, Mary could not make out his expression except as being grim and set. Surely he could feel her watching him. Surely he would know that she would watch him. Could he not at least look up, just once?

With a start Mary realized that despite the fact of their horrible argument the night before, she still felt something for him. Some kind of tendre. In the current situation she could not deny it. For he was going to war. He appeared immortal, but he was not. In any battle, even in a mock tourney, there was always the possibility of death. What if he was hurt today, or even killed? She was sickened by the thought. She was horrified by the thought. Mary gripped the rough stone ledge and leaned forward, impulsively calling out. "Stephen! Stephen!"

He did not hear her, immersed in a dialogue with his squire, and Mary was dismayed. She panted, her heart beat hurtfully; she could not let him leave like this. How wrong she had been to let him leave last night! Determination to attract his attention overwhelmed her. "Stephen!" she shouted. "Stephen!"

He heard her and froze. Then, slowly, he turned his head and looked up at her.

Across the distance separating them, their gazes riveted and held. Mary did not know what to say. She wanted to say that she was sorry, but for what, she was not sure—perhaps for the impasse they had been brought to by their mistrust of each other, perhaps for the era in which they lived. Yet she was angry and she was dismayed; he was so easily riding into battle against her father, just days after their wedding, and his crime was so great that she doubted she would ever forget it. Too, she doubted that they could ever recover what they had once enjoyed, and she despaired of the future that lay in wait for them. But he was her husband—perhaps she was even with his child, a possibility that grew each and every day—and she did not want him to die. Dear Lord, she did not. "God keep you," she whispered finally, knowing he could not hear her, and that even if he guessed what she said, it probably made little difference to him now.

Stephen turned away. Mary wished she had been able to see his face more clearly, to see into his eyes, to glimpse his soul. Too late, she wished they had not fought, she wished she had defused his anger, that she had spent more time denying what he falsely believed, had succeeded in convincing him of her innocence. She wished, too, impossibly, that she had not accused him of treachery. And mostly she wished that last night had been spent altogether differently, not her alone, cold and weary, emotionally beaten and physically battered, in punishment, but the two of them together the way it had been before.

She watched him slip on his helmet. The Norman helm with its nosepiece instantly transformed him, making his appearance sinister and frightening. Stephen mounted his war-horse. Mary inhaled. Fully armed and armored, astride the destrier, he was unrecognizable except as a stranger and an enemy. The urge to cry overcame her.

The knights began to swiftly form into organized lines. She could hear the harsh grating noise of the portcullis being winched up, and the groaning of the wooden drawbridge being lowered. It was hard to breathe, hard to see. She watched through a sudden mist, one formed from the moisture in her eyes, as Stephen rode to the head of one of the columns. The troops moved out.

Mary watched Stephen leave the bailey; quickly he passed through the barbican, and she could not see him anymore.

Still, she watched all of the troops as they left, until the large court was empty and silent, until she heard the portcullis slamming closed, the sound reverberating with finality. She gazed upon the vast, empty bailey, then, as servants began to appear, hurrying to their tasks, she turned and returned to the bed.

She was numb with cold. Before she had barely noticed; now she shivered violently, her teeth chattering. Crawling under the covers, she recalled Stephen as she had last seen him. It was impossible not to be aware of her feelings, which were far from hatred. Mary realized that she had a lot of thinking to do in the time left to her until Stephen returned.

Three days later, as dusk settled over the land, Stephen stood in the entrance of the tent he shared with his father on the edge of the ground that had been turned into a large, muddy battlefield. Once, this land had been green, verdant, and unblemished; now pieces of metal, twisted or broken, and shreds of wool littered the arena; more than a few dead horses were rotting carcasses yet to be removed, picked at by the greedy vultures, and even several human corpses still remained. The stench of death was pervasive.

Stephen stepped outside. Sounds from the makeshift camp drifted to him, most of it weary laughter but some of it female, coming from the many camp whores who always materialized after war to earn a few coins as they relieved the bloodlust of the men. Stephen was very tired and very dirty, and as He was in no mood to talk, he was thankful that he was alone.

Alone for the first time since the battle had begun, Stephen picked his way carefully amongst the leftover debris of war, until the bloody battleground was far behind him. He paused on the edge of a stream, his back shielded by pine trees, and pulled off his leather boots, and then all of his clothing. Stark naked, he waded into the frigid water, then doused himself completely.

He came up shivering and gasping, but it was not enough. Nothing would ever be enough, he suspected, to cleanse either his body or his soul after battle. He submerged himself again.

It had been a long, bloody two-day battle, but Carlisle had fallen, as had been inevitable.

Carlisle was a large town guarded by one single keep which had been built in haste some dozen years ago, and the walls surrounding it were still the original wood. Such construction usually dictated recourse to fire in battle, but the past month's endless rain had determined a wiser course of action, one including both catapult and battering ram. The rotten walls, which should have been replaced years ago, had fallen instantly. The keep had surrendered within the hour.

The real fighting had begun shortly after that when the local lairds had rallied to the area's defense, but they were routed by nightfall, their numbers seriously decimated. When Malcolm's army had next appeared at dawn and attacked in the hope of regaining Carlisle, the Norman forces had already taken up strategic positions and were firmly in control. Still Malcolm had attacked, and the savage warfare had continued for another day.

When the Scot army had finally retreated, seeing their cause as lost—and rightly so—Stephen had seen Malcolm standing in his stirrup irons and shaking his fist at him. It was clear that Canmore was cursing him and vowing revenge.

Stephen sighed, but as his teeth were chattering so badly, it sounded more like a moan. Hurriedly he dressed in the clean clothes he had brought with him. He did not want to recall Malcolm in his defeat and his fury, for to think of him reminded him of his wife. *His wife.* He did not want to think of her either. In fact, he had avoided thinking about her ever since he had ordered her confined to her chamber.

There was a new hardening in his heart. There was also bitterness, one stemming from a horrendous disillusionment, one a man of his age and experience had no right to. Stephen knew he was a fool, but the knowledge did not soothe him.

For Mary had surprised him in the days following their wedding. The sneaky, politically wise, too clever minx had been transformed overnight into a gentle and womanly wife. She had become the perfect wife with such ease, as if she had yearned for such a role her entire life. Stephen knew that could not be true. His wife was no common woman, and no ordinary princess either; the role she would have yearned after undoubtedly could only suit a man. Mary would have much preferred to sit at the war table than at the spinning wheel, or so he would have thought. But once wed to him, it was as if nothing else mattered, as if he were her fondest dream.

His mouth turned down. There was the flash of pain in his chest again, and the very rotten, roiling feeling of betrayal. It had all been an illusion, now shattered thoroughly.

Had he not known it would come to this?

Had he not known that when forced to choose, she would ally herself with Malcolm?

Stephen felt no more guilt, no more regret. He had done his duty, as he must always do. His own personal feelings could not ever interfere in his loyalty to his King. In a savage way, he was glad it had come to this. The King's treacherous invasion of Carlisle had revealed Mary for what she was, a traitor in his own home.

How it hurt.

Briefly he had been overwhelmed with her, briefly he had thought their union a success beyond all expectation. Briefly he had forgotten the short, hate-filled history they shared. How she had pleased him in the past few days! He had known each and every small way she had interjected herself into his life, he had been aware of each and every effort, no matter how small or how large, that she had made to ease his existence, and he had been profoundly pleased and absurdly grateful. It had seemed as if she took joy in what she did for him, in the pleasure she gave him. It had seemed as if she had grown genuinely fond of him. It had almost seemed as if she loved him.

Stephen laughed out loud, the sound bitter and self-mocking. Perhaps he was the weak, besotted fool she had taken him for. His wife did not love him. It had all been a ploy on her part; there was no other explanation. To mend his clothes, see to his meals, even anticipate his moods, to lie with him with the passion of a strumpet, and then, then to spy upon him as he sat in a conference of war—it could only mean that her actions as his wife were insincere.

Stephen paced across foul battleground and ducked into his tent. It was the act of deception that haunted him. It was posing as a perfect wife, not the act of betrayal, spying upon him and his family, that was the source of his ice-cold rage.

He should have known. Mary had lied to him repeatedly from the moment he had first met her, and from that same moment she had been unwavering in her devotion to her country and her kin. He should have known that she would not change, could not change, not in her loyalty, and that the minx could never metamorphose into a dear and gentle wife. He should have known it was an outrageous act. Had she continued to openly defy him after the marriage, and then dared to spy, he might have forgiven her, for he would at least understand her, and even, perhaps, respect her. But she had played a dangerous game, with him and his feelings, and there would not be any forgiveness.

Now that he knew, of course, he would be more careful.

She would not have the opportunity to spy again, or do worse. And still she would be his wife, in fact and in deed, if nothing else. She would manage his household and see to all of his needs. He would give her children; she would bear them, raise them. Yes, she would be his wife in deed, but not in any other way—not in his heart. Never could such a woman have a place in his heart. And the worst of it was that just before he had discovered her treachery and her deception, he had been falling in love with her.

Stephen knew that sleep would elude him for most of this night. Now that the war no longer preoccupied him, it would be impossible to chase his treacherous wife from his thoughts. If only she had denied what she had done. If only . . .

He was a man who dealt in realities, so he must not yearn for what would not be. Tomorrow he was returning to Alnwick. Where once there was joy and comfort in the thought, no more. He settled down upon his pallet, fully clothed. He thought about the greeting he would receive the next day, thought about returning home to a woman who was a more dangerous adversary than any he had ever met upon the battlefield because of the position she held in his home. God, he was tired. So sick and tired of politics and intrigue. How he yearned to return home to open arms and a real embrace. Instead, he would return to Alnwick, where Mary awaited him, his beautiful, traitorous wife.

He pressed his cheek into the straw. A lump rose suddenly in his throat. Dear God, if he faced the truth, he would admit that he felt like a boy of six again, alone and abandoned, confronting his very first bitter betrayal.

Chapter 20

Mary sat on the edge of the bed, her feet dangling over, her back straight, her shoulders erect, her hands clasped in her lap. She had finger-brushed her hair the best that she could and rebraided it, replacing her wimple. Unfortunately she had no clean gown to change into, but she had been able to wash herself somewhat with the water that was brought to her each day. She hoped she looked well. She tried to appear calm and dignified. In case Stephen should come to her directly.

He and his men had ridden into the bailey a few minutes ago. It was impossible not to hear them, they entered with such loud, animated conversation, with a fanfare of horns and happy cries and even some laughter. Mary had been waiting for Stephen to return, aware that it could be just a few days before he did, but her first reaction was dismay. She understood the tenor of the hubbub the returning knights were making well enough—they were victorious. Carlisle had fallen.

How could she not be saddened? She knew that this was only the beginning. Even if the Normans would be satisfied with just this addition to their territory, it could not stop here. Malcolm had never intended to keep the peace anyway, and now he would seek revenge. And this time he was undoubtedly doubly furious, for one of the principals who had betrayed him was his daughter's husband, and not just his daughter's husband but his age-old enemy as well.

She would not think about Carlisle and the political future anymore. Not when her husband had just returned. Not when, even now, he might be climbing the stairs and walking towards her chamber. It was hard to breathe slowly, evenly. It was hard to be calm. What would happen when they next met? Mary trembled.

It had been a half sennight since she had been imprisoned in her room—since she and Stephen had fought so bitterly. Mary knew he was all right, unhurt by the battle, because she had been unable to restrain herself, and she had flown to the window slit to watch as the knights entered the bailey. She had spotted her husband at once, sitting his brown destrier tall and erect, his mail splashed with mud, his helm in the crook of his arm. Had he been wounded, he would not be mounted so. Mary was relieved.

She had brooded many long hours upon her feelings for her husband, upon her past relationship with him and upon the future that now lay in wait for them. Mary had never guessed that she could love such a man, but no matter how it hurt, she did. She was not pleased to love him; how could she be? He had betrayed her father and family for the sake of ruthless, greedy ambition. And he had betrayed her and their marriage. It was unforgivable. But forgive him, she would.

And her forgiveness had less to do with love than it had to do with practicality. She would remain his wife even if she hated him, even if she never forgave him, even if she denied him until he raped her and defied him until he beat her. But she did love him, God help her. So Mary was forgiving him all, and she could only hope that her sensible response to the insanity of the situation would be matched, in the near future, by the mellowing of his own temper and feelings.

And she was not prepared to speculate further. She was not prepared to analyze the extent of her own wants, her own needs, and her own secret longings. It would be enough if an enduring peace could be established between them. She would do her best to continue to see to his comfort, and maybe, one day, he would understand her loyalty. Maybe, in time, he would forget that she had spied upon him, maybe he would one day believe her innocence. She must try to convince him of her innocence now as she had not even attempted to do before.

Mary stiffened as the door to her chamber was unbolted and unlocked. An eternity passed as the heavy door slid open. Disappointment seared her when she saw a servant on the threshold, not her husband. She blinked back a blinding tear, then realized that a big copper bathtub was being carried into the room. More important, Stephen was walking in behind the servants bearing the steaming water.

Mary was frozen. She regarded him uncertainly, fixedly. He did not look at her, entering with a tired, slow stride, his page already helping him out of his mail. Realizing how exhausted he was wrung a response from Mary that, given his recent antipathy towards her, she would have preferred to ignore. But it was impossible; her instinct was to rush to him and help him, soothe him.

She did not. Mary realized that she was not breathing, that her heart was hammering much too quickly, and she took a few steadying breaths. Stephen had shrugged out of the leather vest he wore beneath the armor. She realized that he was finally looking at her.

"Good day, madame," he said, inclining his head.

"Good day, my lord," she breathed.

Silence reigned. The page quickly stripped her husband, a job that belonged to Mary since she was present. Stephen had turned his back to her. As she knew very well that he had no modesty, it was an obvious rejection. Small but real, and it hurt. The tub was full, the servants gone. Stephen lowered himself into the bath, facing away from her, another sign that all was not yet well. Then he told the young squire that he might go. The boy obeyed and they were left alone.

Mary was uncertain. Stephen was obviously calm and rational. Yet she did not think he had forgotten her trespass, or forgiven her for it. Giving her his back, not once but twice, was significant. Perhaps it was a warning, a signal to her to keep her distance.

The last time she had helped him bathe flashed through Mary's mind. Hopelessly she succumbed to intense yearning. She was quite sure that there would never be a repeat of such unabashed, open passion, such mutually flagrant need.

"Shall I help you, my lord?"

Stephen was in the midst of sponging himself with soap and water. He did not turn his head when he spoke. Although fatigue was evident in his tone, he said, "Perhaps another time."

Mary could not move. She had not misread him at all. He had not forgotten anything, he had not forgiven anything. Mary almost sobbed but managed to muffle the sound of despair instead. This man was as far removed from the warm, ardent lover he had been before their fight as he could be.

She was uncertain. She decided to tend the fire, having nothing else to do. She jammed the poker at the dead wood, releasing some of her anger and frustration, but by no means enough of it. Clearly he was intent on avoiding her. But for how long? Recalling the impossibly high stakes—their future—she knew this situation could not continue. She must not allow it to continue in this vein.

Stephen had finished washing himself, and now he lunged to his feet. Mary turned, trembling. A second later he had wrapped his powerful, naked body in a blanket. He did not look at her.

Stephen began to dress. He did not speak. Mary was afraid to approach in order to help him, quite certain her efforts would be rejected yet again. He was making himself very clear. She could not keep her silence. "Will you shun me for the rest of our lives, my lord?"

"Shun you?" Stephen whirled. "I have no intention of shunning you, madame. But if you think to get a warm welcome from me, you have been mistaken."

Her head came up, her nostrils flared. "You are still angry."

He laughed, the sound harsh, unpleasant. "I am still angry, but do not fear. I am in complete control." His gaze was open now, so open that she could see the anger in it, and it was hard and cold.

"I have been punished. But I have not apologized." Knowing she was innocent of treachery made it difficult to continue. "I am sorry."

He stared in some amount of incredulity. "How sincere you seem!"

"I *am* sorry!" Mary cried. "Stephen, I swear to you that I never intended to betray you to my father."

He cocked his head. "Do you not think your avowal a bit untimely?"

"It may be untimely, but 'tis the truth."

"I doubt you comprehend the meaning of the word 'truth,' madame."

Mary inhaled. "You are cruel."

"Why do you seek to convince me now? Were you not spying?"

"Yes, but—"

"Do you plot anew against me? Do you seek to soften me once again, in order to wield another blow?"

"No!"

"If I thought your regret sincere,'twould be enough—I could not ask for more than genuine repentance. But no apology, sincere or not, is enough to undo my regrets, nor my anger. I do not take betrayal lightly, not from my wife, never from my wife."

"But I swear I am telling you the truth—I never intended betrayal!"

"As you swore before God to honor and obey me?" He held up a hand; his eyes flashed warningly, dangerously.

Mary could not back down. "I did not break my vows."

"I have had enough of this, madame," Stephen said very tightly.

He was staring at her. Mary realized she was glaring at him through a veil of tears. She fought for composure.

"Your confinement is ended, if that is any help," Stephen told her. "I expect you to join us downstairs for dinner. My bath is still warm. Why do you not take advantage of it?"

"How charitable you are."

His own fists clenched, his eyes darkened even more. "Once I was very charitable towards you, or have you forgotten? You are lucky, madame, extremely lucky, that I am ending your punishment, as light as it was, and that I am intent on keeping you as my wife, as deceitful as you are."

Mary was quick to protest, unable to keep the bitterness from her tone. "You have no choice, my lord, and you know it. We are wed before God until death!"

"There are many ways to end a marriage such as ours," Stephen remarked pointedly.

Mary was shaken, frightened and aghast. Surely she was misunderstanding—he could not be threatening her with— "What—what do you say, my lord?"

"I am suggesting that you tread cautiously, madame, if you wish to fare well with me."

"Would you ask for an annulment?" she asked in horror.

"Did I say that? No, madame, I would never ask for an annulment. You have yet to give me my heir; need I remind you of that?"

Mary met his cool stare.

Then he smiled, but it was hardly pleasant. "Should there be another instance of treachery, madame, I will exile you. If I am generously disposed, it would be to Tetly, a personal manor of mine on the coast; if not, a convent in France."

Mary was white. "And—if I should bear your heir?"

Stephen's smile was cold and brief. "That would change nothing, madame; children are born to exiled wives every day, as you well know." Stephen turned on his heel. "Do not keep us waiting." He shut the door behind him.

Mary was still, but only for a moment. Then she picked up his helm, which lay on the chest beside her, and threw it furiously at the door. It made a resounding crash, which barely pleased her. She sank onto the chest, scattering his clothes and mail, shaking.

Dear God. She felt as if she were a hairsbreadth away from a fate almost as horrible as death, and perhaps as irrevocable. Exile. He had no feelings left for her, and he would exile her in an instant. That, too, seemed abundantly clear. Mary wanted to cry.

Mary cradled her abdomen with her hands. He had said he would exile her even if she was with child. His statement was proof that he still expected her to give him an heir. She was glad she had not said anything. She was likely with child, for this month she'd had no flux. The secret she kept might very well prove to be the only weapon she had left, if ever she dared to use it. That was why she did not go to him and tell him what he would be glad to hear. And her restraint had nothing to do with ridiculous romanticism. Certainly now, after the past hour, she could not be such a fool to think that there would come a time of ease between them, a time of light and laughter, a time when she might bring him such joyous tidings in love, instead of undeclared war.

At dinner Mary learned the details of what had transpired at Carlisle. The countess wanted to be apprised of it all, and her questions were sharp, pointed, and endless. The earl had remained in the North, restoring order, Geoffrey had returned to Canterbury, but Brand, on his way back to London with his men, had stopped at Alnwick for the night. However, it was Stephen who answered his mother's questions, his tone level and dispassionate. How easily he spoke of his triumph over her land and her people.

Mary listened and said nothing. After the disastrous encounter with her husband earlier, she was in a sore and wary mood, and to hear of how quickly Carlisle had fallen did nothing to improve it.

Too, it was the first time that Mary had seen anyone other than Stephen since being punished for spying. She was guilty of eavesdropping but innocent of treachery, yet she was afraid to look the countess in the eye. She knew how intelligent that woman was, how much she loved her husband and Alnwick, which had once been a Saxon fief belonging to her father. Mary imagined that Lady Ceidre was furious with her—as well as terribly disappointed.

So Mary was startled when the countess addressed her, her tone kind. "I am sure this must be difficult for you, Mary."

Mary looked up, startled, finally meeting the countess's gaze. "Your pardon, madam?"

"How difficult this must be for you, to be married to my son, a Norman, who wars upon your country—and your family."

Mary was pale. She felt every eye at the long table below upon her, as well as her husband's, who sat beside her on the dais. Yet the countess was genuinely sympathetic, Mary was sure. But how could that be? "Yes," she finally croaked. "It is very difficult, very upsetting." To her horror, a tear slipped from her eyes.

The countess sat on Stephen's other side, but she leaned across her son to pat Mary's hand. "Stephen probably has not told you, but he told me that all of your family is well, Mary."

Mary drew in a breath. She had worried, too, about one of her brothers or her father being hurt or killed. It seemed that, even though she had learned just how ruthless Malcolm could be, she could not be oblivious to him—he would always be her father. Unable to keep the eagerness from her voice, she faced her husband for the first time since she had come downstairs. "You are certain?"

He stared at her. "As certain as can be. I believe that Edgar was wounded, but I saw him fighting until the end, so it could not have been too grave."

"Edgar!" Mary's heart twisted. "You are sure he is well enough?"

Stephen nodded, still watching her.

Mary sighed with relief, trembling. It struck her that her current predicament could be so much worse. She and Stephen could be at this impasse, yet it could be complicated by the death of someone she loved. Mary prayed that would never be. But if Northumberland's forces kept clashing with Malcolm's, was it not inevitable? She shivered, struck with horrible premonition.

"It was not easy for me either, once upon a time," the countess was saying.

When Mary looked at the countess again, she could not help peeking at Stephen, who now regarded his glass of wine, grimly. Had she somehow displeased him again?

Mary turned to his mother, her curiosity genuine. "Because you were Saxon?"

"I was not just Saxon, but my father's by-blow," Lady Ceidre admitted candidly. "And Rolfe, as you must have heard, was one of the Conqueror's most trusted men. The gulf between us could not have been wider, especially as he personally was given the responsibility for bringing the North to its knees. Although William determined the policy, it was brutal and cruel. When I first met my husband, he was ordering a small village burned to the ground for harboring Saxon archers, archers who had ambushed his men. He ordered it burned, every square inch of it, even the corn, which meant that one and all would not just freeze that winter, but starve as well. I begged him for mercy, but he refused. How I hated him."

Mary stared, stunned. "But—if you hated him so, how could you have come to love him as you do?" As Mary waited for the countess to reply, she was even more aware of Stephen sitting beside her. Only an inch or two separated their bodies, so it had been impossible not to be aware of him and become somewhat distressed by his proximity the longer they sat together, but now he did not move and did not breathe, as keenly interested in the conversation between her and his mother as she was, or so it seemed.

"Well—" Lady Ceidre smiled slightly "—he is one of the handsomest men you have ever seen, is he not? I could not help noticing. And, as you know, my husband is a good man—he was obeying his King, nothing more, as we all must do. Although I secretly supported my rebel brothers, I fell in love with him. To make matters worse, he was soon married to my sister, Alice, my father's legitimate daughter. We were enemies from the start, but we fell in love." For a moment she was obviously lost in the past, her face suddenly young, a trick of the rosy light, her eyes shining, which was no trick at all. She sighed. "It was not easy. I betrayed him again and again, believing it to be my duty. He was so furious. But . . . time heals all wounds, Mary. Time healed ours. And when the wounds were less painful, the love was still there, stronger than before."

Mary wondered what had happened to Alice, the earl's first wife. Obviously she had died in a timely manner, allowing the earl to marry his lady love. " 'Tis somehow a sad story," Mary said, aware of Stephen listening to her intently, "but beautiful, so beautiful."

"I am a very lucky woman," Ceidre said. She smiled gently. "And so are you, my dear, even if you do not yet know it. Sometimes the path to happiness is long and difficult, but the trial in getting there makes the final reward so much sweeter."

Mary looked down at the trencher she shared with her husband. Although they shared it, although he chose her portions for her as he should, there had been no warmth, no love, in his actions. They had been politeness and duty and nothing more. Mary was assaulted by the foolish romanticism she sought to avoid. How she found herself wishing for the kind of love that the countess had found with the earl, a love strong enough to endure the worst of times— a love grand enough for all time.

The hall was unusually quiet. Mary realized that the many retainers seated below them had been listening to the countess's every word—and hers. Suddenly she looked up, well aware of what everyone was thinking, the countess included. They were all convinced of her guilt. Thinking that she, like the Lady Ceidre, had committed treachery against her husband, foolishly but deliberately. In a love story told on a full belly and in the haze brought on by good wine, it was acceptable and even romantic; in reality it was not. She met the countess's gaze. "I did not betray my husband, madame," she said to her alone. But her voice rang clear, and everyone heard it. "I would never break my wedding vows."

Stephen avoided retiring for the night. Even though he was exhausted, enough so that, as he sat in the Great Hall before the dying fire, the many retainers asleep on their pallets, his mother and sister long since gone to their beds, and his wife as well, he could feel his lids growing heavier by the moment. But still he stared into the glowing cinders and watched the occasional flame. Mary's vehement denial of duplicity echoed in his mind.

The front door groaning open and then banging closed roused him. Brand sauntered into the hall. He saw Stephen and started, then grinned. "What? You are not yet to bed?" He came closer. There was no mistaking what had kept him out so late. He wore a heavy, sated air, and when he slid into the seat beside his brother, Stephen remarked that his blond hair was tousled, disheveled with straw.

"If I had such a bride, I would not linger here," Brand said, grinning.

"Perhaps that is the problem."

Brand's smile died. "What ails you, Stephen? Your unhappiness is evident."

"You need to ask?" He heard how bitter he sounded, and resolved to speak with more detachment.

"I know you were not pleased to go to war against Scotland," Brand said slowly. "But you had no choice. Surely she understands."

"She does not understand me—nor do I understand her." Stephen stood, placing his back to his brother. Brand did not respond, so he turned slightly. "Tell me, brother, what do you think of my wife?"

Brand grew wary. " 'Tis quite the question."

"Does she not appear the angel? Beauty, perfection, and innocence?"

"Yes."

Stephen laughed, once. "There is nothing perfect or innocent about her."

Brand stood. "Stephen, I know what happened. Geoffrey told me."

"Then you know that she is a little liar."

Brand hesitated. " 'Tis a good thing that you have found out her true inclinations. Now forget it. Go and get an heir upon her, and then, if she dares to repeat her behavior, banish her as you must do."

"How simple you make it sound." Stephen faced Brand, his smile mocking. "I fear I will be reluctant to send her into exile if the time should come that I must."

Brand stared. "You would have to, Stephen. This time her spying came to naught, but what if she had succeeded in warning Malcolm? Many Normans would be dead this day—perhaps even you or I."

His jaw was tight. "You think I do not know this? I know it too well!"

"Then just make sure you do not forget it," Brand said very seriously. Then he smiled and gripped his brother's shoulder. "It is late. I know the cure for what ails you. Go to your beautiful bride and beget that heir. I guarantee it will ease your mind." Brand grinned.

Stephen watched him walk across the hall to the pallet he had made. He could not reveal to his brother that he lingered in the hall because he was afraid. Celibacy, even if only in regard to his wife, was out of the question—at least until she had conceived or given him an heir. Thus he had every intention of taking Mary as he willed, as he must in order to beget an heir, but how could he control himself? For he was afraid he might still be overwhelmed by uncontrollable passion, in spite of her treachery. If that was the case, Mary would recognize it immediately and would gain the upper hand.

Every instinct he had was raised in warning in a manner similar to that when he entered the lists or a great war. Undoubtedly he would be entering dangerous territory when he entered her bed. He would be giving her immense power over him, power he dared not trust her with.

And if his threats to exile her were only idle threats, she would soon comprehend that, too. Mary was too clever by far. His threats must not be idle. If given cause, he must do what he must, he must send her away, no matter how distasteful.

If not, Mary could become the agent of his destruction.

Stephen quickly turned. He was no coward. To be afraid of his wife was the height of cowardice. He had always done what he must do. If she gave him cause, he would exile her immediately. And he would control himself in bed, so she would not guess how obsessed with her he had become. Hadn't he learned, a long time ago, when a small boy held hostage at Court, how to chase his feelings into oblivion? Then it had been a matter of survival. Now it might be a matter of survival, too.

Mary did not pretend to sleep. As was customary, she lay naked beneath the blankets and furs of her bed, her hair unbound, uncovered, and brushed out. It shone in the flickering firelight. As Stephen had suggested, she had bathed before dinner, although not in his bath, which had been filthy. She had washed her hair as well as her body, knowing very well how Stephen had once admired it.

Mary cradled a pillow, thinking of Stephen anxiously. Would he sleep with her tonight? Would he try to make love to her? She did not think he would inconvenience himself and sleep on a pallet in the hall below, no matter how he might wish to avoid her. At dinner he had acted casually towards her, which indicated to her that he would indeed share their bed tonight. But she dared not guess if he would touch her.

How glad she was that she had not told him she had conceived. Then he would have every excuse to shun her, and he would likely assuage his lust elsewhere. Just the thought of him going to another woman made Mary rigid. She thought she could tolerate almost anything, but not that. Not his infidelity.

Her thoughts wandered to Stephen's mother. She became wistful. She easily imagined how Lady Ceidre must have felt as a young girl, her father dead, her brothers dispossessed and in hiding, planning their rebellion, while falling in love with the enemy, a man married to her sister. It was a tragic story, one seemingly impossible to resolve. Yet there had been a glorious resolution. The bastard Saxon girl had become the Countess of Northumberland, wife to her lover, the mother of three strong sons and one beautiful daughter, powerful and elegant and beloved.

Mary could not help yearning for such a future, too. But she must be mad. It would be enough, she thought, to be in Stephen's good graces. She would never receive that kind of love from him. But—her heart turned over—there would be children. Or at least a child. Perhaps their mutual love for that child would bring them closer together, perhaps one day he would become genuinely fond of her. Yet could that ever be enough?

Mary stiffened, hearing Stephen's footsteps. All hopes, all deliberations upon what might be their future, fled in that instant. She was frozen, unmoving, not daring to breathe. The door groaned softly as he opened and closed it. Her shoulders were so stiff, they hurt. She listened to him disrobing. First his sword belt, which grated loudly as he laid it down. Other belts dropped to the floor without ceremony. Mary heard the soft whisper of fabric as he removed his tunics. She could visualize him standing bare-chested in his boots, braies, and hose. The boots thumped as they hit the floor. More fabric whispered teasingly.

What kind of woman am I? Mary wondered as he slid into the bed with her. His body did not touch hers, but she could not relax. Her own body was pulsing in acute awareness of him. How could he have such an effect upon her? Her life was a shambles, desperately in need of salvaging, yet she barely cared. Instead, she lay rigid, hoping he would touch her. Knowing he would not.

He did not. Long, slow, torturous minutes ticked by. Mary wondered if he thought her to be asleep. She did not think he would show her any consideration, not under the present circumstances. It became clear to Mary that he had no intention of touching her. Despite his words of earlier that day, he was in fact shunning her. Dear God, if they did not at least have passion, then they had nothing and there was no hope! And no amount of desperate wishing was going to make him turn to her!

Mary was terrified. Could he have become indifferent to her, almost overnight? Could the treachery he had perceived have doused the brilliant fires of their passion?

She thought with frantic speed. Passion was a woman's ancient weapon. For them, it could be another beginning, or at least one single form of intimacy, perhaps the only form, for them to share. Seduction was also a timeless method of reconciliation. And Stephen would not refuse her, would he? Could she not seduce him?

In an act of both desperation and bravery, Mary turned over to face him. He lay on his side, facing away from her. Dreading his rejection, Mary touched his shoulder.

He was as stiff as a board. "What are you doing?" he gritted.

There was no possible answer she could make, so Mary slid her hand down his thick bicep, then pressed the length of her body against his, her breasts to his back, her hips cupping his buttocks. And she touched her mouth to the sweet spot on his neck, just below his ear.

He jerked. "Cease, madame. I am warning you."

His voice was raw. Mary was frozen, wondering if his tone was due to anger—or desire. "Stephen, I am your wife."

He said nothing. But she could hear his harsh, uneven breathing.

Mary pressed closer, wanting to tell him that she loved him, sweeping her hand across his chest and down his abdomen. She gasped. The too ripe tip of him quivered against her hand. He was thick and swollen, slick and aroused. Exultation rushed through her. Regardless of the chasm between them, he desired her—and how.

"Stephen," she whispered, but it sounded much like a moan. And as she spoke, her fingers curled around him. He inhaled once, hard and long.

"You are a witch," he said harshly through clenched teeth.

She realized he was fighting her, and she could not understand why. "No, I am your wife," she returned. Her own painful excitement made her unthinkably bold. She caressed him as he had taught her to do. He gasped with strangled pleasure. Mary began to shake. "Please, Stephen. Come into me, oh dear, please."

"Damn you," he said. But he rolled over with lightning swiftness, pinning her beneath him. Mary embraced him hard, spreading her thighs wide to accommodate him. His phallus nudged her, but he was frozen and unmoving over her.

Their gazes met. His was tortured.

"Why do you fight yourself?" she cried. "Why do you fight me? Come, darling, please!"

Stephen moved. Wordlessly he thrust into her, burying his hard length to the hilt. Mary gasped in pleasure. He withdrew slowly, his entire body shaking as he held himself in check. And very, very slowly he entered her again.

Mary wept. Never had she known such pleasure. Yet she sensed he was forcing an inexplicable kind of self-control upon himself, but why?

"Stephen," she panted, "I cannot . . . stand . . . this."

He moaned. And his control shattered. Mary cried out when he began to move, fast and hard and mindless. Mary threw her head back, exultant, sobbing her intense pleasure, instinctively realizing that she had won even though she barely understood the prize.

Stephen paused to kiss her. Mary wept. Stephen's kiss was openmouthed, hot and devouring, and if he felt nothing for her out of bed, here, at least, he felt all. His kiss brought her to another stunning peak of ecstasy, startling them both.

Stephen's growl came low and long in his throat. He forced himself into her deeper, more intimately, plunging with abandon, captive to his lust. Still Mary welcomed him.

Their passion spiraled out of control. The lovers wrestled upon the bed, across it, and nearly slid to the floor. He rose to his knees; she rose to hers. Again they kissed, their tongues mating now as their bodies just had. Lithely Stephen turned her away from him. She gripped the head of the bed. His hands splayed out over her wet, swollen heat. He whispered in her ear, an endearment, followed by something terribly graphic. It was too much for Mary. As he entered her from behind, filling her womb with his hot, potent seed, she keened wildly, ecstatically, wracked by violent pleasure. And when she had died and been reborn, she smiled to herself. There was hope after all.

"Please do not turn from me, Stephen."

Stephen lay upon his back, the covers up to his waist, one arm flung across his face. He had regained his sanity some time ago, but was reluctant to move his arm and regard her. He knew well enough that she could not discern his expression. Hadn't he already revealed enough? He regretted every instance of the past hour, the way a drunkard does the previous night's ale, with the full knowledge that there was no avoiding such self-destructive behavior again and again.

Slowly he removed his arm. Mary was sitting up unabashedly in bed beside him, her small breasts naked, her small nipples erect from the cold, her hair streaming over her shoulders, tinged with gold from the firelight. She looked as content as any kitten that had lapped up all the cream. Her tone in addressing him had been simple; her smile was not. It was suggestive, teasing, and satisfied all at once.

Stephen damned himself. The sight of her, and her expression, and the knowledge of how well matched they were, was even now causing his groin to stir. His worries had been justified. His passion had been out of bounds, and she knew it—and was more than pleased. In fact, the woman sitting beside him was adorable enough to pounce upon again—yet he knew, he damn well knew, there was nothing about her he should adore. "You look pleased, madame," he said frostily.

"I am." She was arch, still smiling. "You have pleased me."

Stephen sat, dwarfing her. "I did not lie with you to please you."

"No, you chose to suffer rather than to turn to me. Why? Because of some misplaced pride?"

"You ask far too many questions, madame. I am your lord. I need not answer a single one."

She was hurt. "We have just shared a grand passion, but you will pretend it was nothing, will you not? So you can continue to castigate me for a treachery I swear I did not commit!"

"We shared nothing more than mutual lust," he said harshly, telling himself that he must not believe her—he must not. The facts were clear. He would be mad to believe her in spite of the facts.

She was angry. "My lord," she said, her tone too sweet, "I will have you know that I have seen men and women coupling, more than once. And I assure you their efforts were nothing—nothing—like ours! Do not think me a fool?"

"You have watched men and women coupling?" he echoed. Disbelief suddenly became unquenchable amusement. Of course Mary had; her curiosity was indomitable. "Madame, you tell me you have spied upon lovers and you do not even blush?"

"Well, I do have six brothers, Stephen, and it was impossible to restrain myself. I wondered time and again why they chased the women so. In truth, once faced with the act itself, I thought it all quite amusing, not anything else."

He laughed despite himself, too easily imagining Mary lurking in the bushes and spying upon an amorous couple. Mary laughed with him. When he realized, he quickly sobered. Then, to his dismay, she gave him a long, bold look. "I thought it all very amusing, the groping and the panting—until you taught me that there is nothing at all amusing about it."

He forced himself to break glances with her, while his manhood stiffened involuntarily. "You may believe whatever it is you choose to believe, madame, and if you choose to believe our passion special, so be it. I want a son. I want a son from you, the sooner, the better. That is the sum of it."

Mary stared at him unblinkingly. Then she dared to smile yet again, this time smugly. "If you say so, my lord. If you say so."

And that morning she awoke him with her hands and her mouth, and afterwards she dared to challenge him with more of her sweet laughter.

Mary knew that she was terribly lucky. For whatever reason, fate had decided to treat her well. For she and Stephen, it seemed, were well into a sturdy truce.

By night he made love to her, his passion belying his ridiculous words. He could not keep his hands from her, he gloried in her body; their passion was undeniable, and by no means ordinary. At night, in their chamber, in their bed, Mary knew sublime pleasure, supreme confidence, and sweet hope.

By day he was polite. In return, Mary was equally courteous. She was astute enough to know that he had not forgiven her, nor had he forgotten; he did not trust her yet. But he treated her in the manner in which most decent men treated their wives. That was enough. For now. It was the beginning they had needed, the beginning she had craved. In time, she dared to hope that he might send her an intimate look, a warm, lingering regard, as he had before. In time, there might even be more gifts, further proof of appreciation, and maybe even the seeds of his love. In time there might even be another rose.

Several days passed. Mary was in no rush. As long as Stephen continued to shower her with passion at night, as long as their exchanges were pleasant by day, their marriage was well on the road to recovery.

The one small blot upon it all was the fact of Mary's pregnancy. She had not told him. Not yet. She could not help being anxious, both because she hated being dishonest and because she could guess what his reaction would be if he learned the truth himself. This time he would be right in accusing her of deceit. Of course, she would have to tell him soon, but she would wait another month. Her monthly time had always been undependable, so he would not be able to accuse her of trickery. Trickery it was, but Mary had no choice. Their marriage was not on a firm enough footing yet. Mary was determined that they retain their passion, for it was the only form of intimacy they shared. She sensed that if Stephen were to know that she was pregnant, he would immediately cease making love to her. As much as he gloried in her body, he disliked his own capitulation, and she knew it. He was not ready to admit that he needed her. Mary was not about to give him any reason to escape her bed and find his pleasure elsewhere.

Because all was going so well, Mary was very surprised when Stephen sought her out in the middle of the morning in the kitchens. To her knowledge, that was a place he had never entered even once in his entire life. She froze at the sight of him, as did every cook and maid, every skivvy and every lad. His expression was dark and grim. Foreboding claimed Mary. She shoved the meat pie she had been inspecting at the maid standing beside her and rushed towards her husband. "My lord? What is it?"

His smile was a parody of good cheer; indeed, it hinted at distaste. He took her arm, leading her outside. "You have a visitor, madame."

"A visitor?" Mary was confused. "But who?"

He smiled again, this time very unpleasantly. "Your brother Edward."

Mary froze. She drained of all color. "Edward?"

Stephen's smile had transformed itself into a snarl. "Why are you surprised, my dear? Have you not been expecting just such a visit?"

All of her efforts at reconciliation were in dire jeopardy, and Mary knew it. Stephen stared at her as if she were a loathsome traitor. "No!" she cried, grabbing his sleeves.

"No! No! I have not summoned Edward! I do not know what this means!"

"If you have not summoned him and if you do not know what this means," Stephen said coldly, "I am sure that in no time you will. He awaits you in the hall, madame wife."

Chapter 21

Stephen escorted her out of the kitchens and across the backyard to the keep. Mary had to run to keep up with his long, determined strides. He gripped her hand so she could not balk. There was no question that he was angry, that he thought the worst. "Stephen! Stop! Please!"

They paused at the back door, used only by servants to carry hot food quickly into the hall, face-to-face. Mary was desperate and unable to believe her misfortune—Edward's timing could not have been worse. Why could he have not come next month or the month after, when Stephen was convinced of her innocence, or when, at least, the instance of her eavesdropping was so far in the past as to be nearly forgotten? Mary thought her hope was not ill-placed, for she believed that within another month or so, he would be close to capitulation; that they would be sharing more than just heated passion, that they would be sharing trust.

"Do you not wish to greet your brother, madame?"

"No!" The word was out of Mary's mouth before she even thought it in her mind. And the instant she had spoken, she knew she could refuse to see Edward, and by doing so, regain so much more of Stephen's trust. She should refuse

301

to see him. If she turned her back on her family, especially now, in such a blatant way, Stephen would have to accept the fact that her loyalty now belonged to him.

But she could not. Her very nature rebelled at the notion. She was innocent of treachery to begin with, she was being the best wife she could to her husband, and she did not want to cut her ties to her family, not now, not ever. She would not.

Too, Edward would have news of her family. After the battle of Carlisle, with so much renewed animosity between her family and Stephen's, not to mention the sporadic acts of war that were still a daily occurrence, there had been no correspondence between her and Scotland.

"You do not wish to speak with Edward?" Stephen asked, his eyes narrowed.

Tears came to Mary's eyes. A dark premonition swept her, that she would quickly come to rue this day. "No, I must speak with him." Her voice was at once both fierce and broken.

His smile was broken, as well. He gestured. "After you, madame wife."

His tone was mocking, bitter. Mary looked him in the eye. "Do not believe the worst. Please. My lord, I will not betray you."

"We shall soon see, shall we not?" Stephen returned coolly.

Mary was angry then. How quick he was with his false assumptions! She hurried into the hall, ignoring him.

It was deserted, a rare event. Except for her brother, of course, who sat at the long trestle table, accompanied by Fergus, one of her father's closest kinsmen. Mary's heart gladdened despite her predicament. How she loved Edward, and it had been so long. She struggled free of her husband's grasp and rushed across the large chamber into her oldest brother's arms.

She cried a little as he embraced her. Edward loved her. From the time she could first walk, he had always been there to rescue her from her mischievous adventures, and after, he had always been there to defend her lack of restraint. He was not just her older brother and something of a hero, he was her dear, dear friend, a friend she had sorely missed, a friend she desperately needed. Finally Edward gave her over to Fergus for a gigantic bear hug. Mary wiped away her tears when the big redhead released her. Somehow she was both joyous and sad at the very same time.

"How you glow, little sister," Edward said softly while smiling and appraising her. When he smiled he was one of the handsomest men that she knew. His teeth were very white, his skin very tanned, his hair so dark an auburn that sometimes it seemed black. "Marriage must agree with you."

Mary almost laughed. A few days ago she would have agreed wholeheartedly. Then she realized that Stephen stood behind her, silently listening, silently observing. Her smile became determined. "I am not sorry to be wed." That was the truth. She hoped Stephen understood.

The look Stephen gave her was decidedly hostile. Mary almost backed away from him. He gave her a mocking smile. "Enjoy your visitors, madame. As you undoubtedly wish a private moment, I shall leave you to see to my own affairs."

Stephen was walking away. Mary forgot about her brother, racing after him. "Wait! My lord!" She caught up to him. "Stephen, what are you doing? Why would you leave me alone with Ed? Why do you not stay with us?" She spoke in a low, rapid whisper.

"Do you not trust yourself, Mary?"

She winced. "You think to test me?"

"I think to let you hang yourself," he said, and then he strode past her with the force of a whirlwind. The heavy front door of the keep thudded closed behind him.

Mary trembled. Dear God, Stephen did not trust her at all, and had he not just told her why he had left her alone, she would think him mad. But he was not mad. For instead of sitting with her and her brother, not giving her a chance to play at treachery, he was coldly and deliberately allowing her the privacy to scheme against him if she willed.

"He does not appear very pleased by my visit," Edward sighed. "He appeared murderous while we were embracing. Unfortunately, I do not think it was because of misbegotten jealousy."

"No, he is most definitely not jealous of you, Ed," Mary managed.

"Are you all right, Mary?" Edward asked while Fergus scowled.

"A' course she is na all right," Fergus said roughly in his thick brogue. "She's married to the Devil himself, an' hateful he is, too. We should take the lassie home wi' us, Ed."

"No!" Mary cried, genuinely shocked by the idea. "He is not so bad, Fergus, really." She took a calming breath. "I am just surprised that he would leave us alone." But her surprise was wearing off. Did he think to trick her into revealing herself? For it occurred to her that he would never leave her alone to scheme against him—he must have spies about. And—her heart quickened—as that was not her intention, his spies would have nothing to report.

"Mary?" Edward took her arm. "Are you really not sorry to be wed to him?" His voice was low, so that any spies might not hear him. Edward was also astute.

"No, Ed, I am not sorry to be Stephen's wife." She spoke normally. Let the spies hear me now, she thought with sudden satisfaction. "But it has not been easy. You see, I have been trying so hard to win my husband's trust. He has accused me of treachery, for he caught me spying upon him."

Edward paled. "Mary—you heeded Father? You would spy upon your husband?"

"No! No! Father told you that he asked me to spy? I would never spy upon my husband! I was curious, though, and you know how I am when curious." She felt hot tears rise. "How I regret my foolish actions. We had discovered how pleasant marriage could be, when Stephen caught me eavesdropping. And now we are just recovering from that incident; Stephen was so close to forgiving me, perhaps even about to realize my innocence, when you came. I am glad to see you, I am, but now Stephen thinks me a traitor again. For he thinks that you are here to receive information from me or to plot and scheme with me against him."

Edward sighed, leading her to the table. "I am sorry. In truth, Malcom sent me to find out why you failed to warn him about the invasion. I will be glad to tell him that you have no intention of breaking your wedding vows. Indeed, I already said as much, knowing you as I do."

Mary hugged her brother. "Thank you, Ed." It was on the tip of her tongue to ask Edward how their father could ask such a terrible thing of her, but the topic was still too painful, and she did not.

Instead, she thought of her husband, imagining the report his spies would make to him. Her spirits lifted immeasurably. "Now, no more politics. Is Edgar well? I heard he was wounded at Carlisle."

Edward and Fergus stayed for dinner. Mary's mood was joyous. She laughed readily and smiled constantly. What had begun as a disastrous blow to her marriage had now turned into a wonderful boon! For Stephen's spies would report the conversation between her and her brother in exact detail—and he would know that she had not spied upon him, that she never would.

Obviously Stephen had yet to speak with his spies, for he did not appear to be pleased during their noon meal. He ignored Mary, and every time her laughter rang out, his mouth pressed hard together. She did not mind. Soon, very soon, he would know the truth, and he would hardly ignore her then.

At first there was much tension between Stephen and his guest, Edward. It was not their first meeting; they had spoken in London at Court, both before their wedding and during it. Mary vaguely recalled that they had gotten along very well then. Now, so soon after Carlisle, Edward was grim and quiet, Stephen displeased and brooding. As Mary's attempts at making conversation were firmly rebuffed by her husband, it was left to the countess to smooth things over.

And Lady Ceidre was an expert at managing hostile factions in social settings. Swiftly she drew both Edward and Stephen into innocuous and pleasant conversation. Once broken, the tension swiftly died. It soon became apparent that Stephen and Edward liked each other despite the recent battle for Carlisle, despite the history of warfare and politics that lay like a gaping chasm between them. They began to converse with increasing amiability. Following the countess's lead (and she was now obviously satisfied and sitting back quietly to observe her handiwork), they steered carefully clear of all topics politic.

As Mary watched her brother and her husband, her joy grew. One day Edward would be King of Scotland, she had no doubt, and it would be a great thing for Northumberland. Perhaps, because Edward was less of a fighter than her father, not any less brave, but more peaceful of character and less truculent, the constant battling in the border country would diminish and even end. Mary could imagine a day when peace reigned, she could even imagine more meals like this one, with her husband and brother at the same table, both amiable and well disposed towards each other.

Edward and Fergus took their leave after the dinner. They had come to Alnwick with a considerable force, and their men had been awaiting them outside Alnwick's walls all this time. Mary watched them leave from the ramparts, feeling both terribly hopeful and unbearably sad. She wondered when she would see him again—she wondered if her dreams would ever really come true.

Mary was restlessly pacing the bedchamber, waiting for Stephen, when he finally appeared that night. He had disappeared after the noon meal, and she had not seen him since. She had been eagerly awaiting this moment all afternoon and evening. By now Stephen had learned of her innocence, and her final exoneration was near.

He seemed surprised to see her awake. Then his cool gaze slid right past her and he began to undress.

Mary was stunned. Wasn't he going to say something? Or did he have so much pride that he could not admit he was at fault? Or did he no longer care? No—that was impossible! "My lord? Let me help you." She sprang forward.

He did not look at her. "I can manage myself," he said, removing her hands from his belt. "Go to bed."

Mary froze. *Something was not right.* "Stephen?" She laid her palm on his back. He had yet to shrug out of his undertunic, but he turned quickly away, and her hand slid off of his body.

"Do not bother me, Mary."

"What—what is wrong?"

"What is wrong?" He laughed harshly. "Nothing, dear wife, nothing at all."

"But have you not spoken with your spies?" Mary asked frankly.

He looked at her as he dropped his undertunic on the floor. Firelight played over his wide, bare, muscular chest. "My spies?"

Mary's heart began to sink. "Did you not have spies listening to my conversation with Edward today?"

"No, Mary, I did not."

Mary was so stunned with disappointment that she could not speak. Tears finally crept into her eyes.

"How distressed you are." He sat and kicked off his boots, one by one.

"Why?" she whispered, her vision so blurred, she could not see his face clearly. "Why not?"

"For precisely the reason you wished for me to have spies present, madame." He stood, naked, and moved past her to the bed. "My spies would learn nothing of value, as you would admit nothing except what you wanted them to hear and relay back to me."

Mary was aghast. She backed away from him automatically. She had been ecstatic all that day, thinking to be proven innocent at long last, dreaming of the joy that would come again into their life, dreaming of how Stephen would hold her, the endearments he might whisper in her ear, and now she crashed sickeningly and found herself at pit bottom. "I never thought in that manner," she whispered. But hadn't she, in a way? Hadn't she been thinking of his spies as she spoke every single word?

"Come now, Mary, a clever lass like you? I would not waste my time spying upon you when you fully expected it." His glance was brief but searing. Then he climbed into the bed.

Mary stared at the fire, unseeing. "I am not so clever," she whispered finally. She turned to look at her husband, who was stretched out on his back, his eyes closed, as if asleep. And she was angry.

She pounced on the bed, on him. She hit him with her fists. He grabbed them instantly, restraining her, his own expression dark. "What is this?"

"I hate you," she cried. In that moment it was true. "I have worked so hard . . ."

He lifted her to her knees, so they were face-to-face. "You have worked so hard, Mary? At what? At tricking me with your sweet body into trusting you, into forgetting the past?"

"No!" She tried to twist free of him and failed. "I have worked so hard to convince you that I would never break my vows!"

"If only that were true." Stephen released her. "If only that were true."

"It is true, damn you! I spied because I am a Scot, and it was obvious you were planning treachery against Scotland! That, I admit! But I did not try to warn Malcolm, nor did I intend to try!"

"You look like an avenging angel." Stephen touched her hair briefly. "A man would be mad to doubt you."

She was still, disbelieving.

He smiled as if forced to swallow bilious medicine. "A man would also be mad to believe you."

" 'Tis not fair!"

"Why would your wedding vows mean so much to you, Mary? When you have spent your entire life hating me, hating Normans, hating England?"

Mary took a moment to answer carefully. For her answer was a painful gamble. "I have hated Normans, yes, but— not you."

He looked at her.

She reddened, hoping he would not remark it. If only she had less pride. Her pride did her no good now. Her voice was a whisper. "I have never hated you, my lord." And she was thinking about the first time she had seen him, how mighty and invincible he appeared, how proud, how noble, how powerful and male. She had fallen in love with him then and there at Abernathy two long years ago.

Finally Stephen found his voice, and his tone was mocking. "Now the grand confession—that you love me?"

Mary choked. "You make it so very hard."

He stared, silent.

"You do not deserve love from me," she said after a long pause. His cruel doubt, his mockery, made it impossible for her to tell him the whole truth of her feelings for him. That her love had been so forbidden that her only recourse had been to hide behind a wall of hatred. She wiped a tear away with the back of her hand.

"And undoubtedly I do not have it," he said caustically.

Mary turned away.

Stephen grabbed her. She gasped when he flung her on her back, beneath him. His eyes blazed. "You are playing dangerous games, madame."

She shook her head in denial, unable to speak. He was furious, she was frightened. Yet she was suddenly excited and breathless and acutely aware of being beneath him and completely subject to his whim.

"If you love me," he said, low and hoarse, "I suggest you prove it."

Mary was sweating. She licked her lips. "Have I not proved it, my lord?" Her voice was husky and unrecognizable.

His smile was no smile, but more of an animal-like snarl. "You will never prove your love to me in bed, Mary. That is not what I am speaking about."

Their gazes held. The primal thrill was gone. Mary's heart sank with comprehension. Then Stephen turned away from her, and he did not touch her again that night.

The following day Prince Henry appeared at Alnwick. He was not alone; he traveled with a full contingent of troops. His many men were camped just outside the castle's walls, covering the moors for as far as the eye could see. The landscape was changed into a small, raucous village. Local maids hid for fear of rape, local farmers swallowed their grief as their livestock was slaughtered to feed the vast numbers, both upon Stephen's command and without it. It had been raining for days, but now the weather cleared. Which was fine with the mercenaries, who were restless and sick of the inclement English weather. Mock jousts were set up, more maids hunted down, anything to amuse the men.

Mary was glad that they only intended to spend one night. One of the kitchen maids had suffered at the hands of the men, and Mary had seen firsthand their cruel brutality. She had tended the poor weeping girl herself. True, she was no stranger to the proclivities of soldiers fresh from battle, but Henry's mercenaries were worse than any she had ever so far seen.

Although she was very disturbed by the events of the night before, although she was angry enough to want to ignore Stephen as he now ignored her, she could not hold her tongue. She searched him out in order to protest vehemently about the presence of the undisciplined Normans—and to find out why they were there in the North.

"It is only for this day and this night," he told her. "Henry could not restrain them even if he wanted to, which he does not."

"But you do not allow your men to ravage the countryside and rape and maim as they choose," Mary flared. She glared at her husband, trembling with anger, an anger having far more to it than that induced by the subject they were on.

"My men are not mercenaries," Stephen said, and then he dismissed her before she could question him any further.

Mary had not anticipated Stephen being able to rectify the situation. She would not protest again, and she would guard her people the best that she could. She ordered the guards in the barbican to allow all locals free entry into the bailey to escape the Norman knights. As she did so, she was very aware of the irony of her actions. Stephen saw her as an outsider, but she had already taken his people and his home to her heart, and genuinely felt it her duty to protect Alnwick and those bound to it. Hopefully her husband would not find out about her efforts on his behalf, and if he did, she did not think him barbaric enough to countermand her.

But what in God's name was the prince doing there? Although common gossip held that he went to Carlisle to relieve the current garrison there, Mary was terribly afraid that his presence signified far more than that.

And Henry made her nervous. In fact, he made her far more nervous than his marauding troops. She did not trust him. He had sharp, roving eyes, eyes that searched out far too much, that saw far too much. However, Mary knew better than to be anything other than pleasant to him.

He sat on the dais with her and Stephen and the countess, between her husband and her mother-in-law. Mary was glad that Stephen shielded her from him, at least with his physical bulk. If Henry got too close to her for too long, he would soon discern that something was wrong.

She had hardly slept last night. She had tried to seduce Stephen after he had turned away from her, instinctively knowing that she must quickly recover the territory she had lost that day, territory that had been painstakingly regained in the past week. She could not let their marriage continue this downslide. Yet she had been firmly rebuffed. His blatant rejection, one not even politely disguised, had been the final blow. She had sagged in bed beside him, for the first time in her life bewildered and feeling defeat.

That morning she glimpsed the dark circles beneath her eyes in Isobel's looking glass. She was a sore sight. And now Henry was here, and his keen gaze had slid over her, covering every inch of her, making her exceedingly uncomfortable. Mary suspected he found her desirable. When he looked at her she suspected his thoughts were shameful. She did not want to guess at them, but because Stephen had initiated her so thoroughly into the many manners of lovemaking, she could guess too well what they might be.

They spoke little at supper. Conversation in general was light. Henry openly stated that he would relieve the troops at Carlisle. Afterwards he planned to return to his holdings in Normandy. She did not particularly care what transpired in Normandy, as long as it did not affect Northumberland or Scotland, but she knew, as did practically everyone, that William Rufus coveted his brother Robert's Norman duchy and would probably go to war one day to gain it. Would the prince once again go to war for one brother, against the other? And if so, which brother would he support this time?

After dinner there was the usual entertainment, a minstrel, a bard, jongleurs, a clown. Mary excused herself early, frankly pleading fatigue. But instead of going to her bed, she sought a moment of fresh air on the ramparts outside.

In all likelihood the morrow would bring more rain, if the starless night was any indication.

The watchmen murmured polite greetings, then ignored her, leaving her to her own thoughts. Mary had wrapped herself in a fur-lined cloak and she hugged it to her, staring out at the many dying campfires spread out on the moors below. Laughter and song, some of it female, and the sad, slow tune of a gittern, drifted to her. She had no urge to go inside, to go to the chamber she shared with Stephen. She suspected he would stay up late, plotting and planning with Henry now. The two of them got on very well; they seemed to be solid friends. She could not understand why. Henry did have a certain magnetism, but he was ruthless in a way her husband was not, and it frightened her. Like Stephen, he was powerful; unlike Stephen, he was the youngest son, and the Conqueror had given him nothing but immense wealth. Henry had taken for himself what he needed, and today he had power well suited to a prince. Perhaps Stephen's friendship with Henry was more political than personal. Unfortunately, Mary did not think so.

Mary did not want to think about Stephen. Not if she could avoid it. Instead, she looked out upon the night-blackened moors, the rough landscape illuminated slightly by the many small, glowing fires, and her heart tightened. She realized that she was facing north, facing Scotland, but she was not homesick. She had not been homesick in a very long time.

What has happened to me? she wondered. I love my country, but it is no longer my home. How did that happen, and so swiftly? Alnwick has become my home. Today I wanted to kill the men for hurting my bondswoman—*my* bondswoman. Dear God, perhaps I am becoming an English-woman after all.

But would it be so bad? Her destiny was now Northumberland; one day she would be its countess. And she was one-half English, a fact she had ignored for most of her lifetime—her mother was the granddaughter of a Saxon King. Mary's smile was sad. She had always felt complete-ly Scottish, and she still did, but somehow she had gone further than coming to accept her marriage and her new home, somehow she had grown sincerely loyal, sincerely fond, of this place and its people. She was even accepted by them all, by the greatest vassal and the lowest serf. No, she thought quickly, with a terrible pang, she was not accepted by them all. She was not accepted by her lord, who still saw her as an outsider and worse—as a vile traitor.

In one instant their marriage had crumbled again. And she had even told him, in so many words, that she loved him. And he had laughed at her, mocked her, in so many words accusing her of lying. Mary wanted to hate him. But she could not.

A hand was laid on her from behind. Mary jumped in fright. Henry smiled at her. "I did not mean to startle you."

Quickly Mary's glance slid past him—but her husband was not behind Henry. She and the prince were alone. For an instant the icy fingers of panic curled about her. No, she thought wildly, they were not alone—the two guards were also on the ramparts. She spotted them with relief.

Henry guessed her feelings. "Do not fear, my lady, your reputation is safe. We are chaperoned." As usual, there was dry mockery in his tone.

Mary managed a smile. "I am not worried, my lord. Why should I be?"

Henry smiled and leaned against the wall, facing her, his eyes intent. Mary tensed, not liking the gleam she saw there. "Imagine my surprise," he said softly, "taking a moment of air and finding you here."

It was an unfortunate coincidence, but Mary did not say so. She hugged the fur to her more tightly. "Has Stephen gone to bed?"

"No," Henry purred, his smile one that had probably set more than a few female hearts pounding, "he is downstairs, contemplating the fire."

"Perhaps I should go." If Mary had any doubts before, Henry's smile chased them all away. He did find her attractive, and his manner was definitely predatory. She did not think herself in any real jeopardy, not here, in her husband's keep, but she did not like the way he looked at her, and she despised his manner, for it was not just predatory, it was also amused—he enjoyed toying with her. Mary moved to go past Henry, but he restrained her with one hand, the same confident, amused smile flashing. "Are you afraid of me, Mary?"

"Lady Mary," she said breathlessly. He had not released her arm. She could not believe it. But she would pretend that nothing untoward was happening. "And no, why should I be?"

"I think you dissemble." His laughter was pleased. Then it died. He searched her gaze. "You appear to have spent a bad night. Is all well?"

"Of course," she lied. Again she moved, hoping to discreetly dislodge his grip, but he was unshakable. It was a careful game they were playing. Mary did not want to overtly protest. Right now they were both ensconced in propriety. And Henry knew the game well, knew her fears of ending it well. He pretended politeness, pretended to have a casual hand upon her, when there was nothing casual about his intent. He knew she would not demand he release her, and in so doing, expose the polite exchange as a sham, subjecting them both to open hostility.

"The last time I saw you, Mary, you glowed. Rarely have I seen a woman more beautiful. Clearly marriage—and Stephen—agreed with you."

Mary could not smile. He spoke in the past tense.

"How tired you now appear. How distraught. Does not Stephen please you anymore?"

Mary could not hold her tongue a moment longer. "What kind of question is that! Of course he pleases me."

Henry laughed. "I do not mean in bed, my dear. Do not look shocked. I have known Stephen since we were both boys, he six, myself just one year older. We have wenched together on many occasions—I know just what he is capable of."

Mary made no more pretenses. She yanked her arm free. "How dare you," she hissed. She knew now, with a combination of fury, horror, and indignation, that Henry had imagined all the ways Stephen made love to her. She felt as if he had actually been in their chamber spying upon them. "How dare you intrude upon us that way!"

"Have I intruded?" He still laughed, his gaze feigned innocence. "How have I intruded, Mary? Because I know Stephen well? Because I know him better even than you in some ways?"

Mary said nothing, boiling.

"Has he forgiven you, Mary? Will he? I do not think so." Henry still smiled. "You were very foolish, as was he. I cannot believe he allowed you to visit alone with your brother. Do not look surprised. I know every happenstance of import in this realm."

"You keep a spy here?" Mary gasped.

"All great men keep spies everywhere, Mary; surely you know that. Does not your father keep you here?"

Mary tried to slap him. He caught her arm, and suddenly her cape fell away and she was pressed against the rough stone wall—and Henry's hard body was pressed against hers. "Release me, this instant. Stephen will kill you." She did not call out, though. She saw that the guards were on the other side of the ramparts, their backs to them, and thus unaware of what was happening. As Henry obviously knew.

"Or I will kill him." Henry laughed. Mary was horrified. "But I won't tell him about our tête-à-tête if you do not."

Mary stared at his handsome face, at his glittering eyes. She wanted to spit and claw, but he held her too tightly. She knew she would say nothing, because Henry was the King's brother, and because he was also a fearless knight. She did not want to take the chance of him killing her husband.

"Relax," Henry said huskily. "You are a beauty, to be sure, but in truth I am only protecting Stephen—and my own interests. I have no intention of raping you, sweet, no matter how I'd like to feel you beneath me. Surely it is your body that keeps Stephen derelict in his duty to himself and his patrimony. I am more than curious, I admit. Now, an invitation is another matter. That, I would accept." Henry straightened, releasing her.

Mary was still cornered by his body, her back to the wall. She shook, she so badly wanted to strike him. "You will never get an invitation of any kind from me!" Her bravery was a sham. For she was also shaking with fright. Had the guards been absent, Henry could have raped her in an instant, and she would have been powerless to stop him. She did not put such behavior past him. Not anymore.

"But you are a real woman, beneath that fragile, seemingly innocent facade, I know; I sensed it the moment we met. You cannot do without a man. And Stephen will not suffer your treachery for long. One day you will make a fatal mistake, Mary. Fatal. He will never forgive you, and he will send you away as he should have already done. But do not fear. I will not forget you. Even if you are cloistered, I will not forget you."

Mary did not move. Henry's confidence and arrogance were frightening. She could not miss the intent behind his words. If she was exiled, as he thought she would soon be, he would be there to ease her distress. Sexually. She shuddered. God help her, but if she was ever sent away, she had not a doubt that Henry would come to her door. "I will never betray him."

Henry was quiet, regarding her. Then he said, "How strange, I almost believe you."

"He errs. I have not betrayed him, and I will not. Not ever."

"No? Perhaps I have judged you wrongly. Perhaps you have yet to betray your husband, my friend. But what if I tell you the real purpose for my visit this night to Alnwick?"

Mary's heart began to beat with dread. "What real purpose? Surely you seek a bed and a roof over your head—nothing more!"

Henry laughed. "I know you are not so naive! I have already told Stephen, now I shall tell you, news he will undoubtedly keep to himself. Your father, your illustrious sire, is amassing the largest army Scotland has ever seen."

Mary could not move. She tried to speak, but no words came out. She had to swallow and wet her lips first. "Why?" It was a croak. She already knew.

"To retaliate, of course. More specifically, Malcolm has sworn to bring England to its knees, and his invasion of Northumberland is imminent."

Chapter 22

Mary fled. She thought that Henry's soft laughter followed her, but in her shock, she could not be sure. She rushed down the steep, spiral stairs and fell. Fortunately she was at the bottom when she did, and it was only down the last step, but it was enough to make her pause before getting up, panting.

She clutched her abdomen. Dear God, what was she doing? She must take care! She would never forgive herself if she lost her babe through her own lack of caution, her own recklessness. For the child's sake, she must begin to use restraint.

Mary rose to her feet. Her head pounded, but she forced herself to think. She did not doubt Henry's words—how she wished she did. But she knew her father. He would never let a transgression go unchecked. She moaned. He had to be stopped! She could only imagine what a full-scale war would do to them all, the Scots, the Normans, Malcolm, Stephen, herself.

"Mary?"

Mary jerked at the sound of her husband's voice. He stood in the narrow, dark hall, holding up a taper. Mary realized

317

that she was clinging to the wall, not having moved from
the foot of the stairwell where she had fallen. She stared at
Stephen as if he were a stranger.

"Are you all right? Did you fall?" Swiftly he came forward.

He was obviously concerned. With a small, glad cry,
Mary leapt into his arms. Not only did he care about her
a little, she needed him now! She needed him to be her
ally in this dark, frightening time, she needed comfort and
hope, she needed his strength. To her dismay, Stephen did
not hold her. Firmly he set her away, his face grim, as if
he did not want to touch her. "Did you fall?" he repeated.
"Are you hurt?"

"I am all right," she said, clenching her fists so she would
not reach out to him again. He might be concerned, but he
had yet to forgive her anything, and Edward's visit was obviously still fresh upon his mind. "Is it true? Does Malcolm
intend war? Does he plan an invasion of Northumberland
even now? Is it imminent?"

Stephen's eyes narrowed. "And how, dare I ask, did you
find out about such things?"

She had been certain Henry spoke the truth, but even so,
she cried out in anguish when Stephen's words confirmed it.
Still, she could not miss his bitter sarcasm. "I did not spy!"
she shouted. She shook. "Your dear friend Henry told me.
Think you on that!"

Mary pushed herself abruptly from the wall and marched
past Stephen. He instantly came to life, catching her arm
and hustling her forward into their chamber. He released her
in order to shut the door. Mary went to the fire to warm
herself, putting her back to him, still shaking, with anger,
with fearful dread.

She knew Stephen watched her. Finally she turned to meet
his stare, which was piercing. "Henry told me," she repeated.
"Even now he is on the ramparts. Ask him if you doubt me."

"I do not doubt you, not this time," Stephen said quietly.
"Henry thinks himself a puppeteer, pulling the strings of all
those around him. But, unlike the puppeteer, he is never
quite certain what actions his puppets will take. I think that
is where he gains most of his enjoyment."

"And he is your friend?"

"As much of a friend as one who is not family can be," Stephen said. "Henry enjoys causing trouble. I imagine he has caused enough this night. Now what? Are you going to weep and shriek and beg me to avoid this encounter?"

"If my father invades your land, you must defend what is yours. Your armies shall meet head-on." Mary trembled, imagining two gigantic armies rushing at one another, hearing the ringing blows of metal upon metal, hearing the screams of anguish and death.

"Yes."

Mary suddenly froze. A horrible inkling, a premonition of disaster, of death, struck her. Who? Who would it be? Not Stephen! Please, God, not Stephen. She swallowed and found her voice. "But it does not have to be. It is not yet too late. Malcolm has not yet invaded. Please, Stephen, you must go to him!"

"You would send me into the jaws of the enemy on the eve of war?"

Mary rushed to her husband and gripped his hands. "This war can be avoided!"

He flung them off. "Are you mad? Or do you think me mad?"

"You do not understand!" she cried. Her mind was whirling, her pulse roared in her ears. She would beg if she must, on her hands and her knees, the stakes were so high. The war between her father and her husband must be stopped, she could not bear it. And still she was shaken by the premonition, one she fully believed, it was so strong. Someone was going to die, someone cherished and dear—she knew it, she felt it—but not if this horrible confrontation never took place.

"Oh, well do I understand you, madame," Stephen said coldly.

Mary jerked. "You do not think I send you into a trap?!"

"Could you be such a treacherous bitch?"

Mary backed up. "No, Stephen, you have not understood me—once again." Her voice shook. But she comprehended why he thought as he did—because yesterday she had met privately with Edward.

"What fable will you tell me now?"

"You must parley with my father!" she screamed, close to hysteria. "Can you not see that? Words, Stephen, words, might restore a truce—and avert catastrophe!"

"I do not believe that you are so naive, Mary, to truly think to send me to your father to speak of peace. You send me to my death—or to a lifetime of imprisonment. I do not like it." His last words came out as a low growl. Mary had been holding out her hands in the gesture of one making a plea, and he pushed them away. His eyes were black with fury.

"No," Mary whispered, stumbling from the shove. "I am sincere."

"You are sincere? You expect me to believe that you are sincere? You have fought me since we first met, despising everything about me, especially my name and country. You fought our marriage until the end. Not a few days after making your wedding vows, you broke them in a heart-beat." Stephen's smile was cold. "And your brother was here yesterday."

Mary shrank away from Stephen, who loomed over her now, his face etched with tightly reined in fury. "No!" she cried. But she realized how it must seem. Edward's untimely visit was the coup de grace. Stephen could not think it innocent, not with war brewing, not so soon after Carlisle's defeat, and not after her supposed treachery. In his mind, Edward's visit was no mere coincidence, but an event filled with purpose. How her plea did seem like enticement, like a trap. "No, Stephen, you are wrong."

Stephen straightened. "I am weary of your games, madame," he said very coldly. "Listen well. Tomorrow I go to war. There is no avoiding it."

"Stephen, please! This time you must trust me!"

He turned his back on her. A moment later he had left the room. When Mary arose the next morning after a long and sleepless night, he still had not returned. It was many weeks before she saw him again.

Mary dared not think about where Stephen had slept that night. Instead, she thought about the war soon to sweep the land. Four times Malcolm had invaded England, invading de Warenne territory, and four times he had been defeated and forced to swear fealty to the English King. Mary saw no reason to believe that this time would be any different, yet this time was so very different. For this time she was on the other side of the Scot border. This time she would not be with her mother at Edinburgh, awaiting word, praying and cheering wholeheartedly for a Scot victory. Any victory would be a tragedy for Mary. Should her father miraculously win, Stephen would lose, and how could she be gladdened by that? Yet if Malcolm lost again, she would also weep. She could not be impervious to the beating Scotland suffered, not ever. There would be a victor in the war to come, but it would not be Mary; she had already lost.

No, she thought resolutely. She had not already lost. Not if she took matters into her own hands.

Perhaps, after all, she had been wrong to ask Stephen to go to Malcolm to plead for peace. Despite the marriage, they were enemies. But what if she, Mary, Malcolm's own daughter, went in his stead?

Paralyzing excitement swept through Mary. And with it came fear.

It would be the biggest gamble of her life, and she knew it well. Even if Stephen had not left Alnwick already, she could not ask him for his permission. He would not believe her sincere, he would suspect treachery again. Therefore she would have to leave Alnwick without his permission and without his knowledge.

Mary did not want to think about what might happen if she left Alnwick and went to Malcolm but failed to convince him to turn his armies around. It was far too frightening.

This time I must be mad, she managed to think as she planned her escape, for who am I to avert a war between two great houses? But she could not live with herself if she did not try. She yearned for peace as she had never before. Peace in the land, and peace between her and Stephen.

When Mary slid from the bed and dressed, Stephen and all the de Warenne men were gone. Mary had been awakened by their departure that dawn. Once again, it had been obvious that the assembled men were leaving to make war. This time, though, their numbers were few—many men-at-arms were being left behind. To defend Alnwick? Mary knew that there could be no other explanation. Yet she was disbelieving. Did the earl and Stephen think a siege even remotely possible? Yet they must, to leave the keep well guarded by some twoscore men.

Mary was horrified. Not because of cowardice, but because she was finding it difficult to imagine her father laying siege to the fortress belonging to her husband, especially with his own daughter a resident there.

She must not think of such a dismaying event. Instead, Mary's quick mind surmised that if Stephen had left so quickly, riders must have been sent out the night before to summon the vassals to war. Which meant that Malcolm's invasion was imminent, as Henry had said, and that Mary had no time to lose.

Henry had continued on to Carlisle as planned. Now Mary understood his real intentions—which were not to relieve the troops there but to reinforce them and prepare for battle. How could Malcolm really think to beat such an army? Why could he not put his great determination to the cause of peace instead of war?

More foreboding settled over Mary. She turned her thoughts to the task at hand. Mary quickly decided to disguise herself as a peasant boy, boldly leave the keep, and in the village steal a donkey or a horse if she could find one. As a young lad, she would have far less trouble traveling alone. And as soon as it was safe, she would reveal herself and gain both a good horse and a Scottish escort.

Alnwick was in a hive of activity when Mary descended the stairs and entered the Great Hall. It was the kind of activity that heightened Mary's fears and strengthened her resolve—preparations were madly under way for the event of a siege. So not only had the earl left many valuable knights behind to defend the keep, he had ordered it to prepare itself for the worst. Mary shuddered. As far as she knew, Alnwick was impenetrable. Yet the earl was both a seasoned military commander and a brilliant strategist. Obviously the kind of war that threatened now was on a scale that Mary had never in her lifetime witnessed.

Breathless, knowing she must somehow succeed in deterring Malcolm from his path, Mary hoped to hurry through the hall and outside without being noticed, surely a feat easily accomplished due to the hubbub within. But the countess saw her immediately and hailed her over.

Hiding her reluctance, Mary obeyed the summons.

"I am glad you are up so early; there is much to be done," Lady Ceidre said, not mincing words. "I will put you in charge of gathering all we shall need for the wounded. If there is a siege, there will be many casualties." Quickly the countess rattled off a list of supplies to be brought into the keep itself.

Mary listened and nodded, knowing she was not going to compile clean linens and moldy bread or anything else, and feeling like a traitor because of it. Yet if she succeeded in swaying Malcolm, she would not be a traitor—she would be a hero. That thought struck her dumb.

She would be a hero, a savior, *the* savior, and finally she would have proved herself to Stephen.

Mary was so stunned by the thought of a final and complete exoneration that she barely heard the countess when she sent her off to begin her task with a small pat on the shoulder.

Mary had been given the perfect excuse to leave the tower. She rushed into the bailey, where servants scurried back and forth, dragging huge barrels of drinking water inside, as well as sacks of grain and dried foodstuffs. Others were moving casks of oil to the walls. If they were truly sieged, the oil would be boiled and placed on top of the walls and overturned on the attackers as they tried to scale them.

No attention was paid to Mary. She thought that she could probably walk right out of the bailey and across the drawbridge, lowered now for the constant influx and outflux of traffic, pedestrian and vehicular alike, but too much was at stake for her to take a chance of being recognized and stopped. Mary hurried towards the back of the keep where the kitchens and pantries were—where several young boys about her size usually worked. One of the lads was lugging a sack of cornmeal into the kitchen. Mary immediately drew him aside. She gave him a penny for his trouble, which delighted him, as well as a cape for his modesty. He assured her that he would have no difficulty replacing his clothing. Mary took everything he wore, his clogs, his hose, his rough wool tunic and his rope-braid belt, and most important, his torn, hooded cloak.

Tucking the clothing under her arm, Mary rushed past the kitchens and turned the corner. She needed absolute privacy to change into her disguise. An empty wagon provided it—or so she thought.

She had just finished dressing and was carefully hiding her own garments in the wagon under some empty sacks when Isobel said, "Whatever are you doing, Lady Mary?"

Mary's heart lurched with sickening force. She straightened, her visage undoubtedly a hundred shades of guilty red. Isobel was wide-eyed, taking in every inch of her appearance. "The cowl is too big," she remarked.

Mary grabbed Isobel and pulled her into the shadows cast by the wagon. Her heart was pounding madly. What reasonable explanation could she offer to the clever girl for her ludicrous manner of dress? She realized she must appeal to the child's sense of adventure, she must trust her with the truth.

"From a distance," she said softly, "do I look like a lad?"

Isobel backed up, regarding her seriously. "Perhaps if you dirty up your face and hands. What are you doing?"

Mary pulled her close again. "Isobel, I need your help. I need your promise of secrecy."

Suddenly Isobel's expression became accusatory. "You are disguised so that you might run away!"

"Yes, but not for the reason that you are thinking!"

Isobel was white. "You would run away from all of us, from Stephen, now? Abandon us? I thought you were a friend!"

"Please listen to me!" Mary was desperate. "I am not running away!"

Isobel stared.

"I am going to my father to beg him to cease his part in this war!"

Isobel appeared shocked. "And Stephen does not know?"

"He does not know. He left before I even thought of this plan. But even if he did know, he would not let me go. A man does not allow his wife to serve such purposes." She would not tell the child that her brother did not trust her, and would think, as Isobel had, that Mary meant to run away.

Isobel's eyes glowed. She smiled eagerly. "If you can stop Malcolm, why, the bards will tell stories about you and the minstrels will sing of you! No longer will they speak only of your beauty—but of your courage! And Stephen—he shall no longer be so angry with you! He will love you again!"

Mary was silent. Her heart was wrenched hard by the child's words, words that accurately reflected her own hopes. How much did Isobel know? More important, how much did Isobel understand? It seemed as if the child comprehended Mary's predicament completely. How could one so young be so astute? "Then you will help me, by keeping silent?"

Isobel regarded her. "You will come back?"

"Of course." She saw that Isobel was uncertain enough to hesitate. "I love Stephen, Isobel."

And Isobel's eyes danced. "I will help you. I will help you to stop this war and I will help you gain Stephen's love again!"

Late that day, as dusk fell upon the land, Mary was escorted by a single rider around the enemy lines—her husband's lines—as they approached the Scottish army's camp.

The Scot who rode with her was a strong lad who had been eager to help her once she had revealed her identity to him and his kin at their small croft on the eastern edge of the Cheviot Hills. It was no secret that Malcolm's huge army was camped on the flats just north of Liddel, just as it was no secret that the Norman armies were camped on the gentle slopes just south of Carlisle. Upon leaving the small farm, they had traveled directly west into the hills, using deer trails. Soon they had turned south. There had been some need for caution. The two armies were firmly entrenched and many leagues south of them, but armed Normans and Englishmen, vassals or allies of her husband, were still riding across the land to join forces with him. They did not dare use the old Roman road, but followed more paths on the hills just above it. Twice Mary and Jamie had to stir their old horses into a gallop and rush off of the trail to hide in a copse of trees or a gully. They had crouched beside their mounts in fright as the fully armed Norman knights pounded by on their big destriers on the road below them, menacing and dangerous. If Mary had not realized how perilous her scheme was before, she certainly realized it now. If she was caught by these knights, not one of them would believe her to be Stephen's wife. Her fate, and Jamie's, did not bear thinking about.

The irony of it was vast. Stephen's troops had become the enemy, when she loved him so dearly.

When the sun was hanging low, the light faded and gray, it was time to leave the old Roman road behind. The River Tyne forked south and the two riders forked west, leaving the road and slipping into the woods, earnestly in search of Malcolm's camp now. Not too many leagues ahead lay Carlisle.

Jamie had a ready wit, which he had used all day to keep Mary distracted from the danger they were in. Now his gap-toothed grin was gone and sweat sheened his fair skin, although it was cold out. Mary perspired as well. Her heart thudded with dread. The Scot army was not far away, but neither was the Norman army, and undoubtedly there would be many patrols out all that night. Both she and the young lad were terrified now at being discovered by a Norman patrol. She still feared a horrible fate, as did he, but more important, capture would mean that her mission had failed—when they were so close to success.

Ten minutes after having left the road, they were challenged by a patrol. The rough Highland burr gave away the scouts as Scots immediately, and Jamie laughed with relief. Mary did, too. Dear God, they had made it! Somehow they had sneaked past hundreds of Norman troops, evading their patrols, and reached safe Scottish territory!

Despite her disguise, Mary was recognized the instant she threw off her cowl, before she could even reveal herself. The big, burly Scotsmen, all on foot and wearing their plaids, were incredulous. No one asked what she was doing there, but their incredulity had given way to pleased grins. Mary knew what they thought. They thought that she was coming home, a traitor to her husband.

Night was falling rapidly, but Mary could see well enough to be shocked at the size of her father's camp. Jamie had boasted about its size, boasts based on rumor, and Mary had not believed him. Now she turned to one of the brawny men striding along beside her tired plow horse. "He must have gathered five hundred men! Why, there must be a dozen different clans here! I see the Douglas colors, and the Macdonalds, and the Fergusons, too! They have not supported us in all the years I can remember!"

The big Scot whom she had addressed flashed her a roguish grin, then winked. "Yer da has taken the bit between his teeth, lassie. He'll win this one, ye can be sure."

Mary was not sure, but defeat was by no means a glaring probability now. What, she wondered, had Malcolm offered these clans in exchange for their support? And what, dear God, would happen when the Scot army met the Norman one? She was afraid. The destruction would be horrendous, the loss of life on a scale impossible to imagine. Now she understood why Alnwick prepared for a siege. Malcolm's army was massive enough, forbidding enough, to raise the specter of such a fearsome event.

Now was not a time to be selfish, but Mary could not help from choking on a sudden lump in her throat. She could imagine herself cowering in the solar at Alnwick with the other women while the tower was bombarded with stone and metal missiles and Greek fire, while the walls were being buffeted by heavy battering rams. If she failed to dissuade him from war, would it come to that? Would her father attempt to destroy Alnwick, her husband's home, even while she remained within its walls?

She must not think so dismally. Mary blinked twice to clear her vision and gazed out upon the panorama of so many weather-stained tents spread out on the rolling green fields ahead. Malcolm's tent was on a small rise, no bigger or grander than anyone else's, and Mary saw him immediately. Malcolm squatted before his campfire, surrounded by many powerful lairds, as well as Edward, Edmund, and Edgar.

Mary forgot about her escort, Jamie, and the scouts. She urged the old horse forward. Edgar saw her first. He stared, shocked. Then he ran towards her, a glad cry escaping his lips. Mary dismounted, sliding into his arms. She was glad to see that he had full use of both of them.

He did not hug her. He shook her wildly instead. "By all the saints! What are you doing here, Mary? Why are you not with your husband?"

"And I'm glad to see you, too," she said tartly, giving him an embrace. He shrugged free. He had never been demonstrative with his affection, thinking it unmanly. Now he was disapproving. "I hope you have a good reason for being here and not at Alnwick, where you belong!"

She looked at his young, stern face. Edgar was never disapproving of her; they had spent their lives defying authority together and defending each other. Mary realized that he might think that she was betraying Stephen, too. "I have only come to have a word with Father. I intend to return to Alnwick this night."

He gaped. His expression was so boyish, so much like the old Edgar, that she smiled. He opened his mouth to speak, but Edward and Edmund were upon them. "Mary?" Edward was also disbelieving. "How in hell did you get here?"

"More importantly, *why* is she here?" Edmund said.

Mary looked at Edward, saw his concern, and looked at Edmund, saw his distrust. "I must speak with Father."

"Do you carry a message from your husband?" Edmund asked skeptically. "Does the mighty bastard now hide behind a woman's skirts?"

Mary clenched her fists, livid. "He would never hide, not from anyone, and especially not from the likes of you!"

Edmund growled, "You show your true colors, sister."

She flushed. Her defense of Stephen had been automatic, but not diplomatic. "I bring no message from Stephen. He does not know I am here."

Edmund raised a skeptical brow. Edward looked worried. "Dear God, Mary, why are you here? You shouldn't have come! There were skirmishes today; we lost three men already, and the fighting has yet to begin! You could have been caught in one of them!"

"I had to come," Mary said stubbornly. "I must speak with Father."

"And what is it that is so important that you rode all this way to see me without your husband's permission?" Malcolm asked.

Mary whirled. Malcolm stood behind her, his face carved in stone, as cold as his tone. He had never addressed her in such a manner before. Her glad cry of greeting died in her throat. She stopped in her headlong rush to embrace him. "Father?"

"I asked you a question."

Mary drew herself upright. "Might we have a private word?" What was going on? *What was wrong?*

"Why? Have you something to hide from your brothers?"

"Why are you speaking to me so coldly?" Mary asked, trembling. "You act as if you're angry—as if you hate me!"

"I am angry!" Malcolm roared, his deep voice carrying through the night. Men at other tents and fires turned to look at them. "You disobeyed me, and I've not forgotten it! Did I not explain to you why I allowed you to marry that bastard in the first place? I could have sent you to France! I could have married you to some old, poor northern laird! But 'twas the perfect opportunity—to have my own daughter married to one of them, well within their midst."

Mary was frozen.

"You failed to warn me of Carlisle's invasion—because of your treachery, Carlisle is lost."

Mary could not breathe. She felt close to fainting. She wanted, then and there, to die.

"Speak your piece and quickly," Malcom said. "I have no time now to dawdle. But if you come here as Edmund has suggested, to speak words your husband should bear, do not bother. There shall be no more words between us. The time for words is done. The time for swords has come."

"I did not betray you," Mary finally managed. The darkening night blurred her vision, or was it tears? "I took vows, father, vows to obey my husband. 'Twas wrong of you to ask me to break them. 'Twas even more wrong of you to agree to the marriage thinking to make me a spy from the start."

Malcolm raised his hand. Mary screamed. Edward and Edgar leapt upon their father, restraining him before he could strike her down. Yet he came to his senses, and panting, he dropped his clenched fist. "You are no more my daughter," he said harshly.

"Father!" Mary cried out.

"Do you hear me?" Malcolm shouted. "You are no more my daughter!"

"But I love you!"

Malcolm ignored her, livid. "My daughter is a brave, loyal Scottish lass, not one such as you! *You are not my daughter!"*

She had been crying, but silently and soundlessly, and now miraculously she stopped. Somehow she straightened her spine, her shoulders. Inside she felt dead. Dead and old—so very old. But her mind wasn't dead. And in her mind there was her husband's powerful image. Her father was wrong to disown her, but it did not matter now. She belonged to another, to Stephen de Warenne. "I took vows before God," she whispered. She heard herself and was surprised that she could sound so calm and dignified when her heart was so shattered, so broken.

"Vows made to the enemy are meant to be broken! Especially vows made to the likes of Stephen de Warenne." Malcolm fought for calm. His ruddy face was flushed. He towered over the daughter he had just disowned. "Now, madame, what is it you have to say? Speak quickly and be gone."

Mary lifted her chin ever so slightly. "I have come to plead with you to end this folly. Please, retreat. Please retreat before hundreds of men die, before this border is awash in innocent blood."

Malcolm was incredulous. "Your husband did send you! Is he a coward after all? Afraid to face me on the battlefield?" Malcolm laughed. "He knows that this time I canna lose! This time I will win! Never has there been such a Scot army, and victory is ours!"

"But at what price?" Mary whispered.

"No price is too great!" Malcolm cried.

Mary turned away. More silvery tears fell down her cheeks. Someone, Edward, put his arm around her and led her away. Mary told herself that she must not cry. She had failed to avert a war. It had been sheer insanity to think that she could dissuade Malcolm from warfare.

Stephen. How she needed him now. Stephen! *She must return home immediately.* She must return home before he ever found out that she had been gone—before he thought the worst.

"I will go now, Ed," Mary said unsteadily sometime later. Her smile was so sad that it brought tears to Edward's blue eyes. "I was mad to think I could persuade him from his course. Can you get me a fresh horse and an escort?"

Edward tilted her face up, then gripped her arms gently. "Mary, he does not mean it. He cannot understand, or accept, that you owe your loyalty now to de Warenne first. He will get over it. In time."

She looked at her brother tearlessly. "He has disowned me."

Edward inhaled. Her too bright gaze and her almost even tone distressed him far more than any shrieking or weeping could. But he knew his brave little sister. She would never descend into such hysterical behavior. Then it occurred to him that he hardly knew her at all anymore. When she had slipped away from Liddel to rendezvous with Doug Mackinnon, she had been a reckless child. The valiant woman who faced him now with a broken heart she attempted to hide was just that, a brave and peerless woman. "He will change his mind. I am sure of it." He was careful to make certain that she could not see into his eyes, for he was hardly sure of the words he spoke.

Mary pursed her lips and did not speak for some time. "I do not know him, do I?"

Edward stroked her arm. "You have always seen him as a mighty god, but in truth, Malcolm is merely a man. He is not a bad man, Mary, but he has his flaws, as we all do."

She looked at him and choked.

"If you cry, you will feel better," Edward said, taking her into his arms.

But she pushed him away. "No. I will not cry." She sniffled once. "It does not matter. All that matters is that I have failed. There will be a horrible war. Men will die. Perhaps even . . ." She choked. "Please, God," she whispered, "not Stephen."

Edward took her hands. "He is a great knight, Mary; do not fear for him."

"But I do." She gazed at him, trembling. "And what will be next? There is no hope for a future of peace between our families, Ed, not now, not once this war begins."

Edward paused. "I believe in the future, Mary. I believe that it is up to us, the sons, to rectify the wrongs of the fathers, to defy the past."

"What are you saying? That you think that one day, when you are King, this bloody border warfare will stop?"

"I believe so."

Mary stared, then she gripped Edward's hands, hard. "You know something that I do not! I can see it in your eyes! What is it?"

"There is hope," Edward said after a moment's hesitation. "There is hope, if Stephen is a man of his word. Is he?"

"Yes."

"I think so, too."

"What has he promised you, Ed?" Mary gasped.

"One day, when the time is right, Stephen will support me in my quest for Scotland's throne." He paused, then added, "God willing."

Mary gasped again.

Edward smiled and patted her hand. "So feel better, little sister. All is not lost. Your husband and I will become allies. In time."

"When was this alliance made?" Mary cried. "How come I was not told?"

Edward laughed. "That's my Mary! Dear, why in God's name should you be told of a pledge made in secret between two men?"

"Does Malcolm know?"

"He knows, but he does not think Stephen will keep his word, and he is too inflamed by Carlisle to care much now about the future." Edward's tone was somber—sad. " 'Twas your bride-price, Mary."

"Oh, God!" Mary moaned. She covered her face with her hands.

"What is it?" Edward asked, worry rising instantly. Mary was usually indomitable, but tonight, tonight he sensed that she was far from that. Her fragility frightened him.

"I comprehended that I was a political sacrifice," she finally said in a low whisper. She was crying. "But for you—I would not have minded. How I wish I had known the truth sooner—but now it changes nothing."

Edward did not know what to say. The secret alliance did not change the fact that Malcolm had so cruelly disowned his daughter on this day, an act Edward feared Malcolm might obstinately refuse to reverse. Malcolm was hardly a reasonable man when he held a grudge. "You love your husband, and that is what matters now, Mary."

She raised her gaze to his, her eyes shining. "He will do it, you know." She started to choke on tears again.

"What is disturbing you so greatly, Mary? 'Tis not just Father, is it?"

"I must get home." Her voice pitched high. "I must get home immediately—before it is too late."

"Mary," he began, uncertain of how to continue.

She interrupted, her fingers upon his like claws. "Can you arrange the horse and escort, Ed? *I must leave now!*"

"Mary, I cannot."

"What?"

"Listen to me," he said urgently. She was pale with shock. If he had slapped her face, it could not be worse. "You took a terrible chance coming here as you did, on a plow horse escorted by a farmer who carried nothing more than a rusty knife! God's blood, Mary!"

"I had to try," Mary said weakly.

Edward saw that she was beginning to shake. " 'Tis too dangerous to go back now, Mary. Even if I sent you back amidst fifty men. For tomorrow at dawn the battle begins." He hesitated only slightly, but Mary was so distraught that she did not notice. He decided to say nothing about Malcolm's plans for Alnwick, but he would not send her there, not now. "You must trust me. 'Tis too dangerous, and I will not send you back."

"I see," Mary said faintly. Her voice was barely audible. Edward worried that she was close to fainting—a feat he would have never dreamed his boyish sister capable of. But she did not faint. She stood, unsteadily. "I understand," Mary repeated. She tried to smile but failed. " 'Tis only a delay. When all is finished, I will go home."

"Yes," Edward agreed. But he looked at her strangely, his heart wrenching even though he knew it was as it should be. "When it is all over, you can go home, Mary." And he trembled, unable not to feel sad. Mary no longer belonged to Scotland.

"I am suddenly very tired. Should I sleep in your tent?"

"Good God, no! I am afraid you will not sleep this night, Mary. I will not allow you to stay here in our camp. I am sending you to Edinburgh, where you will be safe."

And Mary turned deathly white.

That same night, just a few miles away but several hours later, Stephen lay upon his pallet, unable to sleep. Soon it would be dawn. Yet he had only just gone to bed, for he had been in a counsel of war. His father and his brothers had been present amongst the dozen magnates who would lead the Norman troops. As always, Rolfe's military stratagems were indispensable, while Geoffrey was commanding Canterbury's forces, Brand a captain of the royal troops. Prince Henry had also attended, for he had been persuaded to field his own Norman mercenaries in the name of his brother, the King. And the King, a shrewd general himself, had come to command them in this time of war.

Everyone was fully aware that the army they faced on the morrow was far greater than any Malcolm had ever before assembled. The coming war would be the bloodiest waged in years, and perhaps, just perhaps, victory might elude them.

Stephen wondered if the peace he so dearly sought might ever be obtained upon the border. It did not seem likely, it seemed like a dream. Stephen's regret was vast.

But this time it was also bitter. For if ever a real peace ruled the land, there might be a real peace between him and his wife.

Stephen was angry. Their relations should not hang in the balance of war and peace. She owed him her loyalty and love whether or not he fought in battle, and regardless of with whom. And because his responsibilities were such a great burden, he needed her. Never before in his life had he allowed himself to feel such a need for anyone, to admit to such a need. He was only a mortal man, hardly invincible. He needed his wife standing beside him in all matters great and small. But she did not stand beside him, she stood behind him—with a dagger poised at his back.

Mary had tried to send him to the enemy, into a trap. It would take more than this lifetime to forget it.

He regretted allowing her the rope to hang herself. God, he did.

He regretted falling in love with her. He regretted loving her now.

How had his life come to this?

He was hardly strong, and it was his own secret. He was weak, in love with a woman who had tried to deceive, outwit, and betray him numerous times. How could there be so much pain when there was love? How could he withstand this torment for the rest of his life?

If only . . . He was not a man to waste his time in idle dreams, but the haunting refrain came to him, not for the first time. *If only she were as she seemed.* He could forgive her anything if he could but trust her.

Which he knew he could not.

He laughed aloud, once, the sound pain-filled, echoing harshly in the dead silence of the night. He had almost believed her last night. He had wanted to believe her. And that was why Mary had become so very dangerous. *He had wanted to believe her sincere.* And for a moment he had.

Which was insanity.

And he still wished to trust her. Stephen closed his eyes. Perhaps, just perhaps, he should consider, again, the very minute possibility that Mary's words had been honest last night. Stephen knew that Mary saw Malcolm only as a daughter should, as a hero, not as the man he truly was. She had no idea that her father was a ruthless liar and an ambitious cheat. She could not know that he broke his word as often as the wind changed its course. She could not know that Malcolm loved war and revenge far more than he could ever love peace.

Stephen could not be unkind in this instance. He hoped the day never came when she learned the truth.

And of course, although Stephen knew Malcolm for exactly what he was, he did respect him. He was a dangerous opponent, for he was a clever man as well as a strong leader. Had he not been ruthless, dishonest, and self-serving, he would have never united the ever-warring Scot clans into one nation, then kept them under his heel for thirty-five long years. As a King, Malcolm was without peer.

But such a leader would never harken to his daughter's wish for peace, especially not when it came from the mouth of his sworn enemy.

Stephen tightened his fists. Here was the real danger that Mary poised to him. He knew better than to believe that she had sought for him to go to Malcolm and convince him to seek peace instead of war, knew it with every breath he took, yet he lay awake in the night, succumbing to her charm, even from afar. He was only a heartbeat away from choosing to believe the best of her, instead of the worst.

If he continued in this vein, surely, one day, she would destroy him.

Stephen stood and walked outside. The night was very cold, and his breath made puffs of vapor in the air; he welcomed the chill. It was cloudy, too, and tomorrow might well bring snow instead of rain. He rubbed his hands together to warm them. He would not think about Mary anymore. There was just too much pain.

Stephen stilled, listening. Someone was approaching through the shadows. He realized that it was his father. It was too early for Rolfe to be up, and his father was an old campaigner, one fully capable of deep sleep just before battle. Foreboding filled Stephen. He could only be bringing bad news.

Rolfe paused. "I have just received a messenger from Alnwick."

Stephen's jaw clenched. It could not have anything to do with his wife, he told himself. *It could not.*

"Your wife is gone."

"Gone?"

Rolfe explained that Mary had disguised herself as a peasant lad and had escaped Alnwick. Stephen's shock was so great that he did not hear any more. It was so great that he reeled, causing his father to reach out in order to steady him. But Stephen was not aware of Rolfe.

She had left him.

Mary had run away, to her family, to Scotland. On the eve of war, she had left him, proving her treachery once and for all.

His wife had left him.

And something in his heart died a little, then something else, powerful and consuming, roared to life.

"Stephen?" Rolfe asked.

He did not answer. He could not. Instead, Stephen felt the fury, and he welcomed it.

Chapter 23

Mary raced towards Edinburgh. The night was thickly black and icy cold, promising snow. Clouds of vapor hung in the air, formed by their blowing mounts. The pace of Mary's escort was relentless. They kept their straining horses at a hard gallop, as if pursued by the Norman army, but in truth both armies were now far behind them. Mary suspected that they were under orders to see her to safety as soon as possible and to rejoin their troops immediately. She could not care. With every pounding hoofbeat that brought her closer to the home of her childhood, Mary was also brought one step closer to her doom.

She was numbed with exhaustion from having ridden all that day and most of that night, but not so numb that she could not still feel the heartbreaking pain of her father's cruel rejection. But that hardly seemed to matter, considering that her destiny was being wrenched from her own control and set upon a course leading to disaster and heartbreak. Far more important was the fact that she was being sent to Edinburgh. She should be racing towards Alnwick, where she belonged. Alnwick was now her home. She should be there when Stephen returned from war. Instead, she was being swept deep into the heart of Scotland, into the stronghold of Stephen's enemies, enemies he would soon be engaged with in mortal combat.

This time, she thought, he would never understand; this time, she knew, he would never forgive her.

She did not want to ride north. As they galloped on, pushing their lathered mounts past the limits of exhaustion, again and again Mary had the urge to suddenly saw hard on the reins and whip her mare around and flee for home. It was insanity. She might be able to elude her escort, but her poor horse would never be able to race all the way back to Alnwick, and even if the brave mare could, it was suicide to ride through the war that would soon begin.

And at dawn, at that time when, some miles to the south, the horns of battle were blowing, the first heavy swords clashing, when the sun was just breaking the ash gray sky with pale slivers of ghostly white light, Edinburgh loomed ahead. The dark, near black burgh of weathered wood and ancient stone was set upon the same precipitous hill as the keep, a steep upthrusting of rocky mountain that had protected the burgh and castle since time immemorial from any would-be invaders. Above the village the fortress of the King of Scotland, as dark and black as the rocky island it sat upon, thrust into the sky. The premonition of doom rushed over Mary again.

They raced through the burgh, past an old woman pushing a cart of firewood, past two boys hawking salted herring, past a pack of scavenging dogs, and up the steep, frozen path to the fortress. The gates were thrown open, and within moments Mary was inside walls that should have been familiar and comforting. Instead, as the portcullis slammed down behind her, her skin tingled alarmingly. The sensation of being locked inside a prison was unmistakable.

But this was not a prison, this was her home, Mary told herself. She could not shake her bleak spirits. Sliding down from her horse, barely able to stand, Mary thanked the two burly men who had been her escort. She did not have to ask after her mother. At this hour Margaret would still be in the chapel celebrating the early morning mass of prime.

Mary hurried to the chapel as fast as her tired body could manage it.

At last, the sight that greeted her was reassuring. The slight, elegant form of Margaret, kneeling before the altar in a moment of private, personal prayer, the mass obviously concluded, brought Mary to a quick halt. She gulped down a deep breath, feeling perilously close to tears. If she needed anyone right now, she thought, she needed her mother. She needed to be able to tell her everything: how Stephen mistrusted her, how she had left Alnwick in the hope of averting a war, and how endangered their marriage now was. She needed to tell her mother, too, about the horrible interview with her father. And she would tell her about the child. Wiping a stray tear from her cheek, Mary impulsively moved forward and sank down beside her mother. Margaret did not acknowledge her, but Mary had not expected her to. She bowed her own head and prayed.

She prayed for a speedy end to the war and she prayed for a lasting peace. She prayed for the safe return of her father and her brothers, and a safe return for Stephen.

She wiped away another tear. She hesitated. It did not seem right to ask God for help with her own problems, not when she had never been devout or obedient before. Yet somehow she saw God as benevolent and understanding, not a deity one bargained one's good behavior with. She took another breath and made the most important request of all.

"Dear God, please guide Stephen to see the truth," she whispered aloud. Then she added, "Please let him love me."

Mary remained kneeling for a long moment, blessedly unthinking, suddenly somewhat unburdened and almost relieved. She realized that she was more exhausted than she had ever been in her life. Not moving was welcome. Her body ached from the endless hours she had been in the saddle that day, and her mind was now, finally, numb. Then she saw that her mother was standing. Mary rose also, her muscles protesting the effort.

Mary had her first good look at her mother. Margaret's eyes were deeply shadowed as if she had spent many sleepless nights, and they were also dark with worry. Mary gasped, for her mother was not just obviously fatigued, but thinner than she had ever been, and pale enough to make Mary wonder if she had been ill. "Mother." Mary hugged her. "Have you been sick?"

"No." There was a catch to Margaret's voice. "What are you doing here?"

"I have been a terrible fool," Mary confessed. "I tried to convince Father to turn back from this war. And Edward deemed it too dangerous for me to return to Alnwick, so he sent me here instead."

Margaret took her hand. "Well, I am glad to see you, dear. This time, alone here with just my women, waiting for word—I cannot bear it." Margaret's eyes sparkled with unshed tears, and her hand, in Mary's, trembled.

"Mother, what is it?" If her mother had not been ill, then either she was sick now, or terribly distressed.

Margaret's mouth quivered slightly. "I cannot shake this feeling I have, a terrible feeling of disaster. I have never been so frightened in all of my life." She closed her eyes briefly. "I am so afraid for Malcolm and my boys."

Mary squeezed Margaret's hand, but her own heart was beating heavily, and she recognized the feeling roiling within her as dread. Had she not had the same premonition? "They will be fine, Mother," she said very brightly. "Malcolm is the greatest warrior in this land, he is invincible; surely you know that. And my brothers are all of the same line. Do not fear. You are worrying yourself needlessly."

"If only you are right," Margaret managed listlessly.

Mary had never seen her mother like this before. Queen Margaret was calm by nature, poised and serene, not a woman to be stricken with anxiety to such excess. Mary had wanted to unburden herself and confess all to her mother, but found she could not do so now. Later, she told herself. When the war is over and Father and the boys are on their way home, then I will have all the time in the world to tell her of my problems.

Mary smiled at Margaret with forced cheer. "Let us break the night's fast, Mother. I don't know about you, but I am famished."

*   *   *

Margaret spent the entire day sitting in her chair in the women's solar by the hearth, her needle moving mechanically over a delicate piece of embroidery, awaiting word of the outcome of the first battle. And when that word came later that evening, amidst a light flurry of snow, it was uplifting—at least for the Scots.

The Scot army had not made any progress in its effort to retake Carlisle, but that no longer seemed significant. For while the Scots and Normans were brutally engaged in Cumbria, another force, led by Malcolm himself, had slipped around Carlisle and into the western reaches of Northumberland—and then into the heart of the fief itself. Alnwick was now under siege.

There was great rejoicing in the hall among the servants and women. Except for Margaret, who did not smile even once, whose face remained a mask of fear. And except for Mary, who was so shocked that she could not remain on her feet. She sank shaking into a chair.

Alnwick was under siege.

Her very first thought was for Isobel and the countess. *Dear God, let them be all right!* Mary closed her eyes, stricken with anguish. The countess was a strong, determined woman. If anyone could hold Alnwick together in the face of this attack, she could. Then Mary realized exactly where her loyalty lay. She had no sympathy for the attackers, only for the besieged. Only for the de Warennes.

And the full implications of what was happening struck Mary fully. Malcolm, her father, had attacked Alnwick—his own daughter's home. His vengeance knew no bounds.

But she was no longer his daughter, was she? She had been disowned.

Mary looked at the messenger, a short, bulky man who, though tired, was too elated to sit down. He was reassuring Margaret that all was well with Malcolm and her sons. Mary turned to him. "Is it possible that they can take Alnwick?"

The man faced Mary with flashing eyes. " 'Tis only a matter of time."

"But you do not have time. When my husband finds out that his home is threatened—he will ride with his men for Alnwick to rescue it."

The man faced her directly, in the stance of one ready
to do battle, with his legs braced apart. "But your husband,
Lady de Warenne, is currently engaged in a vicious battle,
one he cannot easily leave. And unless someone at Alnwick
dares to sneak past your father's army in the hope of sending
de Warenne a message begging for rescue, 'twill be a long
time before anyone learns of the siege." He smiled. " 'Tis
as Malcolm planned."

Mary was aghast. But the messenger was right. Stephen
was in the midst of battle, and no one at Alnwick would
have any way of sending him word about their dire straits.
If Mary had not been sitting, she would have undoubtedly
collapsed.

How clever Malcolm had been. Mary was furious.

Then Mary became aware of the silence of the hall.
Every single person within was staring at her, except for
her mother, who gazed unseeingly at the fire. And each and
every person there stared at her with loathing and accusation.
Mary surged to her feet and fled the room.

That night the snow began to fall heavily, the winds
howling so loudly that sleep was impossible. Mary listened
to the eerie, horrible sound, trying not to dwell upon what
was happening to her family and her home. She thought
about her mother, so distraught that she was unquestionably
ill, she thought about her brothers, fighting in battle, perhaps
even a part of the siege itself. She tried not to think about
her father, but that was impossible. He had disowned her,
he had attacked Alnwick. For an instant, a wave of hatred
washed over her, but then it was gone, and she was weak
and exhausted and numb.

Stephen probably had yet to learn that she had escaped
Alnwick. Mary was hardly relieved. She had made a monu-
mental mistake in fleeing without his permission, she had
failed in her mission, and when he learned what she had done,
he would be convinced of her treachery. After Edward's visit
to Alnwick, he would think her escape some prearranged
scheme; he would think that she had fled from him to his
enemy. But the great irony was that in her flight, she had
been confronted with the ironclad truth—as much as she
loved her kin and country, as much as she loved Scotland,

her home was Alnwick, and her loyalty was owed the red rose of Northumberland.

Mary knew that her very life depended upon convincing Stephen to believe her innocence. And the more time that passed, the more convinced he would be that she had run away from him. Despite his mistrust, she loved him wholly, she belonged to him and she always would, and she wanted to be with him, the way it had been before. If he would exile her, she could not bear it. Too clearly Mary recalled his very explicit threat to do just that. She must return home immediately, yet how could she? How long would this war go on? If Malcolm was successful, she realized with sudden horror, the war would never end. Stephen and his father and the other Normans would fight until they died to avenge the destruction of Alnwick.

Mary sat upright and shivered. She must hope for a speedy end to the war, she realized, which meant she must hope for Malcolm's defeat. After his terrible rejection, she owed him no loyalty, yet she could not find it in her heart to yearn for his downfall. She had been his daughter for too many years.

Mary listened to the roaring, high-pitched wind. Outside the night was white from the blizzard. Was she insane enough to take a horse and try to return to Alnwick by herself? Did she love Stephen enough to risk her life for him?

Mary swallowed. She was not a madwoman, to venture out into a snowstorm and risk death. But she did love Stephen enough to risk her life for him, if ever she had to. That time had not yet come; hopefully it never would. But Mary knew now that she could not sit idly by and wait for a truce in order to return home, if ever a truce might come. She would wait for the blizzard to end and for the roads to become passable. If the war had not yet ended, she would set out for home by herself. And nothing and no one would stop her.

When Mary finally dozed, her decision made, she felt better, even hopeful. Yet when she awoke the next day, she doubted whether she might be able to leave anytime soon. The snow had stopped, as had the maddening winds, but outside the world was blanketed six feet deep in white.

More importantly, Margaret's maid told Mary that her mother had passed another completely sleepless night. She had gone to the chapel at midnight for matins, and had stayed there until dawn. She only broke the fast with a few sips of water and two bites of bread. By now Mary knew that her mother had barely eaten or slept in a fortnight, not since Malcolm had left Edinburgh. It had become clear that the Queen was haunted by her own terrible demons. And nothing Mary did or said could convince her to eat or sleep. Mary contemplated drugging her in order to get her to rest.

The second day was endless. While Margaret again took up her place before the hearth, sewing, Mary could do nothing but pace. It made the other waiting women crazy, she knew, but they dared not say anything to her. The morning dragged into noon. No one could eat. Dusk slipped upon them. Still no word came. The heavy snow had obviously delayed news of the second day of fighting. The night sky became black, starkly dark against the pale and ice-encrusted loch below the fortress. Word came that another messenger had arrived.

"Bid him enter," Margaret said. She was as starkly white as the snow on the trees outside. She had spoken so low, one could barely hear her.

Mary instinctively moved to her mother's side. She put a comforting hand on her shoulder. She was growing very afraid. She should have forced Margaret to eat something at nooning.

The messenger entered, shaking the wet snow from his mantle. He was a young man, his boots covered with frozen mud, one arm bandaged, the linens black with blood. He was unsmiling and gray with exhaustion. Mary took one look at his face and went absolutely still. It was clear to her that the Scots had suffered a terrible loss that day.

"The King is dead," he said.

Mary knew she had misheard him. She opened her mouth to protest—surely she could not have construed him correctly.

"Malcolm is dead," the youth said, and this time his words were choked on a sob.

"No," Mary began, disbelieving. "This cannot—"

Mary's words were cut off. A loud thump sounded. Mary started and turned to see Margaret upon the floor. Her eyes were closed, her face lifeless and as pale as death. "Mother!"

All the women rushed to the Queen. Mary took her mother's face in her hands and felt the faint flutter of her breath; she pressed her ear to her breast and heard the faint but steady heartbeat. Tears of relief gathered quickly. She looked up. "Bring ice-cold rags so I can revive her. Hurry! She has only fainted from the shock!"

As several maids fled to obey, Mary tried to revive her mother gently. She shook her and spoke to her, but she could not bring her to consciousness. Mary grew desperate. She was too aware of Margaret's strange state of mind and her poor state of health. All her relief vanished. Margaret was too vulnerable in her condition. Finally Mary struck her across the face. Margaret's eyes flew open.

"Thank God!" Mary cried.

Margaret looked at her daughter, her own eyes filling with tears. The tears poured down her cheeks in a steady stream. Her lids drifted down while the tears poured and she curled up into a ball. She did not make a sound.

Mary gathered her mother into her arms, white with fright, rocking her as she wept silently. "Bring me wine and valerian," Mary said with a calm she did not feel. "And send for two men; we must get the Queen to her bed."

One or two hours later, Mary could not be sure exactly, Margaret opened her eyes. She looked directly at Mary. "I knew it," she said hoarsely. Her words were barely audible.

Mary had been so worried about her mother that she had not had time to dwell upon the news of her father's death. Now she grasped her mother's hands firmly, leaning urgently over her as she lay in her bed. "Mother, you must be strong. You must eat some of this gruel Jeanne made. Please."

"I must pray," Margaret said. "Help me up. I must pray for your father's soul."

Mary realized that her mother intended to go to the chapel.

"No, Mother," she said firmly. "Father Joseph will come here. He is downstairs."

Margaret sank back upon the pillows, her eyes closing, her lips moving in silent prayer. Mary rushed to the door, outside of which all of Margaret's ladies waited. Each and every one of them loved their Queen dearly, as did everyone who knew Margaret, and they were all now somber and pale with anxiety. At Mary's bidding, Lady Matilda rushed downstairs to fetch the priest.

Mary returned to her mother's bedside, sinking down onto her knees. She refused to think about Malcolm's death at the hands of her husband's army. She could not. She must not. She had to take care of her mother. She turned off her thoughts with an iron will.

The priest entered the room. He, too, was a lifelong friend—and mentor—of the Queen's. Mary rose as Father Joseph rushed forward. Margaret opened her eyes. "Did he have the last rites?"

Mary saw the grim truth in the priest's eyes as he lied to Margaret in order to ease her distress.

While Margaret prayed silently with the priest, Mary slipped from the chamber. Outside she leaned against the wall. Her mother's women surrounded her, bombarding her with whispered questions.

Mary pushed away from them, knowing their concern was genuine, that each and every one of them was deathly afraid for their Queen, but she did not answer a single question. She did not know the answers. Somehow she ran downstairs.

The youth who had brought them news of Malcolm's death was in the Great Hall at the table, eating ravenously. Mary sank down on the bench beside him. The sight of food nauseated her. "How can it be true?" she managed huskily. "How can Malcolm be dead?"

The youth shoved his trencher aside. His blue eyes filled with tears. "His army was attacked from behind. Then, he got cut off from his men. It should have never happened." The messenger looked away from her.

Mary grabbed his arm with a strength she had not known she still possessed. *"Which army?"*

"Northumberland's."

Mary felt dizzy; the table swam in front of her. Had Stephen led the attack that killed Malcolm? Had he?

"Princess," the messenger said hoarsely, "there is more."

Mary rubbed her eyes, hoping it would help her vision to clear. The table righted itself, but her whole world had become blurry. "No," she said, "there cannot be more."

He wet his lips. "Edward was wounded."

"No!" Mary gripped the table to keep from reeling, to keep from falling. "He's not . . ."

" 'Tis bad. But he was alive when I left."

"He will live," Mary said with certainty. She closed her eyes, dizzy now with relief. "No damn Norman can kill Ed," she whispered. She fought the sudden fit of trembling. She could not give in to any hysteria now. "And . . . Alnwick?"

"We have been pushed back to Cumbria. The tide has turned. We are almost back where we started," the boy said grimly. "The battle still rages over Carlisle. And now, without Malcolm, without Edward . . ."

Mary closed her eyes. "Edmund is a great warrior. And the other leaders . . ."

"The chiefs all fight among themselves, Princess; 'twas only Malcolm who was strong enough to keep them united." The boy hesitated. "Not all of the men trust Edmund."

Mary could not respond to that. Her brother's character was not the best. But with Ed wounded and Malcolm dead . . . Instantly she shut off her thoughts. She would not think about her father, she would not. Instead, she would pray for Ed.

And she must not think about Stephen either, not now, not when his men had killed her father and wounded her brother—she must not.

"Mother, please, drink some of this. It is your own special brew," Mary pleaded.

Margaret did not respond to her, and it was as if she did not even hear her. Since Father Joseph had left many hours ago, Margaret had fallen into a sleeplike state. She could not be roused; thus it was no ordinary sleep. If Mary had not been able to discern that she was still breathing, albeit very faintly, she would think her to be dead.

Mary was beside herself. She had not slept in days, and she dared not leave her mother, not now, not when it seemed as if Margaret was dying before her very eyes. Mary was resolved. She would not let her die. She could not. But what could she do?

She took her mother's icy hands in hers and warmed them briskly. A sharp knock at the door was an instant relief, diverting her attention. Mary froze when Edgar walked into the room. She had last seen him three nights ago, just before the first battle outside of Carlisle.

He was unrecognizable. Edgar was pale and exhausted, dark circles ringing his eyes; he appeared a wasted man of middle years, not a merry lad of seventeen. His glance passed quickly over Mary and skidded to halt on their mother. "I do not understand this," he said in a hoarse voice. "They told me below that she is at death's door."

Mary rose to her feet, her knees stiff and aching terribly from the long hours she had spent kneeling at her mother's side. Indeed, her entire body ached and hurt, but that was nothing compared to the pain in her chest. "She did not take the news of Malcolm's death well," Mary said unsteadily. Edgar's appearance threatened to unravel her precious emotional control. She took a deep, calming, breath. "When I arrived here I found her in a frightful state. She hadn't eaten or slept in days, she had worried herself sick. It seems," she said, and her voice cracked, "that she had a premonition of Malcolm's death."

Tears glazed Edgar's eyes. "He died a warrior's death. He died the way he wanted to die, the way all men hope to die, in the midst of battle, proudly, bravely."

Mary shuddered. Quickly she crossed her arms and hugged herself. She must not think about Malcolm now, she must not. Tomorrow, when Margaret was better, why, then she could allow herself to grieve.

Edgar interrupted her thoughts. "Edward is dead."

Mary cried out.

Edgar moved quickly, crossing the small chamber and taking her into his arms. Mary screwed her eyes closed tight. Hot tears gathered against her lids, exerting pressure, but she refused to open them and release the flood. *Edward,*

not Edward, her oldest brother, her dear friend, her hero!
She did not believe it, she would not!

Edgar spoke into her ear, one of his hands stroking her back. Edgar—who had never embraced her or openly shown his love for her in any tender way. Edgar, who yesterday had been a boy of seventeen, and who today had become a man of fifty. "The wound was mortal. He lost too much blood. He died in his sleep, thank God for that, without pain."

Edward was dead. "I cannot," Mary began in a hoarse voice.

Suddenly Edgar pushed away from Mary. "Your husband is at their head," he spat.

Mary straightened.

"He is the invincible one! He has pushed far into our ranks, alone and repeatedly, exposing himself to our men again and again—yet no one can approach him without falling victim to his sword. He strikes down all in his path. They say he is possessed; either that, or he is Death himself." Suddenly Edgar fought for some degree of calm and gained it.

Mary was rigid, unmoving. Somehow Stephen had learned of her escape. She had not one doubt. Stephen was not possessed by the Devil, merely possessed by an inhuman rage. And she was chilled with fear.

Edgar jerked on her arm. "He has sworn to beat a path of destruction to your door, Mary. He released one of the prisoners to convey that message to us. His exact words are that he wants you back, not in spite of your treachery—but because of it."

Mary began to tremble. "He wishes to punish me," she whispered.

"I imagine he wishes to kill you," Edgar said. "I glimpsed his face at Alnwick, and even I was struck with terror."

Mary whimpered. She had seen Stephen in a red rage. Could he hate her now so much that he wished to kill her? Could he wish her dead?

Two days later, Margaret was dead.

Mary was numb, shocked, exhausted. She realized that she still knelt beside her mother's body, holding her stiff hands. How long had she been kneeling in such a manner? She forced her body to obey her mind, and she managed to rise awkwardly and painfully to her feet.

The sound of anguished wailing, a sound that had begun some time ago, reverberated within the chamber. It was the way of the Scottish people to grieve loudly and openly and without restraint. Mary listened to Margaret's women, just outside the door, keening hysterically, she listened to the men and women in the hall below, also wailing and weeping, and to those gathered outside in the bailey. The rending communal wailing wafted over her again and again, until the pain of it finally began to pierce through some of Mary's shock.

She felt a huge bubble gathering itself inside her breast, welling and welling, robbing her of air. She choked on it.

Dead. Mary choked aloud. *Dead.* God, the word was so final. She looked at Margaret, as serene in death as she had been in life. *Dead!* It did not seem possible. *Not Margaret, not Mother!*

Mary wanted to keen, too, she wanted to scream and wail and rip her hair, as the women in the hall outside were doing. But she did not. She must hold her grief at bay just a little longer. She had her brothers to think about now. They would need her to see them through this terrible time of loss.

Mary suddenly gasped. "Mother, I love you so much!" It did not seem possible. Margaret was dead! Margaret, her dear mother, was dead, Malcolm was dead, and Edward was dead! It was unfair! She could not bear it, she could not!

She turned blindly in a circle, needing comfort when none was to be found. She finally pressed her cheek to the rough stone wall, clutching it, embracing it. And she began to weep.

She wept and wept, then she beat the walls until her hands were bloody, screaming her grief. She hated him then, for his part in their deaths—in their murders. She hated her husband. They were all dead, Malcolm, Margaret, Edward, and it was forever—she would never see them again.

Finally she could cry no more. Mary found herself prostrate on the floor. God, she was so tired! She could barely sit up. She could not continue like this, she could not, not when she was so exhausted, she doubted she could even walk.

But then her mind told her to think. Her mind told her to think of the danger that lurked without Edinburgh, a danger threatening not just her, but her brothers, even Scotland. Mary wiped away the last traces of her tears. She had no time for tears. Too much was at stake. Lives were at stake; a kingdom was at stake.

Malcolm was dead. Scotland was a kingdom without a King. The seat of the kingdom was Edinburgh, and soon the strongest clans in the land would be descending upon it, hoping to seize power for themselves. Even now, a dozen great chiefs must be closing in upon Edinburgh in a mad race for the crown.

Her brothers all had legitimate claims to the throne. Edmund she did not care about—he could take care of himself, as he undoubtedly was doing—and Ethelred was safe, being a man of God. But she owned the responsibility for guarding her three other brothers; each and every one of whom posed a real threat to Scotland's next King. It did not occur to Mary that, as Edgar was older than herself, the responsibility was his.

Mary forced herself to her feet. She moved like a very old woman.

She paused. She realized that the sounds invading the chamber had changed. Her heart lurched with instinctive dread as she strained to comprehend what she was hearing. She thought she could hear distant thunder, but the sky outside was a clear and cloudless blue. Mary gasped.

What she was hearing through the loud wailing of the castle was not distant thunder but the rumbling reverberations of a huge invading army. Dear God, not so soon! Would there not ever be any respite?

And then Edgar burst into the room. Mary listened in white-faced shock as he told her that Donald Bane had been named tanist, and that Edmund had betrayed them and joined forces with their uncle to usurp the throne. Meanwhile, outside, the thunder grew steadily louder.

For one moment Mary and Edgar stared at each other. Mary knew no relief; Edmund would be as ruthless as any stranger in these circumstances—or more so.

Mary straightened. "Gather up the boys! Do it now! Bring a cart round for—" She looked at Margaret. Her hard-won control slipped and she choked. "For the Queen. We will bury her at the Abbey at Dunfermline, where we can seek sanctuary. Hurry!"

Edgar turned on his heel and left. Mary could not stop shaking, not now, and she gripped the prie-dieu to keep herself from collapsing. Grief, fear, and utter exhaustion overwhelmed her, immobilized her.

It took a great effort, but Mary went to her mother and covered her. Edgar burst back through the door. He gave her one long look, then rushed forward to Margaret. Effortlessly he lifted their mother into his arms.

Mary pushed herself to keep pace with him. "How could Edmund abandon us?"

"He's not a part of this family anymore," Edgar spat as they raced downstairs and outside into the bailey, where the sunlight was so strong, it was briefly blinding. Her brothers were already mounted, all of them except, of course, the traitor Edmund. The next to youngest, Alexander, was trying to comfort little Davie, who was crying. Edgar laid their mother in the horse-drawn cart.

It was then that Mary realized that the bailey had become eerily silent. All of the crazed wailing had ceased, as had every other possible sound. The silence was unnatural, terrifying. Mary knew that she was listening for something, but she did not know what. And then it struck her—the ominous drumming beat of the invading army had ceased.

Mary cried out as Edgar boosted her onto a mount and leapt onto his own steed. The army had halted—to position itself for an attack! " 'Tis Donald Bane, is it not?"

Edgar rode up to her. "No."

Mary froze. "Then . . . who?"

The glance he shot her was long and dark. And Mary knew. She felt it all then, love, hate, fear, and dread. *"No."*

" 'Tis Northumberland's bastard," Edgar spat. "The bastard's led his army right to Edinburgh. Is he coming to claim the throne for himself?"

Mary was faint. "No," she whispered. "He's coming to claim me."

Part Four

Exiled

Chapter 24

*T*he Abbey of Dunfermline was situated on a knoll just across the Firth of Forth from Edinburgh. It was enclosed by thick stone walls of a medium height, but these walls were primarily intended to be a boundary, and while a barrier to vagabonds and outlaws, they could not be a barrier to an invading army. And that was just what the abbey now faced, the abbot thought dismally.

A hundred mounted, armed knights, their armor mostly hidden by the heavy cloaks one and all wore to ward off the freezing cold, lined the snow-clad hillside. Sunlight glinted on a hundred shields and a hundred helms, and a hundred huge horses pawed the snowy ground, churning up dark mud. A black, white, and gold banner waved from the front ranks, a short-stemmed bloodred rose in its center, the red rose of Northumberland. If that were not enough to make the abbot's knees weak, and it was, the leader of these Normans faced him directly now from the great height of his great war-horse. And the leader himself was a huge man, imposing enough surely should he be standing on foot. He did not wear his helm, so the abbot could see his face clearly.

357

His visage dismayed him even more than his great display of power in the face of the abbey's real lack of fortifications. It was thoroughly chilling in its coldness.

The abbot of Dunfermline had decided to greet his visitor rather bravely, opening the narrow side door inset in the walls and stepping outside it. The passage could admit a man on foot, but not one in mail and heavily armed, much less a troop of mounted knights. For that they would need him to unbolt the two front gates. He clutched his mantle to his thin body, hardly aware of the cold. For he had deliberately decided not to open the front gates. Yet he was well aware that if the man facing him chose to enter the abbey against his will, there was nothing he could do to stop him. "What is it you wish, my lord?"

"You harbor the princess Mary. You will release her at once."

The abbot was afraid. Not for himself or the abbey, not for the monks or the nuns, but for the young woman who had come to him for refuge for herself and her brothers in the dead of a winter's night. He could imagine easily enough what this knight might do to the very beautiful and so very anguished princess, and he had no intention of giving in to him. He said a silent prayer to God. He certainly needed His help now. "Sir, you know that this is the Lord's house. She has taken sanctuary here. I cannot allow you to violate that sanctuary."

His teeth gleamed in a wintry smile. It was feral. "Sir Abbot, I prefer not to violate God's house, but if I have to, I will."

It was as he had thought. The abbot shuddered. He knew that the lord meant it. "I cannot allow you to enter, sir."

"Are you aware, Sir Abbot, that she is my wife?"

The abbot swallowed. Of course, he was aware of the fact. "Still, sir, it is a question of duty to God. I cannot allow you to enter."

His teeth flashed again, but not in a smile. "I am going to enter with force."

The abbot raised his chin, set his mouth, and did not move.

Stephen turned. He lifted his hand. Two knights instantly detached themselves from the troops. "Break down the gates," he said.

Geoffrey was mounted at Stephen's flank. His face was ashen. But he said nothing.

The two knights rode forward, lifting their great lances. They charged the gates. The wood cracked and groaned, but the iron bolts did not give. Another charge was successful; the two doors flew open with a tearing roar.

The abbot looked at Lord de Warenne. His face was haggard and shadowed as if he had not slept in days, yet his eyes gleamed with anticipation—with furious, hate-filled anticipation. No man could appear more beastly. He lifted his hand again in a short motion and spurred his destrier forward. A dozen men followed him into the cloister.

Inside, Stephen slid to his feet. His glance took in the abbey church with its long nave, situated at the northern end of the complex. Inside, the sanctuary was at the church's eastern side, facing Jerusalem. Stephen's glance did not flicker even once towards the rest of the buildings—the rectangular cloister where the monks worked at stalls between the pillars and strolled for exercise, the chapter house, the refectory, the dormitory. He gave Geoffrey one single look. "Do not allow anyone to leave."

Stephen strode across the frozen courtyard, heading directly for the church. He flung open the door and stepped inside. He paused one moment as his eyes adjusted to the dim light within.

Edgar stood in the center of the nave, his hand on his sword. Behind him, similarly posed, were his younger brothers, Alexander and Davie. Ethelred appeared from the shadows of the pews, clearly unarmed and in his habit, to stand beside Edgar and confront Stephen as well. Mary was nowhere to be seen.

"You will go to hell, my lord," Ethelred said quietly. "It is not worth it."

"Where is she?" Stephen asked coldly.

"She is gone," Edgar snarled. "She will never return to you, never."

Stephen's chest rose hard. His anger was so immense. "Where has she gone to, Edgar? Answer me. Do not make me cut it out of you." His own hand was on his own sword. He meant every word he said. His control was so precarious that if denied, he would lose it and he would cut Mary's brother to pieces in order to get the information he wanted— in order to get to her.

Ethelred stepped forward. "I will not allow you to taint this church with blood and war! She is not gone." He gave Edgar a dark glance. "She is in the dormitory. She refused to claim sanctuary here, my lord. Think on that."

Stephen's smile was frightening. And he did not give a damn why she had refused to join her brothers in the sanctuary. He strode outside and across the cloister. He correctly guessed which building was the dorter. Opening a door, he was greeted by a long, narrow hall. Small chambers, each with a pallet, lined it. Stephen moved down the hall, glancing into each bedchamber. All the chambers were empty. When he had glanced cursorily into some two dozen such cubicles, when he had reached the very end of the hall, he found her.

She stood in the very last bedchamber, against the wall, facing the threshold, waiting for him.

Stephen could barely breathe, he was so choked with fury. For a long moment he did not move. He silently told her to keep silent, because if she offered one word of explanation, one more damned lie, he knew he would lose all control and kill her.

But it was too much to hope for. Mary was trembling, and she was as white as the snow outside on the bare oaks, but she spoke. "My lord," she said hoarsely. "Please, please listen—"

As he had known it would, his control snapped. His hand arched out. There was a cracking sound as his open palm hit her face. Mary gasped as she fell back against the wall with a thud and then to the floor.

Stephen turned from her, panting, shaking, hating himself—but not as much as he hated her. "Do not," he finally said, when he could speak, "offer me one single lie. There is not a word you could speak which I wish to hear."

Mary pushed herself up with her hands into a sitting position on the cold stone floor. The room seemed to spin, and with it, Stephen's huge, powerful form. Pain washed over her in waves. She managed to wonder if he had broken her jaw. It felt like it. She managed to wonder if it was truly over for them.

Stephen turned, looking at her. "I warned you. No—do not dare speak. When I tell you I do not wish to hear you, I mean it. I am sending you to Tetly."

Mary blinked at him. The pain washing over her was changing, taking on a different nature. He was sending her into exile. At least he would not kill her, for she had been unsure of what to expect when finally they met. It had taken no small amount of courage to remain in her chamber, awaiting him, instead of hiding in the sanctuary. He was not going to kill her, but she could not be relieved. Exile was a fate she dreaded as she would true death. For was it not the death of their marriage?

And he would not let her speak in her own defense. Mary wanted to speak, she must speak—but she was terrified of him now, afraid he was so out of control that he would hit her again, this time killing her and the child unintentionally. Or maybe his intent was there in his breast, dark and deadly and sinister, needing only the briefest pricking of a spur to be roused, a spur her desperate words would provide.

Mary started to cry again, as she so often did these past few days.

A series of images flashed through her mind. Malcolm cold and furious, telling her that she was not his daughter anymore. Edward leading her away, embracing her, comforting her. Her mother kneeling in the chapel at Edinburgh in prayer.

And they were all dead. It was too much, far too much for her to bear, but now, now there was even more, now there was this.

Her husband, the father of her unborn child, a man she had hated briefly and should hate still but could not, hated her. He hated her enough to send her away, undoubtedly forever. And if she was not careful, his hatred might move him to unwittingly murder her and their child.

"Your tears do not affect me," Stephen said coldly. "You will never affect me again."

Mary wanted to tell him about the child. Perhaps if she told him about the life blossoming within her, he would soften, maybe even love her again. She was desperate. She would do anything to make him love her again. But then he said, "After you bear me my heir, I will exile you to France."

Mary was frozen, stunned. If she gave him a son, he would send her away to France. And that, she knew, would be irrevocable. Once she was locked away in France, she would never be able to reach out to him again, never be able to change his mind—for she would never see him again.

For just an instant, she was so sick, she thought she would retch.

Stephen paced to the door and paused. He half-turned to her. "I am too angry to even think of lying with you again at any time in the near future. But you are young. And my anger cannot possibly remain as it is. When the need visits me, I will visit you. I will have my son." He faced her fully, loathing in his eyes.

Mary whimpered, her eyes closed tightly. *And then he would send her away and it would truly be over for them.*

Then Stephen said, harshly, "And once I have my son, there will be no more need."

Mary watched him turn and walk away. Then she collapsed on the floor, moaning. But she was no longer aware of her bruised face, just the pain in her breast, the distress. Her heart had been ravaged. Torn into many tiny pieces, leaving only shattering pain.

Geoffrey came to escort Mary outside. Mary saw that he was aghast at the sight of her face. The side of her jaw was already swollen and mottling; soon it would be purple.

His disposition had been stern; now it eased fractionally. "Are you all right?" he asked, coming to take her arm.

Mary looked at him, her eyes again glazing over. "No, sir. I will never be right again."

Geoffrey was grim. "He will never forget this, Mary, but in time, he will bend a little; in time, I think he will forgive."

Mary closed her eyes briefly. "How I wish I believed

you." She opened them. "I did not run away from him, my lord. I did not. I only wanted to stop the war. I thought my father would listen to my pleas." Tears flowed. "I love Stephen." With great effort she managed to control her raging emotions. "Even after he has done something like this, I still love him. I have loved him for a very long time. Since Abernathy."

Geoffrey was uncomfortable but intense. "Perhaps you should tell him that, Mary."

"How can I? He refuses to believe me. And now he is so furious that I am afraid of him. I am not only afraid to speak to him, I am afraid to go near him."

"You must let some time pass. The next time you see Stephen, you will surely be able to converse without fear of his brutality. It is not like him."

"Of course," Mary said dully, as another hot wave of anguish crested, then crashed upon her. Could she survive these next few minutes, much less these next few days?

If she wanted Stephen back, she would have to. She could not imagine when she would see Stephen again. She would have to do far more than survive these next few days. She might have to survive many months before having the chance to face him again—to face him and defend herself and win him back to her side.

And if it was more than a month or two from now that they again met, her pregnancy would be obvious. Undoubtedly he would be furious with her for not having told him of it. But if she told him now, he would send her away and not even come to "visit" her in her exile. Mary knew that once again her only hope for salvaging their relationship lay in their desire for each other. If that desire still existed on his part. She was not confident.

Mary was exhausted, from her encounter with her husband, the loss of her parents and brother, the many days she had spent caring for her mother as she lay dying, the audience with her father, and her mad escape from Alnwick. She was quite certain that she was unable to bear anything more. Geoffrey led her outside. Mary had to fight to control her ravaged emotions. Although she had good cause to cry, she did not want to be hysterically distraught while being forcibly removed from the abbey by Stephen, in front of his brother, his men, the monks, and the good abbot. Her pride was all that she had left.

Then something fluttered low in her abdomen, making her catch her breath. How wrong she was—she had the child.

As she approached, escorted by the archdeacon, the armed knights looked away from her. Geoffrey helped her onto his horse, then mounted behind her. Mary dried her moist eyes. Her glance met Stephen's. Quickly, coldly, he, too, looked away from her.

How he hated her.

Then Mary saw her three brothers, Edgar, Alexander, and Davie, mounted side by side in the midst of the Norman knights. "What are they doing here?" she asked tersely.

Geoffrey regarded her. "They are not safe here, Mary."

"Of course they are safe here!"

"Did not Stephen break in to get you?"

Mary paused. Her glance flew to Stephen's broad back. If he could enter an abbey and break God's law, she knew that someone like her uncle Donald, or, God forbid, her brother Edmund, could do so as well. She shuddered. They had seized power the day she and the boys had fled Edinburgh— word had arrived that very same night. She did not want to dwell on the thought that Donald Bane or Edmund might seek to harm her brothers in order to secure the throne.

"Where is Stephen taking them?" Mary asked in a low whisper.

"To Alnwick, at least for now."

Mary was relieved. Her brothers would be safe at Alnwick for as long as they should remain there. For a time, at least, she would not have to worry about them, too, when she had so much to worry about herself.

The troops, with Stephen at their head and Mary mounted behind Geoffrey, her brothers in their midst, now prisoners, filed out of the abbey gates. Despite her exhaustion, Mary realized that, although it was against her nature, she must be patient now. Whatever her destiny might be, whatever the fate of her brothers, for the moment, all was out of her control. The time had come for waiting. No matter how bad at waiting she was, Mary realized that she desperately needed a respite. And it appeared that Stephen was inadvertently giving her one by exiling her to Tetly.

Her exile began inauspiciously. Not long after they had crossed the River Tweed and entered Northumberland, Stephen's forces split up. Geoffrey and two dozen soldiers veered east, taking Mary with them. Stephen and the rest of his troops continued south towards Alnwick with her three brothers.

Mary was allowed the barest and briefest of good-byes. She hugged Edgar, Alexander, and Davie each in turn, admonishing them not to worry about her or anything else. "All will be well in the end, I promise you," she said with what she hoped was utter conviction. Her certainty was a complete lie, for she was filled with fear and doubt. To make matters worse, not only did her brothers look as doubtful as she felt, Mary succumbed to hot, sorrowful tears at their parting.

She did not say farewell to Stephen. She was not given the chance. He removed himself from the vicinity of the leave-taking, remaining mounted and with his back to her. No gesture could have been more eloquent. As Mary remounted, she knew that Stephen had used his iron will to strike her from his heart.

Late that afternoon they turned directly east and came upon Tetly. Mary's low spirits plummeted even further when she first glimpsed the lonely keep. It was situated upon a remote and barren cliff just above the channel where the coast met the River Tyne. One twisting, precarious path led to its rusty gates. In such a situation, invasion and siege were impossible. Mary later learned that Tetly's site had been picked for precisely that reason, and for the same reason it had long since fallen into irrelevance and disuse.

There was no need of a drawbridge. The portcullis opened directly upon the steep, rutted road. Apparently Stephen had sent a few servants, a steward, and a chatelaine ahead, for the fanged gate, obstinate from lack of use, was raised immediately. They entered through dark stone walls into a small, dark bailey. The ground underfoot was frozen mud. Mary looked around with despair. The few outer buildings had long since fallen into disrepair. Walls had crumbled and roofs caved in. These sheds were unusable. She saw that a lean-to had been newly erected to stable the men's mounts and to keep a few pigs.

Mary turned towards the keep. It consisted of one lonely black tower which stood with its back to the cliff and the coast, exposed on three sides and constantly buffeted by high channel winds. On its front steps stood her staff, two maids, a young serf, an elderly steward, and a plump, worried-looking chatelaine.

Mary pulled her cloak to her more tightly. It was freezing out there on the cliff in the brunt of the wind, but her action was due more to deep dismay than chilling cold. She was to live here. For how long? And how long would it be until Stephen came to "visit" her? As Geoffrey helped her dismount, Mary was seized with panic and she clung to his hand. "You are not going to leave, are you?" she cried.

His expression was somber. "I have sent Archbishop Anselm word that I am delayed. I will stay a few days, Mary, to oversee some repairs and make sure you are settled in comfortably."

"Comfortably?" Mary was bitter.

"Tetly has seen better days, that's true, but you will not lack for a thing. I promise you that."

Geoffrey's words proved to be mostly accurate. Tetly had been well supplied in advance of her arrival. Obviously Stephen had been prepared when he had handed out his verdict to her. And the steward was efficient and eager to please, the chatelaine kind although pitying. Mary's rooms were constantly warmed by a big fire to ward off the ever-present cold. Anything she desired was served to her in the way of food and drink. Mary had no appetite, she was too sore at heart, but she thought of the child and ate more than she normally would.

Geoffrey stayed a sennight. Mary was grateful. During the day she helped the chatelaine. Mary had nothing else to do and she was determined to keep herself busy in order not to think about the tragedy that had struck her. It would be so easy to grieve, for her parents and brother, for herself. At night she conversed with Geoffrey in front of the fire. If only he could have stayed indefinitely. He was cheerful and considerate. But once the stable had been repaired, he left. And Mary had no choice but to face the nights alone.

And it was the nights that threatened her sanity. The wind howled like a banshee, making sleep difficult at best, and restless and broken when achieved. She was tortured by longings that were impossible dreams. She desperately missed Edward and Margaret. She could not believe that she would never see them again. And she desperately wished that her last few conversations with her father had never taken place. She was shaken to the very core of her being. Suddenly Malcolm was a stranger to her in her memory, not the wonderful father-King he had always been. Mary wanted to remember him as she had known him all her life, not as she had last seen him. She wished she could be sure that he had loved her despite his cruel words, despite his use of her and his rejection, but she could not. And now, now she would never know.

And she desperately needed Stephen. Not the cold, hate-filled man he had become, but the ardent lover, the respectful husband, the just and honorable man. She needed him. She had never needed him more. But he would come when it suited him, not her, and then only to use her.

The days passed monotonously. January slid into February. One snowstorm followed another; the winds were relentless. Mary hated Tetly. Sometimes she hated Stephen. Hating him was far better than loving him, and God knew she had reason to hate him. The blaze of anger would never last. It always gave way to an uncontrollable yearning.

Mary cherished the unborn baby.

Her body had changed. In her tunics only the fullness of her breasts were obvious, but when naked, Mary was delighted to see a small, firm tummy protruding. At least she had this baby, she thought. Already she was deeply in love with her child. Already she had become protective and maternal. She was not crazy, but being so alone, she had taken to talking to it, and sometimes she sang old Gaelic lullabies. The servants looked at her with fear, the chatelaine with fear and pity. They knew she was with child, for Mary made no attempt to hide her condition. When they saw her whispering to herself, to the babe, they crossed themselves or made old pagan signs and hurried away. Mary did not care what they thought. If she had not been carrying this child, she might very well lose all hope, and even her sanity.

Mary lost track of the days. But the snows ceased. It had been, the chatelaine said, a particularly frigid winter. Now there was only the winds, but one afternoon the sun began to peek through the low, thick clouds. And one day, when Mary was taking some air in the bailey, she saw green shoots of grass poking up through the mud.

She looked up at the sky. It was a pale, washed-out blue, but it was blue nevertheless, and the sun was a bright, clear yellow. Mary smiled. It was sometime in March, and now she could smell spring in the air. She took a deep breath. Her depression lifted in that moment. She had survived a long, dark, and dreary winter, and suddenly she was filled with hope. Spring meant renewal and rebirth. At the very least she could look forward to pleasant days and, with summer's advent, the birth of her child. How her heart leapt at the thought.

And it could not be very long now before Stephen would come.

"Riders, my lady!"

Mary looked up from the dais where she sat alone at her noon meal. She dropped her knife. "Riders?"

"They're too far off for me to make them out, but 'tis a goodly sized contingent, flying a banner, my lady," the man said. He had just come running in from the single watchtower and was breathless.

Mary did not move, but her heart thundered so hard, she was faint. 'Twas Stephen. She knew it. Oh, God, she knew it. She was filled with elation, with excitement and fear. Oh, God, she must do everything right! She must win him back!

Mary lurched to her feet. She was five months pregnant, but as her build was so small to begin with, her condition was still not obvious while she was fully clothed. Of course, he would notice that she had gained weight immediately; her face was fuller, her breasts heavier. Suddenly Mary was doubly afraid. What if she was no longer as pretty as she had been?

She fled up the stairs and to her room to check her clothes and pat every hair back into place beneath her wimple. Then she froze. Stephen so loved her hair. Married women did not wear it unbound, but it was her glory now that she had lost her figure. Mary hesitated . . . She would let it down. With a banging heart, her hands shaking, she quickly unpinned and unbraided it. It fell in a riotous, brilliant, sun gold mass past her waist. If Mary was sure of one thing, it was that her hair had never looked better. Yet her hands still trembled while she quickly brushed it.

Mary was so nervous now that she felt sick. She had heard the men entering the hall below. Mary tried to take a few deep breaths. Oh, God. What if he still hated her?

Mary paused at the door to her chamber and said a quick, brief prayer. Then she straightened her shoulders and held her head high. She slid the heavy door open, paused, then went slowly down the stairs.

She entered the hall and stopped. Her eyes widened in disbelief. There was a man sitting at the table, but it was not Stephen. Instead, on the dais as if he were Tetly's lord, Prince Henry lounged. And when he saw her he smiled, and in that smile was all of his intent. As he had promised that dark, solitary night out upon the ramparts at Alnwick, he had come to her in her exile.

Mary stared. Henry stared back. His regard was amused in response to her shock, and it wandered over her, going first from her face and then to her hair and finally down her body. When he looked back at her, his gaze had become intense. "How beautiful you are," he said.

Mary's heart lurched in dread.

His gaze moved to her voluptuous breasts, which strained the fabric of her tunic. "You have never been more beautiful, Mary," the prince said.

Mary's heart slammed. She came to life, regretting her foolish action in letting her hair down. But it was too late now. Pale, frightened, and resolved to send Henry on his way—after she had learned of Stephen's whereabouts and doings—she slowly came forward. "Good day, my lord," she said with a slight curtsy. "This is a surprise."

He waved her up, then took her hand and helped her ascend the dais. Mary instantly slipped her palm free of his. His gaze was again amused. "Why have I surprised you?" he asked. "Did I not tell you I would come to you in your exile?"

Dread again washed over Mary. But with outward calm she sat down beside him. "It is very kind of you to come visit me in such a lonely time," she said, refilling his cup of wine. "But I find it hard to believe that kindness was your sole motivation. Tetly is out of the way for all travelers."

"Indeed, it is isolated and forsaken. What a dreadful place! But you appear to be faring more than well. You glow, Mary. Are you so happy apart from your husband, then?" Henry sipped his wine, but his eyes never left hers.

Mary turned to face him. "I am not happy apart from Stephen, my lord. I love him. I long for the day when he will forgive me and call me back to his side."

Henry smiled. "I do not think that day shall ever come, Mary. You betrayed him, and he is not a man who ever forgives his enemies."

"I am not his enemy. I am his wife."

"A dangerous combination. A fatal combination, as he well knows."

Mary looked away, angry. She forced herself to be calm. This was her first visitor all winter, and she was determined to learn of Stephen and her brothers and Scotland. They'd had no news these past few months, none at all. "How is he?"

"He is well."

That told Mary nothing. "And . . . my brothers?"

"They are well, also. They are enjoying William Rufus's hospitality. Edmund, of course, enjoy's Scotland's throne, with your uncle Donald Bane."

Mary said nothing, for the news that her brothers were now royal prisoners was hardly surprising.

Henry eyed her. "You are so calm. Did you know that Stephen is there, as well? He has been there for most of the winter."

Mary could hardly believe it. Stephen hated the Court. Her brothers had been summoned there, and Stephen had undoubtedly escorted them, but she could not understand why Stephen had remained as well. "What is Stephen doing there?" she asked cautiously.

Mary had tried very hard these past few months not to think about what her husband might be doing to take care of his very virile needs while apart from her, and she had been successful. No more. There were so many beautiful women at Court with the morals of whores. Mary thought that she could bear his using a whore—prostitutes were dirty and ugly, and a man's use of one was impersonal. But she could not stand the idea of his bedding a beautiful lady, and if he had been at Court for so long, he would not solicit whores.

"There is little to do at Alnwick in the long winter months, as you must know. I imagine he is amusing himself with all sorts of intrigues," Henry said blandly.

Mary looked at him. He was cruel. She knew he was not referring to political intrigue. And suddenly she had had enough.

She was Stephen's wife. This estrangement had gone on for far too long. If Stephen had taken another woman as his mistress, she would vent a fury such as he had never seen. She could imagine him entwined with Adele Beaufort. It was a horrible thought. She was his wife. If he had needs, he could sate himself on her.

"What of Adele Beaufort?"

"She married Ferrars in February," Henry said with a grin. "Not that that stops her from her wicked pursuits." His grin widened. "She has not left the Court, either."

Mary's bosom heaved. Was Henry insinuating that Adele and Stephen had resumed their relationship? Impulsively she leaned forward. "Take me with you when you leave. I wish to go to Court and join my husband there."

Henry's eyes widened, then he laughed. "How much gall you have! I cannot bring you with me, Mary, although it would almost be worth it to see the look on Stephen's face when you arrived. But he has exiled you, and rightly so. If I were your husband, I would have put you away in a convent for the rest of your days."

"But you are not my husband, are you?" Mary's tone was tart.

"No." Henry leaned close. "And your husband is not here." He smiled at her. "The winter must have been long and hard for you."

"Not as long nor as hard as you would like," Mary said coldly. "I am not interested in your attentions, my lord. Despite all that has passed, I love my husband and I shall remain faithful to him."

"Even when I tell you he is not faithful to you?"

God, how those direct words hurt. "Even so."

"I think I admire you, madame," Henry said. He sat back in his chair with a sigh. But his eyes gleamed.

That night, Mary could not sleep. Henry's words haunted her. She ached with hurt over Stephen's infidelity. She kept imagining him with the beautiful, immoral Adele Beaufort, who must now be Adele le Ferrars. Mary tried to think of a way to escape Tetly and go to Court, to reclaim her husband and her position as his wife. But escape from Tetly was impossible. The only way out was through the front gates, and she was expressly forbidden past them. Had Henry come with a wagon, she would attempt to hide in it as it left, but he had not. Mary tossed in her bed, finally turning onto her side. The only thing she could do was to send a letter with Henry. Surely the self-serving prince would deliver a missive to Stephen for her.

Mary stiffened. Through the racket of the roaring wind and the distant thunder of the surf breaking on the shore, Mary thought she had heard the creak of a wood door. Henry had the only other chamber on this topmost floor, and by now he must be fast asleep. She strained to hear, and thought it came again. Surely Henry was asleep, and there was no one else on this floor to be creeping about. Mary's pulse raced. But when the wind finally quieted for a moment, when there was only the soft, lulling sound of the waves beating the shore far below the keep at the base of the cliffs, she was reassured, for she heard nothing.

But only for a moment. In the next heartbeat Henry had slid into bed behind her with a chuckle, pressing his long,

aroused body against hers, holding her close. Mary gasped
in shock.

"Don't be surprised, sweet," Henry murmured, rubbing
his distended groin against her bare buttocks. With one
hand he fondled her full breasts. "I know you must yearn
for a man."

Mary could not reply. Henry, thank God, had yet to
undress for bed, but she was stark naked. And—dear lord—
it had been so very long since she had felt a man's touch,
and her own body was so starved that the feel of him had
sent her pulses rioting. She loved Stephen, but Henry was
a virile man, and her body knew it.

"You are hot," Henry said thickly, squeezing her breast
gently and toying with her nipple. "God, I knew it." He
kissed her neck.

Mary recovered her sanity. "Get out of my bed! Get out
of my bed—this instant!"

"You want it," he returned, rubbing himself lazily against
her.

Mary closed her eyes, wishing it were Stephen lying there
with her, then in the next breath cursing him for leaving her
like this, so she might be in such a situation. And for one
second, she allowed herself to feel the sensations stealing
across her body. Then she took a deep breath—and jammed
her elbow into Henry's rib cage with all of her might.

He gasped. Mary scrambled to her hands and knees. Henry made an angry sound. He jerked her abruptly back down
on her belly, hard.

Mary cried out as he came down on top of her, fumbling
with his braies. "The babe, damn you! You'll hurt my
babe!"

Henry froze. An instant later he had lifted himself off of
her, his hand on her protruding belly. He froze again.

Mary scrambled out from under him and off of the bed.

Henry sat up. "God's blood," he said, clearly shaken.

Mary stood before the fire, looking wildly around for a
weapon. Her eyes settled upon the poker. She grabbed it and
held it up threateningly.

Henry stared at her. His gaze focused instantly on her
round, obviously pregnant belly. Then he looked at the vee

between her thighs and at her quivering breasts. He sat up straighter. "There's no need for that," he said dryly. "Rape was never my intention."

"It was not?" Mary asked, her voice high and cracked. She began to shake. She did not care what he said. The prince had almost raped her.

Henry's answer was to slide from the bed and light a taper. He held it up, looking at her again. "Stephen doesn't know." His voice had changed, all the dryness gone—it was cold and hard. It was the voice of a displeased aristocrat.

Mary realized that she was naked. She set the poker down and whipped a fur from the bed, wrapping it quickly around herself. She forced herself to be calm, to meet the prince now carefully, in full possession of all her wits. "No, Stephen does not know."

"Is it his?"

Mary bristled. "Yes, my lord, 'tis Stephen's." Her voice was a hiss. "I have never lain with another man, and I never will." Tears suddenly blurred her gaze. "No matter how hungry my body might be."

Henry was grim. " 'Tis his right to know."

Mary was in agreement, but she froze. Her only hope of seeing Stephen lay in his thinking her not pregnant, so that he would come to get her with child. Of course, what had happened with Henry would happen with him. The minute he got her tunic off, he would see that she was already with child—if he did not guess as much before. But at least he would be there with her, face-to-face. She must confront him; it was her only chance of righting their relationship. But if Henry told him she was already with child, he would send her away as he had promised to do. Mary was stricken with a horrible thought. A scene flashed through her mind that was far worse than anything that had already happened to her: giving birth to her babe and having it taken away from her while she remained behind, locked up in a cloister in France, forever. "You cannot tell him!"

"I shall tell him. He must know immediately!"

"What a fine friend you are!" Mary spat. Tears came. She hated to beg, but beg she would. "Please, let me tell him."

"When? After the child is born?" Henry was sarcastic.

"No." It occurred to her that the solution to her dilemma—the answer to her prayers—had just arrived. "I asked you before, but for a different reason. Now I ask you again. *Take me with you.* I will tell him the moment I see him. Please. 'Tis my right."

Henry stared. Mary could not discern what was going on in his mind; his eyes were opaque and unreadable. Yet finally he nodded.

Mary swooned with relief. She was going to Court—to Stephen. To tell him of the child, and to fight for her life.

Part Five

Promise of
the Rose

Chapter 25

Adele had not seen Geoffrey de Warenne since her wedding to Henry Ferrars, but she would see him today.

The litter she had traveled in had halted. As Adele had traveled with the curtains open, she could see that she had arrived at her destination. Although still surrounded by two dozen of her husband's best knights, she could see the soaring cathedral of Canterbury proudly butting up against a very blue sky just a dozen steps ahead of her.

She had not seen Geoffrey in an achingly long time. She had been married on the first of February, and it was now April's day for fools. It was a terrible waste—her husband had been ensconced at Tutberry these past few weeks, many miles to the west of Essex, where she lingered, alone and increasingly desperate. Adele had sent Geoffrey numerous missives—but he had not come.

Adele made no move to leave her litter. So many heated emotions rampaged throughout her that she could not move, not yet. She was furious, furious at his obvious rejection, and she was afraid.

She, the most coveted woman in the realm, was afraid that the archdeacon had tired of her.

Their affair had been convoluted from the start. After his brother's wedding he had continued to see her for several days, until called away to the invasion of Carlisle in the North. But afterwards he had not returned to her as Adele had expected him to do. Endlessly she waited for her lover to appear, but he never had.

Adele began to send him missives, at first coaxing him, then urging him, finally demanding that he come. His replies were brief. His affairs detained him; she must busy herself with her own interests.

Adele was not just afraid that he had tired of her, she was furious. It seemed clear to her that he hinted that she should take another lover. But no other man could possibly interest her now. And more important, she was hurt—but that emotion she refused to identify.

Meanwhile her wedding to the middle-aged Ferrars approached. And then, just two weeks prior to the event she dreaded, Geoffrey sent her a message requesting a meeting. It had been ten long, interminable weeks since they had seen each other, and its tone was urgent. Adele guessed at the nature of his urgency. She intended to deny him, tease him, torture him—in short, she would punish him for his neglect. But when he arrived, they fell upon each other like rabid animals. Within seconds he had shredded her clothes with his dagger and was impaling her. They both reached their peaks immediately, but Geoffrey did not leave her; instead, he took her again and again. As always, he was masterful and insatiable, and Adele had been, for the first time in her life, exhausted afterwards. But also terribly, smugly pleased.

It was hardly over for them.

She was even more pleased when Geoffrey came to her that next day and every day for the following fortnight. On the eve of her wedding, she lay in Geoffrey's powerful arms, replete and unrepentant.

And she knew he was unhappy. She saw it in every line of his face, she saw it in his eyes. Adele was thrilled. He loves me, she thought happily, and is heartsick because I marry another.

The next day she said her wedding vows, swearing to honor and obey her new husband, to be chaste. Geoffrey attended the mass but not the wedding feast. He left the ceremony early, refusing to look at her even once—and she had not seen him since.

Adele was still angry that she had been given to Ferrars. She did not care how skilled Henry Ferrars was on the battlefield, or how loyal he had been to the King and his father before him. As far as she was concerned, he was a lowborn upstart, and nothing would ever change that.

Adele's new husband was ardent. Adele knew that he was as pleased with the marriage as she was distraught. It was clear to her that he was infatuated with her, perhaps even in love. Adele had no intention of defying him or denying him, no matter how she felt about him. She had never been a fool. If her fate was to be Lady Ferrars, then she would do her best to make sure that her husband worshiped her. While the knight was a powerful man, he retained none of that power when it came to Adele. Within a fortnight she had wrapped him around her little finger. He might outmaneuver his friends and foes alike, but he could not outmaneuver his new wife.

Unlike the archdeacon of Canterbury, whom Adele barely controlled, if at all. But now, now that was about to change.

Adele wanted Geoffrey desperately. She must see him. She was quite certain she could not live without him. He had become an obsession. Instead of taking a lover, she used herself, while thinking of him. Once they were together, once they were in each other's arms, she would know that her fears were foolish and misplaced. He loved her; she was sure of it. And as he would not come to her, she had been daring—she had gone to him.

Besides, she had something to tell him, something that would change their relationship forever, something that could not wait. And after this day, Geoffrey would not be able to elude her, not ever again. After this day, the bond between them would never be revoked.

Geoffrey was incredulous. He paused as he leaned over a long table spread with scrolls, gazing up at the young deacon who stood in the chamber's doorway. They were in one of the chambers in Canterbury's cathedral, from which most of the see's business was conducted. "I beg your pardon?"

"There is a Lady Ferrars here, my lord, and she wishes to speak with you."

Geoffrey straightened. He was disbelieving and furious, but fortunately Anselm was in London. Dear God, hadn't she understood what his refusal to come to her meant?

It was not that his huge lust had died. Hardly. But she was married now, and Geoffrey would not cuckold a man he happened to respect. Other men might have no qualms about doing so, but he was not like other men—he had never been like other men. Indeed, this added factor finally meant that he would be the victor in his own private war with himself. "Show her in," he said irritably.

Adele swept into the room. Geoffrey's body tightened. She wore a red wool mantle, and the hot color suited her. Despite his resolve, which remained firm, she was ravishing.

"My lord," she whispered, curtsying.

Geoffrey murmured a nonsensical greeting, but did not touch her to help her to rise. The deacon had gone, unfortunately, leaving them alone. "Lady Ferrars, I see that matrimony agrees with you," Geoffrey said briskly. The sooner she was gone, the better. He did not trust himself after all.

Adele's gaze blackened and her sultry smile died. "Of course it does," she managed.

"And how is the groom?"

Her eyes blazed. Pointedly she shot a dark look at the open door, but Geoffrey ignored it. "Henry is in Tutberry," she finally said. "He has been there for several weeks."

"So I have heard," Geoffrey said wryly. Adele had sent him a dozen messages, each and every one reminding him that she was alone. "How can I help you, Lady Ferrars?"

She stared with unspoken urgency. "I am on my way to my brother's estate in Kent. I wish to pass the night here, my lord."

Geoffrey was furious. Such a request was common and could not be refused, for travelers were always granted a bed and meal in any abbey they happened to pass by. St. Augustine's was just across the way. "You are speaking with the wrong man, lady," he murmured. "The abbot will gladly put you up." But what did Adele think to achieve by this effort on her part? he wondered. She would not be able to sneak out of the abbey gates after dark—or did she hope to gain an afternoon rendezvous in a wooded glade? Knowing her as he did, it was entirely possible.

And despite himself, knowing what such a rendezvous promised, he grew hard and thick.

"I am very tired," Adele said. "I thought to stop here and rest first."

Geoffrey was silent, so that no evidence of arousal would linger in his tone. "Of course, Lady Ferrars, as you wish."

Her eyes snapped. "Indeed, I do not feel well. I think I might have to remain for several days before continuing my journey south."

Geoffrey was about to make a comment when he realized what she was doing. She had taken her hand and placed it beneath her mantle upon her silk-clad abdomen. She caressed herself.

In a low voice, her gaze holding his, she said, "Perhaps I should not be traveling at all."

'Twas not his place to ask—not if they were unfamiliar with each other—but her gesture was unmistakable. Swiftly Geoffrey went to the door and shut it. He faced her, disbelieving. "If you are with child, Lady Ferrars, you should not be on the roads."

"Then I have erred," she said huskily. But she was smiling, triumphant.

Geoffrey was frozen. Adele was with child. *Was it his?*

Adele suddenly swayed. "I feel quite faint," she murmured.

Geoffrey caught her before she swooned, and she leaned heavily in his arms. A heartbeat later she had turned in his embrace, smiling up at him. "At long last," she said hoarsely, making no attempt to hide her excitement.

For one instant, his gaze wandered from her lush mouth to her heaving bosom. Her mantle had opened, and as she wore not one thing under her fine silk tunic, her nipples, large and erect, were clearly visible, as was every inch of her voluptuous figure. Geoffrey saw no sign of a pregnancy. "Are you with child?" He set her away abruptly.

Instantly she was back in his arms. "We must meet!"

Geoffrey gripped her wrists, forcing her to break her hold upon him. "No, Adele, it is over."

She inhaled. Then she twisted wildly. "I will kill you!"

Geoffrey forced her against the wall while she struggled wildly, hissing and spitting like a cat. Finally he subdued her, but he was not pleased, for she had felt his rigid manhood and she was laughing, exultant. "You need me, darling, you cannot deny it!"

Geoffrey did not want to be cruel, but she was toying with him when she spoke of a child, and he could not allow it. "I want only a woman's body, Adele, and it need not be yours."

She choked in fury. "And I have only missed your big cock, you whoreson," Adele cried.

Geoffrey was too agitated to laugh. "You are always so ladylike, Adele."

She went still, panting. She finally looped her arms around him, groaning, pressing her own quivering body closer to his. "No, Geoff, you know that's not the truth. Of course I have missed you," she said huskily. "You are the only man for me, I swear it."

"I doubt it," he said, very grim. He shrugged free of her. He had no wish to have someone walk in on them, alone and embracing—the repercussions would be vast. Especially now, if his spies were correct.

Adele moved to him, a stalking, determined tigress, and one of her long, tapered nails skimmed his cheek. "No one is as good as you."

"It is over, Adele, over."

She hissed in displeasure. He caught her arm before her talon could claw down his cheek. "Is there someone else? Who?!" she cried.

"There is no one else."

"I do not believe you!" Suddenly she seized his hard shaft. "Or maybe I do!"

He batted her hand away. "Obviously you are not tired, and obviously you are not ill. I will have you escorted to the abbey. If you make a scene, Adele, we will both pay a terrible price. Accept that it is over."

"No. It will never be over!" And she smiled. She blazed with triumph.

Geoffrey was touched with foreboding, and the skin at the nape of his neck tingled. "You are with child, aren't you?"

She laughed once, the sound husky and exultant. "It will be a boy. A gypsy told me so last week." Staring at Geoffrey, she added, "Henry will be so pleased."

Geoffrey's face was tight, his nostrils flared. His tone was dangerous. *"Could it be mine?"*

She laughed with delight. She shrugged.

He jumped on her. She had turned her back as if to leave, but he whirled her about. *"Whose child is it?"*

"What do I get if I tell you?" she asked coyly.

He had never hit a woman before. He almost hit her now. "When is the child due, Adele? Answer me, before I damn you to hell!"

Adele blanched. "In seven months."

Geoffrey made a rapid calculation. "So it could be Ferrar's—or it could be mine."

Adele watched him, both wary and excited.

Geoffrey walked away from Adele, his shoulders rigid, his eyes arctic blue. He was shaking. *Was he the father?*

And Adele was smiling.

Geoffrey had no children. It was no surprise, considering that, although hardly celibate, he fought his sexual proclivities the best that he could. Still, he had had his first woman at the age of thirteen—would he not have created a child by now? It occurred to him that he might not have a potent seed. He had not brooded upon this before. In his position, a child would be a liability and an embarrassment. A child could wreck all that he had worked for, it could destroy his future.

But . . . dear God, how he yearned for a child!

Dear, dear God, how he hoped that the babe Adele carried was his!

In spite of the fact that he could never claim the child openly and in spite of the consequences he might have to pay if ever the truth were revealed—he wanted this child to be his.

Geoffrey looked at Adele. She was smiling and smug with satisfaction. He was furious. "You will be sorry if you continue to toy with me, Adele."

Her smile vanished. " 'Tis yours. I know it."

"How can you be sure? I was in your bed every day for two weeks, but immediately after, you were married to Ferrars. How can you be sure?"

"I am sure!"

Geoffrey knew better than to believe her. It was impossible for her to be sure—wasn't it? In this instance, either he or Ferrars could be the father, and the child's actual birth date would prove nothing, for a child could be born early or late.

And as Ferrars was also fair, unless the child's looks were unmistakable, that also would prove nothing—and if it did, it would be many years from now when the child was well into adulthood.

Adele had come to stand behind him, one of her hands upon his shoulder. "You are the father," she said seductively. "I am sure of it. Your seed could only be powerful and potent, as you are."

Geoffrey hardly heard her. In that instant he realized that in all likelihood he would never know the truth. And it was also the moment when he realized that the child would bind him to Adele forever, in a way far more important than mere lust ever could.

And for a moment, a moment of insanity, even knowing Adele as he did, he coveted her as his wife.

"I will have you escorted to the abbot. If you wish, I will send him a brief missive."

"Geoffrey!"

His gaze was opaque, unreadable. "The child changes nothing, Adele. 'Tis over between us."

"But I love you," Adele cried. She flushed, the telltale color betraying her words as the truth.

"Then I am sorry," Geoffrey said. "Then I am truly sorry, sorrier than you will ever know."

Adele was not a woman who cried. It had been many years since she had shed tears of grief, and that had been when she was a ten-year-old child who had just learned that her parents had been killed by outlaws, leaving her orphaned. She did not cry two years later after her corruption by her stepbrother, Roger Beaufort, a corruption her wicked body had eagerly participated in. But that night, alone on a hard pallet in St. Augustine's Abbey, she wept, brokenhearted.

Now that she had said the words, she knew they were true. She loved him. He was powerful, pure, and good—unlike her. He was the epitome of manhood, and despite his lapse from celibacy, he was virtuous in a way Adele could hardly understand, but could somehow admire.

For the first time in her life, Adele wished she were a virtuous woman. She wished she were someone else, someone worthy of Geoffrey de Warenne, a woman he might want not just in his bed, but as his wife. For the first time, she regretted her nature, her affairs, everything. But she could not regret him.

She knew her child was his. It could not be Henry's; every instinct she had told her that. It must be his! If not, she had truly lost him.

Adele was suddenly dry-eyed. She had spent the past six years since her parents' death alone, scheming in order to survive—and not just to survive, but to survive well. She had hardly ever lost a single battle in that span of time— she would not lose now.

Geoffrey was not unmoved by the news of the child. Adele was determined. This separation could not be final. She wanted Geoffrey back. *He belonged to her.*

There was time, she decided finally, wiping away her tears. As she had concluded long ago, 'twas fortunate that he was of the Church, so she had nothing to fear from another woman. And she did not fear his virtue. He still desired her, and she was an expert at seduction. Tomorrow she would try again. Tomorrow she would succeed. And if not tomorrow, then the day after that.

She would never give up.

Adele was shown by the young deacon to the chamber where Geoffrey worked. Even though she was announced,

Geoffrey did not move. He stood by one of the open windows, drenched in sunlight. His beautiful, golden profile was stark, ravaged.

Adele was frozen. Something was terribly wrong.

Geoffrey turned his head slightly towards her. His gaze was strangely flat. "What now, Adele?"

He was weary, and Adele longed to hold him. Then she realized that he held a scroll in his hand. The scroll's seal was broken. And it was unmistakable, for it was royal.

Adele tensed, knowing that Geoffrey must have received another summons from the King, and knowing as she did how he had fought Rufus for control over many matters pertinent to both Crown and Church alike, she was afraid. How often she had wanted to warn him to cease his mad war against the Crown, but had refrained, not wanting him to comprehend the depth of her passion for him. "Geoffrey— what news do you have?"

His mouth curled slightly. "Why, I have just attained all that I have dreamed of."

His tone was strangely mocking. The hairs upon Adele's nape rose. "Darling," she whispered, forgetting the open door, "what has passed?"

Then his eyes glittered and his expression changed, his jaw flexing, as if a threshold had been crossed, a decision made. "The King has appointed me Bishop of Ely."

Adele gasped. A thrill swept over her. "Bishop of Ely!" she cried. "My God, that's wonderful!"

Geoffrey said nothing, standing tall, straight, and unmoving, his eyes brilliant but opaque.

"But you and the King have been fighting for four years— ever since Lanfranc died," Adele said. Her brow furrowed. "Why would Rufus appoint you to such a position of power and preeminence?"

"Do you not see?" he asked dryly. "I am being bought, Adele. The King thinks to remove a prickly rose thorn from his side."

Adele looked at Geoffrey, proud and cold and indomitable, and shuddered. She was more than afraid. She knew him. From the next Bishop of Ely, the King would expect unwavering loyalty, but Geoffrey was not the kind of man to compromise his cause. And his cause was the Church.

Adele's fears increased. The subtle kind of warfare Geoffrey and the King had so far engaged in had been nothing compared to what would erupt if Geoffrey, once invested, continued upon his present course. 'Twould be suicide! "You must not do anything foolish once this appointment comes to pass! You must cease your mulish confrontation with the Crown!"

Geoffrey regarded her. "What? Could it be that you have some fondness for me after all—outside of the bedchamber?"

Adele shivered, his tone frightening her. And she could not help glancing at the open door, but no one lurked there who could overhear them. Still, Geoffrey was never so careless. "Of course I do."

His lifted brow spoke of pure skepticism.

Adele's fear grew. "Geoffrey, what is happening to you? Dear God, you have just received a great honor from the King, an appointment other men would die for, cheat for, steal and lie for—but you have attained it honestly! Yet you hardly seem pleased!"

"I am pleased." He smiled, but it was not mirthful. "How could I not be pleased?"

Suddenly Adele realized that his appointment could be deterred, and Geoffrey had many enemies. He had said so himself. "You will have the appointment—will you not?"

"Indeed I will. I have received another missive this morn, from Anselm, who returns on the morrow to ordain me. He promises his full support, which means that election by the cathedral chapter is assured. Investiture shall be a mere formality."

Adele could not breathe easier. She was thrilled with his appointment—God, how it suited him—but already he had changed. She was dismayed as well as overjoyed. For he seemed aloof, remote, distant.

And the power she had seen in him from the first was magnified, emanating from him in cool, undulating waves.

Adele trembled. Geoffrey de Warenne faced her from across the chamber in his long, dark robes and heavy gold cross, strikingly male, reeking of virility, blond, blue-eyed, and beautiful. She shook. He was one of the premier prelates in the realm, and one of the King's most powerful vassals. He was the Bishop of Ely, and dear God, he was not quite twenty-three.

Even she was awed.

Chapter 26

Mary did not want to face Stephen again at Court after all of the time that had passed. She wanted no large audience to witness their exchange. Prince Henry took her directly to the door at Graystone. Mary politely thanked him for his efforts on her behalf, and as politely invited him in. He grinned. "I would not miss this for the world, Mary."

Mary had hoped he would decline. She was angered once again, especially because he made no attempt to hide his anticipation of the scene that would surely follow. Mary had enough to worry about without having the enigmatic prince around.

She was not feeling brave at all. Her heart was in her throat and she was sick to her stomach. It had taken two days to get to London. Because of her condition, she had ridden in a litter. During those two days she had not been able to eat or sleep. Fear consumed her. So much was at stake. Her future was at stake. She could imagine, with dread, what Stephen's reaction upon seeing her would be. At the very best he would coldly order her to return to Tetly; at the worst, he would be enraged that she had defied him yet again.

She could not, however, even begin to imagine what his response to her pregnancy might be. Although she had good reason to have denied him the news until now, he would hardly see it that way. She was regretting the deception with every breath she drew. What should be a joyous moment was one clogged with fear and dread.

Mary pulled her cloak and cowl more closely about her, the prince at her side, and walked to the front door. It was late in the day, dusk was falling rapidly, and there was a strong chance that Stephen would be home. The large contingent Henry traveled in had made a commotion as it halted in the meadow across the road, so their advent was no surprise. The Earl of Northumberland stood in the open doorway, watching them approach. He smiled in greeting at Henry.

His gaze slid back to her, unsmiling and searching. Although Mary hoped to hide her face—and identity—for as long as possible, she suspected that her small size gave her away.

"What brings you here, Henry?" Rolfe asked.

"I am delivering a surprise," Henry said with a chuckle.

Mary followed the two men inside. Her heart dropped to her feet. She wished to disappear. Standing facing them, his broad back to the hearth, was Stephen de Warenne.

"A surprise?" Rolfe asked with skepticism.

Henry only laughed.

Stephen stared. Mary cringed. He knew. For disbelief clouded his features, warring with rage. He had known her instantly.

"You bring her here?" he asked Henry incredulously, but his hard gaze was on Mary.

Mary pushed her hood back, filled with despair. "Stephen, it was my idea."

Stephen either ignored her or did not hear her. He addressed the prince again. "You bring her here when you know how I feel about her?"

"She has the most urgent need to see you," Henry remarked dryly.

Stephen advanced. Fury tightened his features. "I left you at Tetly, madame, for a reason. Surely you cannot have forgotten why?" He had raised his voice. It thundered.

Mary managed to stand her ground. "Enough is enough, Stephen," she said. She blinked back tears. "Could we have a private word, please?"

"I have nothing to say to you," Stephen said coldly. "You are returning to Tetly at once. This minute, in fact, is not soon enough."

"No," Mary whispered desperately.

"Stephen, you had better hear what she has to say," Henry said calmly, though there was no mistaking the command in his voice.

Stephen wheeled, facing his friend, furious with him as well, but he visibly controlled his anger. Then, abruptly, he grabbed Mary's arm. He made no effort to be gentle, and his grip hurt. Mary cried out. Stephen half-dragged her to the stairs.

"Have a care with her, Stephen," Henry said sharply.

Stephen did not pause, but his hold eased. Nevertheless, he did not release her, propelling her quickly up the short flight of stairs and into the first chamber on the floor. He slammed the door shut behind them.

Nervously Mary backed away from him.

"Your tears do not move me," Stephen said. Mary wiped her eyes. "Will you never forgive me?"

"No."

Mary sobbed plaintively, sorrowfully. She flung off her cloak. "Damn you," she whispered.

"You are getting fat," Stephen said harshly.

Mary blinked at him and molded her gown to her belly with her hands. In case he might still be in doubt, she turned sideways. Stephen stared.

"Do not ask. If you dare to ask, I will kill you. The babe is yours. I have lain with no other man, and I never will," Mary cried.

Stephen did not move, did not speak. He did not seem capable of either speech or movement. He stared in shock at the profile of her protruding belly.

Finally Mary dropped her hands and took a step over to the bed. She sank down on it in exhaustion. " 'Twill come, I think, in July."

Stephen recovered. His voice was strangely hoarse, though, when he spoke. "That means you conceived soon after we met. Before we were wed. And you have known this entire time."

She looked at him directly. She would not let him cow her, not anymore. "I guessed immediately, as immediately as possible for a woman whose monthly times were never precise. I wanted to tell you before the war. I was saving the news for a special time." Tears clouded her vision. "I wanted to bring you this news as a gift of love in a moment of love. Foolish me!"

"And still you did not tell me at Dunfermline," Stephen said, pale now. They both remembered how he had hit her and knocked her down in the abbey in rage.

"I knew you would delight in finding another reason to fault me, to accuse me of disloyalty. I did not tell you. You made it clear that you would send me away to have the child—I could not accept that."

"And when, pray tell, were you going to tell me?" His tone had become dangerous.

"When you came to Tetly to visit me, as you promised." Mary looked at him, her eyes huge and hurt. "But you never came."

Stephen stared back at her.

Mary clenched her fists, long-hidden anger spilling forth. "Have you been well amused here at Court, my lord? Is the reason you did not come to me because you are enamored of another woman? Your latest lover, perhaps?"

"Your questions are impertinent," Stephen said softly.

Mary blinked back more tears. "Sometimes," she whispered, "I hate you. And it is a relief."

"I do not care." He paced forward to tower over her. "You see, Mary, I am glad you have conceived, but nothing more. It changes not what you have done, or what you are. As soon as you have recovered from the ordeal of the journey, I am sending you back to Tetly. *Nothing has changed.*"

Mary choked on a sob and covered her face with her hands. It was as she had feared. Stephen had not forgotten, nor had he forgiven her, and he intended for her to bear his babe in exile.

Slowly he walked to the door and paused on the threshold without turning to face her.

Mary looked up. "Stephen," she whispered. It was a plea. He did look back, but reluctantly.

"Take me back. I love you. I need you. How I miss you."

His jaw tightened. He turned and left the room.

The household was asleep.

Except for Stephen, who knew sleep would never come to him that night. He stood alone in the hall before the dying fire. He was anguished.

It had not been easy, these past few months. He hated Court but, once delivering Malcolm's three sons into Rufus's care, he had chosen to stay. The decision had been a cold, calculated one. Although he did feel obligated to make certain the three boys were well cared for, he mostly wished to remain as far from his treacherous wife as was possible.

The distance that separated them, though, could not wipe away the memories. She remained a part of his mind. He could not shake her from his thoughts no matter how he tried. He woke up to her image, sometimes playful, sometimes serious, sometimes wanton and wicked. He went to sleep with her image. She haunted him far better than any ghost could.

Stephen stared at the fire, but he saw only Mary. Mary, his wife, who had become even more beautiful, as if she had not suffered at all during the long winter of her exile. Beautiful and so very pregnant. He could not tamp down the rush of choking emotions. Dear God—he had actually missed her.

These past few months he had thought that he hated her, and he had allowed his hatred to consume him, nourishing it, even relishing it. He knew that he would never be able to forgive her leaving him in a time of war, pledging her loyalty to her home and kin instead of him. The hatred was so welcome, because it eased the hurt. A hurt he must not, at all costs, feel.

But feel it, he did. The hurt consumed him, too.

But he had been lying to himself. He did not hate her after all.

For he had given her the greatest gift that he ever could, that day when he had given her the rose; he had given her his undying love. If only he could take it back. But he could not. A man such as he only loved once and forever.

It would not do. Stephen paced. He must be insane. Tonight he confronted feelings he did not want to face, much less to own, but he could not rid himself of them. Perversely, he did not even want to really be rid of them.

But how a man could miss a woman who had committed such treachery escaped all logic. How a man such as he, with such an iron will, could love such a woman, such a treacherous woman, defied all rationality. But now he understood the greatest mystery of the universe, too late. How obvious, how profound, it was. Love was not rational, could never be rational; its mere definition defied rationality. Love was sown not in the power of the mind, but in the power of the heart.

He must not cave in to his obsessive love, his obsessive need for her. He must not cave in to the burning desire.

If he gave in to his desire, he would lose, not just the battle, but the war. How well he knew that.

For no other woman could give him satisfaction; he had discovered that well in these past months of separation. There had been a few other women, all whores, women whose faces he did not remember and whose names he had forgotten, but the encounters had been brief, impersonal, and merely a physical outlet for his perfunctory lust. Nothing at all like being with Mary.

Stephen closed his eyes. He ached for her. Even now, knowing better, he was as hard as a rock, desperate for the release only she could give him. He was desperate for the release she would provide his loins, and desperate for so much more. In truth, was he not desperate for her love? A love she would never give him.

He would not go to her, he would not.

For if he did, even once, he would be lost.

How tempted he was.

She had not changed—he kept repeating that lifesaving litany to himself—thus he could not allow her back into his bed . . . and his life. She was too dangerous. She still had power over him. That had not changed, either.

He knew that he had made the right decision. As soon as a physic pronounced her fit, he would send her back to Tetly. It was his only hope.

The only problem was, he did not know how he could stay away from her now that he had seen her again, now that she was there in his house, just up the stairs, asleep in his bed.

While Stephen paced in front of the fire at Graystone, Henry lounged in a chair on the dais in the Great Hall at the White Tower. The hall was a shambles. It had been a long evening, with much entertainment and feasting. Most of the visitors lolled drunk on the benches of the endless table, a few copulated freely in the shadows with serving maids— and serving boys—and many snored from their places on the floor.

Beside Henry, his brother the King was finishing yet another liter of wine, as well as the explanation of his latest plans. William Rufus had decided that the time had come to put his beloved friend Duncan upon the throne of Scotland.

Henry quirked a brow. "Between you and me, dear brother, just between you and me, do you really think that if you succeed in putting Duncan on the throne, you can continue to control him?"

Rufus smiled and waved his hand languidly. "You must know the truth, brother of mine. Duncan loves me."

Henry raised a brow. "I do hope it's true." He smiled. "What a merry coil. He pines for you, and you pine for another."

Rufus was no longer smiling. He gave his brother an ugly glance.

Henry laughed. "It shall be interesting, shall it not, to see how Stephen treats his wife now that she has returned, and so pregnantly?"

It was Rufus's turn to smile. "He is no longer infatuated with her. He despises her. He cannot even bear to speak of her. But of course, I knew he would tire of her soon. No woman has ever held his interest for long."

"Fortunately for you," Henry murmured. "Or so you must think."

But Rufus had not heard. "So what think you of my plans?"

"I think it is no easy task to topple a King—and even harder to keep one in one's power."

"Donald Bane is barely Scotland's King. There are many who resent him. No one likes Edmund, who rules by his side."

"And you have promised Duncan, these many years, to see his fondest dreams made true."

"I have never openly promised him anything," Rufus said sharply. "You doubt I can control him."

"Duncan has strong ambitions, and he is much like Malcolm, ruthless and determined. He has schemed after his father's crown for some thirty years. He will not be as easy to manage as you wish him to be. If you need a puppy, why not launch young Edgar? His claim is legitimate. He is young enough that you can easily mold him."

"I disagree." Rufus no longer appeared drunk. He faced his brother with an unpleasant expression. "He is too young, he would need too much support, and he might very well turn to Stephen instead of me. No, I much prefer Duncan, who has ever been loyal. Can I count on you, dear brother?"

Henry leaned back in his chair. He had no wish to involve his army in another war in Scotland that would only strengthen his brother's position there in England, as well as freeing him to concentrate on regaining the duchy of Normandy. "I have no need for more silver or more estates."

"Everyone needs more silver and more estates."

"Do you not have many nobles behind you? Have you not got the great Earl of Northumberland in your pocket? Stephen's son, should it be a boy, will be Malcolm's grandson. They surely envision a cozy relationship with Scotland right now. Why, Duncan will be the child's uncle! Surely you do not need me!"

Rufus scowled. "As you have said,'tis no easy thing to topple a King. You must help me, Henry. Your reward will be great. Perhaps I will take the other Scot princess from the convent and give her to you."

"Now that Malcolm is dead, I hardly see how such an

alliance would interest me," Henry said. "Especially with Duncan on the throne."

"Tell me what does interest you, then."

"I will think on it," Henry said. "Carefully." But his mind was made up already, and his answer was no. Let the other nobles weaken themselves in this war, let them sow the seeds of their own destruction. When all was finished, his army would be the strongest in the realm. And Henry did not mind waiting to realize his dreams, even if it meant a few more years. Patience was his forte. Hadn't he coveted his brother's crown for an entire lifetime?

Mary had been sound asleep, but now she was wide-awake. She did not know what had awakened her, some noise, perhaps, or a dream. She lay on her side, facing the fire that still blazed in the hearth. She recalled instantly where she was. At Graystone, in Stephen's chamber, in his bed. Yearning assailed her.

She heard the door to her chamber closing. Mary sat up abruptly, eyes wide. A man stood in the shadows facing her, unmoving, his identity obscured by the darkness. But Mary knew it was Stephen. There could only be one reason he had come. *"Stephen."*

He did not move, and when he spoke, his voice was low and ragged. "I yearn for you, Mary, the way a drunkard yearns for wine."

Tears filled Mary's eyes; she gripped the bedcovers. "I yearn for you, too, Stephen."

He moved closer, into the glow of firelight. Mary saw the blaze in his eyes and gave a small, glad cry. She did not care that he only came to her to slake his desire, she did not. She held her arms out to him.

Stephen reached her in a single stride. The moment their hands touched, their bodies ignited in a burst of desire. For one brief moment Mary cradled his face in her palms, his beautiful, beloved face, reveling in the hunger she saw in his eyes. Stephen held her gaze, and between them there was a sizzling, wordless communication. Then he was kissing her.

He wrapped her in his arms and pushed her down on the bed, devouring her mouth with his. The kiss was open, wild, and wet. Mary's mood and need matched his exactly, and she met him with equal ardor. It was a long time before their lips parted, and when they did, they were both gasping shamelessly for air.

Mary almost wept. She did not care what he said; his denials were forever after baseless. Any man who kissed in such a manner was consumed by far more than mere desire. She would gamble her future on it—indeed, she would gamble her wildest dreams.

They kissed again but soon broke apart, too impatient for such foreplay. Stephen paused only to run his hands over her swollen breasts, murmuring thick endearments, and to touch her hard, round belly with awe. Then she was on her side, and he was sliding deeply into her.

Mary chanted his name. She loved him so. She told him. She was out of control, completely abandoned, crying her pleasure for all the world to hear, proudly, not caring if it did.

Stephen took her as if he had not had a woman in a very long time. He held back nothing. And when he found his own release, he cried her name, too. Not once, but many times.

Mary burrowed into his arms. This was where she wanted to be, where she belonged. She loved Stephen so much that it physically hurt.

Tears rose hotly, despite her abject happiness to be with Stephen again.

Mary did not want to cry. Not here, not now. *She was happy*. Stephen had returned to her. She was happy. But she had relinquished all control over herself when she had welcomed Stephen into her embrace. Raw, powerful emotions, so carefully defended for so long, had been left naked and exposed, all barriers and shields recklessly laid down. Mary choked on a sob.

"Mary?" Stephen said.

His single word, her name, undid her. And once she started to weep in earnest, she soon found that she could not stop.

Stephen cradled her in his arms, his expression drawn. "Don't cry," he whispered, stricken.

"I-I'm s-sorry." Mary wept even harder.

" 'Twas a lie," Stephen said hoarsely. "Your tears do affect me. Mary, I am not going to send you back."

He was not going to send her back. The long winter of her exile was truly over. Stephen had truly come back to her. Real joy mingled with the pain she had thought firmly buried in some final place she might never see again.

For as she lay sobbing in Stephen's arms, so much hurt throbbed within her breast. The pain of losing those she loved, the pain of her father's rejection, the pain of her exile.

"Why do you cry thus?" he asked harshly. "I am sorry, so sorry, if I have hurt you so."

She clung to him tightly. It was a long time before she could be coherent. "I have lost my mother, my father, my brother, and I almost l-lost y-you. And you ask me why I cry?"

Stephen was silent, trying to be strong, but in truth thoroughly undone. He continued to stroke her and hold her. Gruffly he said, "I am sorry Mary, I am sorry about Malcolm and Margaret and Edward. I wanted to punish you, but never did I wish to see you suffer so for the loss of those you love. I have always been sorry—there was just not the circumstance to tell you."

She needed to tell him. "Malcolm disowned me. When I went to him and asked him to—to stop the war—he t-told me—he t-told me . . ." She could not continue. She collapsed against Stephen's chest. She gripped him hard, as she would a lifeline.

"What did he tell you?" Stephen managed, ashen.

"That I—that I was not his daughter anymore. That his daughter was a brave Scottish lass, not one as I!"

Stephen cursed Malcolm and held his wife, rocking her. "You are a brave Scottish lass, Mary, the bravest I have ever known." He tilted her tear-streaked face up to his. "Did you really go to him to ask him to stop the war?"

Mary looked at him. "I was not running away from you. I swear it, Stephen."

Stephen pressed her head back to his chest and closed his eyes. Once again, he wanted to believe her. He supposed it was possible. If any woman had the daring and audacity to confront a King and attempt to dissuade him from war, that woman would be Mary. And did he have a choice? He had fought her for so long—he just could not continue to do so. He had fought his love for so long, but now he had identified it, realizing it would never leave him be. He could not be the cause of such suffering on her part. She needed him. She had needed him for some time. And he had not been there for her. Stephen was sick at the thought. Dear God, if he had known how he was hurting her, he would have never sent her away. If he had known how she suffered, he would have gone to her immediately. "It does not matter," he finally said. "What matters is that you are my wife, and you carry my child, and that I cannot live apart from you."

Mary stared, stunned. "You cannot live apart from me?"

"Not happily."

"Stephen," she whispered. "Does this mean you will forget the past?"

"I am not a man who can forget easily," Stephen said honestly, gravely. "But I am giving us a third chance. We shall start over from this day, Mary."

Mary blinked up at him, her tears finally subsiding. It seemed miraculous, as if Stephen himself was healing her, for the anguish, the real physical pain which had been searing her breast, had diminished to a dull throb, one she could very well live with. Indeed, there was genuine joy coming forth from somewhere deep in her soul, joy that threatened to displace much of the grief.

He gazed at her steadily. "Promise me, here and now, on the life of the child, that you will not imperil our marriage again. I must believe that I can trust you, Mary."

"You can trust me. I will never disobey you again, Stephen," Mary vowed.

And finally, Stephen's expression eased. His mouth quirked. "I do not dare to hope for such respect, madame. Acting with care and circumspection is enough."

And Mary smiled broadly, snuggling against him. She had won. Stephen was hers again.

Chapter 27

Rufus had just returned from a day of successful hunting, and he was in high spirits. As he descended from his private chambers to the Great Hall, he threw his arm around Duncan, who was at his side. "Undoubtedly today was an omen," he told his longtime friend. "We shall snag far greater prey soon."

"I am counting on it," Duncan said tersely. These days he could hardly smile, he was so tense and anxious. Although the King had only hinted to him of his plans, Duncan had heard enough hearsay to know that soon, very soon, a great Anglo-Norman army would march north to depose Donald Bane and Edmund. He craved the position at that army's head—and then upon Scotland's throne.

Rufus ambled through the hall, which was overflowing with courtiers, pausing repeatedly to exchange words with his favorites. His eyes widened and his spirits lifted even more when he saw a dear and familiar face at his table, close to and just below the dais, a face he so rarely saw. Although Stephen had remained in London since the New Year, when he had escorted the three sons of Malcolm

Canmore to their fate, he rarely came to the Tower, and then only when his personal presence was necessary or summoned.

Rufus stared at his handsome profile for a beat longer than necessary. With reluctance he dragged his gaze from Northumberland's heir and marched through the crowd, which gave way to him immediately, no longer dispensing any conversation.

"Sit with me," Rufus said amiably to Duncan. Together they climbed the dais. Rufus's gaze strayed unerringly to Stephen again. His smile died instantly.

Stephen was feeding his wife a morsel of lamb.

It was only polite, of course, for him to do so. But there was nothing polite about the way he stared at her, or about the way his eyes smoked and his nostrils flared. Indeed, even from this distance, Rufus could smell the scent of his arousal.

He looked at Mary. Her face was full, her breasts big, disgusting. Undoubtedly if she stood, she would waddle and resemble a cow. A woman in her condition should not be out in public, and he was infuriated to have to tolerate her in his hall. Not only that, he knew, beyond any doubt, that Stephen had been bedding her since his damn stupid brother had brought her to London, and that he would do so again. From the look on his face, he would probably plow her the moment they left his table.

Duncan followed his gaze. "Amazing, the power my little half sister holds over that man. Amazing—and dangerous."

Rufus looked at him. "She indeed poses a threat to you, dear Duncan."

"We have never spoken of it, you and I, Sire. But do you think de Warenne covets Scotland?"

Rufus shrugged. In truth, he was almost certain the man did not, but he had an interest now, one he wanted served. "He can never claim the throne himself, my friend, but of course, what man would not want to see his son crowned? De Warenne is like his father, ambitious and determined in the extreme." Purposefully Rufus did not finish his thoughts.

"Perhaps the brat she bears will die."

Rufus laid a restraining palm upon Duncan. "We need

Stephen, Duncan; never forget that. He must support us in our efforts to regain Scotland for you."

Duncan flushed with exultation at hearing the King speak so openly of his fondest dream. And his mind raced forward. Did he dare remove the threat that Mary and her child posed to him and his ambition? He feared her child more than he did her three young brothers, more than he had ever feared her. He could imagine, too well, Stephen declaring himself a Prince Regent.

"Clearly I have erred in arranging the match," Rufus said in a low voice. "Perhaps there will come a time to rectify the matter. Perhaps, when you are secure upon the throne . . ." Rufus trailed off.

Duncan said nothing.

Rufus loudly demanded his wine.

And the meal continued as if the pact had never been made. But Duncan had just been given royal sanction to do what he must to insure that Stephen de Warenne's ties to Scotland's throne were severed once and for all.

"Why do we return to Alnwick now, so suddenly?" Mary asked as Stephen ordered his squire to prepare for their immediate departure. The lad ran from the chamber. "What passes, that we must leave this very day?" Her voice was high.

It was early May. Mary had been at Court for four weeks, but she was not bored. She was too busy rediscovering her husband's body, his smiles, his kindness.

Stephen faced her slowly. "I would prefer you bear the child at Alnwick, Mary. As I must return immediately,'tis ideal for me to escort you to Northumberland."

"But you have not answered my question, my lord!" Mary cried, panicked. For there had been rumors circulating about the Court, rumors she could not help hearing. Rumors, Edgar had told her bitterly, that Rufus was going to attempt to put Duncan on Scotland's throne. But such rumors could not be true.

"You do not wish to go home? You wish to bear our child here in the midst of summer? London is not so pleasant then."

Home. Mary tested the word in her mind. Her heart warmed at the thought of returning to Alnwick and giving birth to their child there. But . . . all was not innocence. Or there would not be this rush to leave. "I will deliver our babe wherever you tell me to," Mary said earnestly. "The choice of Alnwick suits me, Stephen, of course it does. But will you not answer my question?"

He was grave. "I go to war, Mary."

Mary cried out. She had known it. She had known with some shrewd sixth sense that the damnable rumors were true, and that Stephen would be at the head of the army that would invade Scotland and depose her uncle and her traitorous brother. She could not believe that Stephen would break the vow he had given her father, to see his eldest son upon the throne. Edmund had betrayed the family, and Ethelred was a priest, so that left Edgar. Edgar must be Scotland's next King!

And if such a sickening circumstance were not enough, fear consumed her. 'Twas only six months ago that she had lost her parents and brother because of war, and she had yet to stop grieving. Indeed, there were mornings when she awoke consumed with soothing dreams in which they were all together, when she forgot that they were dead. On those mornings she expected to see her mother smiling at her and standing there at the foot of her bed. It was the most dark, grievous moment when the cobwebs of sleep were cleared from her brain and she was struck by rude reality. That her mother, her brother, her father, would never be with her again. She could not help being afraid for Stephen now. She had lost those dearest to her in one war, she could not bear to lose Stephen in another one. She would not be able to live without him. "Do not go," she heard herself say.

Stephen's jaw tightened. "Do not speak like a fool."

Mary closed her eyes. "How can you do this?"

"The King is determined to depose Donald Bane."

Mary stared, blinking at tears. "You despise your King. Must you follow him always?"

Stephen's tone was as sharp as the point of his sword. "Madame, I am his vassal, and as you have sworn to uphold and follow me, I have sworn to uphold and follow him."

She walked away from her husband. She knew she had just angered him even more by turning her back on him with such obvious displeasure, for his breath hissed as he drew it in, but she could not care. Her growing belly had made her somewhat swaybacked now, and unconsciously she rubbed the aching muscles at her spine. She stared out of the window, noticing the profusion of blue wildflowers in the meadow without interest. She was well aware that she must tread carefully. She must not interfere in her husband's affairs. It had almost destroyed them once.

"Would you really have me disobey my King, Mary, to whom I have sworn fealty on bended knee?" Stephen asked tersely.

Mary could not lie. "You uphold your oath to your King, but what of the oath you made to my father—my King?"

Stephen was at once both disbelieving and furious. "I beg your pardon?"

Mary inhaled. "What of the promise you made, the sworn promise, to put Edward upon Scotland's throne?"

Stephen stared.

Mary cried, "Surely you would not default on such a pledge now! Surely you intend to launch Edgar, not Duncan!"

He advanced towards her, only to stop in the center of the room. His countenance was thunderous. *"Did I not make myself clear when we reconciled?"*

Mary lifted her chin. She had gone too far and she knew it, but she could not retreat. The fate of all three of her brothers hung in the balance. They might be treated as exalted guests now, but they were royal prisoners, nothing more. They had nothing to their names, not a single coin, not a single estate, nothing but the clothes upon their backs, Rufus's goodwill, and Stephen's pledge. "Yes, you did," she whispered. "But I am your wife. Your cares are mine. I do not mean to upset you, only we must—"

" *'We'*?"

Tears filled Mary's eyes.

"There is no *we*—not in matters politic."

She blinked back the tears, telling herself it was because of the child; she cried so frequently these days. "What of Edgar?" she heard herself whisper.

Stephen's eyes were black, his jaw rigid. "I do not even want to know how you have discovered my most secret pledge, Mary."

"Edward told me," Mary whispered, "the night before he died."

Stephen's expression changed in an instant—from anger to sympathy. "Edward would have been a great King."

"Edgar will be a great King!"

"You tread dangerously, madame, into the affairs of men."

Recklessly Mary cried, "Can you justify deposing one monster in order to crown another, my lord? Can you?"

Stephen was incredulous—then furious. "You dare to question my actions? My integrity?"

"But I am your wife! If you trusted me . . ." She trailed off. What was there to say? He did not trust her with his secrets—had he not said he would never forget her treachery? The old hurt was there, gnawing at her deep within her bones, for it had never gone away, it had only been buried deeply and purposefully. She had thought she could leave it there in its grave forever; apparently she was wrong.

"You are my wife, and I suggest you behave in a wifely manner, madame, unless you wish to bring this marriage down around our heads." Stephen stalked to the door and through it without giving her another glance.

Once he was gone, Mary rushed as best she could to the door and slammed it closed behind him, as hard as she could. Then she gave in to her tears.

What kind of marriage did they have? Damn him! He was a pigheaded, arrogant man! She had a right to know what he intended, for her brothers were now her responsibility with their parents dead. Their only hope lay in Edgar one day seizing the throne. Even if they were free to depart London, they dared not leave the refuge Rufus had provided them. Men had murdered one another over Scotland's throne; the nation had a long and bloody history. Donald Bane had already issued an invitation to her brothers, one they dared not accept. Undoubtedly the moment they arrived in Scotland, they would become lifetime prisoners, or lifeless corpses.

Thus Edgar had little choice now but to remain at Court in London, currying favor with the King, in the hope that one day Rufus would help him in his quest to gain the Scottish throne. His future hinged upon Rufus's goodwill, as did that of his brothers, who were allied with him. One day, if Edgar became King, they would become great lairds in their own right.

Mary did not want to fight with her husband. These past weeks they had enjoyed a triumphant peace—one she wished to endure for a lifetime. But she was not a woman to remain meek and ignorant, yet he refused to share his affairs with her. Where did that leave them?

Perhaps, if the subject were not so dear to her, it would not matter. But her brothers were her affair—more than Stephen's. She had every right to urge her husband to a solution that would assure their futures. Why could he not understand that?

Because he still does not trust me, she thought bleakly. If he trusted me, I would be his dearest ally, and he would whisper all his secrets willingly.

Mary wanted to be his dearest ally. She wanted that more than anything other than his love. She despaired. If Stephen could not forget the past, it would never come to pass.

There was a knock on the chamber door, and Mary turned as a maid entered. The young woman hesitated, seeing her mistress's distress, undoubtedly having heard some, if not all, of her fight with Stephen. "My lady? I have come to help you pack."

"Please." Mary gestured for the girl to come in. Slowly, her back aching, she focused on the task at hand. But all the joy had gone out of the prospect of going home.

Stephen and Mary did not speak with each other except to maintain a semblance of impersonal courtesy. Although Stephen's goal in returning to Alnwick was to raise troops and summon his vassals quickly to the war, he kept the entourage at a pace befitting his wife's condition, and it took two full days for them to journey to Alnwick. Mary could not be grateful. She was too distraught. She catered to her husband as she should, but the pleasant camaraderie,

the warmth and the lust, had vanished. Stephen was stiff and
formal with her, clearly as upset as she. Quivering tension
strained their relations.

Stephen did not remain at Alnwick for even a night. He
deposited Mary at the keep's front steps while awaiting a
fresh mount. "I bid you adieu, madame. Unfortunately, I
cannot tarry even awhile." Suddenly his expression softened.
"I would delay if I could, madame," he said low, staring at
her, "and put an end to this foolish war once and for all."

Mary almost begged him to stay. She understood his
meaning. He would make love to her and show her with
his body that he was master, but in so doing, he would also
reveal that he was the slave. In bed they were equals. In bed
he gave all of himself to her, without restraint. Mary knew
they would never have such equality out of it—that was a
ridiculous notion—but one day, she vowed, he would give
all of himself willingly outside the cloak of passion.

He misread her expression. Concern tightened his features. "Do not worry, Mary. My mother has reassured me
that she will remain with you for the rest of your confinement. She will arrive here within a sennight. If I do not
return soon, you will not be alone."

Mary was startled. "Do you think to be gone so long?"

"I do not know. Once Duncan seizes power, he cannot be
left alone until his position is secure."

Mary regained her composure. "I am not worried," she
lied. She would not send Stephen off to war with needless
anxiety for her state of mind. In fact, every woman she
knew was afraid of childbirth. Too many died from the
ordeal. She herself was no exception, but so far she had
avoided facing her fear, and she would not do so now, at
their parting.

"Then you are braver than I had thought, Mary. You are
indeed a brave Scottish lass."

Mary looked at her handsome husband, her heart turning
over. He was worried and he was concerned, and his praise
was so dear after the horribly cruel words Malcolm had
insulted her with. Her love threatened to overwhelm her,
rendering her weak-kneed. Dear God, she did not want him
to go to war, especially not for such a cause as this. But she

must be as brave as Stephen thought her to be. "Godspeed, my lord. I know you will triumph."

He leaned down from his mount, holding her gaze with his. "And will you rejoice?"

Mary inhaled but no longer hesitated. It was her place to support him. "Yes." She fought sudden tears, assuring herself that she was not abandoning her brothers. "When you triumph, my lord, I will rejoice."

Stephen stared.

It was hard to smile while crying, but Mary managed it.

"Thank you, madame wife," Stephen said. And his eyes had become suspiciously moist.

In mid-May the army finally moved. It marched unerringly towards Stirling, meeting with little resistance. When an opposing army finally came to fight them, the Normans were already close to the royal tower. The battle was surprisingly short. The Scot forces were in disarray, clearly lacking a unified command. Donald Bane and Edmund both fled the moment defeat became obvious. In the last week of May a victorious Norman army marched into Stirling, with Duncan at its head. He was crowned the very same afternoon.

News of the great event reached Alnwick the following day. There was great rejoicing at the keep. Mary could not participate in the spontaneous celebration. She left the feast, adjourning to her chamber. There she stared out of the window slit, unable not to condemn Stephen no matter how she resolved to be loyal to him.

She thought of her three brothers, having no choice but to remain in London, and she was unbearably saddened. What would happen to them now? Someone, perhaps even Duncan himself, had tried to murder her, and she was no threat compared to them. One day any one of her brothers could claim Scotland's throne, raise an army, and march to seize it by force. How afraid she was for them now! Each and every one of them stood in the way of Duncan's lifelong ambition.

The next day Mary received word from Stephen that he would not be returning immediately—he would spend several weeks in Stirling with his army, as he had forecast. Apparently Duncan's position was not terribly secure.

That did hearten Mary, yet she could not be completely glad, for still she was determined to be loyal to Stephen, even though she disagreed with him, even though she had become very worried over the fates of her brothers. And Mary missed Stephen desperately—as her time drew near, how she yearned for him to come home to her.

No day could be better for an outing, Mary thought with excitement. It was warm and pleasant out, the sun shone brightly, and blue jays cried out cheerfully from the leafy treetops overhead. The countess and Isobel were astride palfreys, both riding beside the litter Mary was in. Two household knights accompanied them, and two maids were on foot. Mary suspected the countess sought to distract her from her increasing boredom and anxiety with this short jaunt. The pregnancy had become endless, while her fears of childbirth had begun to grow. Mary both anticipated and dreaded the moment she must deliver the babe.

Within a few minutes they reached the village that lay just below Alnwick. Mary insisted upon walking, determined to explore the busy summer marketplace. She wanted to buy some trinkets, and she could not browse comfortably among the vendors and stalls while in the litter. And she wanted to buy something for Stephen, a gift that would tell him how much she missed him, how much she loved him. But she never had a chance.

For as Mary walked slowly to a stall to inspect fabrics, with the countess beside her, Isobel running ahead to buy a sweetmeat, someone knocked into Lady Ceidre.

Mary saw the entire incident and she was aghast, because the villein had pushed the countess on purpose. As Ceidre reeled into the merchant's table, tipping it and all his goods to the floor, causing an uproar, the villein jerked Mary roughly to him. He clamped a hand over her mouth, cutting off her cry.

Then he lifted her off her feet and moved her away from the scene of confusion. Realizing his intent, Mary began to struggle.

But an instant later he had thrown her upon a waiting horse, leaping up behind her. Mary screamed.

The countess, finally aware of what was happening, shouted, and the two knights drew their swords.

Terrified, not for herself but for the babe, Mary clung to the horse's mane as it bolted. Another rider, materializing out of the throng, joined them in a dead gallop. Vendors and buyers leapt out of their way as they galloped through the market, knocking over stalls and carts and anything else in their way.

Still Mary clung. In disbelief she glanced over her shoulder. She saw the countess racing after her on foot, hopelessly. The din behind her was deafening, but Mary thought she heard someone cry, "They've stole his lordships's wife!" And then the two knights emerged from the crowd, running for their steeds.

Mary collapsed against the mare's neck, beginning to shake. *Dear God, sweet Mother Mary, she had been abducted!* Coldly, calculatedly abducted! Where were they taking her? Who was responsible? And how, sweet Lord, how would she and her baby survive?

Chapter 28

Stephen was livid. "What do you mean, you did not see any harm in an outing?" he roared.

The countess shrank away from him. "She was so anxious . . ."

Disbelief contorted his features. He could not speak. Rolfe moved between his son and his wife. "Your mother is sick to death with distress. The abduction was not her fault," the earl said harshly. "If anyone is to blame, it is Will and Ranulph."

Stephen's jaw tightened. What his father had said was obvious, yet he could not, would not, forgive his mother. He had left explicit orders that Mary remain within the keep. He turned from her coldly, uncaring of her hurt. Dear God, if anything happened to Mary . . .

Sheer, sickening terror clawed at him. Never in his life had he been afraid, not like this. Even now she was out there somewhere, with her abductors, perhaps hurt and in pain. Or worse. Abruptly he pulled himself together. He had no time to dwell upon the possibilities, he must act. Stephen turned his frozen stare upon the two knights who had failed in their duty to protect Mary. "Tell me again what happened."

Word of Mary's abduction had reached him some five or six hours ago in Edinburgh, where Duncan now held court. He had been roused from his pallet at midnight by his mother's messenger. Stephen had immediately left for Alnwick, pausing only to inform his father of where he was going and why. Rolfe had decided to come with him instantly. Both men had been wished well by Scotland's new King; Duncan had also been roused by the news.

It was now dawn. Stephen had practically killed his horse in order to return so swiftly; he had arrived just a few moments ago. He had quickly learned that Mary had been abducted the afternoon before. She had literally been stolen out from the two knights' midst by two horsemen. His men had tracked the duo into the forest, but once there, they had lost them.

"My lord, they were dressed as common freemen, but they rode like seasoned knights," Will was saying. " 'Tis clear the entire event was planned well before yesterday. I think the men must have been waiting for any opportunity to arise in which they could seize her ladyship."

Stephen already knew it was no common abduction. No lout would dare to abduct his wife, or even be capable of such a feat in the face of his own vassals. The fact was that one of his enemies had captured Mary—and Stephen could only think that it was an act of revenge. And he was sick again with fear.

All denial, all protestations, were useless now. He loved his wife to the point of madness; he would do anything to get her back. And once he had her back, he would give her all that she wanted—he would deny her nothing.

Yet there was little that he could do other than beat a bloody trail across the countryside searching for her. So be it. Once he determined what madman was responsible for his wife's abduction, all those in that lord's domain would suffer as never before. There would be no mercy. In his mind Stephen ticked off those who might hate him enough to dare such a feat. He had a half dozen sworn enemies, but not one of them, he thought, was stupid enough to commit such an outrage.

"We ride now, back to the forest, back to their last sign. Will, Ranulph, you shall lead the way," Stephen commanded tersely.

Stephen and two dozen fully armed knights rode out just after sunrise. But by the end of that day, they had made no progress. The trail had disappeared when the two riders, one overburdened with his captive, had ridden into a stream. Stephen and his men could not find a single sign of them again. Mary had been whisked away without a trace.

Mary knew that they were traveling north into Scotland. Despite her terror, she managed to think. Her wits were all she had left, and she knew she must keep them about her. This made no sense. The Scottish people were her people—who among them would do such a thing as kidnap her? Or was it a ruse? Was her destination Scotland only because Stephen would never think of looking for her there?

Stephen. Her heart clenched painfully at the thought of what he must be going through—and at the thought that she might never see him again. "Stephen," she whispered, unaware she spoke aloud, "I need you, how I need you—please help me now!"

They did not use the Roman road, following one deer path after another deep in the hills, using terrain that no man, other than a Scot, could be so acquainted with. The horsemen stopped twice, first to water their mounts and move Mary from the one horse to the other, and then to change their mounts at a prearranged spot, a small thatch cottage, apparently deserted, where two fresh horses were tethered out back. When some of Mary's courage returned, she tried to question them, hoping to learn who had sent them and where they were taking her, but they refused to speak with her.

They rode well into the night. Mary fell asleep. It was a restless sleep in which she dreamed of Stephen, begging him to come to her and rescue her. She dreamed of the baby being born. It was a boy, whom she held tenderly, and he was so small and defenseless in her arms, but it was not a happy dream, for she fought to protect him from an unseen threat. When she awoke she was more frightened than before.

The night was pitch black, and Mary could not decide where they were or precisely where they were going. The two men kept their horses at a brisk walk now.

"Where are we?" she asked, her mouth parched.

The man riding with her handed her a skin bag of watered ale. Mary drank gratefully. "Not far from Edinburgh, lassie."

Mary froze. Her heart began to pound painfully. Edinburgh? Once that had been her home, but no more. Now it was home to Duncan, Scotland's new King. He might be her half brother, but she was sick with fear.

For she knew now that Duncan was behind this. She could not guess at her fate. If he intended to kill her, he would have already done so. So what did he want with her? Fearfully Mary clutched her belly, praying that she should be so lucky as to find Stephen still at the Scot Court.

Mary was taken to the castle. It was the dead of night, and travelers at such an hour were more than rare and certainly suspect. It was obvious to Mary that her arrival was expected, for when one of her captors called out a code word, the heavy gates were instantly thrown open in order to admit them. Her captors rode swiftly to the keep. A knight and a serving maid were waiting on the front steps for them.

Mary was lifted down from the horse. She found that she could barely walk after the long ordeal, and the knight quickly swept her up into his arms. Mary peered up at him as he carried her inside, hoping to recognize him and thus appeal to him for aid. But she did not. She was taken upstairs and laid abed in a small chamber that had, not so long ago, been shared by her younger brothers.

Mary was grateful for the bed, but that was all. Holding a hand to her forehead, which throbbed, aware of the baby kicking inside her, her body stiff and aching, she watched the knight leave the room without so much as another glance at her. She turned her gaze on the maid. She was a thin, older woman, busy now poking the fire. Even in June, the nights in Edinburgh were cool. The elderly woman turned and approached. "I'll be bringin' ye some hot food, mistress, an' some good ale. I won't be long."

Mary was too exhausted to move; she lay absolutely motionless. "I want to speak with my brother."

"Yer brother?"

"My brother, Duncan."

"You mean your half brother, the King, do you not, my dear?" Duncan said from the doorway.

Mary started, tried to rise, and fell back into the bed with a gasp. A cramp had lanced through her abdomen.

Duncan approached and stared down at her coldly. "I think you should rest, sister dear, unless you want your brat born early."

Fear rushed over Mary. She knew what such a pain could mean; it could mean that the babe wanted to come soon. Babes born early rarely survived, and she was probably three or four weeks from her time. Mary closed her eyes, fighting the fear and the panic.

"A much more sensible course," Duncan said above her. "Although I cannot decide if I should prefer my nephew to live or die."

Mary's eyes flew open. Hatred swamped her. "If you hurt my child—"

"You will what? Hurt me?"

"Stephen will kill you!"

Duncan laughed. "And how will he do that, Mary? I am King. Murderers of kings are beheaded, their rotting heads set upon pikes so all might gaze upon the sight and be forewarned."

Mary fought to keep hysteria at bay. She had a horrible image of Stephen's head impaled in such a manner, and she was nauseous. Duncan was right. Stephen would not kill him.

"What do you want?!" she cried fearfully. Her hands held her belly protectively. "What are you planning for me, for my baby?"

" 'Tis all very simple and very civilized," Duncan said calmly. "You really have no cause to be distraught."

Mary was only half-listening, waiting with dread for another cramp, a sign of the babe's distress. But it did not come, and she relaxed slightly. "You threaten my child. I have every cause."

Duncan regarded her. "I have no intention of harming your brat. If harm befalls the child, it will be due to you, not to me."

Mary wanted to believe him. She could not decide whether he spoke true or not. She licked her dry, cracked lips. "If you wish us no harm, then why have you abducted us?"

" 'Tis not obvious? I do not trust your husband, Mary; in fact, there are many here in Scotland who do not trust him, many who are distraught over his marriage to you. At the moment his power is only pertinent in England, but once your child is born, who knows?"

Mary stared, eyes wide, finally comprehending. Duncan was afraid of her child. In a flash she understood why her child frightened him more than her brothers did. Her brothers had no support. But her unborn son had all of the vast power of Northumberland at his disposal—he would be Stephen's heir. Her child, if a boy, would also be Malcolm's grandson, and one day, perhaps, a contender for the throne himself.

Duncan saw that she understood. "That is the crux of it, sister dear. I need leverage over your husband to keep him in my power. I wish for him to continue to support me— for as long as I live."

Fear clenched Mary hard. She managed to push herself up into a sitting position. Out of breath, she asked, "You have not answered me."

"Oh, but I have. You see, if you are my guest—you and the child—Stephen will not dare oppose me."

Mary blanched. "You will hold me hostage? You will hold us hostage? For how long?"

"Indefinitely."

Mary began to pant. "You are crazy!" But she knew he was not mad. He was very clever. If he had murdered her, Stephen would pursue him, and oppose him, with a vengeance. But if she and her child were hostages, he would have no choice but to support him.

Now Duncan was angry. "If I am mad, then the great Conqueror was mad, too, was he not? After all, Malcolm gave me to the Conqueror as a hostage when I was a small boy; I was to be a guarantee for his good behavior—not that it worked! For Malcolm cared not about my welfare, and he broke his oath to King William as he willed. I am lucky to be alive! Indeed, I am lucky to have even come home—after twenty-two damnable years!"

Mary stared.

"You shall bear the brat here, you shall live here, for as long as I deem it necessary," Duncan said coldly. "Perhaps one day your worth will be less, and I will allow you to leave. But the child—if it is a boy—shall remain here." Duncan smiled. "As I was forced to remain at William's court. Why are you so pale? Edinburgh is your home, and the brat is a quarter Scot. Really, there is little hardship in this if you think about it. You will only suffer if you choose to consider yourself a hostage instead of a guest."

"Stephen will not allow this," Mary found her voice. "He will appeal to the King. Rufus will force you to return me, you shall see."

"No, my dear, you are wrong. For Rufus has decided that he erred when he agreed to your marriage to de Warenne. Just recently, in fact, he gave me carte blanche to do with you and the child as I see fit."

Mary knew that she must regain her strength quickly. Time was not on her side, not with the babe due in a month. She spent the next few days in bed, resting and recovering from the long, hard ride to Scotland. She ate large, hearty meals and drank much water, avoiding wine and ale, which increased her tendency to lethargy. She left her bed to take exercise twice daily in the bailey, working the stiffness from her muscles, hoping to keep her body strong. And she planned her escape.

She would escape. There was no question of that. Mary's determination had never been stronger.

She had ascertained that Stephen had yet to be informed of her whereabouts; Duncan had told her that he was in no hurry to do so. His amusement had been palpable. Mary hated Duncan even more, for it was plain that he was delighting in tormenting her husband. Stephen must be anxious and worried for her, coveting some word that she was well. But

Duncan had no intention of relaying that word, at least not just yet.

Yet even if Stephen knew where she was, it was doubtful whether he would be able to gain her release. Mary thought that Duncan had not lied when he had said that he had Rufus's approval in this endeavor, that Rufus was not on her side. Only too well, chillingly, Mary could recall the last time she had seen Rufus. He had been staring at her with undisguised hatred.

Mary thought that there was a slim chance that Rolfe and Stephen could persuade Rufus to force Duncan to release her, but that was not enough. Mary had not a single doubt that she would be forced to leave her child behind as a guarantee of Stephen's continual support for Duncan, just as Malcolm had given Duncan as a boy over to the Conqueror. Children were used as hostages all the time. The idea of leaving her child behind was as abhorrent as death itself.

It was all the more reason to escape.

Now, before the child was born.

Mary was no fool. She was aware that her condition would not make it easy for her. Still, escape would be far more difficult, even impossible, with a tiny newborn. Mary also knew that she might be risking her own life and the baby's. But she was determined to see them both through the ordeal safely. She thought that her resolve, which had never been greater, and her love for both the babe and her husband, would carry her through to safety. Nothing was going to stop her from being reunited with Stephen again, from bearing her child there in his presence, from rearing their child together. Not Duncan, not anything.

Mary did not need a plan. She had been raised at Edinburgh, and she knew every nook and cranny of the castle better than anyone except, perhaps, her three brothers. Duncan, who was a stranger to his new home, and his soldiers, half of whom were Norman mercenaries, could not know of the secrets the keep held. As with most towers, it had been built with an enemy siege in mind. A secret door let onto a short tunnel that allowed the castle's residents to pass beneath the castle walls and flee to safety beyond the moat.

Mary waited a week. On the eighth night after her arrival at Edinburgh, she knew the time had come. She was becoming ungainly, she waddled instead of walked, but her strength had returned as much as it ever would. Mary could only pray that her swollen body would not slow her down that night.

No guards were posted outside Mary's chamber. Apparently it was beyond anyone's belief that a woman in her condition would attempt to escape. However, the maid slept on a pallet in the hall just outside her door. Mary refused to consider hurting the old woman, who had been nothing but kind to her. Instead, when the Great Hall had finally fallen into silence, when Mary could be certain that Duncan was amused with his latest paramour, she called out loudly for the woman. When Eiric was awakened, hurrying to her side, Mary was sincerely apologetic. "I am sorry, Eiric, I know 'tis late, but I cannot sleep. I fear the babe desires to grow even more, for I am starving! Please, go to the kitchens and bring me beef stew, warm bread, a lamb pie, and some of that salmon we dined on this noon."

Eiric gaped. "My lady, you will get sick!"

"I am starving." Mary was firm. "Go, Eiric, but make sure the salmon is heated, for surely I will get sick if I eat cold leftover fish."

Eiric left with no further protest. Mary was briefly delighted. She would have to rouse other maids to help her with the repast. Mary knew the old serving woman would heat up everything, and as the fires in the kitchens were now out, it would take a long time. Mary thought that she probably had an hour or more of a start on Duncan and his men.

But she had not counted on the dogs.

The night was starry and bright. When Mary first slipped from the tunnel and outside, she was briefly elated. She would not need to light any of the candles she had taken with her, for the half-moon and the galaxy of stars were enough for her to see by. And as she had used the tunnel many times as a child, she knew exactly where she was. So far her escape had been impossibly easy.

But her elation vanished in a heartbeat. The moment she heard the first howl.

Mary stood in the edge of the woods, intending to head directly for town in order to steal some beast of transportation. She froze. The single, solitary wolflike howl chilled her blood and raised the hairs upon her nape. Please, God, she prayed silently, let it be a wild wolf.

And then the braying began.

Mary cried out in terror. Duncan had set loose a pack of wolfhounds. Already she was being pursued. Not a quarter of an hour had passed since she had ordered Eiric to the kitchens. The maid must have returned to her chamber shortly afterwards—Mary had not considered that she might do that. She lifted her skirts and began to hurry—as swiftly as her condition allowed.

Options forced their way through her frightened mind. She had been relying on having an hour or more head start on her enemies. She had hardly any advantage at all. Originally she planned to find a horse in the burgh and ride like the wind for Northumberland. Instead she could steal a boat and row herself across the Firth of Forth to the Benedictine abbey at Dunfermline.

Neither of those plans held out any hope of success now. The wolfhounds were howling with maddened intent. The dogs had been let out of the front gates and had yet to pick up her scent, but soon they would. Mary did not think she could make it to the burgh to steal a boat, much less to the Firth of Forth.

Mary turned and fled into the woods. She was stricken with fear. How could she evade Duncan's men and dogs while fleeing on foot? She had one slim chance of success. She would use the same trick her abductors had used to escape Stephen's men.

Bushes, bracken, and thorns beat her legs and hips, tearing at her skin, but Mary ignored them. She rushed forward on a deer trail she knew by heart, one she had used many, many times before. The braying had become more distant. Thank God. The hounds had gone off in the wrong direction.

Mary's pace slowed. Her heart pumped madly—she could barely breathe. A stitch took her in the side, and for a moment she had to stop, clutching herself, panting wildly. She knew she could not linger now. At any moment the hounds might pick up her scent, and then they would be upon her in minutes.

Mary waited one more heartbeat, to make sure the cramp was only that and nothing more. Then she plunged on down a short, steep incline.

Mary slipped and stumbled and finally dropped to her buttocks to slide down the rest of the way. The ground was wet and damp, as she had known it would be. When she had reached the bottom of the ravine, she was again breathless. How was she going to make her escape if she could not walk more than a few paces without dying for a breath of air?

Her plan had crumbled to dust. Without a horse, she would never make it to Northumberland. Even her will was not strong enough to carry her home; she needed physical strength—physical strength she did not have.

Mary got up. The hounds sounded louder, closer.

But she could tell from their tone that they had yet to find her trail. However, there was no question that the dog handlers had changed direction and were circling back around the keep in the other direction. It was only a matter of time before the wolfhounds would discover her scent— would discover her.

Mary lifted her skirts and stepped into the rushing stream. She cried out at the freezing cold. She had played often enough in the racing stream as a child, but in the warmest summer months of August and early September, for the source of the brook was the far mountains, and the water was always icy cold. She wondered if her fate would be to catch her death instead of being eaten alive.

Mary shuddered, lifted her skirts, and stumbled deeper into the stream. It was shallow, the water only coming up to her thighs. She had attained her goal—but now what?

In that instant, God smiled, and she was inspired. Mary began to fight the current, surging upriver. Duncan would think her heading south, heading home. Although there was nowhere Mary wanted to be as desperately as Alnwick, she would be a fool to try to reach home on foot now. Once Duncan lost her trail in the stream, he would try to outwit her, sending his hounds to the south, hoping for them to pick up her scent again. But she was not going south—and they would not find her trail there.

The going was slow and difficult, and each labored breath Mary took was painful. Every few minutes she had to stop to allow her wild pulse to slow. Then she would push on again. She had long since stopped noticing the cold, for she was so frozen now that she was numb.

Mary did not know how much time had passed or how far she had gone when she heard the hounds howl with renewed fervor. She froze. The water swirled about her, and she had to fight to keep her balance. Their ecstatic braying filled the night, sounding loudly now, sounding impossibly close. Mary shrank with dread. The dogs had found her trail.

Mary glanced wildly around, trying to discern her whereabouts. It was hopeless, she thought. Numb with cold and with fear, being stalked so ruthlessly, she could not recognize a single tree or rock. She pushed through the stream, wading out onto the opposite bank. She peered up through the forest canopy, looking for a star to guide her.

The North Star winked at her. Mary gritted with resolve and pushed on. She stumbled and almost fell. Her hands, she realized, were bloody, from the many trees and boulders she had grasped in her headlong flight through the woods. Worse, she had beaten holes in her slippers in the stream on the rocky bed, but she must not dwell on how painful every step was. The hounds howled and snarled and yapped and yelped, even closer, beginning to fight with one another as they closed in upon her. Mary began to run. It could not be that far, she told herself, it could not be more than a few miles—please God.

Mary was soaking wet, shivering violently, and at the last of her strength. She pounded on the wall, her fists bloody, calling out yet again. But she was so weak, her voice had no power, and the guards on the watchtower did not hear her.

She had been pounding on the wall forever, it seemed, and she was so faint now, she could barely lift her fist. Then it occurred to her that she could no longer hear the hounds—that she hadn't heard them in some time.

But there was no elation, no exultation, no sense of triumph or victory. There was only freezing cold, gut-wrenching pain, and sheer desperation.

"Please," Mary whispered, sobbing, sliding to the ground. "Please, let me in, please." She crumbled into a heap, and then, blessedly, her mind slipped into darkness.

At dawn one of the guards upon the watchtower noticed the small human heap sprawled just to the side of the raised drawbridge. "Some beggar wench, no doubt," he said to himself, and went on about his business.

But the laird of the keep had decided to go hunting that day and had deferred his administrative duties to his steward in order that he might leave at sunrise. The portcullis was raised, the drawbridge opened. A dozen mounted Scotsmen clattered over the wooden bridge behind the young laird.

One of his cousins spotted her instantly. "Doug, it appears we've got some beggar-whore lying at our doorstep."

Doug Mackinnon shrugged, riding on. Then he glimpsed a strand of impossibly bright gold hair, hair he had only seen on one woman, and he whirled his beast around. "No, 'tis not possible," he said beneath his breath. But he spurred his stallion over to the crumpled wench and dismounted, ignoring the guffaws and crude remarks his own men were making.

His heart suddenly in his throat, Doug turned the wretch over. His eyes widened in shock and he gasped, the sound strangled with anguish. Instantly he lifted Mary into his arms. He cried out again as her cloak fell open and her huge, swollen belly was revealed.

"Get a physic," he snapped. "Get a midwife, too. And . . . send word to Stephen de Warenne."

Doug turned and ran across the drawbridge with Mary in his arms.

Mary woke up when hot broth was forced past her lips. The room swayed before her, as if it were in motion, and she still shivered spasmodically, despite the chamber's blazing fire and the many blankets piled upon her. A pain ripped through her insides. Mary blanched, choking off a cry.

"Dear heart,'tis all right now," a familiar voice murmured.

Mary blinked. Gradually her vision steadied and cleared. The man sitting by her hip on the bed, who was also holding her hand, came into focus. She was startled to see that it was Doug Mackinnon, and for a moment, she was confused.

"I found you in a heap upon the ground in front of the watchtower," Doug said softly. He stroked her hair. " 'Tis over now, Mary. Whatever has happened,'tis over."

In a horrid flash, Mary recalled that she had been escaping Duncan and his wolfhounds. She cried out. "Duncan captured me. He was holding me a prisoner, Doug." Tears filled her eyes and she would have gripped Doug's hands, but her own hands were swathed in bandages. Her voice was so hoarse from shouting to the watchmen that it was barely audible, and Doug had to lean close to understand her. "He intended to hold my child as a hostage forever— to insure Stephen's support—my own brother!"

"The bastard," Doug hissed. But he was relieved. He had heard a rumor recently, one that held that Stephen de Warenne was tearing up the countryside, searching for his wife. Doug had, like so many others, heard of how Mary had defected to the cause of Scotland during the war last November. Thus he had been distraught at the thought that she had hated her husband so much that she would run away from him again, for that had been the obvious conclusion to be drawn. He was unable to stop himself from loving Mary, and although she was married to another, he could not want her to be so unhappy. And when he had seen her condition, he had been even more distressed, for her marriage must be unbearable to cause her to flee in such a state. Now, learning the truth, he was inordinately relieved.

Yet perhaps he was also somewhat, secretly, dismayed. Doug barely realized that he caressed Mary's hair. The sight of her, so pregnant and so weak, crying and in his bed, was enough to make all of the old yearning come surging to the fore no matter how much he tried to ignore such emotions.

Doug immediately shoved such disturbing thoughts aside. He was furious with Duncan, a King he would never support, a man he, and many other Scots, considered more English than anything else, and nothing but a puppet of William Rufus's.

Then Mary said, "Where is Stephen? How I need him. Oh, God, how I need him!" She cried out as another pain ripped through her.

Doug felt a piercing deep within him and realized, then and there, no matter how noble and selfless he had tried to be, that deep within his heart, he had still harbored hope for them, and now that hope was finally, irrevocably, laid to rest by her obvious love for her husband.

"Stephen," Mary whispered, her eyes focused not on Doug, but behind him.

"I am here," Stephen said from the doorway.

Doug whirled, standing, pale. But Stephen did not even look at him, having eyes only for Mary. He crossed the room with long, resolute strides, his muddy cloak swirling about him.

Mary half-laughed and half-sobbed, holding out her arms. Stephen sank onto the bed beside her, in the place Doug had vacated, pulling her very gently into his embrace.

Mary wept.

Stephen wept also, but soundlessly.

Silently Doug left the room.

"You have come," Mary finally managed, clinging to him.

"But not soon enough," Stephen said hoarsely. He was heavily bearded, his eyes bloodshot and shadowed, testimony to the fact that he had not slept more than a few hours in the past sennight. He cradled her face, scratched from bushes and branches, in his hands. " 'Twas Duncan. I should have guessed."

"H-How long were you standing there?" Mary asked with some trepidation.

"Long enough to know that Doug Mackinnon still loves you, and long enough to also know that you love me."

Mary collapsed on his chest, in both exhaustion and relief. He held her, stroked her, his silent tears mingling with hers. "How, Mary?" Stephen finally asked when he could speak. His tone was as ravaged as his face. "How did you escape?"

"By a secret tunnel I have used since I was a wee bairn," Mary told him, looking up at him. "B-But he had hounds. I had to run from the hounds."

Stephen embraced her again, far more gently than he wished to, soothing her with his big hands. "Never again, my love, never again will you face such evil. I failed to protect you once, but you shall always be safe, from this day forward, I swear it to you, Mary."

"Do not blame yourself," she cried passionately. Then she cried out again, blanching.

"The child?" Stephen asked urgently, their gazes locking.

Mary nodded, mute and tight-lipped, unable to speak.

Stephen pushed her slowly onto her back. "You must not wear yourself out with words. You must save your strength now in case the child decides to come early."

Mary stared at him out of huge, unwavering eyes. When the spasm had passed, she said wonderingly, "Why were you crying?"

Stephen managed a slight smile. " 'Tis not obvious? You are my life—and I almost lost you." His voice lowered, he touched her cheek. "I told you once before, I cannot live without you, madame."

Tears filled Mary's eyes. "I love you, too, Stephen. I always have."

Stephen fought more unmanly tears. Uncomfortable yet elated, he chided, "Really, madame, you go too far. *Always?*"

"Since I have first seen you," Mary whispered. Then she blanched again, crying out, beating Stephen's hands with her own bandaged fists.

When the spasm subsided and Mary finally relaxed, Stephen forced a smile. "When you first saw me, you hated me, sweetheart, do you not remember?" He wished to distract her from the pain.

Tears of agony filled Mary's eyes, but she shook her head in negation stubbornly. When another cramp had passed, she gasped in relief. "No, s-sir, I beg to d-differ. You see, I first saw you almost three years ago at Abernathy, standing behind King Rufus while my father was on bended knee, swearing homage."

Stephen started. "You were at Abernathy then?!"

She smiled slightly. "I rode with Edgar, disguised as his squire."

"You minx," Stephen said softly. "So that beautiful lad who kept staring at me was you!"

"Y-You saw me?"

He actually blushed. "I saw you. I was most uncomfortable, thinking myself attracted to a boy."

"Oh, Stephen!" They gazed at each other, awed, each wondering privately if their love had been born that winter day in such a strange way, each deciding that it was so.

Stephen leaned forward to brush her mouth with his. "Enough conversation, dear heart. You must rest now quietly." He was smiling, his expression so tender that it was remarkable.

But Mary's pleasure died. She moaned, long and low, her face as white as death. For a very long moment she was wracked with pain. Finally it began to subside, and then it was gone. "S-Stephen," she said huskily. "Please fetch the midwife to me."

Stephen blanched himself. "Wait until I return, Mary. Just this once—do not do anything rash!"

But patience again eluded Mary, or it eluded the child. When Stephen returned, the midwife beside him, he heard a baby's mewling cries. His heart quickened, disbelief etched itself onto his face. He had, in part, been jesting—he had only been gone a few minutes. He flung open the door. Mary lay sprawled limply on the bed, but when she saw him, she smiled. The covers were thrown off of her, and between her legs a tiny, bloody newborn lay.

Stephen saw the blood and, having never witnessed a birth before, thought that he was about to lose his wife. He rushed to her frantically. She laughed softly, low and pleased. Startled, he looked at her. She entwined her arm with his. "I peeked, my lord." Triumph filled her tone. " 'Tis a boy."

She turned to the midwife, who had already cut the babe's cord and wrapped the small mite up. "Show his lordship his son."

The midwife turned, her face creased in a smile, holding up the tiny, wide-eyed infant. "Got all his fingers and all his toes, yer lordship, an' he's a big boy, too, considerin' he's a bit early. An' he's wide-awake now, too!"

Stephen stared in shock. "My son?"

"Your son," Mary said happily, drawing his befuddled gaze. "A stong, brave lad, eager to come into the world and greet his father. Give him the babe, mistress."

Before Stephen could object, the tiny newborn was in his arms, hardly more than two handfuls for his oversized father. Stephen was surprised to see that the infant's eyes were actually wide open—and focused on him. "Why, he's looking at me," he murmured, new, inexplicable feelings washing over him. Then he smiled tenderly. "Look, madame, see how alert he is."

"Like his father," Mary said softly. "Just like his father."

And Stephen smiled at her, filled with a rush of pride. "For this, madame, you will know your every fondest dream."

Mary cocked her head. "I already have my fondest dreams, Stephen, I have the babe and I have you. What more could there possibly be?"

But there was more, of course.

Mary convalesced at Kinross. Stephen remained with her, leaving his own affairs in the hands of his steward and castellan. A month after their babe was born, whom they named Edward after Mary's brother, they returned to Alnwick.

As they approached the looming keep, Mary sensed that something was afoot. Stephen rode beside her litter, and whenever he looked at her and his son, there was something else in his expression other than the tender warmth she had come to expect. The sparkle in his eyes was both secretive and satisfied; she could not decipher its precise meaning. But the man was up to some trick—and he was terribly pleased about it.

They were greeted at the keep by the entire family. Mary was in shock as Stephen helped her from the litter while a nurse held little Ned. The earl and countess rushed upon her, to kiss and embrace her and tell her how thrilled they were that she was safe and well and home. Then the Bishop of Ely swept her up, whispering in her ear that he would baptize the boy, that no one else would have that honor. Brand kissed her smack on the lips, and Isobel oohed and aahed over the newborn babe.

And through all this pandemonium, Mary wept, because standing behind Stephen's family was Edgar, Alexander, and Davie.

She held out her arms. Her brothers rushed forward, whooping. Characteristically they refused to hug her. Edgar lifted her up and twirled her in the air, Alexander socked her shoulder, and Davie demanded the right to hold Ned. Surrounded by the three boys, holding her son proudly, Mary looked at her husband. He smiled at her, and she smiled back.

Mary was exhausted. She crept into the chamber she shared with Stephen, grateful to be alone for this one minute. Her mind was filled to overflowing with wonderful, festive images of her family and Stephen's family carousing during dinner in the hall below. It had been a grand homecoming, indeed.

Mary put the sleeping baby down in the cradle by the bed. Tears formed in her eyes. She felt such a rush of love for her son—and for her dear, beloved husband.

She knew now that this visit signified far more than a mere familial reunion. She was well aware of how brotherly Stephen was to Edgar, Alexander, and Davie, and she was grateful. There was a message that had been conveyed this day: Stephen had taken on the responsibility of her brothers' welfare. And now she knew without being told that she had indeed failed to trust him. She knew in her heart that one day there would come a time when Stephen would act to fulfill the promise he had made to Malcolm; one day he would put Edgar upon the throne. She had no doubt.

Mary realized she was not alone. She turned and froze.

Standing in the doorway was Stephen, and he was holding out a rose.

A single, perfect, short-stemmed red rose.

Mary moved forward, almost afraid to touch it, to touch him. This big, powerful man offering her the gift of a red rose was a sight too beautiful to behold. "Stephen," she whispered, and this time the rush of love was so great, it was almost painful. Now she understood that without pain, there could never be such a grand and consuming love.

Stephen said softly, "It will not prick you again, my love, for its thorns have been shorn."

Smiling through her tears, overwhelmed, Mary reached out and accepted the rose without feeling a single thorn.

"I always keep my word," Stephen said.

She cradled the rose to her breast. "I know."

"I intend to fulfill my pledge to your father, Mary. One day Edgar will be Scotland's King."

"I know that, too." She began to cry. Stephen trusted her, and that was the greatest gift he could give her next to the gift of his love, and he had been giving her that without reserve since he had arrived at Kinross.

"You have all of me, Mary," he said solemnly.

"I know that, too," she whispered. Power, purity, nobility, passion—the promise of the rose. She rose up on her toes and kissed him. "Thank you, my lord."

And he held her hard.

Author's Note

Chronology of Historical Events:

Malcolm III (Malcolm Canmore), King of Scotland, 1058–1093.

William I (William the Conqueror), King of England, 1066–1087; he is also Duke of Normandy.

1070 Lanfranc appointed Archbishop of Canterbury.

1072 Malcolm III forced to swear fealty to William I at Abernathy; Duncan sent to English Court as a pledge of peace.

1079 Malcolm III invades England and fails to advance his frontier, forced to swear fealty again.

William II (Rufus the Red) King of England 1087–1100.

Rebellion of Norman barons led by Odo of Bayeux, Earl of Kent, in 1088; rebels crushed, Odo is banished, his lands forfeit.

1089 Lanfranc dies, the see of Canterbury left vacant for four years.

1089 William II claims Normandy, campaigns there with some success.

1091 Malcolm III is forced to swear fealty to William II at Abernathy.

1092 Carlisle is conquered by William II's forces, its local ruler driven out.

1093 Anselm of Bec appointed Archbishop of Canterbury.

November 13, 1093, Malcolm III killed at Alnwick by the Earl of Northumberland's forces; Edward is fatally wounded.

November 16, 1093, Queen Margaret dies at Edinburgh Castle.

Donald Bane attacks Edinburgh Castle; his nephews flee, taking the Queen, their mother, with them and burying her at Dunfermline. They flee to the Court of William II.

May 1094 An Anglo-Norman army deposes Donald Bane and Edmund; Duncan becomes King of Scotland. His half brother Edgar is one of the charter's signatories.

November 1094 Duncan II is overthrown and murdered by Donald Bane and Edmund.

Donald Bane and Edmund, joint Kings of Scotland, 1094–1097.

1095 Robert, Duke of Normandy, goes on Crusade and mortgages Normandy to William II.

Fall of 1097 Edgar is crowned King of Scotland.

Edgar (the Peaceable), King of Scotland, 1097–1106.

1100 William II dies in a hunting accident or is murdered.

Prince Henry (Henry Beauclerc) seizes the treasury that day; three days later he is crowned at Westminster; a few months later he marries Matilde (Maude), the daughter of Malcolm III and Margaret, taking her out of a convent to do so.

Henry I, King of England, 1100–1135.

1106 Henry I invades Normandy, victorious at Tinchebrai; he unites the kingdom of England and the duchy of Normandy; his brother Robert is imprisoned for the rest of his life.

Alexander I (The Fierce), King of Scotland, 1106–1124.

David I, King of Scotland, 1124–53.

This is a work of fiction, and I have interpreted the above events and the historical characters who moved them with great liberty, and much enjoyment. I tried to adhere to the chronology as closely as possible, but the reader may note that Carlisle was taken in 1092, not 1093. Also, while Edinburgh was not the official seat of the King of Scotland, I made it so because history does show that Mary and her brothers fled the burgh in November 1093 after the deaths of Malcolm, Margaret, and Edward. I hope my readers will forgive me for any errors I might have made. There is much conflicting data for this period, when there is any data at all.

I would like to say a word about the Church in the eleventh century. It was hardly as rigidly defined as it is today. The King still exercised vast powers over many religious affairs, although at this time many reformers in the Church began to argue and fight for complete jurisdiction of all their affairs, such as the right of appointment, investiture, etc. There were high prelates who were irreligious or atheists, men who, it appears, were great knights rewarded with their offices by the Conqueror and his sons—just as there were truly great and saintly men. Some archdeacons in this period were not ordained—like Geoffrey de Warenne.

Finally, a very interesting note. When embarking upon this venture, I was locked into this time period because Stephen was conceived in this book's prequel, *The Conqueror*. My muse told me that his love would be a Scot princess named Mairi. Thus I was compelled to accept Malcolm and Margaret as Scotland's King and Queen—as her parents. I was thrilled when my research unearthed such a rich conflict for me to use. But I was soon stunned. For when I paid closer attention to Malcolm and Margaret personally, I found that not only had they six sons, but two daughters—and the oldest one was named Mary, and she married a Norman count.

Of course, I have fictionalized her life completely. At least, so I think.

Brenda Joyce loves to hear from her readers. You may write to her at P.O. Box 1208, Wainscott, N.Y. 11975.